MELVILLE

⚓

FOREWORD BY

Rear Admiral Edward Ellsberg

U.S.N.R. (RET.)

⚓

Contents

HERMAN MELVILLE: A FOREWORD
by Rear Admiral Edward Ellsberg • 9
U.S.N.R. (RET.)

MOBY DICK

1. Loomings • 17
2. The Carpetbag • 22
3. The Spouter Inn • 26
4. The Counterpane • 41
5. Breakfast • 45
6. The Chapel • 48
7. A Bosom Friend • 51
8. Nightgown • 57
9. Biographical • 58
10. Wheelbarrow • 62
11. Chowder • 69
12. The Ship • 73

Contents

13. All Astir • 90
14. Going Aboard • 94
15. Merry Christmas • 99
16. Ahab • 106
17. The Cabin Table • 112
18. The Quarterdeck • 120
19. Midnight, Forecastle • 131
20. Moby Dick • 139
21. Hark! • 146
22. The Chart • 148
23. The Mat-Maker • 152
24. The First Lowering • 156
25. The Hyena • 171
26. The Spirit Spout • 175
27. The Albatross • 181
28. Squid • 184
29. Stubb Kills a Whale • 187
30. Cutting In • 195
31. The Monkey Rope • 199
32. Cistern and Buckets • 206
33. The Try-Works • 212
34. The Grand Armada • 217
35. The Castaway • 235
36. Leg and Arm • 240
37. Ahab's Leg • 251
38. Ahab and Starbuck in the Cabin • 254
39. Queequeg in His Coffin • 258
40. The Forge • 267

Contents

41. The *Pequod* Meets the *Bachelor* • 272
42. The Whale Watch • 276
43. The Quadrant • 279
44. The Candles • 283
45. The Deck • 293
46. Midnight—The Forecastle Bulwarks • 295
47. The Musket • 298
48. The Needle • 303
49. The Log and Line • 308
50. The Life Buoy • 313
51. The *Pequod* Meets the *Rachel* • 319
52. The *Pequod* Meets the *Delight* • 325
53. The Chase—First Day • 328
54. The Chase—Second Day • 342
55. The Chase—Third Day • 355
    Epilogue • 372

TYPEE

1. Apprehensions of Evil • 377
2. The Stranger Again Arrives in the Valley • 391
3. The Escape • 399

BILLY BUDD

    Author's Preface • 415
    Sections 1–31 Complete • 417

ABOUT HERMAN MELVILLE • 541

Herman Melville

A FOREWORD BY
⚓ *Rear Admiral Edward Ellsberg*
U.S.N.R. (RET.)

"THERE SHE BLOWS! SHE BLOWS, SHE BLOWS!"

And with the echo of that hoarse cry from the masthead ringing in your ears, under the magic spell of Herman Melville's vivid prose you are lowering away with a rush, and in a moment more, with salt spray foaming high under the bow of your whaleboat, you are off, pulling your heart out. Ahead of you, rhythmically spouting, majestically swims Moby Dick, the white whale himself—Moby Dick, the hugest individual of all his Leviathan species and that species the the most massive that since creation's dawn this world has ever seen—whether on the land or on the sea.

With Moby Dick and his monstrous flukes breasting the waves dead ahead, who any longer cares for such automated marvels of this day as satellites and spaceships, or how and when man gets to the moon? You yourself are now back in

man's most primitive role, that of the hunter, ready in another
instant to drop your oar, raise aloft your harpoon and with
your life and that of every man in your boat's crew staked on
the accuracy of your quivering arms, drive home your harpoon into the hump of that eighty-ton monster only inches
away from you, swimming now alongside your frail boat.

Meanwhile, as your captain on that cruise of the *Pequod*
you have its skipper the Yankee fanatic, Ahab, the terror of
whose secret purpose is finally revealed and pledged to by a
delirious, howling crew, your shipmates. Chief among them
are a set of expert harpooners such as any Quaker shipowner
of Nantucket would have bartered his hopes of salvation to
have recruited: brown Queequeg, the tattooed cannibal from
the south seas; red Tashtego, the lithe Indian from Gay Head;
black Daggoo, the gigantic Negro from West Africa; and
yellow Fedallah, the little turbaned Parsee—all of you on the
strangest cruise ever sailed by a Nantucket whaler bound off
round the world in pursuit of the sperm whale.

"Call me Ishmael." So, very simply, Melville begins his first-
person account of that cruise. Before long you find that *you*
are involuntarily that Ishmael, watching in terror while you
take part in this drama of the sea, in which vengeful Ahab on
his ivory leg, the *Pequod* herself with her wide-spreading sails,
white-humped Moby Dick, and those savages—Queequeg,
Tashtego, Daggoo and Fedallah—act out their given roles as
all hands, men, whale and ship, meet their destiny at the fate-
ful Season-on-the-Line.

No writer ever could have done it better. A sailor himself,
a whaler himself, a man whose major interest was, oddly
enough, neither the sea nor whales but man's own inner
nature, Melville has woven from his diverse materials *Moby
Dick,* a tale of adventure at sea unmatched in all literature.

The abridged version of *Moby Dick* presented in this volume retains all the excitement, the wonderful scenes and action and the powerful writing of Melville's original story.

Do cannibals—actual cannibals, not fictional ones—interest you? They vitally interested Herman Melville.

After six endless months at sea aboard a New Bedford whaler with never a glimpse of land to relieve the toil and monotony, Melville decided to escape his brutal skipper by jumping ship at the first opportunity. So at Nukuheva in the Marquesas Islands, the next landfall, once he had set foot on the beach he fled his hated ship. To avoid an involuntary return to her he struggled across the surrounding mountains and disappeared into the jungle beyond, only to find himself there immediately a prisoner of the cannibal Taipis or Typees, literally, one might almost say, leaping from the frying pan into the fire!

In *Typee* you will learn at first hand, from the man who lived daily in the dread that he was being tenderly cared for and fattened only for a future feast, about the cannibal Typees and their south sea island paradise in the days before Gauguin with his paint brush came to idealize them and his French countrymen with their men-o'-war to "civilize" them.

You may well imagine that Melville's experiences of living with these primitive people as both honored guest and possible "puerkee" or porker for a ceremonial feast, impressed him vividly. The exciting solution to Melville's dilemma, told in the final chapters of the book, is included in this volume.

Typee and *Moby Dick* were products of the youthful Melville's adventures in the South Pacific in the early 1840s.

Typee, published soon after his return, and then *Omoo,* rocketed Melville to fame in a dazzling display of adulation. In that glow he hurried to turn out more novels. But after *Moby Dick,* published in 1851, the flame within him ran out of fuel, and like a burned-out rocket he fell swiftly into a sea of literary obscurity. To earn a living thereafter, he put in many weary years as a clerk in the New York Customs House. But during all those years still within him smoldered the spark of the eternal question of the nature of man's soul: Good? Evil? Neither?

Forty years after *Moby Dick* had blazed out upon the public, and only a few months before he died in 1891, Melville finished his investigation of that enigma. *Billy Budd,* unpublished at his death, never published in fact until 1924, is that story, and here it is, entire.

In *Billy Budd* you meet Billy, the "handsome sailor," with no enmity in his heart for any man. You meet Captain Vere, commanding *H.M.S. Indomitable,* a three-decker, ship-of-the-line in Admiral Lord Nelson's fleet blockading France in the tense year of 1797, with the safety of his ship and her seventy-four guns resting heavily on the captain's mind. And finally you meet John Claggart, master-at-arms on that man-o'-war—Claggart, whose dark soul is revolted by Billy's innocence and lack of guile.

No volleys belching from the *Indomitable's* three tiers of heavy guns ever burst out to provide the action in this story. The only blow struck in the whole tale is an involuntary one from Billy Budd's clenched fist. And yet not all the thundering guns of Nelson's fleet at Trafalgar nor of Villeneuve's answering broadsides from the combined French and Spanish ships-of-the-line, can match in dramatic impact what ensues in Captain Vere's cabin as a result of that one unintentional blow.

In *Billy Budd*, the product of Melville's final reflections on life, most of the action takes place in the minds and hearts of men. None the less the book is worthy to stand alongside *Moby Dick*—the action-packed tale of Melville's adventurous youth, in which men and whales are pitted against each other in deadly physical combat of inflexible will versus monstrous strength. These two sea tales are as different as night and day, but both are Melville at his best.

SOUTHWEST HARBOR, MAINE
January, 1964.

MOBY DICK

⚓

A special abridged edition

Chapter 1

Loomings

CALL ME ISHMAEL. Some years ago—never mind how long precisely—having little or no money in my purse, and nothing particular to interest me on shore, I thought I would sail about a little and see the watery part of the world. It is a way I have of driving off the spleen, and regulating the circulation. Whenever I find myself growing grim about the mouth, whenever it is damp, drizzly November in my soul, whenever I find myself involuntarily pausing before coffin warehouses and bringing up the rear of every funeral I meet, and especially whenever my hypos get such an upper hand of me that it requires a strong moral principle to prevent me from deliberately stepping into the street and methodically knocking people's hats off—then I account it high time to get to sea as soon as I can. This is my substitute for pistol and ball.

With a philosophical flourish Cato throws himself upon
his sword; I quietly take to the ship.

There is nothing surprising in this. If they but knew it,
almost all men in their degree, sometime or other, cherish
very nearly the same feelings toward the ocean with me.

Now, when I say that I am in the habit of going to sea
whenever I begin to grow hazy about the eyes and begin
to be over-conscious of my lungs, I do not mean to have it
inferred that I ever go to sea as a passenger. For to go as
a passenger you must needs have a purse, and a purse is
but a rag unless you have something in it. Besides, passengers get seasick—grow quarrelsome—don't sleep of
nights—do not enjoy themselves much, as a general thing.
No, I never go as a passenger. Nor, though I am something of a salt, do I ever go to sea as a commodore or a
captain. I abandon the glory and distinction of such
offices to those who like them. For my part, I abominate
all honorable respectable toils, trials and tribulations of
every kind whatsoever. It is quite as much as I can do to
take care of myself, without taking care of ships, barques,
brigs, schooners and what not.

No, when I go to sea I go as a simple sailor, right before the mast, plumb down into the forecastle, aloft there
to the royal masthead. True, they rather order me about
and make me jump from spar to spar, like a grasshopper
in a May meadow. And at first this sort of thing is un-
pleasant enough. It touches one's sense of honor, particularly if you come of an old established family in the
land, the Van Rensselaers, or Randolphs or Hardicanutes.
And more than all, if just previous to putting your hand

into the tar-pot you have been lording it as a country
schoolmaster, making the tallest boys stand in awe of
you. The transition is a keen one, I assure you, from a
schoolmaster to a sailor, and requires a strong decoction
of Seneca and the Stoics to enable you to grin and bear it.
But even this wears off in time.

What of it, if some old hunks of a sea captain orders me
to get a broom and sweep down the decks? What does
that indignity amount to, weighed, I mean, in the scales
of the New Testament? Who ain't a slave? Tell me that.
Well then, however the old sea captains may order me
about—however they may thump and punch me about, I
have the satisfaction of knowing that it is all right; that
everybody else is one way or other served in much the
same way—either in a physical or metaphysical point of
view, that is. And so the universal thump is passed around
and all hands should rub each other's shoulder blades and
be content.

Again, I always go to sea as a sailor because they make
a point of paying me for my trouble, whereas they never
pay passengers a single penny that I ever heard of. On
the contrary, passengers themselves must pay, and there
is all the difference in the world between paying and being paid.

Finally, I always go to sea as a sailor, because of the
wholesome exercise and pure air of the forecastle deck.

But wherefore it was that after having repeatedly
smelt the sea as a merchant sailor, I should now take it
into my head to go on a whaling voyage; this the invisible
police officer of the Fates, who has the constant surveil-

lance of me, and secretly dogs me and influences me in
some unaccountable way—he can better answer than anyone else. I take it that this part of the bill must have run
something like this:

*Grand Contested Election for the Presidency of the
United States*

WHALING VOYAGE BY ONE ISHMAEL

BLOODY BATTLE IN AFGHANISTAN

Though I cannot tell why it was exactly that those
stage managers, the Fates, put me down for this shabby
part of a whaling voyage when others were set down for
magnificent parts in high tragedies, and short and easy
parts in genteel comedies, and jolly parts in farces—
though I cannot tell why this was exactly; yet, now that
I recall all the circumstances, I think I can see a little
into the springs and motives which being cunningly
presented to me under various disguises, induced me to
set about performing the part I did, besides cajoling me
into the delusion that it was a choice resulting from my
own unbiased free will and discriminating judgment.

Chief among these motives was the overwhelming idea
of the great whale himself. Such a portentous and mysterious monster roused all my curiosity. Then the wild and
distant seas where he rolled his island bulk, the un-
deliverable, nameless perils of the whale; these, with all
the attending marvels of a thousand Patagonian sights

and sounds, helped to sway me to my wish. With other men, perhaps, such things would not have been inducements. But as for me, I am tormented with an everlasting itch for things remote. I love to sail forbidden seas and land on barbarous coasts. Not ignoring what is good, I am quick to perceive a horror, and could still be sociable with it—would they let me—since it is but well to be on friendly terms with all the inmates of the place one lodges in.

By reason of these things, then, the whaling voyage was welcome. The great floodgates of the wonder-world swung open, and in the wild conceits that swayed me to my purpose, two and two there floated into my inmost soul, endless processions of the whale. And midmost of them all, was one grand hooded phantom, like a snow hill in the air.

CHAPTER 2

⚓

The Carpetbag

I STUFFED a shirt or two into my old carpetbag, tucked it under my arm, and started for Cape Horn and the Pacific. Quitting the good city of old Manhatto, I duly arrived in New Bedford. It was on a Saturday night in December. Much was I disappointed upon learning that the little packet for Nantucket had already sailed, and that no way of reaching that place would offer, till the following Monday.

As most young candidates for the pains and penalties of whaling stop at this same New Bedford, thence to embark on their voyage, it may as well be related that I, for one, had no idea of so doing. For my mind was made up to sail in no other than a Nantucket craft, because there was a fine boisterous something about everything connected with that famous old island, which amazingly pleased me. Besides, though New Bedford has of late been gradually monopolizing the business of whaling, and though in this matter poor old Nantucket is now much behind her, yet Nantucket was her great original, the Tyre of this Carthage, the place where the first dead American whale was stranded. Where else but from Nantucket did those aboriginal whalemen, the red men, first sally out in canoes to give chase to the leviathan? And where but from Nantucket, too, did that first adventurous little sloop put forth, partly laden with imported cobblestones, so goes the story, to throw at the whales, in order to discover when they were nigh enough to risk a harpoon from the bowsprit?

Now having a night, a day, and still another night following before me in New Bedford, ere I could embark for my destined port, it became a matter of concernment where I was to eat and sleep meanwhile. It was a very dubious-looking, nay, a very dark and dismal night, bitingly cold and cheerless. I knew no one in the place. With anxious grapnels I had sounded my pocket, and only brought up a few pieces of silver. So, wherever you go, Ishmael, said I to myself as I stood in the middle of a dreary street shouldering my bag, and comparing the gloom toward the north with the darkness toward the south—wherever in your wisdom you may conclude to lodge for the night, my dear Ishmael, be sure to inquire the price, and don't be too particular.

With halting steps I paced the streets, and passed the

sign of THE CROSSED HARPOONS—but it looked too expensive and jolly there. Farther on, from the bright red windows of the SWORDFISH INN, there came such fervent rays, that it seemed to have melted the packed snow and ice from before the house, for everywhere else the congealed frost lay ten inches thick in a hard, asphaltic pavement— rather weary for me when I struck my foot against the flinty projections, because from hard remorseless service the soles of my boots were in a most miserable plight. Too expensive and jolly again, thought I, pausing one moment to watch the broad glare in the street and hear the sounds of the tinkling glasses within. But go on, Ishmael, said I at last. Don't you hear? get away from before the door; your patched boots are stopping the way.

So on I went. I now by instinct followed the streets that took me waterward, for there, doubtless, were the cheapest, if not the cheeriest inns. Such dreary streets! Blocks of blackness, not houses, on either hand, and here and there a candle, like a candle moving about a tomb. At this hour of the night, of the last day of the week, that quarter of the town proved all but deserted.

Moving on, I at last came to a dim sort of light not far from the docks, and heard a forlorn creaking in the air. Looking up, I saw a swinging sign over the door with a white painting upon it, faintly representing a tall straight jet of misty spray, and these words underneath:

THE SPOUTER INN—*Peter Coffin.*

Coffin? Spouter? Rather ominous in that particular connection, thought I. But it is a common name in Nantucket, they say, and I suppose this Peter here is an emigrant from there. As the light looked so dim, and the place, for the time, looked quiet enough, and the dilapidated little wooden house itself looked as if it might have been carted here from the ruins of some burnt district, and as the swinging sign had a poverty-stricken sort of creak to it, I thought that here was the very spot for cheap lodgings, and the best of pea coffee.

CHAPTER 3

⚓

The Spouter Inn

ENTERING that gabled-ended SPOUTER INN, you found yourself in a wide, low, straggling entry with old-fashioned wainscots, reminding one of the bulwarks of some condemned old craft. On one side hung a very large oil painting so thoroughly besmoked, and every way defaced, that in the unequal crosslights by which you viewed it, it was only by diligent study and a series of systematic visits to it, and careful inquiry of the neighbors, that you could any way arrive at an understanding of its purpose. Such unaccountable masses of shades and shadows, that at first you almost thought some ambitious young artist, in the time of the New England hags, had endeavored to delineate chaos bewitched. What most puzzled and confounded you was a long, limber, portentous, black mass of something hovering in the center of the

picture over three blue, dim, perpendicular lines floating
in a nameless yeast. A boggy, soggy, squitchy picture
truly, enough to drive a nervous man distracted. But
stop; does it not bear a faint resemblance to a gigantic
fish? Even the great Leviathan himself?

In fact, the artist's design seemed this, a final theory of
my own, partly based upon the aggregrated opinions of
many aged persons with whom I conversed upon the subject: the picture represents a Cape Horner in a great
hurricane, the half-foundered ship weltering there with
its three dismantled masts alone visible. And an exasperated whale, purposing to spring clean over the craft,
is in the enormous act of impaling himself upon the
three mastheads.

The opposite wall of this entry was hung all over with
a heathenish array of monstrous clubs and spears. And
mixed with these were rusty old whaling lances and harpoons all broken and deformed. Some were storied weapons. With this once long lance, now wildly elbowed, fifty
years ago did Nathan Swain kill fifteen whales between
a sunrise and a sunset. And that harpoon—so like a corkscrew now—was flung in Javan seas, and run away with
by a whale, years afterward slain off the Cape of Blanco.
The original iron entered nigh the tail, and like a restless
needle sojourning in the body of a man, traveled full forty
feet, and at last was found imbedded in the hump.

Crossing this dusky entry, and on through yon low-
arched way—cut through what in old times must have
been a great central chimney with fireplaces all around—
you enter the public room. A still duskier place is this,

with such low ponderous beams above, and such old
wrinkled planks beneath, that you would almost fancy
you trod some old craft's cockpits, especially of such a
howling night, when this corner-anchored old ark rocked
so furiously. On one side stood a long, low shelf-like table
covered with cracked glass cases, filled with dusty rarities
gathered from this wide world's remotest nooks. Projecting from the farther angle of the room stands a dark-look-
ing den, the bar—a rude attempt at a right whale's head.
Be that how it may, there stands the vast arched bone
of the whale's jaw, so wide a coach might almost drive
beneath it. Within are shabby shelves, ranged around
with old decanters, bottles, flasks; and in those jaws of
swift destruction, bustles a little withered old man, who,
for their money, dearly sells the sailors deliriums and
death.

Upon entering the place I found a number of young
seamen gathered about a table, examining by a dim light
divers specimens of *skrimshander*.[1] I sought the landlord, and telling him I desired to be accommodated with
a room, received for answer that his house was full—not
a bed unoccupied. "But avast," he added, tapping his
forehead, "you haint no objections to sharing a harpooneer's blanket, have ye? I s'pose you are goin' a-
whalin', so you'd better get used to that sort of thing."

I told him that I never liked to sleep two in a bed, that
if I should ever do so, it would depend upon who the harpooneer might be, and that if he (the landlord) really had
no other place for me, and the harpooneer was not de-

---

[1] *Scrimshaw:* objects carved from whalebone—ED.

cidedly objectionable, why, rather than wander further about a strange town on so bitter a night, I would put up with the half of any decent man's blanket.

"I thought so. All right; take a seat. Supper? You want supper? Supper'll be ready directly."

I sat down on an old wooden settle, carved all over like a bench on the Battery. At one end a ruminating tar was still further adorning it with his jackknife, stooping over and diligently working away at the space between his legs. He was trying his hand at a ship under full sail, but he didn't make much headway, I thought.

At last some four or five of us were summoned to our meal in an adjoining room. It was cold as Iceland. No fire at all—the landlord said he couldn't afford it. Nothing but two dismal tallow candles, each in a winding-sheet. We were fain to button up our monkey jackets, and hold to our lips cups of scalding tea with our half-frozen fingers. But the fare was of the most substantial kind—not only meat and potatoes, but dumplings; good heavens! Dumplings for supper! One young fellow in a green box coat, addressed himself to these dumplings in a most direful manner.

"My boy," said the landlord, "you'll have the nightmare to a dead sartainty."

"Landlord," I whispered, "that ain't the harpooneer, is it?"

"Oh, no," said he, looking a sort of diabolically funny, "the harpooneer is a dark-complexioned chap. He never eats dumplings, he don't. He eats nothing but steaks, and likes 'em rare."

"The devil he does," says I. "Where is that harpooneer? Is he here?"

"He'll be here afore long," was the answer.

I could not help it, but I began to feel suspicious of this "dark-complexioned" harpooneer. At any rate, I made up my mind that if it so turned out that we should sleep together, he must undress and get into bed before I did.

Supper over, the company went back to the bar-room, where, not knowing what else to do with myself, I resolved to spend the rest of the evening as a looker-on.

Presently a rioting noise was heard without. Starting up, the landlord cried, "That's the *Grampus'* crew. I seed her reported in the offing this morning: a three years' voyage, and a full ship. Hurrah, boys; now we'll have the latest news from the Feejees."

A tramping of sea boots was heard in the entry; the door was flung open, and in rolled a wild enough set of mariners. Enveloped in their shaggy watch coats, and with their heads muffled in woolen comforters, all be-darned and ragged, and their beards stiff with icicles, they seemed an eruption of bears from Labrador. They had just landed from their boat, and this was the first house they entered. No wonder, then, that they made a straight wake for the whale's mouth—the bar—where the wrinkled little old Jonah, there officiating, poured them out brimmers all around. The liquor soon mounted to their heads, as it generally does even with the arrantest topers newly landed from sea, and they began capering about most obstreperously.

I observed, however, that one of them held somewhat

aloof, and though he seemed desirous not to spoil the
hilarity of his shipmates by his own sober face, yet upon
the whole he refrained from making as much noise as the
rest. When the revelry of his companions had mounted
to its height, this man slipped away unobserved, and I
saw no more of him till he became my comrade on the
sea. In a few minutes, however, he was missed by his
shipmates, and being, it seems, for some reason a huge
favorite with them, they raised a cry of "Bulkington!
Bulkington! Where's Bulkington?" and darted out of the
house in pursuit of him.

It was now about nine o'clock. The devil fetch that
harpooneer, thought I, but stop, couldn't I steal a march
on him—bolt his door inside and jump into his bed, not to
be awakened by the most violent knockings? It seemed no
bad idea, but upon second thought I dismissed it. For
who could tell but what the next morning, as soon as I
popped out of the room, the harpooneer might be standing in the entry all ready to knock me down!

Still, looking around me, and seeing no possible
chance of spending a sufferable night unless in some
other person's bed, I began to think that I might be
cherishing unwarrantable prejudices against this unknown harpooneer. Thinks I, I'll wait awhile; he must be
dropping in before long. I'll have a good look at him
then, and perhaps we may become jolly good bedfellows
after all—there's no telling.

But though the other boarders kept coming in by ones,
twos and threes, and going to bed, yet there was no sign
of my harpooneer.

"Landlord!" said I, "what sort of a chap is he? Does he always keep such late hours?" It was now hard upon twelve o'clock.

The landlord chuckled again with his lean chuckle, and seemed to be mightily tickled at something beyond my comprehension. "No," he answered, "generally he's an early bird. Airley to bed and airley to rise—yes, he's the bird what catches the worm. But tonight he went out a-peddling, you see, and I don't see what on airth keeps him so late, unless may be, he can't sell his head."

"Can't sell his head? What sort of a bamboozingly story is this you are telling me?"—getting into a towering rage. "Do you pretend to say, landlord, that this harpooneer is actually engaged this blessed Saturday night, or rather Sunday morning, in peddling his head around this town?"

"That's precisely it," said the landlord, "and I told him he couldn't sell it here; the market's overstocked."

"With what?" shouted I.

"With heads, to be sure; ain't there too many heads in the world?"

"I tell you what it is, landlord," said I quite calmly, "you'd better stop spinning that yarn to me. I'm not green."

"Maybe not,"—taking out a stick and whittling a toothpick, "but I rayther guess you'll be done *brown* if that ere harpooneer hears you a-slanderin' his head."

"I'll break it for him," said I, now flying into a passion again at this unaccountable farrago of the landlord's.

"It's broke a'ready," said he.

"Broke," said I, "*broke*, do you mean?"

"Sartain, and that's the very reason he can't sell it, I guess."

"Landlord," said I, going up to him as cool as Mount Hecla in a snowstorm, "landlord, stop whittling. You and I must understand one another, and that too without delay. I come to your house and want a bed; you tell me you can only give me half a one, that the other belongs to a certain harpooneer. And about this harpooneer, whom I have not yet seen, you persist in telling me the most mystifying and exasperating stories, tending to beget in me an uncomfortable feeling toward the man who you design for my bedfellow—a sort of connection, landlord, which is an intimate and confidential one in the highest degree. I now demand of you to speak out and tell me who and what this harpooneer is, and whether I shall be in all respects safe to spend the night with him. And in the first place, you will be so good as to unsay that story about selling his head, which if true I take to be good evidence that this harpooneer is stark mad, and I've no idea of sleeping with a madman; and you, sir, *you* I mean, landlord, *you*, sir, by trying to induce me to do so knowingly, would thereby render yourself liable to a criminal prosecution."

"Wall," said the landlord, fetching a long breath, "that's a purty long sarmon for a chap that rips a little now and then. But be easy, be easy. This here harpooneer I have been tellin' you of has just arrived from the south seas, where he bought up a lot of 'balmed New Zealand heads (great curios, you know), and he's sold all on 'em but one, and that one he's trying to sell tonight, 'cause tomorrow's Sunday, and it would not do to be sellin' human heads about the streets when folks is goin' to churches. He wanted to, last Sunday, but I stopped him just as he was goin' out of the door with four heads strung on a string, for all the airth like a string of inions."

This account cleared up the otherwise unaccountable mystery, and showed that the landlord, after all, had no idea of fooling me. But at the same time what could I think of a harpooneer who stayed out of a Saturday night clean into the holy Sabbath, engaged in such a cannibal business as selling the heads of dead idolaters?

"Depend upon it, landlord, that harpooneer is a dangerous man."

"He pays reg'lar," was the rejoinder. "But come, it's getting dreadful late, you had better be turning flukes. It's a nice bed; Sal and me slept in that ere bed the night we were spliced. There's plenty room for two to kick about in that bed; it's an almighty big bed that. Come along here, I'll give ye a glim in a jiffy." And so saying he lighted a candle and held it toward me, offering to lead the way. But I stood irresolute, when looking at a clock in the corner, he exclaimed, "I vum it's Sunday—you won't see that harpooneer tonight; he's come to anchor somewhere. Come along then; *do* come; *won't* ye come?"

I considered the matter a moment, and then upstairs we went, and I was ushered into a small room, cold as a clam, and furnished, sure enough, with a prodigious bed, almost big enough indeed for any four harpooneers to sleep abreast.

"There," said the landlord, placing the candle on a crazy old sea chest that did double duty as a washstand and center-table. "There, make yourself comfortable now, and good night to ye." I turned around from eyeing the bed, but he had disappeared.

I sat down on the side of the bed, and commenced thinking about this head-peddling harpooneer. After thinking some time on the bedside, I got up and took off my monkey jacket, and then stood in the middle of the room thinking. I then took off my coat, and thought a little more in my shirt-sleeves. But beginning to feel very cold now, half undressed as I was, and remembering what the landlord said about the harpooneer's not coming home at all that night, it being so very late, I made no more ado but jumped out of my pantaloons and boots, and then blowing out the light tumbled into bed and commended myself to the care of heaven.

Whether that mattress was stuffed with corncobs or broken crockery there is no telling, but I rolled about a good deal, and could not sleep for a long time. At last I slid off into a light doze, and had pretty nearly made a good offing toward the land of Nod, when I heard a heavy footfall in the passage, and saw a glimmer of light come into the room from under the door.

Lord save me, thinks I, that must be the harpooneer, the infernal head peddler. But I lay perfectly still and resolved not to say a word till spoken to. Holding a light in one hand and that identical New Zealand head in the other, the stranger entered the room, and without looking toward the bed, placed his candle a good way off from

me on the floor in one corner, and then began working
away at the knotted cords of his large seaman's bag. I
was all eagerness to see his face, but he kept it averted
for some time while employed in unlacing the bag's
mouth. This accomplished, however, he turned around.
Good heavens! What a sight! Such a face! It was of a
dark purplish, yellow color, stuck over here and there
with large, blackish-looking squares. Yes, it's just as I
thought, he's a terrible bedfellow; he's been in a fight, got
dreadfully cut, and here he is, just back from the surgeon. But at that moment he chanced to turn his face toward the light, so that I plainly saw they could not be
sticking-plasters at all, those black squares on his cheeks.
They were stains of some sort or other. At first I knew
not what to make of this, but soon an inkling of the truth
occurred to me. I remembered a story of a white man—a
whaleman too—who, falling among the cannibals, had
been tattooed by them. I concluded that this harpooneer,
in the course of his distant voyages, must have met with
a similar adventure. And what is it, thought I, after all!
It's only his outside; a man can be honest in any sort of
skin.

Now, while all these ideas were passing through me
like lightning, this harpooneer never noticed me at all.
But, after some difficulty having opened his bag, he commenced fumbling in it, and presently pulled out a sort
of tomahawk, and a sealskin wallet with the hair still on
it. Placing these on the old chest in the middle of the
room, he then took the New Zealand head, a ghastly thing
enough, and crammed it down into the bag. He now took

off his hat, a new beaver hat, when I came nigh singing
out with fresh surprise. There was no hair on his head—
none to speak of at least—nothing but a small scalp-knot
twisted up on his forehead. His bald purplish head now
looked for all the world like a mildewed skull. Had not
the stranger stood between me and the door, I would
have bolted out of it quicker than ever I bolted a dinner.

He continued the business of undressing, and at last
showed his chest and arms. As I live, these covered parts
of him were checkered with the same squares as his face;
his back, too, was covered all over with the same dark
squares. He seemed to have been in a Thirty Years' War,
and just escaped from it with a sticking-plaster shirt. Still
more, his very legs were marked, as if a parcel of dark
green frogs were running up the trunks of young palms.
It was now quite plain that he must be some abominable
savage or other shipped aboard a whaleman in the south
seas, and so landed in this Christian country. I quaked to
think of it. A peddler of heads too—perhaps the heads
of his own brothers. He might take a fancy to mine—
heavens! Look at that tomahawk!

But there was no time for shuddering, for now the savage went about something that completely fascinated
me, and convinced me that he must indeed be a heathen.
Going to his heavy grego, or wrapall, or dreadnought,
which he had previously hung on a chair, he fumbled in
the pockets, and produced at length a curious little deformed image with a hunch on its back.

Remembering the embalmed head, at first I almost
thought that this black manikin was a real baby preserved

in some similar manner. But seeing that it was not at all limber, and that it glistened a good deal like polished ebony, I concluded that it must be nothing but a wooden idol, which indeed it proved to be. For now the savage goes up to the empty fireplace, and removing the papered fireboard, sets up this little hunchbacked image, like a tenpin, between the andirons.

I now screwed my eyes hard toward the half-hidden image, feeling but ill at ease meantime—to see what was next to follow. First he takes about a double handful of shavings out of his grego pocket, and places them carefully before the idol; then laying a bit of ship biscuit on top and applying the flame from the lamp, he kindled the shavings into a sacrificial blaze. Presently, after many hasty snatches into the fire, and still hastier withdrawals of his fingers (whereby he seemed to be scorching them badly), he at last succeeded in drawing out the biscuit; then blowing off the heat and ashes a little, he made a polite offer of it to the little Negro. But the little devil did not seem to fancy such dry sort of fare at all; he never moved his lips. All these strange antics were accompanied by still stranger guttural noises from the devotee, who seemed to be praying in a singsong or else singing some pagan psalmody or other, during which his face twitched about in the most unnatural manner. At last extinguishing the fire, he took the idol up very unceremoniously, and bagged it again in his grego pocket as carelessly as a sportsman bagging a dead woodcock.

All these queer proceedings increased my uncomfortableness, and seeing him now exhibiting strong symptoms of concluding his business operations and jumping into bed with me, I thought it was high time, now or never, before the light was put out, to break the spell in which I had so long been bound.

But the interval I spent in deliberating what to say was a fatal one. Taking up his tomahawk from the table, he examined the head of it for an instant, and then holding it to the light, with his mouth at the handle, he puffed out great clouds of tobacco smoke. The next moment the light was extinguished, and this wild cannibal, tomahawk between his teeth, sprang into bed with me. I sang out; I could not help it now, and giving a sudden grunt of astonishment he began feeling of me.

Stammering out something, I knew not what, I rolled away from him against the wall, and then conjured him, whoever or whatever he might be, to keep quiet and let me get up and light the lamp again. But his guttural responses satisfied me at once that he but ill comprehended my meaning.

"Who-e debel you?" he at last said. "You no speak-e, dam-me, I kill-e." And so saying the lighted tomahawk began flourishing about me in the dark.

"Landlord, for God's sake, Peter Coffin!" shouted I. "Landlord! Watch! Coffin! Angels! Save me!"

"Speake-e! Tell-ee me who-ee be, or dam-me, I kill-e!" again growled the cannibal, while his horrid flourishings of the tomahawk scattered the hot tobacco ashes about me till I thought my linen would get on fire. But thank heaven, at that moment the landlord came into the room light in hand, and leaping from the bed I ran up to him.

"Don't be afraid now," said he, grinning again. "Queequeg here wouldn't harm a hair of your head."

"Stop your grinning," shouted I, "and why didn't you tell me that infernal harpooneer was a cannibal?"

"I thought ye know'd it; didn't I tell ye he was a-peddlin' heads around town? But turn flukes again and go to sleep. Queequeg, look here—you sabbee me, I sabbee you—this man sleep-e you—you sabbee?"

"Me sabbee plenty," grunted Queequeg, puffing away at his pipe and sitting up in bed.

"You gettee in," he added, motioning to me with his tomahawk and throwing the clothes to one side. He really did this in not only a civil but a really kind and charitable way. I stood looking at him a moment. For all his tattooings he was on the whole a clean, comely-looking cannibal. "What's all this fuss I have been making about," thought I to myself. "The man's a human being just as I am; he has just as much reason to fear me as I have to be afraid of him. Better sleep with a sober cannibal than a drunken Christian."

"Landlord," said I, "tell him to stash his tomahawk there, or pipe, or whatever you call it; tell him to stop smoking, in short, and I will turn in with him. But I don't fancy having a man smoking in bed with me. It's dangerous. Besides, I ain't insured."

This being told to Queequeg, he at once complied, and again politely motioned me to get into bed, rolling over to one side as much as to say, "I won't touch a leg of ye."

"Good night, landlord," said I, "you may go."

I turned in, and never slept better in my life.

CHAPTER 4

⚓

The Counterpane

UPON WAKING next morning about daylight, I found Queequeg's arm thrown over me in the most loving and affectionate manner. Though I tried to move his arm, unlock his bridegroom clasp, yet sleeping as he was, he still hugged me tightly, as though naught but death should part us twain. I now strove to rouse him—"Queequeg!"—but his only answer was a snore. I then rolled over, my face feeling as if it were in a horse-collar, and suddenly felt a slight scratch. I threw aside the counterpane; there lay the tomahawk sleeping by the savage's side, as if it were a hatchet-faced baby. A pretty pickle, truly, thought I, abed here in a strange house in the broad day, with a cannibal and a tomahawk! "Queequeg! In the name of goodness, Queequeg, wake!" At length, by dint of much wriggling, and loud and incessant expostula-

tions upon the unbecomingness of his hugging a fellow
male in that sort of style, I succeeded in extracting a
grunt; and presently he drew back his arm, shook himself
all over like a Newfoundland dog just out of the water,
and sat up in bed, stiff as a pikestaff, looking at me and
rubbing his eyes as if he did not altogether remember
how I came to be there, though a dim consciousness of
knowing something about me seemed to be slowly dawning on him. Meanwhile I lay quietly eyeing him, having
no serious misgivings now, and bent upon narrowly observing so curious a creature. When at last his mind
seemed made up touching the character of his bedfellow,
and he became, as it were, reconciled to the fact, he
jumped out upon the floor, and by certain signs and
sounds gave me to understand that if it pleased me he
would dress first and then leave me to dress afterward,
leaving the whole apartment to me. Thinks I, Queequeg,
under the circumstances, this is a very civilized overture;
the truth is, these savages have an innate sense of deli-
cacy, say what you will; it is marvelous how essentially
polite they are. I pay this particular compliment to Queequeg because he treated me with so much civility and
consideration, while I was guilty of great rudeness, staring at him from the bed and watching all his toilet motions, for the time my curiosity getting the better of my
breeding. Nevertheless, a man like Queequeg you don't
see every day; he and his ways were well worth unusual
regarding.

He commenced dressing at the top by donning his beaver hat, a very tall one, by the way, and then, still minus his

trousers, he hunted up his boots. What under the heavens he did it for I cannot tell, but his next movement was to crush himself, boots in hand, and hat on, under the bed. There, from sundry violent gaspings and strainings, I inferred he was hard at work booting himself, though by no law of propriety that I ever heard of is any man required to be private when putting on his boots. But Quee-queg, do you see, was a creature in the transition state, neither caterpillar nor butterfly. He was just enough civilized to show off his outlandishness in the strangest possible manner. His education was not yet completed. He was an undergraduate. If he had not been a small degree civilized, he very probably would not have troubled himself with boots at all; but then, if he had not been still a savage, he never would have dreamt of getting under the bed to put them on. At last, he emerged with his hat very much dented and crushed down over his eyes and began creaking and limping about the room, as if, not being much accustomed to boots, his pair of damp, wrinkled cowhide ones—probably not made to order either—rather pinched and tormented him at the first go-off of a bitter cold morning.

Seeing now that there were no curtains to the window, and that the street being very narrow, the house opposite commanded a plain view into the room, and observing more and more the indecorous figure that Queequeg made, staving about with little else but his hat and boots on, I begged him as well as I could to accelerate his toilet somewhat, and particularly to get into his pantaloons as soon as possible. He complied, and then proceeded to wash himself. At that time in the morning any Christian would have washed his face, but Queequeg, to my amazement, contented himself with restricting his ablutions to his chest, arms and hands. He then donned his waistcoat, and taking up a piece of hard soap on the washstand center table, dipped it into water and commenced lathering his face. I was watching to see where he kept his razor, when lo and behold, he takes the harpoon from the bed corner, slips out the long wooden stock, unsheathes the head, whets it a little on his boot, and striding up to the bit of mirror against the wall, begins a vigorous scraping, or rather harpooning of his cheeks. Thinks I, Queequeg, this is using Roger's best cutlery with a vengeance. Afterward I wondered the less at this operation when I came to know of what fine steel the head of a harpoon is made, and how exceedingly sharp the long straight edges are always kept.

The rest of his toilet was soon achieved, and he proudly marched out of the room, wrapped up in his great pilot monkey jacket and sporting his harpoon like a marshal's baton.

CHAPTER 5

⚓

Breakfast

I QUICKLY followed suit, and descending into the bar-
room accosted the grinning landlord very pleasantly. I
cherished no malice toward him, though he had been sky-
larking with me not a little in the matter of my bedfellow.

The barroom was now full of the boarders who had
been dropping in the previous night, and whom I had not
as yet had a good look at. They were nearly all whalemen: chief mates, and second mates, and third mates, and
sea carpenters, and sea coopers, and sea blacksmiths, and
harpooneers, and shipkeepers—a brown and brawny company, with bosky beards, an unshorn, shaggy set, all
wearing monkey jackets for morning gowns.

You could pretty plainly tell how long each one had
been ashore. This young fellow's healthy cheek is like a
sun-toasted pear in hue, and would seem to smell almost

as musky; he cannot have been three days landed from his Indian voyage. That man next to him looks a few shades lighter; you might say a touch of satinwood is in him. In the complexion of a third still lingers a tropic tawn, but slightly bleached withal; *he* doubtless has tarried whole weeks ashore. But who could show a cheek like Queequeg? Barred with various tints it seemed, like the Andes' western slope, to show forth in one array contrasting climates, zone by zone.

"Grub, ho!" now cried the landlord, flinging open a door, and in we went to breakfast.

After we were all seated at the table, I was preparing to hear some good stories about whaling. To my no small surprise, nearly every man maintained a profound silence. And not only that, but they looked embarrassed. Here were a set of sea dogs, many of whom without the slightest bashfulness had boarded great whales on the high sea—entire strangers to them—and dueled them dead without winking. Yet here they sat at a social breakfast table, all of the same calling, all of kindred tastes, looking around as sheepishly at each other as though they had never been out of sight of some sheepfold among the Green Mountains. A curious sight, these bashful bears, these timid warrior whalemen!

But as for Queequeg—why, Queequeg sat there among them, at the head of the table, too, it so chanced, as cool as an icicle. To be sure I cannot say much for his breeding. His greatest admirer could not have cordially justified his bringing his harpoon in to breakfast with him and using it there without ceremony, reaching over the table with it, to the imminent jeopardy of many heads, and grappling the beefsteaks toward him. But *that* was certainly very coolly done by him, and everyone knows that in most people's estimation, to do anything coolly is to do it genteelly.

We will not speak of all Queequeg's peculiarities here, how he eschewed coffee and hot rolls, and applied his undivided attention to beefsteaks, done rare. Enough that when breakfast was over he withdrew like the rest into the public room, lighted his tomahawk pipe, and was sitting there quietly digesting and smoking with his inseparable hat on when I sallied out for a stroll.

CHAPTER 6

⚓

The Chapel

IN THIS SAME New Bedford there stands a whaleman's chapel, and few are the moody fishermen, shortly bound for the Indian ocean or Pacific, who fail to make a Sunday visit to the spot. I am sure that I did not.

Returning from my first morning stroll, I again sallied out upon this special errand. The sky had changed from clear, sunny cold to driving sleet and mist. Wrapping myself in my shaggy jacket of the cloth called bearskin, I fought my way against the stubborn storm. Entering, I found a small scattered congregation of sailors, and sailors' wives and widows. A muffled silence reigned, only broken at times by the shrieks of the storm. Each silent worshiper seemed purposely sitting apart from the other, as if each silent grief were insular and incommunicable. The chaplain had not yet arrived, and there these silent islands of men and women sat, steadfastly eyeing several marble tablets with black borders, masoned into the wall on either side of the pulpit.

Three of them ran something like the following, but I do not pretend to quote:

SACRED TO THE MEMORY OF
JOHN TALBOT,
WHO, AT THE AGE OF EIGHTEEN, WAS LOST OVERBOARD
NEAR THE ISLE OF DESOLATION, OFF PATAGONIA
NOVEMBER 1ST, 1836.
THIS TABLET IS ERECTED TO HIS MEMORY
BY HIS SISTER.

SACRED TO THE MEMORY OF
ROBERT LONG, WILLIS ELLERY,
NATHAN COLEMAN, WALTER CANNY,
SETH MACY, AND SAMUEL GLEIG,
FORMING ONE OF THE BOATS' CREWS OF
THE SHIP ELIZA
WHO WERE TOWED OUT OF SIGHT BY A WHALE,
ON THE OFF-SHORE GROUND IN THE PACIFIC,
DECEMBER 31ST, 1839.
THIS MARBLE IS HERE PLACED BY THEIR SURVIVING
SHIPMATES.

SACRED TO THE MEMORY OF
THE LATE
CAPTAIN EZEKIEL HARDY,
WHO IN THE BOWS OF HIS BOAT WAS KILLED BY A
SPERM WHALE ON THE COAST OF JAPAN,
AUGUST 3RD, 1833.
THIS TABLET IS ERECTED TO HIS MEMORY BY
HIS WIDOW

It need scarcely to be told, with what feelings, on the eve of a Nantucket voyage, I regarded those marble tablets, and by the murky light of that darkened doleful day read the fate of the whalemen who had gone before me. Yes, Ishmael, the same fate may be thine. But somehow I grew merry again. Delightful inducements to embark, fine chance for promotion, it seems—aye, a stove boat will make me an immortal by brevet. Yes, there is death in this business of whaling—a speechlessly quick chaotic bundling of a man into Eternity. But what then? Methinks we have hugely mistaken this matter of Life and Death. Methinks that what they call my shadow here on earth is my true substance.

Methinks my body is but the lees of my better being. In fact take my body who will. Take it I say, it is not myself. And therefore three cheers for Nantucket, and come a stove boat and stove body when they will, for stave my soul, Jove himself cannot.

CHAPTER 7

⚓

A Bosom Friend

RETURNING to the SPOUTER INN from the chapel, I found Queequeg there quite alone. He was sitting on a bench before the fire, with his feet on the stove hearth, and in one hand was holding close up to his face that little Negro idol of his, peering hard into its face, and with a jackknife gently whittling away at its nose, meanwhile humming to himself in his heathenish way.

But being now interrupted, he put up the image, and pretty soon, going to the table, took up a large book there, and placing it on his lap began counting the pages with deliberate regularity, at every fiftieth page—as I fancied—stopping a moment, looking vacantly around him, and giving utterance to a long-drawn gurgling whistle of astonishment. He would then begin at the next fifty, seeming to commence at number one each time, as

51

though he could not count more than fifty, and it was only by such a large number of fifties being found together that his astonishment at the multitude of pages was excited.

With much interest I sat watching him. Savage though he was, and hideously marred about the face—at least to my taste—his countenance yet had a something in it which was by no means disagreeable. You cannot hide the soul. Through all his unearthly tattooings, I thought I saw the traces of a simple honest heart; and in his large, deep eyes, fiery black and bold, there seemed tokens of a spirit that would dare a thousand devils. And besides all this, there was a certain lofty bearing about the pagan, which even his uncouthness could not altogether maim.

Whilst I was thus closely scanning him, half-pretending meanwhile to be looking out at the storm from the casement, he never heeded my presence, never troubled himself with so much as a single glance; but appeared wholly occupied with counting the pages of the marvelous book. Considering how sociably we had been sleeping together the previous night, and especially considering the affectionate arm I had found thrown over me upon waking in the morning, I thought this indifference of his very strange. But savages are strange beings. At times you do not know exactly how to take them. At first they are overawing; their calm self-collectedness of simplicity seems a Socratic wisdom. I had noticed also that Queequeg never consorted at all, or but very little, with the other seamen in the inn. He made no advances whatever, appeared to have no desire to enlarge the circle of his acquaintances. All this struck me as mighty singular; yet upon second thought, there was something almost sublime in it. Here was a man some twenty thousand miles from home, by the way of Cape Horn, that is—which was the only way he could get there—thrown among people as strange to him as though he were in the planet Jupiter. And yet he seemed entirely at his ease, preserving the utmost serenity, content with his own companionship, always equal to himself. Surely this was a touch of fine philosophy, though no doubt he had never heard there was such a thing as that. But, perhaps, to be true philosophers, we mortals should not be conscious of so living or so striving.

As I sat there in that now lonely room, the fire burning low in that mild stage when, after its first intensity has warmed the air, it then only glows to be looked at, the evening shades and phantoms gathering around the casements and peering in upon us silent, solitary twain, the storm booming without in solemn swells, I began to be sensible of strange feelings. I felt a melting in me. No more my splintered heart and maddened hand were turned against the wolfish world. This soothing savage had redeemed it. There he sat, his very indifference speaking a nature in which there lurked no civilized hypocrisies and bland deceits. Wild he was, a very sight of sights to see; yet I began to feel myself mysteriously drawn toward him. And those same things that would have repelled most others, they were the very magnets

that thus drew me. I'll try a pagan friend, thought I, since
Christian kindness has proved but hollow courtesy. I
drew my bench near him, and made some friendly signs
and hints, doing my best to talk with him meanwhile. At
first he little noticed these advances; but presently, upon
my referring to his last night's hospitalities, he made out
to ask me whether we were again to be bedfellows. I told
him yes, whereat I thought he looked pleased, perhaps a
little complimented.

We then turned over the book together, and I endeavored to explain to him the purpose of the printing, and
the meaning of the few pictures that were in it. Thus I
soon engaged his interest; and from that we went to jab-
bering the best we could about the various outer sights
to be seen in this famous town. Soon I proposed a social
smoke; and producing his pouch and tomahawk, he
quietly offered me a puff. And there we sat exchanging
puffs from that wild pipe of his, and keeping it regularly
passing between us.

If there yet lurked any ice of indifference toward me in
the pagan's breast, this pleasant, genial smoke we had
soon thawed it out and left us cronies. He seemed to take
to me quite as naturally and unbiddenly as I to him. And
when our smoke was over, he pressed his forehead against
mine, clasped me around the waist, and said that henceforth we were married, meaning, in his country's phrase,
that we were bosom friends; he would gladly die for me,
if need should be. In a countryman, this sudden flame of
friendship would have seemed far too premature, a thing

to be much distrusted; but in this simple savage those old rules would not apply.

After supper, and another social chat and smoke, we went to our room together. He made me a present of his embalmed head, took out his enormous tobacco wallet, and groping under the tobacco, drew out some thirty dollars in silver. Then spreading them on the table, and mechanically dividing them into two equal portions, he pushed one of them toward me, and said it was mine. I was going to remonstrate, but he silenced me by pouring them into my trousers' pockets. I let them stay. He then went about his evening prayers, took out his idol, and removed the paper fireboard. By certain signs and symptoms, I thought he seemed anxious for me to join him; but well knowing what was to follow, I deliberated a moment whether, in case he invited me, I would comply or otherwise.

I was a good Christian, born and bred in the bosom of the infallible Presbyterian Church. How then could I unite with this wild idolater in worshiping his piece of wood? But what is worship? thought I. Do you suppose now, Ishmael, that the magnanimous God of heaven and earth—pagans and all included—can possibly be jealous of an insignificant bit of black wood? Impossible! But what is worship? To do the will of God—*that* is worship. And what is the will of God? To do to my fellowman what I would have my fellowman to do to me—*that* is the will of God. Now Queequeg is my fellowman. And what do I wish that this Queequeg would do to me? Why,

unite with me in my particular Presbyterian form of worship. Consequently, I must then unite with him in his;
ergo, I must turn idolator. So I kindled the shavings,
helped prop up the innocent little idol, offered him burnt
biscuit with Queequeg, salaamed before him twice or
thrice, kissed his nose, and that done, we undressed and
went to bed, at peace with our own consciences and all
the world. But we did not go to sleep without some little
chat.

CHAPTER 8

⚓

Nightgown

Wᴇ ʜᴀᴅ ʟᴀɪɴ in bed, chatting and napping at short intervals, when at last by reason of our confabulations, what little nappishness remained in us altogether departed and we felt like getting up again, though daybreak was yet some way down the future.

With our shaggy jackets drawn about our shoulders, we now passed the tomahawk pipe from one to the other, till slowly there grew over us a blue hanging tester of smoke, illuminated by the flame of the new-lit lamp.

Whether it was that this undulating tester rolled the savage away to far distant scenes, I know not, but Queequeg now spoke of his native island, and eager to hear his history, I begged him to go on and tell it. He gladly complied. Though at the time I but ill comprehended not a few of his words, yet subsequent disclosures, when I had become more familiar with his broken phraseology, now enable me to present the whole story such as it may prove in the mere skeleton I give.

⚓

Chapter 9

Biographical

Q UEEQUEG was a native of Kokovoko, an island far away to the west and south. It is not down in any map; true places never are.

When a new-hatched savage, running wild about his native woodlands in a grass clout, followed by the nibbling goats as if he were a green sapling, even then, in Queequeg's ambitious soul, lurked a strong desire to see something more of Christendom than a specimen whaler or two. His father was a high chief, a king, his uncle a high priest, and on the maternal side he boasted aunts who were the wives of unconquerable warriors. There was excellent blood in his veins—royal stuff, though sadly vitiated, I fear, by the cannibal propensity he nourished in his untutored youth.

A Sag Harbor ship visited his father's bay, and Queequeg sought a passage to Christian lands. But the ship, having her full complement of seamen, spurned his suit; and not all the influence of the King, his father, could prevail. But Queequeg vowed a vow. Alone in his canoe, he paddled off to a distant strait which he knew the ship must pass through when she quitted the island. On one side was a coral reef; on the other a low tongue of land, covered with mangrove thickets that grew out into the water. Hiding his canoe, still afloat, among these thickets, with its prow seaward, he sat down in the stern, paddle low in hand; and when the ship was gliding by, like a flash he darted out and gained her side. With one backward dash of his foot he capsized and sank his canoe, climbed up the chains, and throwing himself at full length upon the deck, grappled a ring-bolt there, and swore not to let it go though hacked in pieces.

In vain the captain threatened to throw him overboard, suspended a cutlass over his naked wrists; Queequeg was the son of a king, and Queequeg budged not. Struck by his desperate dauntlessness, and his wild desire to visit Christendom, the captain at last relented, and told him he might make himself at home. But this fine young savage—this sea Prince of Wales, never saw the captain's cabin. They put him down among the sailors and made a whaleman of him. But like the Czar Peter content to toil in the shipyards of foreign cities, Queequeg disdained no seeming ignominy, if thereby he might happily gain the power of enlightening his untutored countrymen. For at bottom—so he told me—he was actuated by a profound desire to learn among the Christians the arts whereby to make his people still happier than they were, and more than that, still better than they were. But, alas! The practices of whalemen soon convinced him that even Christians could be both miserable and wicked, infinitely more so than all his father's heathens. Arrived at last in old Sag Harbor, and seeing what the sailors did there, and then going on to Nantucket and seeing how they spent their wages in *that* place also, poor Queequeg gave it up for lost. Thought he, it's a wicked world in all meridians; I'll die a pagan.

And thus an old idolater at heart, he yet lived among these Christians, wore their clothes, and tried to talk their gibberish. Hence the queer ways about him, though now some time away from home.

By hints, I asked him whether he did not propose going back and having a coronation, since he might now consider his father dead and gone, he being very old and feeble at the last accounts. He answered no, not yet, and added that he was fearful Christianity, or rather Christians, had unfitted him for ascending the pure and undefiled throne of thirty pagan kings before him. But by and by, he said, he would return—as soon as he felt himself baptized again. For the nonce, however, he proposed to sail about, and sow his wild oats in all four oceans. They had made a harpooneer of him, and that barbed iron was in lieu of a scepter now.

I asked him what might be his immediate purpose, touching his future movements. He answered, to go to sea again, in his old vocation. Upon this, I told him that whaling was my own design, and informed him of my intention to sail out of Nantucket, as being the most promising port for an adventurous whaleman to embark from. He at once resolved to accompany me to that island, ship aboard the same vessel, get into the same watch, the same boat, the same mess with me, in short to share my every hap: with both my hands in his, boldly dip into the potluck of both worlds. To all this I joyously assented; for besides the affection I now felt for Queequeg, he was an experienced harpooneer, and as such, could not fail to be of great usefulness to one who, like me, was wholly ignorant of the mysteries of whaling, though well acquainted with the sea as known to merchant seamen.

His story being ended with his pipe's last dying puff, Queequeg embraced me, pressed his forehead against mine, and blowing out the light, we rolled over from each other, this way and that, and very soon were sleeping.

Chapter 10

⚓

Wheelbarrow

Next morning, Monday, after disposing of the embalmed head to a barber, for a block, I settled my own and comrade's bill, using, however, my comrade's money. The grinning landlord, as well as the boarders, seemed amazingly tickled at the sudden friendship which had sprung up between me and Queequeg—especially as Peter Coffin's cock-and-bull stories had previously so much alarmed me about him.

We borrowed a wheelbarrow, and embarking our things, including my own poor carpetbag, and Queequeg's canvas sack and hammock, away we went down to the *Moss*, the little Nantucket packet schooner moored at the wharf. As we were going along the people stared, not at Queequeg so much—for they were used to seeing cannibals like him in their streets, but at seeing him and me upon such confidential terms. But we heeded them not, going along wheeling the barrow by turns, and Queequeg now and then stopping to adjust the sheath on his harpoon barbs. I asked him why he carried such a troublesome thing with him ashore, and whether all whaling ships did not find their own harpoons. To this, in substance, he replied that though what I hinted was true enough, yet he had a particular affection for his own harpoon, because it was of assured stuff, well tried in many a mortal combat, and deeply intimate with the hearts of whales. In short, like many inland reapers and mowers, who go into the farmers' meadows armed with their own scythes—though in no wise obliged to furnish them—even so, Queequeg, for his own private reasons, preferred his own harpoon.

Shifting the barrow from my hand to his, he told me a funny story about the first wheelbarrow he had ever seen. It was in Sag Harbor. The owners of his ship, it seems, had lent him one, in which to carry his heavy chest to his boarding house. Not to seem ignorant about the thing—though in truth he was entirely so, concerning the precise way in which to manage the barrow—Queequeg puts his chest upon it, lashes it fast, and then shoulders the barrow and marches up the wharf. "Why," said I, "Queequeg, you might have known better than that, one would think. Didn't the people laugh?"

Upon this, he told me another story. The people of his island of Kokovoko, it seems, at their wedding feasts express the fragrant water of young coconuts into a large stained calabash like a punchbowl; and this punchbowl

always forms the great central ornament on the braided
mat where the feast is held. Now a certain grand merchant ship once touched at Kokovoko, and its commander
—from all accounts, a very stately punctilious gentleman,
at least for a sea captain—this commander was invited to
the wedding feast of Queequeg's sister, a pretty young
princess just turned ten. Well, when all the wedding
guests were assembled at the bride's bamboo cottage,
this captain marches in, and being assigned the post of
honor, places himself over against the punchbowl, and
between the high priest and his majesty the king, Queequeg's father. Grace being said—for those people have
their grace as well as we—though Queequeg told me that
unlike us, who at such times look downward to our plat-
ters, they, on the contrary, copying the ducks, glance upward to the great Giver of all feasts—grace, I say, being
said, the high priest opens the banquet by the immemorial ceremony of the island: that is, by dipping his con-
secrated and consecrating fingers into the bowl before the
blessed beverage circulates. Seeing himself placed next
to the priest, and noting the ceremony, and thinking himself—being captain of a ship—as having plain precedence
over a mere king, especially in the king's own house, the
captain coolly proceeds to wash his hands in the punchbowl—taking it I suppose for a huge finger bowl. "Now,"
said Queequeg, "what you tink now? Didn't our people
laugh?"

At last, passage paid and luggage safe, we stood on
board the schooner. Hoisting sail, it glided down the
Acushnet river. On one side, New Bedford rose in ter-

races of streets, their ice-covered trees all glittering in the clear cold air. Huge hills and mountains of casks on casks were piled upon her wharves, and side by side, the world-wandering whaleships lay silent and safely moored at last; while from others came a sound of carpenters and coopers, with blended noises of fires and forges to melt the pitch, all betokening that new cruises were on the start; that one most perilous and long voyage ended only begins a second; and a second ended only begins a third, and so on, forever and for aye. Such is the endlessness, yea, the intolerableness of all earthly effort.

Gaining the more open water, the bracing breeze waxed fresh; the little *Moss* tossed the quick foam from her bows as a young colt his snortings. How I snuffed that Tartar air! How I spurned that turnpike earth, that common highway dented all over with the marks of slavish heels and hoofs, and turned to admire the magnanimity of the sea which will permit no records.

At the same foam-fountain, Queequeg seemed to drink and reel with me. His dusky nostrils swelled apart; he showed his filed and pointed teeth. On, on we flew; and our offing gained, the *Moss* did homage to the blast, ducked and dived her bows as a slave before the sultan. Sideways leaning, we sideways darted; every rope yarn tingling like a wire, the two tall masts buckling like Indian canes in land tornadoes. So full of this reeling scene were we, as we stood by the plunging bowsprit, that for some time we did not notice the jeering glances of the passengers, a lubberlike assembly, who marveled that two fellow beings should be so companionable, as though

a white man were anything more dignified than a white-washed Negro. But there were some boobies and bumpkins there, who, by their intense greenness, must have come from the heart and center of all verdure. Queequeg caught one of these young saplings mimicking him behind his back. I thought the bumpkin's hour of doom was come. Dropping his harpoon, the brawny savage caught him in his arms, and by an almost miraculous dexterity and strength sent him high up bodily into the air, slightly tapping his stern in mid-somersault. The fellow landed with bursting lungs upon his feet, while Queequeg, turning his back upon him, lighted his tomahawk pipe and passed it to me for a puff.

"Capting! Capting!" yelled the bumpkin, running toward that officer, "Capting, Capting, here's the devil."

"Hallo, *you* sir," cried the captain, a gaunt rib of the sea, stalking up to Queequeg, "what in thunder do you mean by that? Don't you know you might have killed that chap?"

"What him say?" said Queequeg, as he mildly turned to me.

"He say," said I, "that you came near kill-e that man there," pointing to the still shivering greenhorn.

"Kill-e," cried Queequeg, twisting his tattooed face into an unearthly expression of disdain, "ah! him bevy small-e fish-e; Queequeg no kill-e so small-e fish-e; Queequeg kill-e big whale!"

"Look you," roared the captain, "I'll kill-e *you*, you cannibal, if you try any more of your tricks aboard here, so mind your eye."

But it so happened just then, that it was nigh time for the captain to mind his own eye. The prodigious strain upon the mainsail had parted the weather sheet, and the tremendous boom was now flying from side to side, completely sweeping the entire afterpart of the deck. The poor fellow whom Queequeg had handled so roughly was swept overboard; all hands were in a panic; and to attempt snatching at the boom to stay it, seemed madness. It flew from right to left and back again, almost in one ticking of a watch, and every instant seemed on the point of snapping into splinters. Nothing was done, and nothing seemed capable of being done; those on deck rushed toward the bows and stood eyeing the boom as if it were the lower jaw of an exasperated whale. In the midst of this consternation Queequeg dropped deftly to his knees, and crawling under the path of the boom, whipped hold of a rope, secured one end to the bulwarks, and then flinging the other like a lasso, caught it around the boom as it swept over his head. At the next jerk the spar was that way trapped, and all was safe. The schooner was run into the wind, and while the hands were clearing away the stern boat, Queequeg, stripped to the waist, darted from the side with a long living arc of a leap. For three minutes or more he was seen swimming like a dog, throwing his long arms straight out before him, and by turns revealing his brawny shoulders through the freezing foam. I looked at the grand and glorious fellow, but saw no one to be saved. The greenhorn had gone down. Shooting himself perpendicularly from the water, Queequeg now took an instant's glance around him, and seeming to

see just how matters were, dived down and disappeared.
A few minutes more and he rose again, one arm still striking out, and with the other dragging a lifeless form. The
boat soon picked them up. The poor bumpkin was restored. All hands voted Queequeg a noble trump; the
captain begged his pardon. From that hour I clove to
Queequeg like a barnacle, yea, till poor Queequeg took
his last long dive.

Was there ever such unconsciousness? He did not
seem to think that he at all deserved a medal from the
Humane and Magnanimous Societies. He only asked for
water—fresh water—something to wipe the brine off. That
done, he put on dry clothes, lighted his pipe, and leaning
against the bulwarks and mildly eyeing those around
him, seemed to be saying to himself: "It's a mutual, joint-
stock world in all meridians. We cannibals must help
these Christians."

CHAPTER 11

⚓

Chowder

IT WAS quite late in the evening when the little *Moss*
came snugly to anchor and Queequeg and I went ashore.
So we could attend to no business that day, at least none
but a supper and a bed. The landlord of the SPOUTER INN
had recommended to us his cousin Hosea Hussey of the
TRY-POTS, whom he asserted to be the proprietor of one
of the best kept hotels in all Nantucket. Moreover he had
assured us that Cousin Hosea, as he called him, was
famous for his chowders. In short, he plainly hinted that
we could not possibly do better than try potluck at the
TRY-POTS.

Two enormous wooden pots painted black and suspended by asses' ears, swung from the crosstrees of an
old topmast, planted in front of an old doorway. The
horns of the crosstrees were sawed off on the other side,
so that this old topmast looked not a little like a gallows.
Perhaps I was oversensitive to such impressions at the
time, but I could not help staring at this gallows with a

vague misgiving. A sort of crick was in my neck as I gazed up to the two remaining horns; yes, *two* of them, one for Queequeg, and one for me. It's ominous, thinks I. A Coffin my innkeeper upon landing in my first whaling port, tombstones staring at me in the whalemen's chapel, and here a gallows! And a pair of prodigious black pots too! Are these last throwing out oblique hints touching Tophet?

I was called from these reflections by the sight of a freckled woman with yellow hair and a yellow gown, standing in the porch of the inn, under a dull red lamp swinging there, that looked much like an injured eye, and carrying on a brisk scolding with a man in a purple woolen shirt.

"Get along with ye," said she to the man, "or I'll be combing ye!"

"Come on, Queequeg," said I. "It's all right. There's Mrs. Hussey."

And so it turned out, Mr. Hosea Hussey being away from home, but leaving Mrs. Hussey entirely competent to attend to all his affairs. Upon making known our desires for a supper and a bed, Mrs. Hussey postponed further scolding for the present, ushered us into a little room, and seating us at a table spread with the relics of a recently concluded repast, turned around to us and said, "Clam or cod?"

"What's that about cods, ma'am?" said I with much politeness.

"Clam or cod?" she repeated.

"A clam for supper? A cold clam; is *that* what you

mean, Mrs. Hussey?" says I. "But that's a rather cold and clammy reception in the wintertime, ain't it, Mrs. Hussey?"

But being in a great hurry to resume scolding the man in the purple shirt, who was waiting for it in the entry, and seeming to hear nothing but the word "clam," Mrs. Hussey hurried toward an open door leading to the kitchen, and bawling out "clam for two," disappeared.

"Queequeg," said I, "do you think that we can make out a supper for us both on one clam?"

However, a warm savory steam from the kitchen served to belie the apparently cheerless prospect before us. And when that smoking chowder came in the mystery was delightfully explained. Oh, sweet friends! Harken to me. It was made of small juicy clams, scarcely bigger than hazel nuts, mixed with pounded ship biscuit and salt pork cut up into little flakes, the whole enriched with butter, and plentifully seasoned with pepper and salt. Our appetites being sharpened by the frosty voyage, and in particular, Queequeg seeing his favorite fishy food before him, and the chowder being surpassingly excellent, we dispatched it with great expedition. Then leaning back a moment and bethinking me of Mrs. Hussey's clam and cod announcement, I thought I would try a little experiment. Stepping to the kitchen door, I uttered the word "cod" with great emphasis, and resumed my seat. In a few moments the savory steam came forth again, but with a different flavor, and in good time a fine cod chowder was placed before us.

Supper concluded, we received a lamp and directions from Mrs. Hussey concerning the nearest way to bed; but

as Queequeg was about to precede me up the stairs, the
lady reached forth her arm and demanded his harpoon;
she allowed no harpoon in her chambers. "Why not?" said
I. "Every true whaleman sleeps with his harpoon—but
why not!" "Because it's dangerous," says she. "Ever since
young Stiggs coming from that unfort'n't v'y'ge of his,
when he was gone four years and a half, with only three
barrels of *ile*, was found dead in my first floor back, with
his harpoon in his side, ever since then I allow no
boarders to take sich dangerous weapons in their rooms
a-night. So, Mr. Queequeg" (for she learned his name),
"I will just take this here iron, and keep it for you till
morning. But the chowder; clam or cod tomorrow for
breakfast, men?"

"Both," says I, "and let's have a couple of smoked
herring by way of variety."

CHAPTER 12

⚓

The Ship

IN BED we concocted our plans for the morrow. But to my surprise and no small concern, Queequeg now gave me to understand that he had been diligently consulting Yojo—the name of his black little god—and Yojo had told him two or three times over, and strongly insisted upon it every way, that instead of our going together among the whaling fleet in harbor, and in concert selecting our craft—instead of this, I say, Yojo earnestly enjoined that the selection of the ship should rest wholly with me, inasmuch as Yojo proposed befriending us. And in order to do so, he had already pitched upon a vessel which, if left to myself, I, Ishmael, should infallibly light upon, for all the world as though it had turned out by chance. And in that vessel I must immediately ship myself, for the present irrespective of Queequeg.

Now, this plan of Queequeg's or rather Yojo's, touching

the selection of our craft, I did not like at all. I had not a little relied upon Queequeg's sagacity to point out the whaler best fitted to carry us and our fortunes securely. But as all my remonstrances produced no effect upon Queequeg I was obliged to acquiesce, and accordingly prepared to set about this business with a determined rushing sort of energy and vigor that should quickly settle that trifling little affair.

Next morning early, leaving Queequeg shut up with Yojo in our little bedroom—for it seemed that it was some sort of Lent or Ramadan, or day of fasting, humiliation and prayer with Queequeg and Yojo that day—leaving Queequeg, then, fasting on his tomahawk pipe, and Yojo warming himself at his sacrificial fire of shavings, I sallied out among the shipping. After much prolonged sauntering and many random inquiries, I learnt that there were three ships up for three years' voyages—the *Devil-dam*, the *Tit-bit*, and the *Pequod. Devil-dam*, I do not know the origin of; *Tit-bit* is obvious; *Pequod*, you will no doubt remember, was the name of a celebrated tribe of Massachusetts Indians, now extinct as the ancient Medes. I peered and pried about the *Devil-dam*, from her, hopped over to the *Tit-bit;* and, finally, going on board the *Pequod*, I looked around her for a moment, and then decided that this was the very ship for us.

You may have seen many a quaint craft in your day, for aught I know: square-toed luggers, mountainous Japanese junks, butter-box galliots, and what not; but take my word for it, you never saw such a rare old craft as this same rare old *Pequod*. She was a ship of the old school, rather small if anything, with an old-fashioned claw-footed look about her. Long seasoned and weather-stained in the typhoons and calms of all four oceans, her old hull's complexion was darkened like a French grena-dier's who has alike fought in Egypt and Siberia. Her venerable bows looked bearded. Her masts, cut some-where on the coast of Japan where her original ones were lost overboard in a gale, stood stiffly up like the spines of the three old kings of Cologne. Her ancient decks were worn and wrinkled, like the pilgrim-worshiped flagstone in Canterbury Cathedral where Becket bled.

But to all these her old antiquities were added new and marvelous features, pertaining to the wild business that for more than half a century she had followed. Old Captain Peleg, many years her chief mate before he com-manded another vessel of his own, and now a retired seaman and one of the principal owners of the *Pequod*—this old Peleg, during the term of his chief mateship, had built upon her original grotesqueness, and inlaid it all over with a quaintness both of material and device.

She was a thing of trophies—a cannibal of a craft, trick-ing herself forth in the chased bones of her enemies. All around, her unpaneled open bulwarks were garnished like one continuous jaw with the long sharp teeth of the sperm whale, inserted there for pins to fasten her old hempen thews and tendons to. Those thews ran not through base blocks of land wood, but deftly traveled through sheaves of sea ivory. Scorning a turnstile wheel at her reverend helm, she sported there a tiller; and that tiller was in one mass, curiously carved from the long narrow lower jaw of her hereditary foe. The helmsman who steered by that tiller in a tempest, felt like the Tartar, when he holds back his fiery steed by clutching its jaw. A noble craft, but somehow a most melancholy! All noble things are touched with that.

Now when I looked about the quarterdeck for someone having authority, in order to propose myself as a candidate for the voyage, at first I saw nobody; but I could not well overlook a strange sort of tent, or rather wigwam, pitched a little behind the mainmast. It seemed only a temporary erection used in port. It was of a conical shape, some ten feet high, consisting of the long huge slabs of limber black bone taken from the middle and highest part of the jaws of the right whale.

And half concealed in this queer tenement, I at length found one who by his aspect seemed to have authority; and who, it being noon, and the ship's work suspended, was now enjoying respite from the burden of command.

There was nothing so very particular, perhaps, about the appearance of the elderly man I saw. He was brown and brawny like most old seamen, and heavily rolled up in pilot cloth, cut in the Quaker style, only there was a fine and almost microscopic network of the minutest wrinkles interlacing around his eyes, which must have arisen from his continual sailings in many hard gales, and always looking to windward—for this causes the muscles about the eyes to become pursed together. Such eye wrinkles are very effectual in a scowl.

"Is this the captain of the *Pequod?*" said I, advancing to the door of the tent.

"Supposing it be the captain of the *Pequod,* what dost thou want of him?" he demanded.

"I was thinking of shipping."

"Thou wast, wast thou? I see thou art no Nantucketer—ever been in a stove boat?"

"No, sir, I never have."

"Dost know nothing at all about whaling, I dare say —eh?"

"Nothing, sir; but I have no doubt I shall soon learn. I've been several voyages in the merchant service, and I think that——"

"Marchant service be damned. Talk not that lingo to me. Dost see that leg? I'll take that leg away from thy stern, if ever thou talkest of the marchant service to me again. Marchant service, indeed! I suppose now ye feel considerable proud of having served in those marchant ships. But flukes, man! What makes thee want to go a-whaling, eh? It looks a little suspicious, don't it, eh? Hast not been a pirate, hast thou? Didst not rob thy last captain, didst thou? Dost not think of murdering the officers when thou gettest to sea?"

I protested my innocence of these things. I saw that under the mask of these half-humorous innuendoes, this old seaman, as an insulated Quakerish Nantucketer, was full of his insular prejudices, and rather distrustful of all aliens, unless they hailed from Cape Cod or the Vineyard.

"But what takes thee a-whaling? I want to know that before I think of shipping ye."

"Well, sir, I want to see what whaling is. I want to see the world."

"Want to see what whaling is, eh? Have ye clapped eye on Captain Ahab?"

"Who is Captain Ahab, sir?"

"Aye, aye, I thought so. Captain Ahab is the captain of this ship."

"I am mistaken then. I thought I was speaking to the captain himself."

"Thou are speaking to Captain Peleg. That's who ye are speaking to, young man. It belongs to me and Captain Bildad to see the *Pequod* fitted out for the voyage, and supplied with all her needs, including crew. We are part owners and agents. But as I was going to say, if thou wantest to know what whaling is, as thou tellest ye do, I can put ye in a way of finding it out before ye bind yourself to it, past backing out. Clap eye on Captain Ahab, young man, and thou wilt find that he has only one leg."

"What do you mean, sir? Was the other one lost by a whale?"

"Lost by a whale! Young man, come nearer to me: it was devoured, chewed up, crunched by the monstrousest parmacetty that ever chipped a boat!—ah, ah!"

I was a little alarmed about this energy, perhaps also a little touched at the hearty grief in his concluding exclamation, but said as calmly as I could, "What you say is no doubt true enough, sir; but how could I know there was any peculiar ferocity in that particular whale, though indeed I might have inferred as much from the simple fact of the accident."

"Look ye now, young man, thy lungs are a sort of soft, d'ye see; thou dost not talk shark a bit. *Sure*, ye've been to sea before now; sure of that?"

"Sir," said I, "I thought I told you that I had been four voyages in the merchant——"

"Hard down out of that! Mind what I said about the marchant service—don't aggravate me—I won't have it. But let us understand each other. I have given thee a hint about what whaling is; do ye yet feel inclined for it?"

"I do, sir."

"Very good. Now, art thou the man to pitch a harpoon down a live whale's throat, and then jump after it? Answer, quick!"

"I am, sir, if it should be positively indispensable to do so, not to be got rid of, that is, which I don't take to be the fact."

"Good again. Now then, thou not only wantest to go a-whaling, to find out by experience what whaling is, but ye also want to go in order to see the world? Was not that what ye said? I thought so. Well then, just step forward there and take a peep over the weather bow, and then back to me and tell me what ye see there."

For a moment I stood a little puzzled by this curious request, not knowing exactly how to take it, whether humorously or in earnest. But concentrating all his crow's feet into one scowl, Captain Peleg started me on the errand.

Going forward and glancing over the weather bow, I perceived that the ship swinging to her anchor with the flood tide, was now obliquely pointing toward the open ocean. The prospect was unlimited, but exceedingly monotonous and forbidding—not the slightest variety that I could see.

"Well, what's the report?" said Peleg when I came back. "What did ye see?"

"Not much," I replied. "Nothing but water. Considerable horizon though, and there's a squall coming up, I think."

"Well, what dost thou think then of seeing the world? Do ye wish to go round Cape Horn to see any more of it, eh? Can't ye see the world where ye stand?"

I was a little staggered, but go a-whaling I must, and I would, and the *Pequod* was as good a ship as any—I thought the best—and all this I now repeated to Peleg. Seeing me so determined, he expressed his willingness to ship me.

"And thou mayest as well sign the papers right off," he added—"come along with ye." And so saying, he led the way below deck into the cabin.

Seated on the transom was what seemed to me a most uncommon and surprising figure. It turned out to be Captain Bildad, who along with Captain Peleg was one of the largest owners of the vessel; the other shares, as is sometimes the case in these ports, being held by a crowd of old annuitants, widows, fatherless children, and chancery wards, each owning about the value of a timber head, or a foot of plank, or a nail or two in the ship. People in Nantucket invest their money in whaling vessels the same way that you do yours in approved state stocks bringing in good interest.

Now Bildad, like Peleg, and indeed many other Nantucketers, was a Quaker, the island having been originally
settled by that sect; and to this day its inhabitants in general retain in an uncommon measure the peculiarities of
the Quaker, only variously and anomalously modified by
things altogether alien and heterogeneous. For some of
these same Quakers are the most sanguinary of all sailors
and whale hunters. They are fighting Quakers; they are
Quakers with a vengeance.

So that there are instances among them of men, who,
named with Scripture names—a singularly common fashion on the island—and in childhood naturally imbibing
the stately dramatic *thee* and *thou* of the Quaker idiom,
still, from the audacious, daring and boundless adventure
of their subsequent lives, strangely blend with these un-
outgrown peculiarities, a thousand bold dashes of character, not unworthy of a Scandinavian sea king, or a
poetical pagan Roman.

Bildad, I am sorry to say, had the reputation of being
an incorrigible old hunks, and in his sea-going days, a
bitter, hard taskmaster. They told me in Nantucket,
though it certainly seems a curious story, that when he
sailed the old *Categut* whaleman, his crew upon arriving
home, were mostly all carried ashore to the hospital, sore
exhausted and worn out. For a pious man, especially for a
Quaker, he was certainly rather hardhearted, to say the
least. He never used to swear, though, at his men, they
said; but somehow he got an inordinate quantity of cruel,
unmitigated hard work out of them. When Bildad was a
chief mate, to have his drab-colored eye intently looking

at you, made you feel completely nervous, till you could clutch something—a hammer or a marlinspike, and go to work like mad, at something or other, never mind what. Indolence and idleness perished from before him. His own person was the exact embodiment of his utilitarian character. On his long gaunt body he carried no spare flesh, no superfluous beard, his chin having a soft economical nap to it, like the worn nap of his broad-brimmed hat.

Such, then, was the person that I saw seated on the transom when I followed Captain Peleg down into the cabin. The space between the decks was small; and there, bolt upright, sat old Bildad, who always sat so, and never leaned, and this to save his coattails. His broad-brim was placed beside him; his legs were stiffly crossed; his drab vesture was buttoned up to his chin; and spectacles on nose, he seemed absorbed in reading from a ponderous volume.

"Bildad," cried Captain Peleg, "at it again, Bildad, eh? Ye have been studying those Scriptures, now, for the last thirty years, to my certain knowledge. How far ye got, Bildad?"

As if long habituated to such profane talk from his old shipmate, Bildad, without noticing his present irreverence, quietly looked up, and seeing me, glanced again inquiringly toward Peleg.

"He says he's our man, Bildad," said Peleg, "he wants to ship."

"Dost thee?" said Bildad, in a hollow tone, and turning around to me.

"I *dost*," said I unconsciously, he was so intense a Quaker.

"What do ye think of him, Bildad?" said Peleg.

"He'll do," said Bildad, eyeing me, and then went on spelling away at his book in a mumbling yet quite audible tone.

I thought him the queerest old Quaker I had ever seen, especially as Peleg, his friend and old shipmate, seemed such a blusterer. But I said nothing, only looked around me sharply. Peleg now threw open a chest, and drawing forth the ship's articles, placed pen and ink before him, and seated himself at a little table. I began to think it was high time to settle with myself at what terms I would be willing to engage for the voyage. I was already aware that in the whaling business they paid no wages; but all hands including the captain, received certain shares of the profits called *lays;* and these lays were proportioned to the degree of importance pertaining to the respective duties of the ship's company. I was also aware that being a green hand at whaling, my own lay would not be very large; but considering that I was used to the sea, could steer a ship, splice a rope, and all that, I made no doubt that from all I had heard I should be offered at least the 275th lay—that is the 275th part of the clear net proceeds of the voyage, whatever that might eventually amount to. And though the 275th lay was what they call a rather *long lay,* yet it was better than nothing; and if we had a lucky voyage, it might pretty nearly pay for the clothing I would wear out on it, not to speak of my three years'

beef and board, for which I would not have to pay one
stiver.

While Peleg was vainly trying to mend a pen with his
jackknife, old Bildad, to my no small surprise, considering
that he was such an interested party in these proceedings,
Bildad never heeded us, but went on mumbling to himself out of his book. " '*Lay* not up for yourselves treasures
upon earth, where moth——' "

"Well, Captain Bildad," interrupted Peleg, "what d'ye
say, what lay shall we give this young man?"

"Thou knowest best," was the sepulchral reply, "the
seven hundred and seventy-seventh wouldn't be too
much, would it?—'where moth and rust do corrupt, but
lay——' "

Lay, indeed, thought I, and such a lay! The seven hundred and seventy-seventh! Well, old Bildad, you are
determined that I, for one, shall not *lay* up many *lays*
here below, "where moth and rust do corrupt."

"Why, blast your eyes, Bildad," cried Peleg, "thou dost
not want to swindle this young man! He must have more
than that."

"Seven hundred and seventy-seven," again said Bildad,
without lifting his eyes, and then went on mumbling—
" 'for where your treasure is, there will your heart be
also.' "

"I am going to put him down for the three hundredth,"
said Peleg, "do ye hear that, Bildad! The three hundredth
lay, I say."

Bildad laid down his book, and turning solemnly toward him said, "Captain Peleg, thou hast a generous

heart, but thou must consider the duty thou owest to the other owners of this ship—widows and orphans, many of them—and if we too abundantly reward the labors of this young man, we may be taking the bread from those widows and those orphans. The seven hundred and seventy-seventh lay, Captain Peleg."

"Thou, Bildad!" roared Peleg, starting up and clattering about the cabin. "Blast ye, Captain Bildad, if I had followed thy advice in these matters, I would afore now had a conscience to lug about that would be heavy enough to founder the largest ship that ever sailed round Cape Horn."

"Captain Peleg," said Bildad steadily, "thy conscience may be drawing ten inches of water, or ten fathoms, I can't tell. But as thou art still an impenitent man, Captain Peleg, I greatly fear lest thy conscience be but a leaky one, and will in the end sink thee foundering down to the fiery pit, Captain Peleg."

"Fiery pit! Fiery pit! Ye insult me, man; past all natural bearing, ye insult me. It's an all-fired outrage to tell any human creature that he's bound for hell. Flukes and flames! Bildad, say that again to me, and start my soul-bolts, but I'll—I'll—yes, I'll swallow a live goat with all his hair and horns on. Out of the cabin, ye canting, drab-colored son of a wooden gun—a straight wake with ye!"

As he thundered this out he made a rush at Bildad, but with a marvelous oblique, sliding celerity, Bildad for that time eluded him.

Alarmed at this terrible outburst between the two principal and responsible owners of the ship, and feeling half a mind to give up all idea of sailing in a vessel so questionably owned and temporarily commanded, I stepped aside from the door to give egress to Bildad, who I made no doubt, was all eagerness to vanish from before the awakened wrath of Peleg. But to my astonishment, he sat down again on the transom very quietly, and seemed to have not the slightest intention of withdrawing. He seemed quite used to impenitent Peleg and his ways. As for Peleg, after letting off his rage as he had, there seemed no more left in him, and he, too, sat down like a lamb, though he twitched a little as if still nervously agitated.

"Whew!" he whistled at last, "the squall's gone off to leeward, I think. Bildad, thou used to be good at sharpening a lance, mend that pen, will ye. My jackknife here needs the grindstone. That's he; thank ye, Bildad. Now then, my young man, Ishmael's thy name, didn't ye say? Well then, down ye go here, Ishmael, for the three hundredth lay."

"Captain Peleg," said I, "I have a friend with me who wants to ship, too. Shall I bring him down tomorrow?"

"To be sure," said Peleg. "Fetch him along, and we'll look at him."

"What *lay* does *he* want?" groaned Bildad, glancing up from the book in which he had again been burying himself.

"Oh! never thee mind about that, Bildad," said Peleg. "Has he ever whaled it any?"—turning to me.

"Killed more whales than I can count, Captain Peleg."

"Well, bring him along then."

And, after signing the papers, off I went, nothing

doubting but that I had done a good morning's work, and that the *Pequod* was the identical ship that Yojo had provided to carry Queequeg and me around the Cape.

But I had not proceeded far when I began to bethink me that the captain with whom I was to sail yet remained unseen by me. Though indeed, in many cases, a whale-ship will be completely fitted out, and receive all her crew on board ere the captain makes himself visible by arriving to take command. For sometimes these voyages are so prolonged, and the short intervals at home so exceedingly brief, that if the captain have a family or any absorbing concernment of that sort, he does not trouble himself much about his ship in port, but leaves her to the owners until all is ready for sea. However, it is always as well to have a look at him before irrevocably committing yourself into his hands. Turning back I accosted Captain Peleg, inquiring where Captain Ahab was to be found.

"And what dost thou want of Captain Ahab? It's all right enough; thou art shipped."

"Yes, but I should like to see him."

"But I don't think thou wilt be able to at present. I don't know exactly what's the matter with him, but he keeps close inside the house. A sort of sick, and yet he don't look so. In fact, he ain't sick, but no, he isn't well either. Anyhow, young man, he won't always see me, so I don't suppose he will thee. He's a queer man, Captain Ahab—so some think—but a good one. Oh, thou'lt like him well enough, no fear, no fear. He's a grand, ungodly, god-like man, Captain Ahab. Doesn't speak much, but when he does speak, then you may well listen. Mark ye, be fore-

warned; Ahab's above the common. Ahab's been in col-
leges, as well as 'mong the cannibals, been used to deeper
wonders than the waves, fixed his fiery lance in mightier,
stranger foes than whales. His lance! Ay, the keenest and
the surest that out of all our isle! Oh, he ain't Captain
Bildad; no, and he ain't Captain Peleg; he's *Ahab*, boy,
and Ahab of old, thou knowest, was a crowned king!"

"And a very vile one. When that wicked king was slain,
the dogs, did they not lick his blood?"

"Come hither to me—hither, hither," said Peleg, with a
significance in his eye that almost startled me. "Look ye,
lad, never say that on board the *Pequod*. Never say it anywhere. Captain Ahab did not name himself. 'Twas a foolish, ignorant whim of his crazy widowed mother, who
died when he was only a twelvemonth old. And yet the
old squaw Tistig, at Gay Head, said that the name would
somehow prove prophetic. And perhaps other fools like
her may tell thee the same. I wish to warn thee. It's a lie.
I know Captain Ahab well; I've sailed with him as mate
years ago. I know what he is—a good man. Not a pious
good man, like Bildad, but a swearing good man. Something like me—only there's a good deal more of him. Aye,
aye, I know that he was never very jolly; and I know that
on the passage home he was a little out of his mind for a
spell; but it was the sharp shooting pains in his bleeding
stump that brought that about, as anyone might see. I
know, too, that ever since he lost his leg last voyage by
that accursed whale, he's been a kind of moody—desperate moody and savage sometimes; but that will all pass
off. And once for all, let me tell thee and assure thee,

young man, it's better to sail with a moody good captain than a laughing bad one. So good-bye to thee—and wrong not Captain Ahab because he happens to have a wicked name. Besides, my boy, he has a wife—not three voyages wedded—a sweet resigned girl. Think of that; by that sweet girl that old man has a child; hold ye then there can be any utter, hopeless harm in Ahab? No, no, my lad; stricken, blasted, if he be, Ahab has his humanities!"

As I walked away, I was full of thoughtfulness. What had been incidentally revealed to me of Captain Ahab filled me with a certain wild vagueness of painfulness concerning him. And somehow, at the time, I felt a sympathy and a sorrow for him, but for I don't know what, unless it was the cruel loss of his leg. And yet I also felt a strange awe of him; but that sort of awe, which I cannot at all describe, was not exactly awe; I do not know what it was. But I felt it; and it did not disincline me toward him, though I felt impatience at what seemed like mystery in him, so imperfectly as he was known to me then. However, my thoughts were at length carried in other directions, so that for the present dark Ahab slipped my mind.

⚓

CHAPTER 13

All Astir

A DAY OR TWO PASSED, and there was great activity aboard the *Pequod*. Not only were the old sails being mended, but new sails were coming on board, and bolts of canvas, and coils of rigging; in short, everything betokened that the ship's preparations were hurrying to a close. Captain Peleg seldom or never went ashore, but sat in his wigwam keeping a sharp lookout upon the hands. Bildad did all the purchasing and providing at the stores, and the men employed in the hold and on the rigging were working till long after nightfall.

On the day following Queequeg's signing the articles, word was given at all the inns where the ship's company were stopping, that their chests must be on board before night, for there was no telling how soon the vessel might be sailing. So Queequeg and I got down our traps, resolving, however, to sleep ashore till the last. But it seems they always give very long notice in these cases, and the ship did not sail for several days. But no wonder; there was a good deal to be done, and there is no telling how many things to be thought of before the *Pequod* was fully equipped.

Every one knows what a multitude of things—beds, saucepans, knives and forks, shovels and tongs, napkins, nutcrackers, and what not, are indispensable to the business of housekeeping. Just so with whaling, which necessitates a three-years' housekeeping upon the wide ocean, far from all grocers, costermongers, doctors, bakers, and bankers. And although this also holds true of merchant vessels, yet not by any means to the same extent as with whalemen. For besides the great length of the whaling voyage, the numerous articles peculiar to the prosecution of the fishery, and the impossibility of replacing them at the remote harbors usually frequented, it must be remembered that of all ships, whaling vessels are the most exposed to accidents of all kinds, and especially to the destruction and loss of the very things upon which the success of the voyage most depends. Hence, the spare boats, spare spars, and spare lines and harpoons, and spare everything, almost, but a spare captain and duplicate ship.

At the period of our arrival at the island, the heaviest stowage of the *Pequod* had been almost completed, comprising her beef, bread, water, fuel, and iron hoops and

staves. But for some time there was a continual fetching
and carrying on board of divers odds and ends of things,
both large and small.

Chief among those who did this fetching and carrying
was Captain Bildad's sister, a lean old lady of a most
determined and indefatigable spirit, but withal very kind-
hearted, who seemed resolved that, if *she* could help it,
nothing should be found wanting in the *Pequod,* after
once fairly getting to sea. At one time she would come
on board with a jar of pickles for the steward's pantry,
another time with a bunch of quills for the chief mate's
desk, where he kept his log, a third time with a roll of
flannel for the small of someone's rheumatic back. Never
did any woman better deserve her name, which was
Charity—Aunt Charity, as everybody called her. And like
a sister of charity did this charitable Aunt Charity bustle
about hither and thither, ready to turn her hand and
heart to anything that promised to yield safety, comfort,
and consolation to all on board a ship in which her be-
loved brother Bildad was concerned, and in which she
herself owned a score or two of well-saved dollars.

But it was startling to see this excellent hearted Quakeress coming on board, as she did the last day, with a
long oil ladle in one hand, and a still longer whaling
lance in the other. Nor was Bildad himself nor Captain
Peleg at all backward. Bildad carried about with him a
long list of the articles needed, and at every fresh arrival,
down went his mark opposite the article upon the paper.
Every once in a while Peleg came running out of his
whalebone den, roaring at the men down the hatchways,

roaring up to the riggers at the masthead, and then concluded by roaring back into his wigwam.

During these days of preparation Queequeg and I often visited the craft, and as often I asked about Captain Ahab, and how he was, and when he was going to come on board his ship. To these questions they would answer that he was getting better and better, and was expected aboard every day. Meantime the two captains, Peleg and Bildad, could attend to everything necessary to fit the vessel for the voyage. If I had been downright honest with myself, I would have seen very plainly in my heart that I did but half fancy being committed this way to so long a voyage without once laying my eyes on the man who was to be absolute dictator of it, as soon as the ship sailed out upon the open sea. But when a man suspects any wrong, it sometimes happens that if he be already involved in the matter, he insensibly strives to cover up his suspicions even from himself. And much this way it was with me. I said nothing, and tried to think nothing.

At last it was given out that sometime next day the ship would certainly sail. So next morning, Queequeg and I took a very early start.

⚓

Chapter 14

Going Aboard

I<small>T WAS NEARLY</small> six o'clock, but only gray imperfect misty dawn, when we drew nigh the wharf.

"There are some sailors running ahead there, if I see right," said I to Queequeg, "it can't be shadows. She's off by sunrise, I guess; come on!"

"Avast!" cried a voice, whose owner at the same time coming close behind us, laid a hand upon both our shoulders, and then insinuating himself between us, stood stooping forward a little in the uncertain twilight, strangely peering from Queequeg to me. It was Elijah.[1]

"Going aboard?"

"Hands off, will you," said I.

"Lookee here," said Queequeg, shaking himself, "go 'way!"

"Ain't going aboard, then?"

---

[1] A slightly mad "prophet" who hung about the wharves at Nantucket.

"Yes, we are," said I, "but what business is that of yours? Do you know, Mr. Elijah, that I consider you a little impertinent?"

"No, no, no; I wasn't aware of that," said Elijah, slowly and wonderingly looking from me to Queequeg, with the most unaccountable glances.

"Elijah," said I, "you will oblige my friend and me by withdrawing. We are going to the Indian and Pacific Oceans, and would prefer not to be detained."

"Ye be, be ye? Coming back afore breakfast?"

"He's cracked, Queequeg," said I. "Come on."

"Holloa!" cried stationary Elijah, hailing us when we had gone a few paces.

"Never mind him," said I, "Queequeg, come on."

But he stole up to us again, and suddenly clapping his hand on my shoulder, said, "Did ye see anything looking like men going toward that ship a while ago?"

Struck by this plain matter-of-fact question, I answered, saying, "Yes, I thought I did see four or five men, but it was too dim to be sure."

"Very dim, very dim," said Elijah. "Morning to ye."

Once more we quitted him; but once more he came softly after us, and touching my shoulder again, said, "See if you can find 'em now, will ye?"

"Find who?"

"Morning to ye! Morning to ye!" he rejoined, again moving off. "Oh! I was going to warn ye against—but never mind, never mind. It's all one, all in the family too. Sharp frost this morning, ain't it? Good-bye to ye. Shan't see ye again very soon, I guess, unless it's before the

Grand Jury." And with these cracked words he finally departed, leaving me, for the moment, in no small wonderment at his frantic impudence.

At last, stepping on board the *Pequod*, we found everything in profound quiet, not a soul moving. The cabin entrance was locked within; the hatches were all on, and lumbered with coils of rigging. Going forward to the forecastle, we found the slide of the scuttle open. Seeing a light we went down, and found only an old rigger there, wrapped in a tattered pea jacket. He was thrown at full length upon two chests, his face downward and enclosed in his folded arms. The profoundest slumber was upon him.

"Those sailors we saw, Queequeg, where can they have gone to?" said I, looking dubiously at the sleeper. But it seemed that on the wharf Queequeg had not at all noticed what I now alluded to; hence I would have thought myself to have been optically deceived in that matter, were it not for Elijah's otherwise inexplicable question. But I beat the thing down, and again marking the sleeper, jocularly hinted to Queequeg that perhaps we had best sit up with the body, telling him to establish himself accordingly. He put his hand upon the sleeper's rear, as though feeling if it was soft enough; and then, without more ado, sat quietly down there.

"Gracious! Queequeg, don't sit there," said I.

"Oh! perry dood seat," said Queequeg. "My country way; won't hurt him face."

"Face!" said I, "call that his face? Very benevolent countenance then; but how hard he breathes. He's heaving himself; get off, Queequeg, you are heavy; it's grinding the face of the poor. Get off, Queequeg! Look, he'll twitch you off soon. I wonder he don't wake."

Queequeg removed himself to just beyond the head of the sleeper, and lighted his tomahawk pipe. I sat at the feet. We kept the pipe passing over the sleeper, from one to the other. Meanwhile upon questioning him, in his broken fashion Queequeg gave me to understand that in his land, owing to the absence of settees and sofas of all sorts, the king, chiefs, and great people generally, were in the custom of fattening some of the lower orders for ottomans; and to furnish a house comfortably in that respect, you had only to buy up eight or ten lazy fellows, and lay them around in the piers and alcoves. Besides, it was very convenient on an excursion, much better than those garden chairs which are convertible into walking-sticks. Upon occasion, a chief would call his attendant desiring him to make a settee of himself under a spreading tree, perhaps in some damp marshy place.

While narrating these things, every time Queequeg received the tomahawk from me, he flourished the hatchet side of it over the sleeper's head.

"What's that for, Queequeg?"

"Perry easy, kill-e; oh, perry easy!"

He was going on with some wild reminiscences about his tomahawk pipe, which, it seemed, had in its two uses both brained his foes and soothed his soul, when we were directly attracted to the sleeping rigger. The strong vapor now completely filling the contracted hole began to tell on him. He breathed with a sort of muffledness, then seemed troubled in the nose, then revolved over once or twice, then sat up and rubbed his eyes.

"Holloa!" he breathed at last, "who be ye smokers?"

"Shipped men," answered I, "when does she sail?"

"Ay, ay, ye are going in her, be ye? She sails today. The captain came aboard last night."

"What captain—Ahab?"

"Who but him indeed?"

I was going to ask him some further questions concerning Ahab, when we heard a noise on deck.

"Holloa! Starbuck's astir," said the rigger. "He's a lively chief mate, that; good man and a pious, but all alive now. I must turn to." And so saying he went on deck, and we followed.

It was now clear sunrise. Soon the crew came on board in twos and threes; the riggers bestirred themselves; the mates were actively engaged; and several of the shore people were busy in bringing various last things on board. Meanwhile Captain Ahab remained invisibly enshrined within his cabin.

⚓

CHAPTER 15

Merry Christmas

AT LENGTH, toward noon, upon the final dismissal of the ship's riggers, and after the *Pequod* had been hauled out from the wharf, and after the ever-thoughtful Charity had come off in a whaleboat with her last gift—a nightcap for Stubb, the second mate, her brother-in-law, and a spare Bible for the steward—after all this the two captains, Peleg and Bildad, issued from the cabin, and turning to the chief mate, Peleg said—

"Now, Mr. Starbuck, are you sure everything is right? Captain Ahab is all ready—just spoke to him. Nothing more to be got from shore, eh? Well, call all hands, then. Muster 'em aft here—blast 'em!"

"No need of profane words, however great the hurry, Peleg," said Bildad. "But away with thee, friend Starbuck, and do our bidding."

How now! here upon the very point of starting for the voyage, Captain Peleg and Captain Bildad were going it with a high hand on the quarterdeck just as if they were to be joint commanders at sea, as well as to all appearances in port. And as for Captain Ahab, no sign of him was yet to be seen; only, they said he was in the cabin. But then the idea was that his presence was by no means necessary in getting the ship under weigh, and steering her well out to sea. Indeed, as that was not at all his proper business, but the pilot's; and as he was not yet completely recovered—so they said—therefore Captain Ahab stayed below. And all this seemed natural enough, especially as in the merchant service many captains never show themselves on deck for a considerable time after heaving up the anchor, but remain over the cabin table, having a farewell merrymaking with their shore friends before they quit the ship for good with the pilot.

But there was not much chance to think over the matter, for Captain Peleg was now all alive. He seemed to do most of the talking and commanding, and not Bildad.

"Aft here, ye sons of bachelors," he cried, as the sailors lingered at the mainmast. "Mr. Starbuck, drive 'em aft."

"Strike the tent there!" was the next order. As I hinted before, this whalebone marquee was never pitched except in port; and on board the *Pequod,* for thirty years, the order to strike the tent was well known to be the next thing to heaving up the anchor.

"Man the capstan! Blood and thunder—jump!" was the next command, and the crew sprang for the handspikes.

Now in getting under weigh the station generally occupied by the pilot is the forward part of the ship. And here Bildad who, with Peleg, be it known, in addition to his other offices, was one of the licensed pilots of the port —he was suspected of having got himself made a pilot in order to save the Nantucket pilot fee to all the ships he was concerned in, for he never piloted any other craft— Bildad, I say, might now be seen actively engaged in looking over the bows for the approaching anchor, and at intervals singing what seemed a dismal stave of psalmody to cheer the hands at the windlass, who roared forth some sort of a chorus about the girls in Booble Alley, with hearty goodwill. Nevertheless, not three days previous Bildad had told them that no profane songs would be allowed on board the *Pequod,* particularly in getting under weigh.

Meantime, overseeing the other part of the ship, Captain Peleg ripped and swore astern in the most frightful manner. I almost thought he would sink the ship before the anchor could be got up; involuntarily I paused on my handspike and told Queequeg to do the same, thinking of the perils we both ran in starting on the voyage with such a devil for a pilot. I was comforting myself, however, with the thought that in pious Bildad might be found some salvation, spite of his seven hundred and seventy-seventh lay, when I felt a sudden sharp poke in my rear, and turning around, was horrified at the apparition of Captain Peleg in the act of withdrawing his leg from my immediate vicinity. That was my first kick.

"Is that the way they heave in the marchant service?" he roared. "Spring, thou sheephead; spring, and break thy

backbone! Why, don't ye spring, I say, all of ye—spring!
Quohog! Spring, thou chap with the red whiskers; spring
there, Scotch-cap; spring, thou green pants. Spring, I say,
all of ye, and spring your eyes out!" And so saying, he
moved along the windlass, here and there using his leg
very freely, while imperturbable Bildad kept leading off
with his psalmody. Thinks I, Captain Peleg must have
been drinking something today.

At last the anchor was up, the sails were set, and off we
glided. It was a sharp, cold Christmas; and as the short
northern day merged into night, we found ourselves almost broad upon the wintery ocean, whose freezing spray
cased us in ice, as in polished armor. The long rows of
teeth on the bulwarks glistened in the moonlight; and like
the white ivory tusks of some huge elephant, vast curving
icicles depended from the bows.

Lank Bildad, as pilot, headed the first watch, and ever
and anon, as the old craft deep dived into the green seas,
and sent the shivering frost all over her, and the winds
howled, and the cordage rang, his steady notes were
heard—

> "Sweet fields beyond the swelling flood,
>   Stand dress'd in living green.
> So to the Jews old Canaan stood,
>   While Jordan roll'd between."

Never did those sweet words sound more sweetly to
me than then. They were full of hope and fruition. Spite
of this frigid winter night in the boisterous Atlantic, spite
of my wet feet and wetter jacket, there was yet, it then

seemed to me, many a pleasant haven in store, and meads and glades so eternally vernal that the grass shot up by the spring, untrodden, unwilted remains at midsummer. At last we gained such an offing that the two pilots were needed no longer. The stout sailboat that had accompanied us began ranging alongside.

It was curious and not unpleasing how Peleg and Bildad were affected at this juncture, especially Captain Bildad. For he was loath to depart, yet, very loath to leave for good a ship bound on so long and perilous a voyage—beyond both stormy Capes; a ship in which some thousands of his hard earned dollars were invested, a ship in which an old shipmate sailed as captain—a man almost as old as he, once more starting to encounter all the terrors of the pitiless jaw. Loath to say good-bye to a thing so every way brimful of every interest to him, poor old Bildad lingered long; paced the deck with anxious strides; ran down into the cabin to speak another farewell word there; again came on deck, and looked to windward; looked toward the wide and endless waters, bounded only by the far-off unseen eastern continents; looked toward the land; looked aloft; looked right and left; looked everywhere and nowhere.

At last, mechanically coiling a rope upon its pin, he convulsively grasped stout Peleg by the hand, and holding up a lantern, for a moment stood gazing heroically in his face, as much as to say, "Nevertheless, friend Peleg, I can stand it; yes, I can."

As for Peleg himself, he took it more like a philosopher; but for all his philosophy, there was a tear twinkling in his eye when the lantern came too near. And he too did not a little run from cabin to deck—now a word below, and now a word with Starbuck, the chief mate.

But, at last, he turned to his comrade with a final sort of look about him. "Captain Bildad—come, old shipmate, we must go. Back the mainyard there! Boat ahoy! Stand by to come close alongside, now! Careful, careful! Come, Bildad, boy—say your last. Luck to ye, Starbuck—luck to ye, Mr. Stubb—luck to ye, Mr. Flask—good-bye, and good luck to ye all—and this day three years I'll have a hot supper smoking for ye in old Nantucket. Hurrah and away!"

"God bless ye, and have ye in His holy keeping, men," murmured old Bildad, almost incoherently. "I hope ye'll have fine weather now, so that Captain Ahab may soon be moving among ye—a pleasant sun is all he needs, and ye'll have plenty of them in the tropic voyage ye go. Be careful in the hunt, ye mates. Don't stave the boats needlessly, ye harpooneers; good white cedar plank is raised full three percent within the year. Don't forget your prayers, either. Mr. Starbuck, mind that cooper don't waste the spare staves. Oh! the sail needles are in the green locker! Don't whale it too much a' Lord's Day men; but don't miss a fair chance either; that's rejecting Heaven's good gifts. Have an eye to the molasses tierce, Mr. Stubb; it was a little leaky, I thought. If ye touch at the islands, Mr. Flask, beware of fornication. Good-bye, good-bye! Don't keep that cheese too long down in the hold, Mr. Starbuck; it'll spoil. Be careful with the butter—twenty cents the pound it was, and mind ye, if——"

"Come, come, Captain Bildad; stop palavering—away!"

And with that, Peleg hurried him over the side, and both dropped into the boat.

Ship and boat diverged; the cold, damp night breeze blew between; a screaming gull flew overhead; the two hulls wildly rolled; we gave three heavy-hearted cheers, and blindly plunged like fate into the lone Atlantic.

⚓

CHAPTER 16

Ahab

FOR SEVERAL DAYS after leaving Nantucket, nothing above hatches was seen of Captain Ahab. The mates regularly relieved each other at the watches, and for aught that could be seen to the contrary, they seemed to be the only commanders of the ship; only they sometimes issued from the cabin with orders so sudden and peremptory, that after all it was plain they but commanded vicariously. Yes, their supreme lord and dictator was there, though hitherto unseen by any eyes not permitted to penetrate into the now sacred retreat of the cabin.

Every time I ascended to the deck from my watches below, I instantly gazed aft to mark if any strange face were visible; for my first vague disquietude touching the unknown captain, now in the seclusion of the sea, became almost a perturbation. This was strangely heightened at times by the ragged Elijah's diabolical incoherences un-invitedly recurring to me, with a subtle energy I could not have before conceived of. Whatever it was of appre-hensiveness or uneasiness—to call it so—which I felt, yet whenever I came to look about me in the ship, it seemed against all warrantry to cherish such emotions. For though the harpooneers, with the great body of the crew, were a far more barbaric, heathenish and motley set than any of the tame merchant ship companies which my previous experiences had made me acquainted with, still I ascribed this—and rightly ascribed it—to the fierce uniqueness of the very nature of that wild Scandinavian vocation in which I had so abandonedly embarked.

But it was especially the aspect of the three chief officers of the ship, the mates, which was most forcibly calculated to allay these colorless misgivings, and induce confidence and cheerfulness in every presentment of the voyage. Three better, more likely sea officers and men, each in his own different way, could not readily be found, and they were every one of them Americans: a Nan-tucketer, a Vineyarder, a Cape man.

Now it being Christmas when the ship shot from out her harbor, for a space we had biting polar weather, though all the time running away from it to the south-ward, and by every degree and minute of latitude which we sailed, gradually leaving that merciless winter and all its intolerable weather behind us.

It was one of those less lowering, but still gray and gloomy enough mornings of the transition, when with a

fair wind the ship was rushing through the water with a
vindictive sort of leaping and melancholy rapidity, that
I mounted to the deck at the call of the forenoon watch.
As soon as I leveled my glance toward the taffrail, foreboding shivers ran over me. Reality outran apprehensions: Captain Ahab stood upon his quarterdeck.

There seemed no sign of common bodily illness about
him, nor of the recovery from any. He looked like a man
cut away from the stake, when the fire has overrunningly
wasted all the limbs without consuming them or taking
away one particle from their compacted aged robustness.
His whole high, broad form seemed made of solid bronze,
and shaped in an unalterable mold, like Cellini's cast
Perseus. Threading its way out from among his gray hairs,
and continuing right down one side of his tawny scorched
face and neck till it disappeared in his clothing, you saw
a slender rodlike mark, lividly whitish. It resembled that
perpendicular seam sometimes made in the straight lofty
trunk of a great tree, when the upper lightning tearingly
darts down it, and without wrenching a single twig, peels
and grooves out the bark from top to bottom, ere running
off into the soil, leaving the tree still greenly alive, but
branded.

Whether that mark was born with him, or whether it
was the scar left by some desperate wound, no one could
certainly say. By some tacit consent, throughout the
voyage little or no allusion was made to it, especially by
the mates. But once Tashtego's senior, an old Gay Head
Indian among the crew, superstitiously asserted that not

till he was full forty years old did Ahab become that way branded, and then it came upon him, not in the fury of any mortal fray, but in an elemental strife at sea.

Yet this wild hint seemed inferentially negated by what a gray Manxman insinuated, an old sepulchral man, who, having never before sailed out of Nantucket, had never ere this laid eye upon wild Ahab. Nevertheless, the old sea traditions, the immemorial credulities, popularly invested this old Manxman with preternatural powers of discernment. So that no white sailor seriously contradicted him when he said that if ever Captain Ahab should be tranquilly laid out—which might hardly come to pass, so he muttered—then, whoever should do that last office for the dead, would find a birthmark on him from crown to sole.

So powerfully did the whole grim aspect of Ahab affect me, and the livid brand which streaked it, that for the first few moments I hardly noted that not a little of this overbearing grimness was owing to the barbaric white leg upon which he partly stood. It had previously come to me that this ivory leg had at sea been fashioned from the polished bone of the sperm whale's jaw. "Aye, he was dismasted off Japan," said the old Gay Head Indian once. "But like his dismasted craft, he shipped another mast without coming home for it. He has a quiver of 'em."

I was struck with the singular posture he maintained. Upon each side of the *Pequod's* quarterdeck, and pretty close to the mizzen shrouds, there was an auger hole, bored about half an inch or so, into the plank. His bone leg steadied in that hole, one arm elevated, and holding by a shroud, Captain Ahab stood erect, looking straight out beyond the ship's ever-pitching prow. There was an infinity of firmest fortitude, a determinate, unsurrenderable wilfulness, in the fixed and fearless forward dedication of that glance. Not a word he spoke; nor did his officers say aught to him, though by all their minutest gestures and expressions they plainly showed the uneasy if not painful consciousness of being under a troubled master eye. And not only that, but moody stricken Ahab stood before them with a crucifixion in his face, in all the nameless regal overbearing dignity of some mighty woe.

Ere long, from his first visit in the air, Ahab withdrew into his cabin. But after that morning he was every day visible to the crew, either standing in his pivot hole, or seated upon an ivory stool he had, or heavily walking the deck. As the sky grew less gloomy, indeed, began to grow a little genial, he became still less and less a recluse, as if, when the ship had sailed from home, nothing but the dead wintry bleakness of the sea had then kept him so secluded. And by and by, it came to pass that he was almost continually in the air; but as yet, for all that he said or perceptibly did on the at last sunny deck, he seemed as unnecessary there as another mast. But the Pequod was only making a passage now, not regularly cruising; nearly all whaling preparatives needing supervision the mates were fully competent to do. So there was little or nothing, out of himself, to employ or excite Ahab now; and thus chase away, for that one interval, the clouds that layer upon layer were piled upon his brow, as ever all clouds choose the loftiest peaks to pile themselves upon.

Nevertheless, ere long, the warm warbling persuasiveness of the pleasant holiday weather we came to, seemed gradually to charm him from his mood. More than once did he put forth the faint blossom of a look, which, in any other man, would have soon flowered out in a smile.

CHAPTER 17

⚓

The Cabin Table

IT IS NOON, and Dough Boy, the steward, thrusting his pale loaf-of-bread face from the cabin scuttle, announces dinner to his lord and master, who, sitting in the lee quarter boat, has just been taking an observation of the sun, and is now mutely reckoning the latitude on the smooth medallion-shaped tablet reserved for that daily purpose on the upper part of his ivory leg. From his complete inattention to the tidings you would think that moody Ahab had not heard his menial. But presently, catching hold of the mizzen shrouds, he swings himself to the deck, and in an even unexhilarated voice, saying, "Dinner, Mr. Starbuck," disappears into the cabin.

When the last echo of his sultan's step has died away, and Starbuck, the first emir, has every reason to suppose that he is seated, then Starbuck rouses from his quietude, takes a few turns along the planks, and after a grave peep into the binnacle says, with some touch of pleasantness, "Dinner, Mr. Stubb," and descends the scuttle. The second emir lounges about the rigging awhile, and then slightly shaking the main brace to see whether it be all right with that important rope, he likewise takes up the old burden, and with a rapid "Dinner, Mr. Flask," follows after his predecessors.

But the third emir, now seeing himself all alone on the quarterdeck, seems to feel relieved from some curious restraint; for, tipping all sorts of knowing winks in all sorts of directions, and kicking off his shoes, he strikes into a sharp but noiseless squall of a hornpipe right over the Grand Turk's head; and then, by a dexterous sleight pitching his cap up into the mizzentop for a shelf, he goes down rollicking, as far at least as he remains visible from the deck, reversing all other processions by bringing up the rear with music. But ere stepping into the cabin doorway below, he pauses, ships a new face altogether, and then independent, hilarious little Flask enters King Ahab's presence, in the character of Abjectus, or the slave.

Over his ivory-inlaid table, Ahab presided like a mute, maned sea lion on the white coral beach, surrounded by his warlike but still deferential cubs. In his own proper turn, each officer waited to be served. They were as little children before Ahab, and yet in Ahab there seemed not to lurk the smallest social arrogance. With one mind, their intent eyes all fastened upon the old man's knife as he carved the chief dish before him, I do not suppose that

for the world they would have profaned that moment
with the slightest observation, even upon so neutral a
topic as the weather. No! And when reaching out his
knife and fork, between which the slice of beef was
locked, Ahab thereby motioned Starbuck's plate toward
him, the mate received his meat as though receiving alms,
and cut it tenderly, and a little started if, perchance, the
knife grazed against the plate, and chewed it noiselessly
and swallowed it, not without circumspection.

Like the coronation banquet at Frankfort, where the
German emperor profoundly dines with the seven imperial electors, these cabin meals were somehow solemn
meals, eaten in awful silence. And yet at table old Ahab
forbade not conversation; only he himself was dumb.
What a relief it was to choking Stubb, when a rat made a
sudden racket in the hold below. And poor little Flask, he
was the youngest son and little boy of this weary family
party. His were the shinbones of the saline beef; his
would have been the drumsticks. For Flask to have
presumed to help himself, this must have seemed to him
tantamount to larceny in the first degree. Had he helped
himself at that table, doubtless, nevermore would he have
been able to hold his head up in this honest world. Nevertheless, strange to say, Ahab never forbade him. And had
Flask helped himself, the chances were Ahab had never
so much as noticed it. Least of all, did Flask presume to
help himself to butter. Whether he thought the owners of
the ship denied it to him, on account of its clotting his
clear, sunny complexion, or whether he deemed that on
so long a voyage in such marketless waters butter was at

a premium, and therefore was not for him, a subaltern, however it was, Flask, alas, was a butterless man!

Another thing. Flask was the last person down at the dinner, and Flask is the first man up. Consider! For hereby Flask's dinner was badly jammed in point of time. Starbuck and Stubb both had the start of him; and yet they also have the privilege of lounging in the rear. If Stubb even, who is but a peg higher than Flask, happens to have but a small appetite and soon shows symptoms of concluding his repast, then Flask must bestir himself. He will not get more than three mouthfuls that day, for it is against holy usage for Stubb to precede Flask to the deck. Therefore it was that Flask once admitted in private, that ever since he had risen to the dignity of an officer, from that moment he had never known what it was to be otherwise than hungry, more or less. For what he ate did not so much relieve his hunger as keep it immortal in him. Peace and satisfaction, thought Flask, have forever departed from my stomach. I am an officer; but how I wish I could fist a bit of old-fashioned beef in the forecastle, as I used to when I was before the mast. There's the fruits of promotion now; there's the vanity of glory; there's the insanity of life!

If it were so that any mere sailor of the *Pequod* had a grudge against Flask in Flask's official capacity, all that sailor had to do, in order to obtain ample vengeance, was to go aft at dinnertime, and get a peep at Flask through the cabin skylight, sitting silly and dumfoundered before awful Ahab.

Now, Ahab and his three mates formed what may be

called the first table in the *Pequod's* cabin. After their departure, taking place in inverted order to their arrival, the canvas cloth was cleared, or rather was restored to some hurried order by the pallid steward. And then the three harpooneers were bidden to the feast, they being its residuary legatees. They made a sort of temporary servants hall of the high and mighty cabin.

In strange contrast to the hardly tolerable constraint and nameless invisible domineerings of the captain's table, was the entire carefree license and ease, the almost frantic democracy of those inferior fellows the harpooneers. While their masters, the mates, seemed afraid of the sound of the hinges of their own jaws, the harpooneers chewed their food with such a relish that there was a report to it. They dined like lords; they filled their bellies like Indian ships all day loading with spices. Such portentous appetites had Queequeg and Tashtego, that to fill out the vacancies made by the previous repast, often the pale Dough Boy was fain to bring on a great baron of salt junk, seemingly quarried out of the solid ox.

And if he were not lively about it, if he did not go with a nimble hop-skip-and-jump, then Tashtego had an ungentlemanly way of accelerating him by darting a fork at his back, harpoonwise. And once Daggoo, seized with a sudden humor, assisted Dough Boy's memory by snatching him up bodily and thrusting his head into a great empty wooden trencher, while Tashtego, knife in hand, began laying out the circle preliminary to scalping him. He was naturally a very nervous, shuddering sort of little fellow, this bread-faced steward, the progeny of a bank-rupt baker and a hospital nurse. And what with the standing spectacle of the black terrific Ahab, and the periodical tumultuous visitations of these three savages, Dough Boy's whole life was one continual lip-quiver. Commonly, after seeing the harpooneers furnished with all things they demanded, he would escape from their clutches into his little pantry adjoining, and fearfully peep out at them through the blinds of its door, until all was over.

It was a sight to see Queequeg seated over against Tashtego, opposing his filed teeth to the Indian's; cross-wise to them Daggoo, seated on the floor (for a bench would have brought his hearse-plumed head to the low carlines), at every motion of his colossal limbs making the low cabin framework to shake, as when an African ele-phant goes passenger in a ship. But for all this, the great Negro was wonderfully abstemious, not to say dainty. It seemed hardly possible that by such comparatively small mouthfuls he could keep up the vitality diffused through so broad, baronial and superb a person. But doubtless this noble savage fed strong and drank deep of the abound-ing element of air, and through his dilated nostrils snuffed in the sublime life of the worlds. Not by beef or by bread are giants made or nourished. But Queequeg, he had a mortal, barbaric smack of the lip in eating—an ugly enough sound—so much so, that the trembling Dough Boy almost looked to see whether any marks of teeth lurked in his own lean arms. And when he would hear Tashtego singing out for him to produce himself, that his bones might be picked, the simple-witted steward all but shattered the crockery hanging around him in the pantry, by his sudden fits of the palsy.

And the whetstone, which the harpooneers carried in their pockets for their lances and other weapons, and with which whetstones, at dinner, they would ostentatiously sharpen their knives—that grating sound did not at all tend to tranquilize poor Dough Boy. How could he forget that in his island days Queequeg, for one, must certainly have been guilty of some murderous convivial indiscretions. Alas, Dough Boy! Hard fares the waiter who waits upon cannibals. Not a napkin should he carry on his arm, but a buckler. In good time, though, to his great delight, the three salt sea warriors would rise and depart— to his credulous, fable-mongering ears, all their martial bones jingling in them at every step, like Moorish scimitars in scabbards.

But though these barbarians dined in the cabin and nominally lived there, still, being anything but sedentary in their habits, they were scarcely ever in it except at meal times and just before sleeping time, when they passed through it to their own peculiar quarters.

In this one matter, Ahab seemed no exception to most American whale captains, who, as a set, rather incline to the opinion that by rights the ship's cabin belongs to them, and that it is by courtesy alone that anybody else is, at any time, permitted there. So that, in real truth, the mates and harpooneers of the *Pequod* might more properly be said to have lived out of the cabin than in it. For when they did enter it, it was something as a street door enters a house, turning inward for a moment, only to be turned out the next, and as a permanent thing, residing in the open air. Nor did they lose much hereby; in the cabin was no companionship. Socially, Ahab was inaccessible. Though nominally included in the census of Christendom he was still an alien to it. He lived in the world as the last of the grisly bears lived in settled Missouri. And as when spring and summer had departed, that wild Logan of the woods, burying himself in the hollow of a tree, lived out the winter there, sucking his own paws; so in his inclement, howling old age, Ahab's soul, shut up in the caved trunk of his body, there fed upon the sullen paws of its gloom!

CHAPTER 18

⚓

The Quarterdeck

(Enter Ahab, then, all.)

O NE MORNING shortly after breakfast, Ahab, as was his wont, ascended the cabin gangway to the deck. There most sea captains usually walk at that hour, as country gentlemen, after the same meal, take a few turns in the garden.

Soon his steady, ivory stride was heard, as to and fro he paced his old rounds, upon planks so familiar to his tread that they were dented all over, like geological stones, with the peculiar mark of his walk. Did you fixedly gaze, too, upon that ribbed and dented brow; there also, you would see still stranger footprints—the footprints of his one unsleeping, ever-pacing thought.

But on the occasion in question, those dents looked

deeper, even as his nervous step that morning left a deeper mark. And so full of his thought was Ahab, that at every uniform turn he made, now at the mainmast and now at the binnacle, you could almost see that thought turn in him as he turned, and pace in him as he paced, so completely possessing him, indeed, that it all but seemed the inward mold of every outer movement.

"D'ye mark him, Flask?" whispered Stubb. "The chick that's in him pecks the shell. 'Twill soon be out."

The hours wore on, Ahab now shut up within his cabin, anon pacing the deck, with the same intense bigotry of purpose in his aspect.

It drew near the close of day. Suddenly he came to a halt by the bulwarks, and inserting his bone leg into the auger hole there and with one hand grasping a shroud, he ordered Starbuck to send everybody aft.

"Sir!" said the mate, astonished at an order seldom or never given on shipboard except in some extraordinary case.

"Send everybody aft," repeated Ahab. "Mastheads, there! Come down!"

When the entire ship's company were assembled, and with curious and not wholly unapprehensive faces were eyeing him, for he looked not unlike the weather horizon when a storm is coming up, Ahab, after rapidly glancing over the bulwarks, and then darting his eyes among the crew, started from his standpoint; and as though not a soul were nigh him resumed his heavy turns upon the deck. With bent head and half-slouched hat he continued to pace, unmindful of the wondering whispering among

the men, till Stubb cautiously whispered to Flask that
Ahab must have summoned them there for the purpose of
witnessing a pedestrian feat. But this did not last long.
Vehemently pausing he cried, "What do ye do when ye
see a whale, men?"

"Sing out for him!" was the impulsive rejoinder from a
score of clubbed voices.

"Good!" cried Ahab, with a wild approval in his tones,
observing the hearty animation into which his unexpected question had so magnetically thrown them.

"And what do ye next, men?"

"Lower away, and after him!"

"And what tune is it ye pull to, men?"

"A dead whale or a stove boat!"

More and more strangely and fiercely glad and approv-
ing grew the countenance of the old man at every shout,
while the mariners began to gaze curiously at each other,
as if marveling how it was that they themselves became
so excited at such seemingly purposeless questions.

But they were all eagerness again as Ahab, now half
revolving in his pivot hole, with one hand reaching high
up a shroud, and tightly, almost convulsively grasping it,
addressed them thus:

"All ye mastheaders have before now heard me give
orders about a white whale. Look ye! d'ye see this Spanish ounce of gold?"—holding up a broad bright coin to the
sun. "It is a sixteen dollar piece, men. D'ye see it? Mr.
Starbuck, hand me yon top-maul."

While the mate was getting the hammer, Ahab, without speaking, was slowly rubbing the gold piece against

the skirts of his jacket, as if to heighten its luster, and without using any words was meanwhile lowly humming to himself, producing a sound so strangely muffled and inarticulate that it seemed the mechanical humming of the wheels of his vitality in him.

Receiving the top-maul from Starbuck, he advanced toward the mainmast with the hammer uplifted in one hand, exhibiting the gold with the other, and with a high raised voice exclaiming: "Whosoever of ye raises me a white-headed whale with a wrinkled brow and a crooked jaw, whosoever of ye raises me that white-headed whale, with three holes punctured in his starboard fluke—look ye, whosover of ye raises me that same white whale, he shall have this gold ounce, my boys!"

"Huzza! huzza!" cried the seamen, as with swinging tarpaulins they hailed the act of nailing the gold to the mast.

"It's a white whale, I say," resumed Ahab, as he threw down the top-maul. "A white whale. Skin your eyes for him, men; look sharp for white water; if ye see but a bubble, sing out."

All this while Tashtego, Daggoo, and Queequeg had looked on with even more intense interest and surprise than the rest, and at the mention of the wrinkled brow and crooked jaw, they had started as if each was separately touched by some specific recollection.

"Captain Ahab," said Tashtego, "that white whale must be the same that some call Moby Dick."

"Moby Dick?" shouted Ahab. "Do ye know the white whale then, Tash?"

"Does he fan-tail a little curious, sir, before he goes down?" said the Gay Header deliberately.

"And has he a curious spout, too," said Daggoo, "very bushy, even for a parmacetty, and mighty quick, Captain Ahab?"

"And he have one, two, tree—oh! good many iron in him hide, too, Captain," cried Queequeg disjointedly, "all twisketee be-twisk, like him—him"—faltering hard for a word, and screwing his hand round and round as though uncorking a bottle—"like him—him———"

"Corkscrew!" cried Ahab. "Aye, Queequeg, the harpoons lie all twisted and wrenched in him; aye, Daggoo, his spout is a big one, like a whole shock of wheat, and white as a pile of our Nantucket wool after the great annual sheep-shearing; aye Tashtego, and he fan-tails like a split jib in a squall. Death and devils! Men, it is Moby Dick ye have seen—Moby Dick—Moby Dick!"

"Captain Ahab," said Starbuck, who with Stubb and Flask, had thus far been eyeing his superior with increasing surprise, but at last seemed struck with a thought which somewhat explained all the wonder. "Captain Ahab, I have heard of Moby Dick—but it was not Moby Dick that took off thy leg?"

"Who told thee that?" cried Ahab. Then, pausing: "Aye, Starbuck; aye, my hearties all round; it was Moby Dick that dismasted me, Moby Dick that brought me to this dead stump I stand on now. Aye, aye," he shouted with a terrific, loud, animal sob, like that of a heart-stricken moose. "Aye, aye! It was that accursed white whale that razed me, made a poor pegging lubber of me forever and a day!" Then tossing both arms, with measureless imprecations he shouted out: "Aye, aye! And I'll chase him round Good Hope, and round the Horn, and round the Norway Maelstrom, and round perdition's flames before I give him up. And this is what ye have shipped for, men! To chase that white whale on both sides of land, and over all sides of earth, till he spouts black blood and rolls fin out. What say ye, men, will ye splice hands on it, now? I think ye do look brave."

"Aye, aye!" shouted the harpooneers and seamen, running closer to the excited old man. "A sharp eye for the white whale; a sharp lance for Moby Dick!"

"God bless ye," he seemed to half sob and half shout. "God bless ye, men. Steward! Go draw the great measure of grog. But what's this long face about, Mr. Starbuck? Wilt thou not chase the white whale? Art not game for Moby Dick?"

"I am game for his crooked jaw, and for the jaws of Death too, Captain Ahab, if it fairly comes in the way of the business we follow; but I came here to hunt whales, not my commander's vengeance. How many barrels will thy vengeance yield thee even if thou gettest it, Captain Ahab? It will not fetch thee much in our Nantucket market."

"Nantucket market! Hoot! But come closer, Starbuck; thou requirest a little lower layer. If money's to be the measure, man, and the accountants have computed their great countinghouse the globe, by girdling it with guineas, one to every three parts of an inch, then let me tell thee that my vengeance will fetch a great premium *here!*"

"He smites his chest," whispered Stubb. "What's that for? Methinks it rings most vast, but hollow."

"Vengeance on a dumb brute!" cried Starbuck, "that simply smote thee from blindest instinct! Madness! To be enraged with a dumb thing, Captain Ahab, seems blasphemous."

"Hark ye yet again—the little lower layer. All visible objects, man, are but as pasteboard masks. But in each event—in the living act, the undoubted deed—there, some unknown but still reasoning thing puts forth the moldings of its features from behind the unreasoning mask. If man will strike, strike through the mask! How can the prisoner reach outside except by thrusting through the wall? To me, the white whale is that wall, shoved near to me. Sometimes I think there's naught beyond. But 'tis enough. He tasks me; he heaps me; I see in him outrageous strength, with an inscrutable malice sinewing it. That inscrutable thing is chiefly what I hate; and be the white whale agent, or be the white whale principal, I will wreak that hate upon him. Talk not to me of blasphemy, man; I'd strike the sun if it insulted me. Who's over me? Truth hath no confines. Take off thine eye! More intolerable than fiends' glarings is a doltish stare! So, so; thou reddenest and palest; my heat has melted thee to anger-glow. But look ye, Starbuck, what is said in heat, that thing unsays itself. There are men from whom warm words are small indignity. I meant not to incense thee. Let it go.

Look! See yonder Turkish cheeks of spotted tawn— living, breathing pictures painted by the sun. The pagan leopards—the unrecking and unworshiping things that live and seek, and give no reasons for the torrid life they feel! The crew, man, the crew! Are they not one and all with Ahab in this matter of the whale? See Stubb! He laughs! See yonder Chilean! He snorts to think of it. Stand up amid the general hurricane, thy one tossed sapling cannot, Starbuck! And what is it? Reckon it. 'Tis but to help strike a fin, no wondrous feat for Starbuck. What is it more? From this one poor hunt, then, the best lance out of all Nantucket, surely he will not hang back when every foremost hand has clutched a whetstone? Ah! Con- strainings seize thee; I see! The billow lifts thee! Speak, but speak! Aye, aye, thy silence, that—*that* voices thee. (*Aside*) Something shot from my dilated nostrils; he has inhaled it in his lungs. Starbuck now is mine, cannot oppose me now, without rebellion."

"God keep me!—keep us all!" murmured Starbuck slowly.

But in his joy at the enchanted, tacit acquiescence of the mate, Ahab did not hear his foreboding invocation, nor yet the low laugh from the hold, nor yet the presaging vibrations of the winds in the cordage, nor yet the hollow flap of the sails against the masts, as for a moment their hearts sank in. For again Starbuck's downcast eyes lighted up with the stubbornness of life; the subter- ranean laugh died away; the winds blew on; the sails filled out; the ship heaved and rolled as before. Ah, ye admonitions and warnings! why stay ye not when ye come? But rather are ye predictions than warnings, ye shadows! Yet not so much predictions from without, as verifications of the foregoing things within. For with little external to constrain us, the innermost necessities in our being, these still drive us on.

"The measure! the measure!" cried Ahab.

Receiving the brimming pewter, and turning to the harpooneers, he ordered them to produce their weapons. Then he ranged them before him near the capstan, with their harpoons in their hands, while his three mates stood at his side with their lances, and the rest of the ship's company formed a circle around the group. He stood for an instant searchingly eyeing every man of his crew. But those wild eyes met his as the bloodshot eyes of the prairie wolves meet the eye of their leader, ere he rushes on at their head in the trail of the bison, but alas! only to fall into the hidden snare of the Indian.

"Drink and pass!" he cried, handing the heavy charged flagon to the nearest seaman. "The crew alone now drink. Round with it, round! Short draughts—long swallows, men: 'tis hot as Satan's hoof. So, so; it goes round excellently. It spiralizes in ye, forks out at the serpent-snapping eye. Well done, almost drained. That way it went, this way it comes. Hand it me—here's a hollow! Men, ye seem the years; so brimming life is gulped and gone. Steward, refill!

"Attend now, my braves. I have mustered ye all round this capstan; and ye mates, flank me with your lances; and ye harpooneers, stand there with your irons; and ye, stout mariners, ring me in, that I may in some sort revive an old custom of my fishermen fathers before me. O men, you will yet see that——Ha! Boy, come back? Bad pennies come not sooner. Hand it me. Why, now, this pewter had run brimming again, wert not thou St. Vitus' imp— away, thou ague!

"Advance, ye mates! Cross your lances full before me. Well done! Let me touch the axis." So saying, with extended arm, he grasped the three level, radiating lances at their crossed center; while so doing, he suddenly and nervously twitched them, meanwhile glancing intently from Starbuck to Stubb, from Stubb to Flask. It seemed as though, by some nameless, interior volition, he would fain have shocked into them the same fiery emotion accumulated within the Leyden jar of his own magnetic life. The three mates quailed before his strong, sustained and mystic aspect. Stubb and Flask looked sideways from him; the honest eye of Starbuck fell downright.

"In vain!" cried Ahab, "but may be, 'tis well. For did ye three but once take the full-forced shock, then mine own electric thing, *that* had perhaps expired from out me. Perchance, too, it would have dropped ye dead. Perchance ye need it not. Down lances! And now, ye mates, I do appoint ye three cupbearers to my three pagan kinsmen there—you three most honorable gentlemen and noblemen, my valiant harpooneers. Disdain the task? What, when the great Pope washes the feet of beggars, using his tiara for ewer? Oh, my sweet cardinals! Your own condescension, *that* shall bend ye to it. I do not order ye; ye will it. Cut your seizings and draw the poles, ye harpooneers!"

Silently obeying the order, the three harpooners now stood with the detached iron part of their harpoons, some three feet long, held barbs up before him.

"Stab me not with that keen steel! Cant them, cant them over! Know ye not the goblet end? Turn up the socket! So; so, now, ye cupbearers, advance. The irons! Take them; hold them while I fill!" Forthwith, slowly going from one officer to the other, he brimmed the harpoon socket with the fiery waters from the pewter.

"Now three to three, ye stand. Commend the murderous chalices! Bestow them, ye who are now made parties to this indissoluble league. Ha! Starbuck! But the deed is done! Yon ratifying sun now waits to sit upon it. Drink, ye harpooneers! Drink and swear, ye men that man the deathful whaleboat's bow! Death to Moby Dick! God hunt us all, if we do not hunt Moby Dick to his death!"

The long barbed steel goblets were lifted; and to cries and maledictions against the white whale, the spirits were simultaneously quaffed down with a hiss. Starbuck paled, and turned, and shivered. Once more, and finally, the replenished pewter went the rounds among the frantic crew. Then waving his free hand to them they all dispersed, and Ahab retired within his cabin.

⚓

CHAPTER 19

Midnight, Forecastle

HARPOONEERS AND SAILORS

(Foresail rises and discovers the watch standing, lounging, leaning, and lying in various attitudes, all singing in chorus.)

> Farewell and adieu to you, Spanish ladies!
> Farewell and adieu to you, ladies of Spain!
> Our captain's commanded.—

1ST NANTUCKET SAILOR

Oh, boys, don't be sentimental; it's bad for the digestion! Take a tonic, follow me!

(Sings, and all follow)

> Our captain stood upon the deck,
> A spy-glass in his hand,

A viewing of those gallant whales
   That blew at every strand.
Oh, your tubs in your boats, my boys,
   And by your braces stand,
And we'll have one of those fine whales,
   Hand, boys, over hand!
So, be cheery, my lads! may your hearts never fail!
While the bold harpooneer is striking the whale!

MATE'S VOICE FROM THE QUARTERDECK

Eight bells there, forward!

2ND NANTUCKET SAILOR

Avast the chorus! Eight bells there! d'ye hear, bellboy?
Strike the bell eight, thou Pip! thou blackling! and let me
call the watch. I've the sort of mouth for that—the hogs-
head mouth. So, so, (*thrusts his head down the scuttle,*)
Star—bo-l-e-e-n-s, a-h-o-y! Eight bells there below!
Tumble up!

DUTCH SAILOR

Grand snoozing tonight, matey; fat night for that. I
mark this in our old Mogul's wine; it's quite as deadening
to some as filliping to others. We sing; they sleep—aye,
lie down there, like ground-tier butts. At 'em again!
There, take this copper-pump, and hail 'em through it.
Tell 'em to avast dreaming of their lasses. Tell 'em it's the
resurrection; they must kiss their last, and come to judgment. That's the way—*that's* it; thy throat ain't spoiled
with eating Amsterdam butter.

FRENCH SAILOR

Hist, boys! let's have a jig or two before we ride to anchor in Blanket Bay. What say ye? There comes the other watch. Stand by all legs! Pip! little Pip! hurrah with your tambourine!

PIP

(Sulky and sleepy)

Don't know where it is.

FRENCH SAILOR

Beat thy belly, then, and wag thy ears. Jig it, men, I say; merry's the word; hurrah! Damn me, won't you dance? Form, now, Indian-file, and gallop into the double-shuffle? Throw yourselves! Legs! legs!

ICELAND SAILOR

I don't like your floor, matey; it's too springy to my taste. I'm used to ice floors. I'm sorry to throw cold water on the subject; but excuse me.

MALTESE SAILOR

Me too; where's your girls? Who but a fool would take his left hand by his right, and say to himself, how d'ye do? Partners! I must have partners!

SICILIAN SAILOR

Aye; girls and a green!—then I'll hop with ye; yea, turn grasshopper!

LONG ISLAND SAILOR

Well, well, ye sulkies, there's plenty more of us. Hoe corn when you may, say I. All legs go to harvest soon. Ah! here comes the music; now for it!

AZORE SAILOR

(*Ascending, and pitching the tambourine up the scuttle.*)

Here you are, Pip; and there's the windlass-bits; up you mount! Now, boys!

(*Half of them dance to the tambourine; some go below; some sleep or lie among the coils of rigging. Oaths a-plenty.*)

AZORE SAILOR

(*Dancing*)

Go it, Pip! Bang it, bellboy! Rig it, dig it, stig it, quig it, bellboy! Make fireflies; break the jinglers!

PIP

Jinglers, you say? There goes another, dropped off, I pound it so.

CHINA SAILOR

Rattle thy teeth, then, and pound away; make a pagoda of thyself.

FRENCH SAILOR

Merry-mad! Hold up thy hoop, Pip, till I jump through it! Split jibs! Tear yourselves!

TASHTEGO
(Quietly smoking)

That's a white man; he calls that fun. Humph! I save
my sweat.

OLD MANX SAILOR

I wonder whether those jolly lads bethink them of what
they are dancing over. I'll dance over your grave, I will—
that's the bitterest threat of your night-women, that beat
head winds around corners. O Christ! To think of the
green navies and the green-skulled crews! Well, well; be-
like the whole world's a ball, as you scholars have it; and
so 'tis right to make one ballroom of it. Dance on, lads,
you're young; I was once.

3D NANTUCKET SAILOR

Spell oh!—whew! This is worse than pulling after
whales in a calm—give us a whiff, Tash.

*(They cease dancing, and gather in clusters. Meantime
the sky darkens—the wind rises.)*

LASCAR SAILOR

By Brahma! boys, it'll be douse sail soon. The sky-
born, high-tide Ganges turned to wind! Thou showest thy
black brow, Seeva!

MALTESE SAILOR
(Reclining and shaking his cap)

It's the waves—the snow's caps turn to jig it now.
They'll shake their tassels soon. Now would all the waves

were women, then I'd go drown, and chassee with them
evermore! There's naught so sweet on earth—heaven may
not match it!—as those swift glances of warm wild bosoms
in the dance, when the over-arboring arms hide such ripe,
bursting grapes.

SICILIAN SAILOR
(Reclining)

Tell me not of it! Hark ye, lad—fleet interlacings of the
limbs—lithe swayings—coyings—flutterings! lip! heart!
hip! all graze: unceasing touch and go! not taste, observe
ye, else come satiety. Eh, Pagan? *(Nudging.)*

TAHITIAN SAILOR
(Reclining on a mat)

Hail, holy nakedness of our dancing girls!—the Heeva-
Heeva! Ah! low veiled, high palmed Tahiti! I still rest
me on thy mat, but the soft soil has slid! I saw thee woven
in the wood, my mat! green the first day I brought ye
thence; now worn and wilted quite. Ah me!—not thou nor
I can bear the change! How then, if so be transplanted to
yon sky? Hear I the roaring streams from Pirohitee's
peak of spears, when they leap down the crags and drown
the villages?—The blast! the blast! Up, spine, and meet it!
(Leaps to his feet.)

PORTUGUESE SAILOR

How the sea rolls swashing 'gainst the side! Stand by
for reefing, hearties! the winds are just crossing swords,
pell-mell they'll go lunging presently.

DANISH SAILOR

Crack, crack, old ship! So long as thou crackest, thou holdest! Well done! The mate there holds ye to it stiffly. He's no more afraid than the isle fort at Cattegat, put there to fight the Baltic with storm-lashed guns, on which the sea salt cakes!

4TH NANTUCKET SAILOR

He has his orders, mind ye that. I heard old Ahab tell him he must always kill a squall, something as they burst a waterspout with a pistol—fire your ship right into it!

ENGLISH SAILOR

Blood! But that old man's a grand old cove! We are the lads to hunt him up his whale!

ALL

Aye! aye!

OLD MANX SAILOR

How the three pines shake! Pines are the hardest sort of tree to live when shifted to any other soil, and here there's none but the crew's cursed clay. Steady, helmsmen! steady. This is the sort of weather when brave hearts snap ashore, and keeled hulls split at sea. Our captain has his birthmark; look yonder, boys, there's another in the sky—luridlike, ye see, all else pitch black.

MATE'S VOICE FROM THE QUARTERDECK

Hands by the halyards! In topgallant sails! Stand by to reef topsails!

ALL

The squall! the squall! jump, my jollies! (*They scatter.*)

PIP (*shrinking under the windlass*)

Jollies? Lord help such jollies! Crish, crash! There goes
the jib-stay! Blang-whang! God! Duck lower, Pip, here
comes the royal yard! It's worse than being in the whirled
woods, the last day of the year! Who'd go climbing after
chestnuts now? But there they go, all cursing, and here
I don't. Fine prospects to 'em; they're on the road to
heaven. Hold on hard! Jimmini, what a squall! But those
chaps there are worse yet—they are your white squalls,
they. White squalls? White whale, shirr! shirr! Here I
have heard all their chat just now, and the white whale
—shirr! shirr!—but spoken of once! And only this evening
—it makes me jingle all over like my tambourine—that
anaconda of an old man swore 'em in to hunt him! Oh,
thou big white God aloft there somewhere in yon darkness, have mercy on this small black boy down here; pre-
serve him from all men that have no bowels to feel fear!

⚓

CHAPTER 20

Moby Dick

I, ISHMAEL, was one of that crew; my shouts had gone up with the rest; my oath had been welded with theirs; and stronger I shouted, and more did I hammer and clinch my oath, because of the dread in my soul. A wild, mystical, sympathetical feeling was in me; Ahab's quenchless feud seemed mine. With greedy ear I learned the history of that murderous monster against whom I and all the others had taken our oaths of violence and revenge.

For some time past, though at intervals only, the unaccompanied, secluded white whale had haunted those uncivilized seas mostly frequented by the sperm whale fishermen.

Of late the sperm whale fishery had been marked by various and not unfrequent instances of great ferocity, cunning and malice in the monster attacked; therefore it was, that those who by accident ignorantly gave battle to Moby Dick, such hunters, perhaps, for the most part, were content to ascribe the peculiar terror he bred more, as it were, to the perils of the sperm whale fishery at large, than to the individual cause. In that way, mostly, the disastrous encounter between Ahab and the whale had hitherto been popularly regarded.

And as for those who, previously hearing of the white whale, by chance caught sight of him, in the beginning they had, almost every one of them, as boldly and fearlessly lowered for him as for any other whale of that species. But at length, such calamities did ensue in these assaults—not restricted to sprained wrists and ankles, broken limbs or devouring amputations—but fatal to the last degree of fatality, those repeated disastrous repulses all accumulating and piling their terrors upon Moby Dick, those things had gone far to shake the fortitude of many brave hunters, to whom the story of the white whale had eventually come.

One of the wild suggestions referred to, as at last coming to be linked with the white whale in the minds of the superstitiously inclined, was the unearthly conceit that Moby Dick was ubiquitous, that he had actually been encountered in opposite latitudes at one and the same instant of time.

And knowing that after repeated, intrepid assaults the white whale had escaped alive, it cannot be much matter of surprise that some whalemen should go still further in their superstitions, declaring Moby Dick not only ubiquitous, but immortal (for immortality is but ubiquity in time); that though groves of spears should be planted in his flanks, he would still swim away unharmed; or if indeed he should ever be made to spout thick blood, such a sight would be but a ghastly deception; for again in unensanguined billows hundreds of leagues away, his unsullied jet would once more be seen.

Nor was it his unwonted magnitude, nor his remarkable hue, nor yet his deformed lower jaw, that so much invested the whale with natural terror, as that unexampled, intelligent malignity which, according to specific accounts, he had over and over again evinced in his assaults. More than all, his treacherous retreats struck more of dismay than perhaps aught else. For, when swimming before his exulting pursuers with every apparent symptom of alarm, he had several times been known to turn around suddenly, and bearing down upon them, either stave their boats to splinters, or drive them back in consternation to their ship.

Already several fatalities had attended his chase. But though similar disasters, however little bruited ashore, were by no means unusual in the fishery; yet in most instances, such seemed the white whale's infernal forethought of ferocity, that every dismembering or death that he caused was not wholly regarded as having been inflicted by an unintelligent agent.

Judge, then, to what pitches of inflamed distracted fury the minds of his more desperate hunters were impelled, when amid the chips of chewed boats and the sinking limbs of torn comrades, they swam out of the white curds of the whale's direful wrath into the serene exasperating sunlight, that smiled on as if at a birth or a bridal.

His three boats stove around him, and oars and men whirling in the eddies, one captain, seizing the line knife from his broken prow, had dashed at the whale, as an Arkansas duelist at his foe, blindly seeking with a six-inch blade to reach the fathom-deep life of the whale. That captain was Ahab. And then it was, that suddenly sweeping his sickle-shaped lower jaw beneath him, Moby Dick had reaped away Ahab's leg, as a mower a blade of grass in the field. No turbaned Turk, no hired Venetian or Malay, could have smote him with more seeming malice. Small reason was there to doubt, then, that ever since that almost fatal encounter, Ahab had cherished a wild vindictiveness against the whale, all the more fell, for that in his frantic morbidness he at last came to identify with him, not only all his bodily woes, but all his intellectual and spiritual exasperations.

It is not probable that this monomania in him took its instant rise at the precise time of his bodily dismemberment. Then, in darting at the monster, knife in hand, he had but given loose to a sudden, passionate, corporal animosity. And when he received the stroke that tore him, he probably felt the agonizing bodily laceration, but nothing more. Yet, when by this collision forced to turn toward home, and for long months of days and weeks, Ahab and anguish lay stretched together in one hammock, rounding in midwinter that dreary, howling Patagonian Cape, then it was that his torn body and gashed soul bled into one another, and so interfusing, made him mad.

That it was only then, on the homeward voyage after the encounter, that the final monomania seized him, seems all but certain from the fact that, at intervals during the passage, he was a raving lunatic; and, though unlimbed of a leg, such vital strength yet lurked in his Egyptian chest, and was moreover intensified by his delirium, that his mates were forced to lace him fast, even there, as he sailed, raving, in his hammock. In a straitjacket, he swung to the mad rockings of the gales.

And when running into more sufferable latitudes, the ship with mild stunsails spread floated across the tranquil tropics, to all appearances the old man's delirium seemed left behind him with the Cape Horn swells, and he came forth from his dark den into the blessed light and air. Even then, when he bore that firm collected front, however pale, and issued his calm orders once again, and his mates thanked God the direful madness was now gone, even then, Ahab in his hidden self raved on.

In that broad madness, not one jot of his great natural intellect had perished. That before living agent, now became the living instrument. If such a furious trope may stand, this special lunacy stormed his general sanity, and carried it, and turned all its concentrated cannon upon its own mad mark. So that far from having lost his strength, Ahab, to that one end, did now possess a thou-

sand-fold more potency than ever he had sanely brought
to bear upon any one reasonable object.

Nevertheless, so well did he succeed in dissembling
that when with ivory leg he stepped ashore at last, no
Nantucketer thought him otherwise than but naturally
grieved, and that to the quick, with the terrible casualty
which had overtaken him.

The report of his undeniable delirium at sea was likewise popularly ascribed to a kindred cause. And so too
all the added moodiness which always afterward, to the
very day of sailing in the *Pequod* on the present voyage,
sat brooding on his brow. Nor is it so very unlikely, that
far from distrusting his fitness for another whaling voyage, on account of such dark symptoms, the calculating
people of that prudent isle were inclined to harbor the
conceit, that for those very reasons he was all the better
qualified and set on edge, for a pursuit so full of rage and
wildness as the bloody hunt of whales.

But be all this as it may, certain it is that with the mad
secret of his unabated rage bolted up and keyed in him,
Ahab had purposely sailed upon the present voyage with
the one only and all-engrossing object of hunting the
white whale. Had any one of his old acquaintances on
shore but half dreamed of what was lurking in him then,
how soon would their aghast and righteous souls have
wrenched the ship from such a fiendish man! They were
bent on profitable cruises, the profit to be counted down
in dollars from the mint. He was intent on an audacious,
immitigable, and supernatural revenge.

Here, then, was this gray-headed, ungodly old man, chasing with curses a Job's whale around the world, at the head of a crew, too, chiefly made up of mongrel renegades, castaways and cannibals—morally enfeebled also, by the incompetence of mere unaided virtue or right-mindedness in Starbuck, the invulnerable jollity of indifference and recklessness in Stubb, and the pervading mediocrity in Flask. Such a crew, so officered, seemed especially picked and packed by some infernal fatality to help him to his monomaniac revenge. For one, I gave myself up to the abandonment of the time and the place. But while yet all a-rush to encounter the whale, I could see naught in that brute but the deadliest ill.

Chapter 21

⚓

Hark!

"**H**IST! Did you hear that noise, Cabaco?"

It was the middle watch, a fair moonlight. The seamen were standing in a cordon extending from one of the fresh water butts in the waist to the scuttle-butt near the taff-rail. In this manner they passed the buckets to fill the scuttle-butt. Standing for the most part on the hallowed precincts of the quarterdeck, they were careful not to speak or rustle their feet. From hand to hand the buckets went in the deepest silence, only broken by the occasional flap of a sail and the steady hum of the unceasingly advancing keel.

It was in the midst of this repose that Archy, one of the cordon, whose post was near the after-hatches, whispered to his neighbor, a Cholo, the words above:

"Hist! did you hear that noise, Cabaco?"

"Take the bucket, will ye, Archy? What noise d'ye mean?"

"There it is again—under the hatches. Don't you hear it? A cough—it sounded like a cough."

"Cough be damned! Pass along that return bucket."

"There again—there it is! It sounds like two or three sleepers turning over, now!"

"Caramba! Have done, shipmate, will ye? It's the three soaked biscuits ye eat for supper turning over inside of ye —nothing else. Look to the bucket!"

"Say what ye will, shipmate, I've sharp ears."

"Aye, you are the chap, ain't ye, that heard the hum of the old Quakeress' knitting needles fifty miles at sea from Nantucket; you're the chap."

"Grin away; we'll see what turns up. Hark ye, Cabaco, there is somebody down in the afterhold that has not yet been seen on deck, and I suspect our old Mogul knows something of it too. I heard Stubb tell Flask, one morning watch, that there was something of that sort in the wind."

"Tish! the bucket!"

⚓

CHAPTER 22

The Chart

HAD YOU followed Captain Ahab down into his cabin after the squall that took place on the night succeeding that wild ratification of his purpose with his crew, you would have seen him go to a locker in the transom, and bringing out a large wrinkled roll of yellowish sea charts, spread them before him on his screwed-down table. Then seating himself before it, you would have seen him intently study the various lines and shadings which there met his eye, and with slow but steady pencil trace additional courses over spaces that before were blank. At intervals, he would refer to piles of old log-books beside him, wherein were set down the seasons and places in which, on various former voyages of various ships, sperm whales had been captured or seen.

But it was not this night in particular that, in the solitude of his cabin, Ahab thus pondered over his charts. Almost every night they were brought out; almost every night some pencil marks were effaced, and others were substituted. For with the charts of all four oceans before him, Ahab was threading a maze of currents and eddies, with a view to the more certain accomplishment of that monomaniac thought of his soul.

Now, to anyone not fully acquainted with the ways of the Leviathans, it might seem an absurdly hopeless task thus to seek out one solitary creature in the unhooped oceans of this planet. But not so did it seem to Ahab, who knew the sets of all tides and currents. And by calculating the driftings of the sperm whale's food, and also calling to mind the regular ascertained seasons for hunting him in particular latitudes, he could arrive at reasonable surmises, almost approaching to certainties, concerning the timeliest day to be upon this or that ground in search of his prey.

Besides, when making a passage from one feeding-ground to another, the sperm whales, guided by some infallible instinct—say rather, secret intelligence from the Deity—mostly swim in *veins*, as they are called, continuing their way along a given ocean line with such undeviating exactitude that no ship ever sailed her course by any chart, with one tithe of such marvelous precision.

And hence not only at substantiated times, upon well-known separate feeding-grounds, could Ahab hope to encounter his prey, but in crossing the widest expanse of water between those grounds he could, by his art, so place and time himself on his way, as even then not to be wholly without prospect of a meeting.

Thus far allusion has been made only to whatever wayside, antecedent, extra prospects were his, ere a particular set time or place were attained when all possibilities would become probabilities, and, as Ahab fondly thought, every possibility the next thing to a certainty. That particular set time and place were conjoined in the one technical phrase—the Season-on-the-Line. For there and then, for several consecutive years, Moby Dick had been periodically described, lingering in those waters for a while, as the sun, in its annual round, loiters for a predicted interval in any one sign of the zodiac. There it was, too, that most of the deadly encounters with the white whale had taken place; there the waves were storied with his deeds. There also was that tragic spot where the monomaniac old man had found the awful motive to his vengeance.

Now, the *Pequod* had sailed from Nantucket at the very beginning of the Season-on-the-Line. No possible endeavors then could enable her commander to make the great passage southward, double Cape Horn, and then running down sixty degrees of latitude arrive in the equatorial Pacific in time to cruise there. Therefore, he must wait for the next ensuing season.

Yet the premature hour of the *Pequod's* sailing had, perhaps, been correctly selected by Ahab with a view to this very complexion of things. Because an interval of three hundred and sixty-five days and nights was before him, an interval which instead of impatiently enduring ashore, he would spend in a miscellaneous hunt, if by chance the white whale, spending his vacation in seas far remote from his periodical feeding-grounds, should turn up his wrinkled brow off the Persian Gulf, or in the Bengal Bay, or the China Seas, or in any other waters haunted by his race. So that monsoons, pampas, nor'-westers, harmattans, trades—any wind but the levanter and simoom, might blow Moby Dick into the devious zigzag world-circle of the *Pequod's* circumnavigating wake.

"And have I not tallied the whale," Ahab would mutter to himself, as after poring over his charts until long after midnight he would throw himself back in reveries—"tallied him, and shall he escape? His broad fins are bored and scalloped out like a lost sheep's ear!" And here his mad mind would run on in a breathless race, until a weariness and faintness of pondering came over him; and in the open air of the deck he would seek to recover his strength. Ah, God! What trances of torments does that man endure who is consumed with one unachieved revengeful desire. He sleeps with clenched hands, and wakes with his own bloody nails in his palms.

CHAPTER 23

⚓

The Mat-Maker

I T WAS a cloudy, sultry afternoon; the seamen were lazily lounging about the decks, or vacantly gazing over into the lead-colored waters. Queequeg and I were mildly employed weaving what is called a sword mat, for an additional lashing to our boat. So still and subdued and yet somehow preluding was all the scene, and such an incantation of reverie lurked in the air, that each silent sailor seemed resolved into his own invisible self.

I was the attendant or page of Queequeg, while busy at the mat. As I kept passing and repassing the filling or woof of marline between the long yarns of the warps, using my own hand for the shuttle, and as Queequeg, standing sideways, ever and anon slid his heavy oaken sword between the threads, and idly looking off upon the water, carelessly and unthinkingly drove home every yarn: I say so strange a dreaminess did there then reign all over the ship and all over the sea, only broken by the intermitting dull sound of the sword, that it seemed as if this were the loom of time, and I myself were a shuttle mechanically weaving and weaving away at the fates.

There lay the fixed threads of the warp subject to but one single, ever returning, unchanging vibration, and that vibration merely enough to admit of the crosswise inter-blending of other threads with its own. This warp seemed necessity; and here, thought I, with my own hand I ply my own shuttle and weave my own destiny into these unalterable threads. Meantime, Queequeg's impulsive in-different sword, sometimes hit the woof slantingly or crookedly, or strongly or weakly, as the case might be, and by this difference in the concluding blow producing a corresponding contrast in the final aspect of the completed fabric. This savage's sword, thought I, which thus finally shapes and fashions both warp and woof, this easy indifferent sword must be chance—aye, chance, free will and necessity—no wise incompatible—all interweavingly working together.

Thus we were weaving and weaving away when I started at a sound so strange, long drawn, and musically wild and unearthly, that the ball of free will dropped from my hand, and I stood gazing up at the clouds whence that voice dropped like a wing. High aloft in the crosstrees was that mad Gay Header, Tashtego. His body was reaching eagerly forward, his hand stretched out like a wand, and at brief sudden intervals he continued his cries. To be sure the same sound was that very moment perhaps being heard all over the seas, from hundreds of whalemen's lookouts perched as high in the air; but from few of those lungs could that accustomed old cry have derived such a marvelous cadence as from Tashtego the Indian's.

As he stood hovering over you half suspended in air, so wildly and eagerly peering toward the horizon, you would have thought him some prophet or seer beholding the shadows of Fate, and by those wild cries announcing their coming.

"There she blows! There! There! There! She blows! She blows!"

"Where-away?"

"On the lee beam, about two miles off! A school of them!"

Instantly all was commotion.

The sperm whale blows as a clock ticks, with the same undeviating and reliable uniformity. And thereby whalemen distinguish this fish from other tribes of his genus.

"There go flukes!" was now the cry from Tashtego, and the whales disappeared.

"Quick, steward!" cried Ahab. "Time! Time!"

Dough Boy hurried below, glanced at the watch, and reported the exact minute to Ahab.

The ship was now kept away from the wind, and she went gently rolling before it. Tashtego reporting that the whales had gone down heading to leeward, we confidently looked to see them again directly in advance of our bows. For that singular craft at times evinced by the sperm whale when, sounding with his head in one direction, he nevertheless, while concealed beneath the surface, mills around, and swiftly swims off in the opposite quarter—this deceitfulness of his could not now be in action; for there was no reason to suppose that the fish seen by Tashtego had been in any way alarmed, or indeed knew at all of our vicinity. One of the men selected for shipkeepers—that is, those not appointed to the boats, by this time relieved the Indian at the mainmast head. The sailors at the fore and mizzen had come down; the line tubs were fixed in their places; the cranes were thrust out; the mainyard was backed, and the three boats swung over the sea like three samphire baskets over high cliffs. Outside of the bulwarks their eager crews with one hand clung to the rail, while one foot was expectantly poised on the gunwale. So look the long line of man-of-war's men about to throw themselves on board an enemy's ship.

But at this critical instant a sudden exclamation was heard that took every eye from the whale. With a start all glared at dark Ahab, who was surrounded by five dusky phantoms that seemed fresh formed out of air.

⚓

Chapter 24

The First Lowering

THE PHANTOMS, for so they then seemed, were flitting on the other side of the deck, and with a noiseless celerity were casting loose the tackles and bands of the boat which swung there. This boat had always been deemed one of the spare boats, though technically called the captain's, on account of its hanging from the starboard quarter. The figure that now stood by its bows was tall and swart, with one white tooth evilly protruding from his steel-like lips. A rumpled Chinese jacket of black cotton funereally invested him, with wide black trousers of the same dark stuff. But strangely crowning this ebonness was a glistening white plaited turban, the living hair braided and coiled round and round upon his head. Less swart in aspect, the companions of this figure were of that vivid, tiger-yellow complexion peculiar to some of the aboriginal natives of the Manilas—a race notorious for a certain diabolism of subtlety, and by some honest white mariners supposed to be the paid spies and secret confidential agents on the water of the devil, their lord, whose counting room they suppose to be elsewhere.

While yet the wondering ship's company were gazing upon these strangers, Ahab cried out to the white-turbaned old man at their head, "All ready there, Fedallah?"

"Ready," was the half-hissed reply.

"Lower away then, d'ye hear?" shouting across the deck. "Lower away there, I say."

Such was the thunder of his voice, that spite of their amazement the men sprang over the rail; the sheaves whirled round in the blocks; with a wallow, the three boats dropped into the sea; while, with a dexterous, off-handed daring, unknown in any other vocation, the sailors, goatlike, leaped down the rolling ship's side into the tossed boats below.

Hardly had they pulled out from under the ship's lee, when a fourth keel, coming from the windward side pulled around under the stern, and showed the five strangers rowing Ahab, who standing erect in the stern, loudly hailed Starbuck, Stubb and Flask to spread themselves widely, so as to cover a large expanse of water. But with all their eyes again riveted upon the swart Fedallah and his crew, the inmates of the other boats obeyed not the command.

"Captain Ahab?" said Starbuck.

"Spread yourselves," cried Ahab; "give way, all four boats. Thou, Flask, pull out more to leeward!"

"Aye, aye, sir," cheerily cried little King Post, sweeping around his great steering oar. "Lay back!" addressing his crew. "There!—there!—there again! There she blows right ahead, boys!—lay back! Never heed yonder yellow boys, Archy."

"Oh, I don't mind 'em, sir," said Archy; "I knew it all before now. Didn't I hear 'em in the hold? And didn't I tell Cabaco here of it? What say ye, Cabaco? They are stowaways, Mr. Flask."

"Pull, pull, my fine hearts alive; pull, my children; pull, my little ones," drawlingly and soothingly sighed Stubb to his crew, some of whom still showed signs of uneasiness. "Why don't you break your backbones, my boys? What is it you stare at? Those chaps in yonder boats? Tut! They are only five more hands come to help us— never mind from where—the more the merrier. Pull, then, do pull; never mind the brimstone—devils are good fellows enough. So, so; there you are now; that's the stroke for a thousand pounds; that's the stroke to sweep the stakes! Hurrah for the gold cup of sperm oil, my heroes! Three cheers, men—all hearts alive! Easy, easy; don't be in a hurry—don't be in a hurry. Why don't you snap your oars, you rascals? Bite something, you dogs! So, so, so, then—softly, softly! That's it—that's it! Long and strong. Give way there, give way! The devil fetch ye, ye ragamuffin rapscallions; ye are all asleep. Stop snoring, ye sleepers, and pull. Pull, will ye? Pull, can't ye? Pull, won't ye? Why in the name of gudgeons and ginger cakes don't ye pull? Pull and break something! Pull, and start your eyes out! Here!"—whipping out the sharp knife from his girdle—"every mother's son of ye draw his knife and pull with the blade between his teeth. That's it—that's it. Now ye do something; that looks like it, my steelbits. Start her —start her, my silver spoons! Start her, marlinspikes!"

Stubb's exordium to his crew is given here at large, because he had rather a peculiar way of talking to them in general, and especially in inculcating the religion of rowing. But you must not suppose from this specimen of his sermonizings that he ever flew into downright passions with his congregation. Not at all; and therein consisted his chief peculiarity. He would say the most terrific things to his crew, in a tone so strangely compounded of fun and fury, and the fury seemed so calculated merely as a spice to the fun, that no oarsman could hear such queer invocations without pulling for dear life, and yet pulling for the mere joke of the thing. Besides he all the time looked so easy and indolent himself, so loungingly managed his steering oar, and so broadly gaped—open-mouthed at times—that the mere sight of such a yawning commander, by sheer force of contrast, acted like a charm upon the crew. Then again, Stub was one of those odd sort of humorists whose jollity is sometimes so curiously ambiguous as to put all inferiors on their guard in the matter of obeying them.

In obedience to a sign from Ahab, Starbuck was now pulling obliquely across Stubb's bow; and when for a minute or so the two boats were pretty near to each other Stubb hailed the mate.

"Mr. Starbuck! Larboard boat there, ahoy! A word with ye, sir, if ye please!"

"Holloa!" returned Starbuck, turning around not a single inch as he spoke, still earnestly but whisperingly urging his crew, his face set like a flint from Stubb's.

"What think ye of those yellow boys, sir?"

"Smuggled on board, somehow, before the ship sailed. (Strong, strong boys!)"—in a whisper to his crew, then speaking out loud again—"A sad business, Mr. Stubb! (seethe her, seethe her, my lads!) but never mind, Mr. Stubb, all for the best. Let all your crew pull strong, come what will. (Spring, my men, spring!) There's hogsheads of sperm ahead, Mr. Stubb, and that's what ye came for. (Pull, my boys!) Sperm, sperm's the play! This at least is duty; duty and profit hand in hand!"

"Aye, aye, I thought as much," soliloquized Stubb, when the boats diverged, "as soon as I clapt eye on 'em, I thought so. Aye, and that's what he went into the after-hold for so often, as Dough Boy long suspected. They were hidden down there. The white whale's at the bottom of it. Well, well, so be it! Can't be helped! All right! Give way, men! It ain't the white whale today! Give way!"

Now the advent of these outlandish strangers at such a critical instant as the lowering of the boat from the deck, had not unreasonably awakened a sort of superstitious amazement in some of the ship's company; but Archy's fancied discovery having sometime previous got abroad among them, though indeed not credited then, had in some small measure prepared them for the event. It took off the extreme edge of their wonder; and so what with all this and Stubb's confident way of accounting for their appearance, they were for the time freed from superstitious surmisings, though the affair still left abundant room for all manner of wild conjectures as to dark Ahab's precise agency in the matter from the beginning. As for me, I silently recalled the mysterious shadows I had seen creeping on board the *Pequod* during the dim Nantucket dawn, as well as the enigmatical hintings of the unaccountable Elijah.

Meantime Ahab, out of hearing of his officers, having sided the furthest to windward, was still ranging ahead of the other boats, a circumstance bespeaking how potent a crew was pulling him. Those tiger-yellow creatures of his seemed all steel and whalebone; like five trip hammers they rose and fell with regular strokes of strength, which periodically started the boat along the water like a horizontal burst boiler out of a Mississippi steamer. As for Fedallah, who was seen pulling the harpooneer oar, he had thrown aside his black jacket and displayed his naked chest with the whole part of his body above the gunwale, clearly cut against the alternating depressions of the watery horizon. At the other end of the boat Ahab, with one arm like a fencer's thrown half backward into the air, as if to counterbalance any tendency to trip, Ahab was seen steadily managing his steering oar as in a thousand boat lowerings ere the white whale had torn him. All at once the outstretched arm gave a peculiar motion and then remained fixed, while the boat's five oars were seen simultaneously peaked. Boat and crew sat motionless on the sea. Instantly the three spread boats in the rear paused on their way. The whales had irregularly settled bodily down into the blue, thus giving no distantly discernible token of the movement, though from his closer vicinity Ahab had observed it.

"Every man look out along his oars!" cried Starbuck. "Thou, Queequeg, stand up!"

Nimbly springing up on the triangular raised box in the bow, the savage stood erect there, and with intensely eager eyes gazed off toward the spot where the chase had last been described. Likewise upon the extreme stern of the boat where it was also triangularly platformed level with the gunwale, Starbuck himself was seen coolly and adroitly balancing himself to the jerking tossings of his chip of a craft, and silently eyeing the vast blue eye of the sea.

Not very far distant Flask's boat was also lying breathlessly still, its commander recklessly standing upon the top of the loggerhead, a stout sort of post rooted in the keel, and rising some two feet above the level of the stern platform. It is used for catching turns with the whale line. Its stop is not more spacious than the palm of a man's hand, and standing upon such a base as that, Flask seemed perched at the masthead of some ship which had sunk to all but her trucks. But little King Post was small and short, and at the same time little King Post was full of a large and tall ambition, so that this loggerhead standpoint of his did by no means satisfy King Post.

"I can't see three seas off; tip us up an oar there, and let me on to that."

Upon this, Daggoo, with either hand upon the gunwale to steady his way, swiftly slid aft, and then erecting himself volunteered his lofty shoulders for a pedestal.

"Good a masthead as any, sir. Will you mount?"

"That I will and thank ye very much, my fine fellow; only I wish you fifty feet taller."

Whereupon planting his feet firmly against two opposite planks of the boat, the gigantic Negro, stooping a little, presented his flat palm to Flask's foot, and then putting Flask's hand on his hearse-plumed head and bidding him spring as he himself should toss, with one dexterous fling landed the little man high and dry on his shoulders. And here was Flask now standing, Daggoo with one lifted arm furnishing him with a breastband to lean against and steady himself by.

At any time it is a strange sight to the tyro to see with what wondrous habitude of unconscious skill the whale-man will maintain an erect posture in his boat, even when pitched about by the most riotously perverse and cross-running seas; still more strange to see him giddily perched upon the loggerhead itself, under such circumstances. But the sight of little Flask mounted upon gigantic Daggoo was yet more curious; for sustaining himself with a cool, indifferent, easy unthought of barbaric majesty, the noble Negro to every roll of the sea harmoniously rolled his fine form. On his broad back, flaxen-haired Flask seemed a snowflake. The bearer looked nobler than the rider. Though truly vivacious, tumultuous ostentatious little Flask would now and then stamp with impatience, not one added heave did he thereby give to the Negro's lordly chest. So have I seen Passion and Vanity stamping the living magnanimous earth, but the earth did not alter her tides and her seasons for that.

Meanwhile Stubb, the second mate, betrayed no such fargazing solicitudes. The whales might have made one of their regular soundings, not a temporary dive from mere fright; and if that were the case, Stubb, as his wont in such cases, it seems, was resolved to solace the languishing interval with his pipe. He withdrew it from his hatband, where he always wore it aslant like a feather. He loaded it, and rammed home the loading with his thumb end; but hardly had he ignited his match across the rough sandpaper of his hand, when Tashtego, his harpooneer, whose eyes had been setting to windward like two fixed stars, suddenly dropped like light from his erect attitude to his seat, crying out in a quick frenzy of hurry, "Down, down all, and give way!—there they are!"

To a landsman, no whale, nor any sign of a herring, would have been visible at that moment; nothing but a troubled bit of greenish white water, and thin scattered puffs of vapor hovering over it, and suffusingly blowing off to leeward, like the confused scud from white rolling billows. The air around suddenly vibrated and tingled, as it were, like the air over intensely heated plates of iron. Beneath this atmospheric waving and curling, and partially beneath a thin layer of water, also, the whales were swimming. Seen in advance of all the other indications, the puffs of vapor they spouted seemed their forerunning couriers and detached flying outriders.

All four boats were now in keen pursuit of that one spot of troubled water and air. But it bade fair to outstrip them; it flew on and on, as a mass of interblending bubbles borne down a rapid stream from the hills.

"Pull, pull, my good boys," said Starbuck, in the lowest possible but intensest concentrated whisper to his men, while the sharp fixed glance from his eyes darted straight ahead of the bow, almost seemed as two visible needles in two unerring binnacle compasses. He did not say much to his crew, though, nor did his crew say anything to him; only the silence of the boat was at intervals startlingly pierced by one of his peculiar whispers, now harsh with command, now soft with entreaty.

How different the loud little King Post. "Sing out and say something, my hearties. Roar and pull, my thunderbolts! Beach me, beach me on their black backs, boys; only do that for me, and I'll sign over to you my Martha's Vineyard plantation, boys, including wife, and children, boys. Lay me on—lay me on! O Lord, Lord! But I shall go stark, staring mad! See! See that white water!" And so shouting, he pulled his hat from his head, and stamped up and down on it, then picking it up, flirted it far off upon the sea; and finally fell to rearing and plunging in the boat's stern like a crazed colt from the prairie.

"Look at that chap, now," philosophically drawled Stubb, who, with his unlighted short pipe mechanically retained between his teeth, at a short distance followed after. "He's got fits, that Flask has. Fits? Yes, give him fits—that's the very word—pitch fits into 'em. Merrily, merrily, heart's alive. Pudding for supper, you know—merry's the word. Pull, babes—pull, sucklings—pull, all. But what the devil are you hurrying about? Softly, softly, and steadily, my men. Only pull, and keep pulling; nothing more. Crack all your backbones, and bite your knives in two—that's all. Take it easy—why don't ye take it easy, I say, and burst all your livers and lungs!"

But what it was that inscrutable Ahab said to that tiger-yellow crew of his—these were words best omitted here, for you live under the blessed light of the evangelical land. Only the infidel sharks in the audacious seas may give ear to such words, when, with tornado brow and eyes of red murder and foam-glued lips, Ahab leaped after his prey.

Meanwhile, all the boats tore on. The repeated specific allusions of Flask to "that whale," as he called the ficti-tious monster which he declared to be incessantly tantal-izing his boat's bow with his tail—these allusions of his were at times so vivid and lifelike, that they would cause some one or two of his men to snatch a fearful look over the shoulder. But this was against all rule, for the oarsmen must put out their eyes, and ram a skewer through their necks, usage pronouncing that they must have no organs but ears, and no limbs but arms, in these critical moments.

It was a sight full of quick wonder and awe! The vast swells of the omnipotent sea; the surging, hollow roar they made as they rolled along the eight gunwales, like gigantic bowls in a boundless bowling green; the brief suspended agony of the boat, as it would tip for an instant on the knifelike edge of the sharper waves, that almost seemed threatening to cut it in two; the sudden profound dip into the watery glens and hollows; the keen spurrings and goadings to gain the top of the opposite hill; the headlong, sledlike slide down its other side—all these, with the cries of the headsmen and harpooneers, and the shuddering gasps of the oarsmen, with the wondrous sight of the ivory *Pequod* bearing down upon her boats with outstretched sails, like a wild hen after her screaming brood; all this was thrilling. Not the raw recruit, marching from the bosom of his wife into the fever heat of his first battle; not the dead man's ghost encountering the first unknown phantom in the other world—neither of these can feel stranger and stronger emotions than that man does, who for the first time finds himself pulling into the charmed, churned circle of the hunted sperm whale.

The dancing white water made by the chase was now becoming more and more visible, owing to the increasing darkness of the dun cloud shadows flung upon the sea. The jets of vapor no longer blended, but tilted everywhere to right and left; the whales seemed separating their wakes. The boats were pulled more apart, Starbuck giving chase to three whales running dead to leeward. Our sail was now set, and with the still rising wind we rushed along, the boat going with such madness through the water, that the lee oars could scarcely be worked rapidly enough to escape being torn from the rowlocks.

Soon we were running through a suffusing wide veil of mist, neither ship nor boat to be seen.

"Give way, men," whispered Starbuck, drawing still further aft the sheet of his sail; "there is time to kill fish yet before the squall comes. There's white water again! Close to! Spring!"

Soon after, two cries in quick succession on each side of us denoted that the other boats had got fast; but hardly were they overheard, when with a lightninglike hurtling whisper Starbuck said: "Stand up!" and Queequeg, harpoon in hand, sprang to his feet.

Though not one of the oarsmen was then facing the life and death peril so close to them ahead, yet with their eyes on the intense countenance of the mate in the stern of the boat, they knew that the imminent instant had come; they heard, too, an enormous wallowing sound as of fifty elephants stirring in their litter. Meanwhile the boat was still booming through the mist, the waves curling and hissing around us like the erected crests of enraged serpents.

"That's his hump. *There, there,* give it to him!" whispered Starbuck.

A short rushing sound leaped out of the boat; it was the darted iron of Queequeg. Then all in one welded commotion came an invisible push from astern, while forward the boat seemed striking on a ledge; the sail collapsed and exploded; a gush of scalding vapor shot up near by; something rolled and tumbled like an earthquake beneath us. The whole crew were half suffocated as they were tossed helter-skelter into the white curdling cream of the squall. Squall, whale, and harpoon had all blended together; and the whale, merely grazed by the iron, escaped.

Though completely swamped, the boat was nearly unharmed. Swimming around it we picked up the floating oars, and lashing them across the gunwale, tumbled back to our places. There we sat up to our knees in the sea, the water covering every rib and plank, so that to our downward gazing eyes the suspended craft seemed a coral boat grown up to us from the bottom of the ocean.

The wind increased to a howl; the waves dashed their bucklers together; the whole squall roared, forked and crackled around us like a white fire upon the prairie, in which, unconsumed, we were burning, immortal in these jaws of death! In vain we hailed the other boats; as well roar to the live coals down the chimney of a flaming furnace as hail those boats in that storm. Meanwhile the driving scud, rack and mist grew darker with the shadows of night; no sign of the ship could be seen. The rising sea forbade all attempts to bail out the boat. The oars were useless as propellers, performing now the office of life preservers. So, cutting the lashing of the waterproof match-keg, after many failures Starbuck contrived to ignite the lamp in the lantern; then stretching it on a waif pole, handed it to Queequeg as the standard-bearer of this forlorn hope. There, then, he sat, holding up that imbecile candle in the heart of that almighty forlornness. There, then, he sat, the sign and symbol of a man without faith, hopelessly holding up hope in the midst of despair.

Wet, drenched through, and shivering cold, despairing of ship or boat, we lifted up our eyes as the dawn came on. The mist still spread over the sea; the empty lantern lay crushed in the bottom of the boat. Suddenly Queequeg started to his feet, hollowing his hand to his ear. We all heard a faint creaking, as of ropes and yards hitherto muffled by the storm. The sound came nearer and nearer; the thick mists were dimly parted by a huge vague form. Affrighted, we all sprang into the sea as the ship at last loomed into view, bearing right down upon us within a distance of not much more than its length.

Floating on the waves we saw the abandoned boat, as for one instant it tossed and gaped beneath the ship's bows like a chip at the base of a cataract; and then the vast hull rolled over it, and it was seen no more till it came up weltering astern. Again we swam for it, were dashed against it by the seas, and were at last taken up and safely landed on board. Ere the squall came close to, the other boats had cut loose from their fish and returned to the ship in good time. The ship had given us up, but was still cruising, if haply it might light upon some token of our perishing—an oar or a lance pole.

⚓

CHAPTER 25

The Hyena

THERE ARE CERTAIN queer times and occasions in this strange mixed affair we call life when a man takes this whole universe for a vast practical joke, though the wit thereof he but dimly discerns, and more than suspects that the joke is at nobody's expense but his own. However, nothing dispirits, and nothing seems worthwhile disputing. He bolts down all events, all creeds and beliefs and persuasions, all hard things visible and invisible, never mind how knobby, as an ostrich of potent digestion gobbles down bullets and gun flints. And as for small difficulties and worryings, prospects of sudden disaster, peril of life and limb; all these, and death itself, seem to him only sly, good-natured hits and jolly punches in the side bestowed by the unseen and unaccountable old joker. That odd sort of wayward mood I am speaking of, comes over a man only in some time of extreme tribulation; it

171

comes in the very midst of his earnestness, so that what just before might have seemed to him a thing most momentous, now seems but a part of the general joke. There is nothing like the perils of whaling to breed this free and easy sort of genial, desperado philosophy; and with it I now regarded this whole voyage of the *Pequod,* and the great white whale its object.

"Queequeg," said I when they had dragged me, the last man, to the deck, and I was still shaking myself in my jacket to fling off the water. "Queequeg, my fine friend, does this sort of thing often happen?" Without much emotion, though soaked through just like me, he gave me to understand that such things did often happen.

"Mr. Stubb," said I, turning to that worthy, who, buttoned up in his oil jacket, was now calmly smoking his pipe in the rain. "Mr. Stubb, I think I have heard you say that of all whalemen you ever met our chief mate, Mr. Starbuck, is by far the most careful and prudent. I suppose then, that going plump on a flying whale with your sail set in a foggy squall is the height of a whaleman's discretion?"

"Certain. I've lowered for whales from a leaking ship in a gale off Cape Horn."

"Mr. Flask," said I, turning to little King Post, who was standing close by. "You are experienced in these things and I am not. Will you tell me whether it is an unalterable law in this fishery, Mr. Flask, for an oarsman to break his own back pulling himself back foremost into death's jaws?"

"Can't you twist that smaller?" said Flask. "Yes, that's

the law. I should like to see a boat's crew backing water up to a whale, face foremost. Ha, ha! The whale would give them squint for squint, mind that!"

Here then, from three impartial witnesses, I had a deliberate statement of the entire case. Considering, therefore, that squalls and capsizings in the water and consequent bivouacks on the deep were matters of common occurrence in this kind of life, considering that at the superlatively critical instant of going on to the whale I must resign my life into the hands of him who steered the boat—oftentimes a fellow who at that very moment is in his impetuousness upon the point of scuttling the craft with his own frantic stampings, considering that the particular disaster to our own particular boat was chiefly to be imputed to Starbuck's driving on to his whale almost in the teeth of a squall, and considering that Starbuck, notwithstanding, was famous for his great heedfulness in the fishery, considering that I belonged to this uncommonly prudent Starbuck's boat, and finally considering in what a devil's chase I was implicated, touching the white whale: taking all things together, I say, I thought I might as well go below and make a rough draft of my will. "Queequeg," said I, "come along; you shall be my lawyer, executor, and legatee."

It may seem strange that of all men sailors should be tinkering at their last wills and testaments, but there are no people in the world more fond of that diversion. This was the fourth time in my nautical life that I had done the same thing. After the ceremony was concluded upon the present occasion, I felt all the easier; a stone was rolled away from my heart. Besides, all the days I should now live would be as supplementary clean gain of so many months or weeks as the case might be. I survived myself; my death and burial were locked up in my chest. I looked round me tranquilly and contentedly, like a quiet ghost with a clean conscience sitting inside the bars of a snug family vault.

Now then, thought I, unconsciously rolling up my sleeves, here goes for a cool collected dive at death and destruction, and the devil fetch the hindmost.

⚓

CHAPTER 26

The Spirit Spout

D AYS, weeks passed, and under easy sail, the ivory *Pequod* had slowly swept across four separate cruising-grounds: that off the Azores; off the Cape de Verdes; on the Plate (so-called), being off the mouth of the Rio de la Plata; and the Carrol Ground, an unstaked, watery locality, southerly from St. Helena.

It was while gliding through these latter waters that one serene and moonlight night when all the waves rolled by like scrolls of silver, and by their soft suffusing seethings made what seemed a silvery silence, not a solitude; on such a silent night a silvery jet was seen far in advance of the white bubbles at the bow. Lit up by the moon, it looked celestial, seemed some plumed and glittering god uprising from the sea. Fedallah first descried this jet. For of these moonlight nights, it was his wont to mount the mainmast head, and stand a lookout there with the same

precision as if it had been day. And yet, though herds of
whales were seen by night, not one whaleman in a hundred would venture a lowering for them. You may think
with what emotions, then, the seamen beheld this old
Oriental perched aloft at such unusual hours, his turban
and the moon, companions in one sky. But when, after
spending his uniform interval there for several successive
nights without uttering a single sound, when after all this
silence, his unearthly voice was heard announcing that
silvery, moonlit jet, every reclining mariner started to his
feet as if some winged spirit had lighted in the rigging,
and hailed the mortal crew. "There she blows!" Had the
trump of judgment blown, they could not have quivered
more; yet still they felt no terror, rather pleasure. For
though it was a most unwonted hour, yet so impressive
was the cry, and so deliriously exciting, that almost every
soul on board instinctively desired a lowering.

Walking the deck with quick, side-lunging strides,
Ahab commanded the t'gallant sails and royals to be set,
and every stunsail spread. The best man in the ship must
take the helm. Then, with every masthead manned, the
piled-up craft rolled down before the wind. The strange,
upheaving lifting tendency of the taffrail breeze filling
the hollows of so many sails, made the buoyant hovering
deck to feel like air beneath the feet, while still she
rushed along, as if two antagonistic influences were
struggling in her—one to mount direct to heaven, the
other to drive yawingly to some horizontal goal. And had
you watched Ahab's face that night, you would have
thought that in him also two different things were war-

ring. While his one live leg made lively echoes along the deck, every stroke of his dead limb sounded like a coffin tap. On life and death this old man walked. But though the ship so swiftly sped, and though from every eye, like arrows, the eager glances shot, yet the silvery jet was no more seen that night. Every sailor swore he saw it once, but not a second time.

This midnight spout had almost grown a forgotten thing, when, some days after, lo! at the same silent hour it was again announced: again it was described by all; but upon making sail to overtake it, once more it disappeared as if it had never been. And so it served us night after night, until no one heeded it but to wonder at it. Mysteriously jetted into the clear moonlight or starlight, as the case might be, disappearing again for one whole day, or two days or three, and somehow seeming at every distinct repetition to be advancing still further and further in our van, this solitary jet seemed forever alluring us on.

Nor with the immemorial superstition of their race, and in accordance with the preternaturalness, as it seemed, which in many things invested the *Pequod,* were there wanting some of the seamen who swore that whenever and wherever descried, at however remote times or in however far apart latitudes and longitudes, that unnearable spout was cast by one selfsame whale; and that whale, Moby Dick. For a time there reigned, too, a sense of peculiar dread at this flitting apparition, as if it were treacherously beckoning us on and on in order that the monster might turn round upon us, and rend us at last in the remotest and most savage seas.

These temporary apprehensions, so vague but so awful, derived a wondrous potency from the contrasting serenity of the weather, in which, beneath all its blue blandness, some thought there lurked a devilish charm, as for days and days we voyaged along through seas so wearily, lonesomely mild that all space, in repugnance to our vengeful errand, seemed vacating itself of life before our urnlike prow.

But at last, when turning to the eastward, the Cape winds began howling around us, and we rose and fell upon the long, troubled seas that are there, when the ivory-tusked *Pequod* sharply bowed to the blast and gored the dark waves in her madness until, like showers of silver chips, the foam-flakes flew over her bulwarks. Then all this desolate vacuity of life went away, but gave place to sights more dismal than before.

Close to our bows, strange forms in the water darted hither and thither before us, while thick in our rear flew the inscrutable sea ravens. And every morning, perched on our stays, rows of these birds were seen; and spite of our hootings, for a long time obstinately clung to the hemp, as though they deemed our ship some drifting, uninhabited craft, a thing appointed to desolation, and therefore fit roosting-place for their homeless selves. And heaved and heaved, still unrestingly heaved the black sea, as if its vast tides were a conscience, and the great mundane soul were in anguish and remorse for the long sin and suffering it had bred.

Cape of Good Hope, do they call ye? Rather Cape Tormentoto, as called of yore. For long allured by the per-

fidious silences that before had attended us, we found ourselves launched into this tormented sea, where guilty beings transformed into those fowls and these fish, seemed
condemned to swim on everlastingly without any haven
in store, or beat that black air without any horizon. But
calm, snow-white and unvarying, still directing its fountain of feathers to the sky, still beckoning us on from before, the solitary jet would at times be descried.

During all this blackness of the elements, Ahab, though
assuming for the time the almost continual command of
the drenched and dangerous deck, manifested the gloom-
iest reserve and more seldom than ever addressed his
mates. In tempestuous times like these, after everything
above and aloft has been secured, nothing more can be
done but passively to await the issue of the gale. Then
captain and crew become practical fatalists. So, with his
ivory leg inserted into its accustomed hole, and with one
hand firmly grasping a shroud, Ahab for hours and hours
would stand gazing dead to windward, while an occasional squall of sleet or snow would all but congeal his
very eyelashes together. Meantime, the crew driven from
the forward part of the ship by the perilous seas that
burstingly broke over its bows, stood in a line along the
bulwarks in the waist; and the better to guard against the
leaping waves, each man had slipped himself into a sort
of bowline secured to the rail, in which he swung as in a
loosened belt. Few or no words were spoken; and the
silent ship, as if manned by painted sailors in wax, day
after day tore on through all the swift madness and glad-
ness of the demoniac waves. By night the same muteness

of humanity before the shrieks of the ocean prevailed; still in silence the men swung in the bowlines; still wordless Ahab stood up to the blast. Even when wearied nature seemed demanding repose, he would not seek that repose in his hammock. Never could Starbuck forget the old man's aspect, when one night going down into the cabin to mark how the barometer stood, he saw him with closed eyes sitting straight in his floor-screwed chair; the rain and half-melted sleet of the storm from which he had some time before emerged, still slowly dripping from the unremoved hat and coat. On the table beside him lay unrolled one of those charts of tides and currents which have previously been spoken of. His lantern swung from his tightly clenched hand. Though the body was erect, the head was thrown back so that the closed eyes were pointed toward the needle of the telltale that swung from a beam in the ceiling.[1]

"Terrible old man!" thought Starbuck with a shudder. "Sleeping in this gale, still thou steadfastly eyest thy purpose."

[1] The cabin compass is called the telltale, because without going to the compass at the helm, the captain while below can inform himself of the course of the ship.

CHAPTER 27

⚓

The Albatross

SOUTHEASTWARD from the Cape, off the distant Crozetts, a good cruising ground for Right Whalemen, a sail loomed ahead, the *Goney* (Albatross) by name. As she slowly drew nigh, from my lofty perch at the foremast head, I had a good view of that sight so remarkable to a tyro in the far ocean fisheries—a whaler at sea, and long absent from home.

As if the waves had been fullers,[1] this craft was bleached like the skeleton of a stranded walrus. All down her sides this spectral appearance was traced with long channels of reddened rust, while all her spars and her rigging were like the thick branches of trees furred over with hoar frost. Only her lower sails were set. A wild sight

---

[1] Grooving tools—ED.

it was to see her long-bearded lookouts at those three
mastheads. They seemed to be clad in the skins of beasts,
so torn and bepatched the raiment that had survived
nearly four years of cruising. Standing in iron hoops
nailed to the mast, they swayed and swung over a fathom-
less sea; and though, when the ship slowly glided close
under our stern, we six men in the air came so nigh to
each other that we might almost have leaped from the
mastheads of one ship to those of the other, yet those for-
lorn-looking fishermen, mildly eyeing us as they passed,
said not one word to our own lookouts while the quarterdeck hail was being heard from below.

"Ship ahoy! Have ye seen the white whale?"

But as the strange captain, leaning over the pallid bulwarks, was in the act of putting his trumpet to his mouth,
it somehow fell from his hand into the sea; and the wind
now rising amain, he in vain strove to make himself heard
without it. Meantime his ship was still increasing the distance between. While in various silent ways the seamen
of the *Pequod* were evincing their observance of this
ominous incident at the first mere mention of the white
whale's name to another ship, Ahab for a moment paused;
it almost seemed as though he would have lowered a boat
to board the stranger, had not the threatening wind
forbade. But taking advantage of his windward position
he again seized his trumpet, and knowing by her aspect
that the stranger vessel was a Nantucketer and shortly
bound home, he loudly hailed—"Ahoy there! This is the
Pequod, bound round the world! Tell them to address all
future letters to the Pacific Ocean! And this time three

years, if I am not at home, tell them to address them to—"

At that moment the two wakes were fairly crossed, and instantly, then, in accordance with their singular ways, shoals of small harmless fish that for some days before had been placidly swimming by our side, darted away with what seemed shuddering fins, and ranged themselves, fore and aft with the stranger's flanks. Though in the course of his continual voyagings Ahab must often before have noticed a similar sight, yet, to any monomaniac man, the veriest trifles capriciously carry meanings.

"Swim away from me, do ye?" murmured Ahab, gazing over into the water. There seemed but little in the words, but the tone conveyed more of deep helpless sadness than the insane old man had ever before evinced. But turning to the steersman, who thus far had been holding the ship in the wind to diminish her headway, he cried out in his old lion voice—"Up helm! Keep her off round the world!"

Chapter 28

⚓

Squid

SLOWLY wading through the meadows of brit,[1] the *Pequod* still held on her way northeastward toward the island of Java, a gentle air impelling her keel, so that in the surrounding serenity her three tall, tapering masts mildly waved to that languid breeze, as three mild palms on a plain. And still, at wide intervals in the silvery night, the lonely, alluring jet would be seen.

But one transparent blue morning, when a stillness almost preternatural spread over the sea, unattended however with any stagnant calm, when the long burnished sun-glade on the waters seemed a golden finger laid across them, enjoining some secrecy, when the slippered waves whispered together as they softly ran on—in this

---

[1] Masses of minute, yellow, marine animals, upon which the right whale largely feeds.

profound hush of the visible sphere a strange specter was seen by Daggoo from the mainmast head.

In the distance, a great white mass lazily rose, and rising higher and higher and disentangling itself from the azure, at last gleamed before our prow like a snowslide new slid from the hills. Thus glistening for a moment, as slowly it subsided and sank. Then once more it rose and silently gleamed. It seemed not a whale. And yet is this Moby Dick? thought Daggoo. Again the phantom went down, but on reappearing once more, with a stilettolike cry that startled every man from his nod, the Negro yelled out—"There! there again! There she breaches! Right ahead! The white whale, the white whale!"

Upon this, the seamen rushed to the yardarms, as in swarming-time the bees rush to the boughs. Bareheaded in the sultry sun, Ahab stood on the bowsprit, and with one hand pushed far behind in readiness to wave his orders to the helmsman, cast his eager glance in the direction indicated aloft by the outstretched motionless arm of Daggoo.

Whether the flitting attendance of the one still and solitary jet had gradually worked upon Ahab, so that he was now prepared to connect the ideas of mildness and repose with the first sight of the particular whale he pursued; however this was, or whether his eagerness betrayed him—whichever way it might have been—no sooner did he distinctly perceive the white mass, than with a quick intensity he instantly gave orders for lowering.

The four boats were soon on the water, Ahab's in advance, and all swiftly pulling toward their prey. Soon it went down, and while with oars suspended we were awaiting its reappearance, lo! In the same spot where it sank once more it slowly rose. Almost forgetting for the moment all thoughts of Moby Dick, we now gazed at the most wondrous phenomenon which the secret seas have hitherto revealed to mankind. A vast pulpy mass, furlongs in length and breadth, of a glancing cream color, lay floating on the water, innumerable long arms radiating from its center and curling and twisting like a nest of anacondas, as if blindly to clutch at any hapless object within reach. No perceptible face or front did it have, no conceivable token of either sensation or instinct, but undulated there on the billows, an unearthly, formless, chancelike apparition of life.

As with a low suckling sound it slowly disappeared again, Starbuck, still gazing at the agitated waters where it had sunk, with a wild voice exclaimed—"Almost rather had I seen Moby Dick and fought him, than to have seen thee, thou white ghost!"

"What was it, sir?" said Flask.

"The great live squid, which, they say, few whaleships ever beheld, and returned to their ports to tell of it."

But Ahab said nothing. Turning his boat, he sailed back to the vessel, the rest as silently following.

CHAPTER 29

⚓

Stubb Kills a Whale

I

IF TO Starbuck the apparition of the squid was a thing of portents, to Queequeg it was quite a different object.

"When you see him 'quid," said the savage, honing his harpoon in the bow of his hoisted boat, "then you quick see him 'parm whale."

The next day was exceedingly still and sultry, and with nothing special to engage them, the *Pequod's* crew could hardly resist the spell of sleep induced by such a vacant sea. For this part of the Indian Ocean through which we then were voyaging is not what whalemen call a lively ground; that is, it affords fewer glimpses of porpoises, dolphins, flying-fish and other vivacious denizens of more stirring waters than those off the Rio de la Plata, or the inshore ground off Peru.

It was my turn to stand at the foremast head; and with

my shoulders leaning against the slackened royal shrouds, to and fro I idly swayed in what seemed an enchanted air. No resolution could withstand it; in that dreamy mood losing all consciousness, at last my soul went out of my body, though my body still continued to sway as a pendulum will, long after the power which first moved it is withdrawn.

Ere forgetfulness altogether came over me, I had noticed that the seamen at the main- and mizzen-mastheads were already drowsy. So that at last all three of us lifelessly swung from the spars, and for every swing that we made there was a nod from below from the slumbering helmsman. The waves, too, nodded their indolent crests; and across the wide trance of the sea east nodded to west, and the sun over all.

Suddenly bubbles seemed bursting beneath my closed eyes; like vices my hands grasped the shrouds; some invisible gracious agency preserved me; with a shock I came back to life. And lo! Close under our lee, not forty fathoms off, a gigantic sperm whale lay rolling in the water like the capsized hull of a frigate, his broad glossy back of an Ethiopian hue glistening in the sun's ray like a mirror. But lazily undulating in the trough of the sea, and ever and anon tranquilly spouting his vapory jet, the whale looked like a portly burgher smoking his pipe of a warm afternoon. But that pipe, poor whale, was thy last. As if struck by some enchanter's wand, the sleepy ship and every sleeper in it all at once started into wakefulness; and more than a score of voices from all parts of the vessel, simultaneously with the three notes from aloft, shouted forth the accustomed cry, as the great fish slowly and regularly spouted the sparkling brine into the air.

"Clear away the boats! Luff!" cried Ahab. And obeying his own order, he dashed the helm down before the helmsman could handle the spokes.

The sudden exclamations of the crew must have alarmed the whale; and ere the boats were down, majestically turning, he swam away to the leeward, but with such a steady tranquility, and making so few ripples as he swam, that thinking after all he might not as yet be alarmed, Ahab gave orders that not an oar should be used, and no man must speak but in whispers. So seated like Ontario Indians on the gunwales of the boats, we swiftly but silently paddled along, the calm not admitting of the noiseless sails being set. Presently, as we thus glided in chase, the monster perpendicularly flitted his tail forty feet into the air, and then sank out of sight like a tower swallowed up.

"There go flukes!" was the cry, an announcement immediately followed by Stubb's producing his match and igniting his pipe, for now a respite was granted. After the full interval of his sounding had elapsed, the whale rose again, and being now in advance of the smoker's boat, and much nearer to it than to any of the others, Stubb counted upon the honor of the capture. It was obvious now that the whale had at length become aware of his pursuers. All silence or cautiousness was therefore no longer of use. Paddles were dropped and oars came loudly into play. And still puffing at his pipe, Stubb cheered on his crew to the assault.

Yes, a mighty change had come over the fish. All alive to his jeopardy, he was going "head out," that part obliquely projecting from the mad yeast which he brewed.[1]

"Start her, start her, my men! Don't hurry yourselves; take plenty of time—but start her; start her like thunder-claps, that's all," cried Stubb, spluttering out the smoke as he spoke. "Start her, now; give 'em the long and strong stroke, Tashtego. Start her, Tash, my boy—start her, all; but keep cool, keep cool—cucumbers is the word—easy, easy—only start her like grim death and grinning devils, and raise the buried dead perpendicular out of their graves, boys—that's all. Start her!"

"Woo-hoo! Wa-hee!" screamed the Gay Header in re-ply, raising some old war whoop to the skies as every oars-men in the strained boat involuntarily bounced forward with the one tremendous leading stroke which the eager Indian gave.

But his wild screams were answered by others quite as wild. "Kee-hee! Kee-hee!" yelled Daggoo, straining for-ward and backward on his seat like a pacing tiger in his cage.

"Ka-la Koo-loo!" howled Queequeg, as if smacking his lips over a mouthful of grenadier's steak. And thus with

[1] The sperm whale's enormous head, though apparently the most massive, is by far the most buoyant part about him. So that with ease he elevates it in the air, and invariably does so when going at his utmost speed. Besides, such is the breadth of the upper part of the front of his head, and such the tapering cut-water formation of the lower part, that by obliquely elevating his head, he thereby may be said to transform himself from a bluff-bowed, sluggish galliot into a sharp-pointed New York pilot boat.

oars and yells the keels cut the sea. Meanwhile, Stubb re-
taining his place in the van, still encouraged his men to
the onset, all the while puffing the smoke from his mouth.
Like desperadoes they tugged and they strained, till the
welcome cry was heard—"Stand up, Tashtego!—Give it to
him!" The harpoon was hurled. "Stern all!" The oarsmen
backed water; the same moment something went hot and
hissing along every one of their wrists. It was the magical line. An instant before, Stubb had swiftly caught two
additional turns with it around the loggerhead, whence
by reason of its increased rapid circlings, a hempen blue
smoke now jetted up and mingled with the steady fumes
from his pipe. As the line passed round and round the loggerhead, so also, just before reaching that point, it blister-
ingly passed through and through both of Stubb's hands,
from which the handcloths, or squares of quilted canvas
sometimes worn at these times, had accidentally dropped.
It was like holding an enemy's sharp two-edged sword
by the blade, and that enemy all the time striving to wrest
it out of your clutch.

"Wet the line! wet the line!" cried Stubb to the tub
oarsman (him seated by the tub) who, snatching off his
hat, dashed the seawater into it.[1] More turns were taken,
so that the line began holding its place. The boat now
flew through the boiling water like a shark all fins. Stubb
and Tashtego here changed places—stem for stern—a

[1] Partly to show the indispensableness of this act, it may here be
stated, that, in the old Dutch fishery, a mop was used to dash the run-
ning-line with water; in many other ships, a wooden piggin, or bailer, is
set apart for that purpose. Your hat however, is the most convenient.

staggering business truly in that rocking commotion.

From the vibrating line extending the entire length of the upper part of the boat, and from its now being more tight than a harpstring, you would have thought the craft had two keels—one cleaving the water, the other the air— as the boat churned on through both opposing elements at once. A continual cascade played at the bows, a ceaseless whirling eddy in her wake; and, at the slightest motion from within, even but of a little finger, the vibrating, cracking craft canted over her spasmodic gunwale into the sea. Thus they rushed, each man with might and main clinging to his seat to prevent being tossed to the foam, and the tall form of Tashtego at the steering-oar crouching almost double in order to bring down his center of gravity. Whole Atlantics and Pacifics seemed passed as they shot on their way, till at length the whale somewhat slackened his flight.

"Haul in—haul in!" cried Stubb to the bowsman. And facing around toward the whale, all hands began pulling the boat up to him, while yet the boat was being towed on. Soon ranging up by his flank, Stubb, firmly planting his knee in the clumsy cleat, darted dart after dart into the flying fish; at the word of command, the boat alternately sterning out of the way of the whale's horrible wallow, and then ranging up for another fling.

The red tide now poured from all sides of the monster like brooks down a hill. His tormented body rolled not in brine but in blood, which bubbled and seethed for furlongs behind in their wake. The slanting sun playing upon this crimson pond in the sea, sent back its reflection into every face, so that all glowed to each other like red men. And all the while, jet after jet of white smoke was agonizingly shot from the spiracle of the whale, and vehement puff after puff from the mouth of the excited headsman, as at every dart, hauling in upon his crooked lance (by the line attached to it), Stubb straightened it again and again by a few rapid blows against the gunwale, then again and again sent it into the whale.

"Pull up—pull up!" he now cried to the bowsman, as the waning whale relaxed in his wrath. "Pull up!—close to!" and the boat ranged along the fish's flank. Then reaching far over the bow, Stubb slowly churned his long sharp lance into the fish and kept it there, carefully churning and churning, as if cautiously seeking to feel after some gold watch that the whale might have swallowed, and which he was fearful of breaking ere he could hook it out. But that gold watch he sought was the innermost life of the fish. And now it is struck; for, starting from his trance into that unspeakable thing called his "flurry," the monster horribly wallowed in his blood, overwrapped himself in impenetrable, mad boiling spray, so that the imperiled craft instantly dropping astern, had much ado blindly to struggle out from that frenzied twilight into the clear air of the day.

And now abating in his flurry, the whale once more rolled out into view, surging from side to side, spasmodically dilating and contracting his spout-hole with sharp, cracking, agonized respirations. At last, gush after gush of clotted red gore, as if it had been the purple lees of red wine, shot into the frighted air, and falling back again ran dripping down his motionless flanks into the sea. His heart had burst!

"He's dead, Mr. Stubb," said Daggoo.

"Yes; both pipes smoked out!" and withdrawing his own from his mouth Stubb scattered the dead ashes over the water, and for a moment stood thoughtfully eyeing the vast corpse he had made.

CHAPTER 30

⚓

Cutting In

It was a Saturday night, and such a Sabbath as followed! Ex-officio professors of Sabbath-breaking are all whalemen. The ivory *Pequod* was turned into what seemed a shamble, every sailor a butcher. You would have thought we were offering up ten thousand red oxen to the sea gods.

In the first place the enormous cutting tackles, among other ponderous things comprising a cluster of blocks generally painted green, and which no single man can possibly lift—this vast bunch of grapes was swayed up to the maintop and firmly lashed to the lower masthead, the strongest point anywhere above a ship's deck. The end of the hawserlike rope winding through these intricacies was then conducted to the windlass, and the huge lower block of the tackles was swung over the whale. To this block the great blubber hook, weighing some one hundred pounds, was attached. And now suspended in stages over the side, Starbuck and Stubb, the mates, armed with their long spades, began cutting a hole in the body for the insertion of the hook just above the nearest of the two side fins.

This done, a broad semicircular line is cut around the hole, the hook is inserted, and the main body of the crew striking up a wild chorus, now commence heaving in one dense crowd at the windlass. Then instantly the entire ship careens over on her side; every bolt in her starts like the nailheads of an old house in frosty weather; she trembles, quivers and nods her frighted mastheads to the sky. More and more she leans over to the whale, while every gasping heave of the windlass is answered by a helping heave from the billows. At last a swift startling snap is heard; with a great swash the ship rolls upward and backward from the whale, and the triumphant tackle rises into sight dragging after it the disengaged semicircular end of the first strip of blubber.

Now as the blubber envelopes the whale precisely as the rind does an orange, so is it stripped off the body precisely as an orange is sometimes stripped, by spiralizing it. For the strain constantly kept up by the windlass continually keeps the whale rolling over and over in the water, and the blubber in one strip uniformly peels off along the line called the "scarf," simultaneously cut by the spades of Starbuck and Stubb. And just as fast as it is thus peeled off, and indeed by that very act itself, it is all the time being hoisted higher and higher aloft until its upper end grazes the maintop. The men at the windlass then cease heaving, and for a moment or two the prodigious blood-dripping mass sways to and fro as if let down from the sky, and every one present must take good heed to dodge it when it swings, else it may box his ears and pitch him headlong overboard.

One of the attending harpooneers now advances with a long keen weapon called a boarding sword, and watching his chance he dexterously slices out a considerable hole in the lower part of the swaying mass. Into this hole the end of the second alternating great tackle is then hooked so as to retain a hold upon the blubber in order to prepare for what follows. Whereupon this accomplished swordsman, warning all hands to stand off, once more makes a scientific dash at the mass, and with a few sidelong, desperate lunging slices, severs it completely in twain; so that while the short lower part is still fast, the long upper strip called a blanket-piece swings clear, and is all ready for lowering.

The heavers forward now resume their song, and while the one tackle is peeling and hoisting a second strip from the whale, the other is slowly slackened away. Down goes the first strip through the main hatchway right beneath, into an unfurnished parlor called the blubber room. Into this twilight apartment sundry nimble hands keep coiling away the long blanket-piece as if it were a great live mass of plaited serpents.

And thus the work proceeds: the two tackles hoisting and lowering simultaneously, both whale and windlass heaving, the heavers singing, the blubber room gentlemen coiling, the mates scarfing, the ship straining, and all hands swearing occasionally by way of assuaging the general friction.

⚓

CHAPTER 31

The Monkey Rope

IN THE tumultuous business of cutting in and attending to a whale, there is much running backward and forward among the crew. Now hands are wanted here, and then again hands are wanted there. There is no staying in any one place; for at one and the same time everything has to be done everywhere. It is much the same with him who endeavors the description of the scene. We must now retrace our way a little. It was mentioned that upon first breaking ground in the whale's back, the blubber hook was inserted into the original hole there cut by the spades of the mates. But how did so clumsy and weighty a mass as that same hook get fixed in that hole? It was inserted there by my particular friend Queequeg whose duty it was, a harpooner, to descend upon the monster's back for the special purpose referred to. But in many cases, circumstances require that the harpooner shall remain on the whale till the whole flensing or stripping operation is concluded. The whale, be it observed, lies almost entirely submerged, excepting the immediate parts operated upon. So down there, some ten feet below the level of the deck, the poor harpooneer flounders about, half on the whale, and half in the water, as the vast mass revolves like a treadmill beneath him. On the occasion in question, Queequeg figured in the Highland costume—a shirt and socks—in which to my eyes, at least, he appeared to uncommon advantage; and no one had a better chance to observe him, as will presently be seen.

Being the savage's bowman, that is, the person who pulled the bow-oar in his boat (the second one from forward), it was my cheerful duty to attend upon him while taking that hard-scrabble scramble upon the dead whale's back. You have seen Italian organ boys holding a dancing ape by a long cord. Just so from the ship's steep side did I hold Queequeg down there in the sea, by what is technically called in the fishery a monkey rope, attached to a strong strip of canvas belted around his waist.

It was a humorously perilous business for both of us. For before we proceed further, it must be said that the monkey rope was fast at both ends, fast to Queequeg's broad canvas belt, and fast to my narrow leather one. So that for better or for worse, we two, for the time were wedded; and should poor Queequeg sink to rise no more, then both usage and honor demanded that instead of cutting the cord, it should drag me down in his wake. So, then, an elongated Siamese ligature united us. Queequeg was my own inseparable twin brother, nor could I in any way get rid of the dangerous liabilities which the hempen bond entailed.

So strongly and metaphysically did I conceive of my situation then, that while earnestly watching his motions, I seemed distinctly to perceive that my own individuality was now merged in a joint-stock company of two; that my free will had received a mortal wound; and that another's mistake or misfortune might plunge innocent me into unmerited disaster and death. Therefore I saw that here was a sort of interregnum in Providence; for its even-handed equity never could have sanctioned so gross an injustice. And yet still further pondering—while I jerked him now and then from between the whale and the ship, which would threaten to jam him—still further pondering, I say, I saw that this situation of mine was the precise situation of every mortal that breathes. Only in most cases he, one way or other, has this Siamese connection with a plurality of other mortals. If your banker breaks, you snap; if your apothecary by mistake sends you poison in your pills, you die. True, you may say that by exceeding caution you may possibly escape these and the multitudinous other evil chances of life. But handle Queequeg's monkey rope heedfully as I would, sometimes he jerked it so that I came very near sliding overboard. Nor could I possibly forget that, do what I would, I only had the management of one end of it.[1]

[1] The monkey rope is found in all whalers; but it was only in the *Pequod* that the monkey and his holder were ever tied together. This improvement upon the original usage was introduced by no less a man than Stubb, in order to afford the imperiled harpooneer the strongest possible guarantee for the faithfulness and vigilance of his monkey-rope holder.

I have hinted that I would often jerk poor Queequeg from between the whale and the ship, where he would occasionally fall from the incessant rolling and swaying of both. But jamming was not the only jeopardy he was exposed to. Unappalled by the massacre made on them during the night, the sharks were now freshly and more keenly allured by the pent blood which now began to flow from the carcass. The rabid creatures swarmed around it like bees in a beehive.

And right in among those sharks was Queequeg, who often pushed them aside with his floundering feet. A thing altogether incredible were it not that, attracted by such prey as a dead whale, the otherwise miscellaneously carnivorous shark will seldom touch a man.

Nevertheless it may well be believed that since they have such a ravenous finger in the pie, it is deemed but wise to look sharp to them. Accordingly, besides the monkey rope with which I now and then jerked the poor fellow from too close a vicinity to the maw of what seemed a peculiarly ferocious shark, he was provided with still another protection. Suspended over the side in one of the stages, Tashtego and Daggoo continually flourished over his head a couple of keen whale-spades, wherewith they slaughtered as many sharks as they could reach. This procedure of theirs, to be sure, was very disinterested and benevolent of them. They meant Queequeg's best happiness, I admit; but in their hasty zeal to befriend him, and from the circumstance that both he and the sharks were at times half hidden by the blood-muddled water, those indiscreet spades of theirs would come nearer amputating a leg than a tail. But poor Queequeg, I suppose, straining and gasping there with that great iron hook—poor Queequeg, I suppose only prayed to his Yojo, and gave up his life into the hands of his gods.

Well, well, my dear comrade and twin brother, thought I, as I drew in and then slacked off the rope to every swell of the sea. What matters it, after all? Are you not the previous image of each and all of us men in this whaling world? That unsounded ocean you gasp in, is Life; those sharks, your foes; those spades, your friends; and what between sharks and spades you are in a sad pickle and peril, poor lad.

But courage! there is good cheer in store for you, Queequeg. For now, as with blue lips and bloodshot eyes the exhausted savage at last climbs up the chains and stands all dripping and involuntarily trembling over the side, the steward advances and with a benevolent consolatory glance hands him—what? Some hot cognac? No! Hands him, ye gods! Hands him a cup of tepid ginger and water!

"Ginger? Do I smell ginger?" suspiciously asked Stubb, coming near. "Yes, this must be ginger," peering into the as yet untasted cup. Then standing as if incredulous for a while, he calmly walked toward the astonished steward slowly saying, "Ginger? Ginger? And will you have the goodness to tell me, Mr. Dough Boy, where lies the virtue of ginger? Ginger? Is ginger the sort of fuel you use, Dough Boy, to kindle a fire in this shivering cannibal? Ginger! What the devil is ginger?—sea coal?—firewood? —lucifer matches?—tinder?—gunpowder? What the devil

is ginger, I say, that you offer this cup to our poor Queequeg here?

"There is some sneaking Temperance Society movement about this business," he suddenly added, now approaching Starbuck who had just come from forward.
"Will you look at that cannikin sir; smell of it, if you
please." Then watching the mate's countenance, he
added: "The steward, Mr. Starbuck, had the face to offer
that calomel and jalap to Queequeg there, this instant
off the whale. Is the steward an apothecary, sir? And
may I ask whether this is the sort of bellows by which he
blows back the breath into a half-drowned man?"

"I trust not," said Starbuck; "it is poor stuff enough."

"Aye, aye, steward," cried Stubb, "we'll teach you to
drug a harpooneer; none of your apothecary's medicine
here; you want to poison us, do ye? You have got out in-
surances on our lives and want to murder us all, and
pocket the proceeds, do ye?"

"It was not me," cried Dough Boy, "it was Aunt Charity
that brought the ginger on board, and bade me never
give the harpooneers any spirits, but only this ginger-
jub—so she called it."

"Ginger-jub! You gingerly rascal! Take that! And run
along with ye to the lockers and get something better. I
hope I do no wrong, Mr. Starbuck. It is the captain's
orders—grog for the harpooneer on a whale."

"Enough," replied Starbuck, "only don't hit him again,
but——"

"Oh, I never hurt when I hit, except when I hit a whale

or something of that sort, and this fellow's a weasel. What were you about saying, sir?"

"Only this: go down with him and get what thou wantest thyself." When Stubb reappeared, he came with a dark flask in one hand and a sort of tea caddy in the other. The first contained strong spirits, and was handed to Queequeg; the second was Aunt Charity's gift, and that was freely given to the waves.

⚓

CHAPTER 32

Cistern and Buckets

N IMBLE AS A CAT, Tashtego mounts aloft, and without altering his erect posture runs straight out upon the overhanging main yardarm, to the part where it exactly projects over the hoisted tun.[1] He has carried with him a light tackle called a whip, consisting of only two parts, traveling through a single sheaved block. Securing this block so that it hangs down from the yardarm, he swings one end of the rope until it is caught and firmly held by a hand on deck. Then, hand over hand down the other part, the Indian drops through the air, until dexterously he lands on the summit of the whale's head. There—still high elevated above the rest of the company, to whom

---

[1] The case, or upper part of the whale's head, often containing some 500 gallons of the purest sperm oil—ED.

206

he vivaciously cries—he seems some Turkish muezzin calling the good people to prayers from the top of a tower. A short-handled sharp spade being sent up to him, he diligently searches for the proper place to begin breaking into the tun. In this business he proceeds very heedfully, like a treasure hunter in some old house, sounding the walls to find where the gold is masoned in. By the time this cautious search is over, a stout ironbound bucket, precisely like a well-bucket, has been attached to one end of the whip, while the other end, being stretched across the deck, is there held by two or three alert hands. These last now hoist the bucket within grasp of the Indian, to whom another person has reached up a very long pole. Inserting this pole into the bucket, Tashtego downward guides the bucket into the tun, till it entirely disappears; then giving the word to the seamen at the whip, up comes the bucket again, all bubbling like a dairymaid's pail of new milk. Carefully lowered from its height, the full-freighted vessel is caught by an appointed hand, and quickly emptied into a large tub. Then remounting aloft, it again goes through the same round until the deep cistern will yield no more. Toward the end, Tashtego has to ram his long pole harder and harder, and deeper and deeper into the tun, until some twenty feet of the pole have gone down.

Now the people of the *Pequod* had been bailing some time in this way. Several tubs had been filled with the fragrant sperm, when all at once a queer accident happened. Whether it was that Tashtego, that wild Indian,

was so heedless and reckless as to let go for a moment
his one-handed hold on the great-cabled tackles suspending the head, or whether the place where he stood
was so treacherous and oozy, or whether the Evil One
himself would have it to fall out so, without stating his
particular reason; how it was exactly, there is no telling
now; but, on a sudden, as the eightieth or ninetieth
bucket came suckingly up—my God! Poor Tashtego—like
the twin reciprocating bucket in a veritable well, dropped
head foremost down into this great Tun of Heidelburgh,
and with a horrible oily gurgling went clean out of sight!

"Man overboard!" cried Daggoo, who amid the general
consternation first came to his senses. "Swing the bucket
this way!" and putting one foot into it so as the better to
secure his slippery hand-hold on the whip itself, the
hoisters ran him high up to the top of the head, almost before Tashtego could have reached its interior bottom.
Meantime, there was a terrible tumult. Looking over the
side, they saw the before lifeless head throbbing and
heaving just below the surface of the sea, as if that moment seized with some momentous idea, whereas it was
only the poor Indian unconsciously revealing by those
struggles the perilous depth to which he had sunk.

At this instant, while Daggoo on the summit of the
head was clearing the whip, which had somehow got
foul of the great cutting tackles, a sharp cracking noise
was heard; and to the unspeakable horror of all, one of
the two enormous hooks suspending the head tore out,
and with a vast vibration the enormous mass sideways

swung, until the drunk ship reeled and shook as if smitten by an iceberg. The one remaining hook, upon which the entire strain now depended, seemed every instant to be on the point of giving way, an event still more likely from the violent motions of the head.

"Come down, come down!" yelled the seamen to Daggoo, but with one hand holding on to the heavy tackles, so that if the head should drop he would still remain suspended, the Negro having cleared the foul line, rammed down the bucket into the now collapsed well, meaning that the buried harpooner should grasp it, and so be hoisted out.

"In heaven's name, man," cried Stubb, "are you ramming home a cartridge there? Avast! How will that help him, jamming that ironbound bucket on top of his head? Avast, will ye!"

"Stand clear of the tackle!" cried a voice like the bursting of a rocket.

Almost in the same instant, with a thunder-boom the enormous mass dropped into the sea, like Niagara's Table Rock into the whirlpool. The suddenly relieved hull rolled away from it, to far down her glittering copper, and all caught their breath, as half-swinging—now over the sailors' heads, and now over the water—Daggoo, through a thick mist of spray, was dimly beheld clinging to the pendulous tackles, while poor, buried-alive Tashtego was sinking utterly down to the bottom of the sea! But hardly had the blinding vapor cleared away when a naked figure with a boarding sword in its hand was for one swift moment seen hovering over the bulwarks. The next, a loud splash announced that my brave Queequeg had dived to the rescue. One packed rush was made to the side, and every eye counted every ripple as moment followed moment, and no sign of either the sinker or the diver could be seen. Some hands now jumped into a boat alongside and pushed a little off from the ship.

"Ha! ha!" cried Daggoo, all at once, from his now quiet swinging perch overhead; and looking farther off from the side we saw an arm thrust upright from the blue waves, a sight as strange to see as an arm thrust forth from the grass over a grave.

"Both! both! It is both!" cried Daggoo again with a joyful shout. And soon afterward Queequeg was seen boldly striking out with one hand and with the other clutching the long hair of the Indian. Drawn into the waiting boat they were quickly brought to the deck; but Tashtego was long in coming to, and Queequeg did not look very brisk.

Now, how had this noble rescue been accomplished? Why, diving after the slowly descending head, Queequeg with his keen sword had made side lunges near its bottom, so as to scuttle a large hole there. Then dropping his sword, he had thrust his long arm far inward and upward, and so hauled out our poor Tash by the head. He averred that upon first thrusting in for him, a leg was presented; but well knowing that that was not as it ought to be, and might occasion great trouble, he had thrust back the leg, and by a dexterous heave and toss had wrought a somersault upon the Indian, so that with the next trial he came forth in the good old way—head foremost. As for the great head itself, that was doing as well as could be expected.

And thus through the courage and great skill in obstetrics of Queequeg, the deliverance, or rather delivery of Tashtego was successfully accomplished—in the teeth, too, of the most untoward and apparently hopeless impediments, which is a lesson by no means to be forgotten.

forth in the good old way—head foremost. As for the great
head itself, that was doing as well as could be expected.
And thus through the courage and great skill in obstetrics of Queequeg, the deliverance, or rather delivery of
Tashtego, was successfully accomplished, in the teeth,
too, of the most untoward and apparently hopeless impediments; which is a lesson by no means to be forgotten.

CHAPTER 33

⚓

The Try-Works

BESIDES her hoisted boats, an American whaler is out-
wardly distinguished by her try-works. She presents the
curious anomaly of the most solid masonry joining with
oak and hemp in constituting the completed ship. It is as
if from the open field a brick kiln were transported to her
planks.

The try-works are planted between the foremast and
mainmast, the most roomy part of the deck. The timbers
beneath are of a peculiar strength, fitted to sustain the
weight of an almost solid mass of brick and mortar some
ten feet by eight square and five in height. The founda-
tion does not penetrate the deck, but the masonry is
firmly secured to the surface by ponderous knees of iron
bracing it on all sides, and screwing it down to the timbers. On the flanks it is cased with wood, and at top com-

pletely covered by a large, sloping, battened hatchway. Removing this hatch we expose the great try-pots, two in number, and each of several barrels' capacity.

Removing the fireboard from the front of the try-works, the bare masonry of that side is exposed, penetrated by the two iron mouths of the furnaces, directly underneath the pots. These mouths are fitted with heavy doors of iron. The intense heat of the fire is prevented from communicating itself to the deck by means of a shallow reservoir extending under the entire enclosed surface of the works. By a tunnel inserted at the rear, this reservoir is kept replenished with water as fast as it evaporates. There are no external chimneys; they open direct from the rear wall. And here let us go back for a moment.

It was about nine o'clock at night that the *Pequod's* try-works were first started on this present voyage. It belonged to Stubb to oversee the business.

"All ready there? Off hatch, then, and start her. You, cook, fire the works." This was an easy thing, for the carpenter had been thrusting his shavings into the furnace throughout the passage. Here be it said that in a whaling voyage the first fire in the try-works has to be fed for a time with wood. After that no wood is used, except as a means of quick ignition to the staple fuel. In a word, after being tried out, the crisp, shriveled blubber, now called scraps or fritters, still contains considerable of its unctuous properties. These fritters feed the flames. Like a plethoric burning martyr, or a self-consuming misanthrope, once ignited, the whale supplies his own fuel and burns by his own body. Would that he consumed his own smoke! For his smoke is horrible to inhale, and inhale it you must, and not only that, but you must live in it for the time. It has an unspeakable, wild, Hindoo odor about it, such as may lurk in the vicinity of funeral pyres.

By midnight the works were in full operation. We were clear from the carcass; sail had been made; the wind was freshening; the wild ocean darkness was intense. But that darkness was licked up by the fierce flames, which at intervals forked forth from the sooty flues, and illuminated every lofty rope in the rigging, as with the famed Greek fire. The burning ship drove on, as if remorselessly commissioned to some vengeful deed. So the pitch- and sulphur-freighted brigs of the bold Hydriote, Canaris, issuing from their midnight harbors, with broad sheets of flame for sails, bore down upon the Turkish frigates, and folded them in conflagrations.

The hatch, removed from the top of the works, now afforded a wide hearth in front. Standing on this were the Tartarean shapes of the pagan harpooneers, always the whaleship's stokers. With huge pronged poles they pitched hissing masses of blubber into the scalding pots, or stirred up the fires beneath, till the snaky flames darted, curling, out of the doors to catch them by the feet. The smoke rolled away in sullen heaps. To every pitch of the ship there was a pitch of the boiling oil, which seemed all eagerness to leap into their faces. Opposite the mouth of the works, on the farther side of the wide wooden hearth, was the windlass. This served for a sea sofa. Here lounged the watch, when not otherwise employed, looking into the red heat of the fire, till their eyes felt scorched in their heads. Their tawny features, now all begrimed with smoke and sweat, their matted beards, and the contrasting barbaric brilliancy of their teeth—all these were strangely revealed in the capricious emblazonings of the works. As they narrated to each other their unholy adventures, their tales of terror told in words of mirth; as their uncivilized laughter forked upward out of them, like the flames from the furnace; as to and fro the harpooneers wildly gesticulated with their huge pronged forks and dippers; as the wind howled on, and the sea leaped, and the ship groaned and dived, and yet steadfastly shot her red hell further and further into the blackness of the sea and the night, and scornfully champed the white bone in her mouth, and viciously spat around her on all sides; then the rushing *Pequod,* freighted with savages and laden with fire, and burning a corpse, and plunging into that blackness of darkness, seemed the material counterpart of her monomaniac commander's soul.

So seemed it to me, as I stood at her helm, and for long hours silently guided the way of this fire ship on the sea. Wrapped for that interval in darkness myself, I but the better saw the redness, the madness, the ghastliness of others. The continual sight of the fiends' shapes before me, capering half in smoke and half in fire, these at last begat kindred visions in my soul as I began to yield to that unaccountable drowsiness which ever would come over me at a midnight helm.

But that night in particular, a strange (and ever since inexplicable) thing occurred to me. Starting from a brief standing sleep, I was horribly conscious of something fatally wrong. The jawbone tiller smote my side, which leaned against it; in my ears was the low hum of sails, just beginning to shake in the wind. I thought my eyes were open; I was half conscious of putting my fingers to the lids and mechanically stretching them still further apart. But, in spite of all this, I could see no compass before me to steer by; though it seemed but a minute since I had been watching the card, by the steady binnacle lamp illumining it. Nothing seemed before me but a jet gloom, now and then made ghastly by flashes of redness. Uppermost was the impression that whatever swift rushing thing I stood on was not so much bound to any haven ahead as rushing from all havens astern. A stark bewildered feeling, as of death, came over me. Convulsively my hands grasped the tiller, but with the crazy conceit that the tiller was, somehow, in some enchanted way, inverted. My God! What is the matter with me? thought I. Lo! In my brief sleep I had turned myself about and was fronting the ship's stern, with my back to her prow and the compass. In an instant I faced back, just in time to prevent the vessel from flying up into the wind, and very probably capsizing her. How glad and how grateful the relief from this unnatural hallucination of the night, and the fatal contingency of being brought by the lee!

CHAPTER 34

⚓

The Grand Armada

THE long and narrow peninsula of Malacca, extending southeastward from the territories of Burma, forms the most southerly point of all Asia. In a continuous line from that peninsula stretch the long islands of Sumatra, Java, Bali and Timor, which with many others, form a vast mole or rampart lengthwise connecting Asia with Australia, and dividing the long unbroken Indian Ocean from the thickly studded Oriental archipelagoes. This rampart is pierced by several sally-ports for the convenience of ships and whales, conspicuous among which are the straits of Sunda and Malacca. By the straits of Sunda, chiefly, vessels bound to China from the west emerge into the China seas.

Those narrow straits of Sunda divide Sumatra from Java. Standing midway in that vast rampart of islands,

217

and buttressed by that bold green promontory known to
seamen as Java Head, they not a little correspond to the
central gateway opening into some vast walled empire.
And considering the inexhaustible wealth of spices and
silks and jewels and gold and ivory with which the
thousand islands of that Oriental sea are enriched, it
seems a significant provision of nature that such treasures,
by the very formation of the land, should at least bear the
appearance, however ineffectual, of being guarded from
the all-grasping western world. The shores of the straits
of Sunda are unsupplied with those domineering fort-
resses which guard the entrances to the Mediterranean,
the Baltic and the Propontis. Unlike the Danes, these
Orientals do not demand the obsequious homage of lowered topsails from the endless procession of ships before
the wind, which for centuries past, by night and by day,
have passed between the islands of Sumatra and Java,
freighted with the costliest cargoes of the east. But while
they freely waive a ceremonial like this, they do by no
means renounce their claim to more solid tribute.

Time out of mind the piratical proas of the Malays,
lurking among the low shaded coves and islets of Sumatra, have sallied out upon the vessels sailing through
the straits, fiercely demanding tribute at the point of
their spears. Though by the repeated bloody chastise-
ments they have received at the hands of European
cruisers, the audacity of these corsairs has of late been
somewhat repressed, yet, even at the present day, we
occasionally hear of English and American vessels which,

in those waters, have been remorselessly boarded and pillaged.

With a fair, fresh wind, the *Pequod* was now drawing nigh to these straits; Ahab purposing to pass through them into the Javan sea; and thence, cruising northward over waters known to be frequented here and there by the sperm whale, sweep inshore by the Philippine Islands, and gain the far coast of Japan in time for the great whaling season there.

By these means, the circumnavigating *Pequod* would sweep almost all the known sperm whale cruising grounds of the world, previous to descending upon the Line in the Pacific. There Ahab, though everywhere else foiled in his pursuit, firmly counted upon giving battle to Moby Dick in the sea he was most known to frequent, and at a season when he might most reasonably be presumed to be haunting it.

But how now? In this zoned quest, does Ahab touch no land? Does his crew drink air? Surely, he will stop for water. Nay. For a long time, now, the circus-running sun has raced within his fiery ring, and needs no sustenance but what's in himself. So Ahab. Mark this, too, in the whaler. While other hulls are loaded down with alien stuff to be transferred to foreign wharves, the world-wandering whaleship carries no cargo but herself and crew, their weapons and their wants. She has a whole lake's contents bottled in her ample hold. She is ballasted with utilities, not altogether with unusable pig lead and kentledge. She carries years' water in her. Clear old prime

Nantucket water which, when three years afloat, the Nantucketer in the Pacific prefers to drink, before the brackish
fluid but yesterday rafted off in casks from the Peruvian
or Indian streams. Hence it is that while other ships may
have gone to China from New York and back again,
touching at a score of ports, the whaleship in all that interval may not have sighted one grain of soil, her crew
having seen no man but floating seamen like themselves;
so that did you carry them the news that another flood
had come, they would only answer—"Well, boys, here's
the ark!"

Now as many sperm whales had been captured on the
western coast of Java in the near vicinity of the straits of
Sunda, indeed as most of the ground round about was
generally recognized by the fishermen as an excellent
spot for cruising, therefore as the *Pequod* gained more
and more upon Java Head, the lookouts were repeatedly
hailed and admonished to keep wide awake. But though
the green palmy cliffs of the land so loomed on the starboard bow that with delighted nostrils the fresh cinna-
mon was snuffed in the air, yet not a single jet was descried. Almost renouncing all thought of falling in with
any game hereabouts, the ship had well-nigh entered the
straits when the customary cheering cry was heard from
aloft, and ere long a spectacle of singular magnificence
saluted us.

But here be it premised, that owing to the unwearied
activity with which of late they have been hunted over all
four oceans, the sperm whales, instead of almost invari-

ably sailing in small detached companies, as in former times, are now frequently met with in extensive herds, sometimes embracing so great a multitude that it would almost seem as if numerous nations of them had sworn solemn league and covenant for mutual assistance and protection. To this aggregation of the sperm whale into such immense caravans, may be imputed the circumstance that even in the best cruising grounds, you may now sometimes sail for weeks and months together without being greeted by a single spout, and then be suddenly saluted by what sometimes seem thousands on thousands.

Broad on both bows at the distance of two or three miles, and forming a great semicircle embracing one half of the level horizon, a continuous chain of whale jets were up-playing and sparkling in the noonday air. Unlike the straight perpendicular twin jets of the right whale, which, dividing at top, fall over in two branches, like the cleft drooping boughs of a willow, the single forward-slanting spout of the sperm whale presents a thick curled bush of white mist, continually rising and falling away to leeward.

Seen from the *Pequod's* deck, then, as she would rise on a high hill of the sea, this host of vapory spouts, individually curling up into the air and beheld through a blending atmosphere of bluish haze, showed like the thousand cheerful chimneys of some dense metropolis, descried of a balmy autumnal morning by some horseman on a height.

As marching armies approaching an unfriendly defile in the mountains accelerate their march, all eagerness to place that perilous passage in their rear and once more expand in comparative security upon the plain; even so did this vast fleet of whales now seem hurrying forward through the straits, gradually contracting the wings of their semicircle, and swimming on in one solid but still crescentic center.

Crowding all sail the *Pequod* pressed after them, the harpooneers handling their weapons and loudly cheering from the heads of their yet suspended boats. If the wind only held, little doubt had they, that chased through these straits of Sunda, the vast host would only deploy in the Oriental seas to witness the capture of not a few of their number. And who could tell whether, in that congregated caravan, Moby Dick himself might not temporarily be swimming, like the worshiped white elephant in the coronation procession of the Siamese! So with stunsail piled on stunsail, we sailed along, driving these Leviathans before us, when, of a sudden, the voice of Tashtego was heard loudly directing attention to something in our wake.

Corresponding to the crescent in our van, we beheld another in our rear. It seemed formed of detached white vapors, rising and falling something like the spouts of the whales, only they did not so completely come and go; for they constantly hovered, without finally disappearing. Leveling his glass at this sight, Ahab quickly revolved in his pivot hole, crying, "Aloft there, and rig whips and buckets to wet the sails! Malays, sir, and after us!"

As if too long lurking behind the headlands until the *Pequod* should fairly have entered the straits, these rascally Asiatics were now in hot pursuit to make up for their overcautious delay. But when the swift *Pequod,* with a fresh leading wind, was herself in hot chase. How very kind of these tawny philanthropists to assist in speeding her on to her own chosen pursuit—mere riding whips and rowels to her that they were. As with glass under arm, Ahab to and fro paced the deck, in his forward turn beholding the monsters he chased, and in the after one the bloodthirsty pirates chasing *him,* some such fancy as the above seemed his. And when he glanced upon the green walls of the watery defile in which the ship was then sailing, and bethought him that through that gate lay the route to his vengeance, and beheld how that through that same gate he was now both chasing and being chased to his deadly end; and not only that, but a herd of remorseless wild pirates and inhuman atheistical devils were infernally cheering them on with their curses —when all these conceits had passed through his brain, Ahab's brow was left gaunt and ribbed, like the black sand beach after some stormy tide has been gnawing it, without being able to drag the firm thing from its place.

But thoughts like these troubled very few of the reckless crew. And when after steadily dropping and dropping the pirates astern, the *Pequod* at last shot by the vivid green Cockatoo Point on the Sumatra side, emerging at last upon the broad waters beyond, then the har-

pooneers seemed more to grieve that the swift whales had
been gaining upon the ship, than to rejoice that the ship
had so victoriously gained upon the Malays. But still
driving on in the wake of the whales, at length they
seemed abating their speed. Gradually the ship neared
them, and the wind now dying away, word was passed
to spring to the boats. But no sooner did the herd, by
some presumed wonderful instinct of the sperm whale,
become notified of the three keels that were after them,
though as yet a mile in their rear, than they rallied again,
and forming in close ranks and battalions, so that their
spouts all looked like flashing lines of stacked bayonets,
moved on with redoubled velocity.

Stripped to our shirts and drawers, we sprang to the
white-ash, and after several hours' pulling were almost disposed to renounce the chase, when a general pausing
commotion among the whales gave animating token that
they were now at last under the influence of that strange
perplexity of inert irresolution, which when the fishermen
perceive it in the whale, they say he is gallied. The compact martial columns in which they had been hitherto
rapidly and steadily swimming, were now broken up in
one measureless rout; and like King Porus' elephants in
the Indian battle with Alexander, they seemed going
mad with consternation. In all directions expanding in
vast irregular circles, and aimlessly swimming hither and
thither, by their short thick spoutings they plainly betrayed their distraction of panic. This was still more
strangely evinced by those of their number, who, com-

pletely paralyzed as it were, helplessly floated like water-logged dismantled ships on the sea. Had these Leviathans been but a flock of simple sheep, pursued over the pasture by three fierce wolves, they could not possibly have evinced such excessive dismay.[1]

Though many of the whales, as has been said, were in violent motion, yet it is to be observed that as a whole the herd neither advanced nor retreated, but collectively remained in one place. As is customary in those cases, the boats at once separated, each making for some one lone whale on the outskirts of the shoal. In about three minutes' time, Queequeg's harpoon was flung; the stricken fish darted blinding spray in our faces, and then running away with us like light, steered straight for the heart of the herd. Though such a movement on the part of the whale struck under such circumstances, is in no wise unprecedented, and indeed is almost always more or less anticipated, yet does it present one of the more perilous vicissitudes of the fishery; for as the swift monster drags you deeper and deeper into the frantic shoal, you bid adieu to circumspect life and only exist in a delirious throb.

As, blind and deaf, the whale plunged forward as if by

[1] This occasional timidity is characteristic of almost all herding creatures. Though banding together in tens of thousands, the lion-maned buffaloes of the west have fled before a solitary horseman. Witness, too, all human beings, how when herded together in the sheepfold of a theatre's pit, they will, at the slightest alarm of fire, rush helter-skelter for the outlets, crowding, trampling, jamming and remorselessly dashing each other to death. Best, therefore, withhold any amazement at the strangely gallied whales before us, for there is no folly of the beasts of the earth which is not infinitely outdone by the madness of men.

sheer power of speed to rid himself of the iron leech
that had fastened to him; as we thus tore a white gash in
the sea, on all sides menaced as we flew, by the crazed
creatures to and fro rushing about us; our beset boat was
like a ship mobbed by icebergs in a tempest, striving to
steer through their complicated channels and straits,
knowing not at what moment it may be locked in and
crushed.

But not a bit daunted, Queequeg steered us manfully,
now sheering off from this monster directly across our
route in advance, now edging away from that, whose
colossal flukes were suspended overhead. All this time,
Starbuck stood up in the bows, lance in hand, pricking
out of our way whatever whales he could reach by short
darts, for there was no time to make long ones. Nor were
the oarsmen quite idle, though their wonted duty was now
altogether dispensed with. They chiefly attended to the
shouting part of the business. "Out of the way, Commodore!" cried one, to a great dromedary that of a sudden
rose bodily to the surface and for an instant threatened
to swamp us. "Hard down with your tail, there!" cried a
second to another, which, close to our gunwale, seemed
calmly cooling himself with his own fanlike extremity.

All whaleboats carry certain curious contrivances, originally invented by the Nantucket Indians called
"druggs." Two thick squares of wood of equal size are
stoutly clenched together, so that they cross each other's
grain at right angles. A line of considerable length is then
attached to the middle of this block and the other end of

the line being looped, it can in a moment be fastened to a harpoon. It is chiefly among gallied whales that this drugg is used. For then, more whales are close around you than you can possibly chase at one time. But sperm whales are not every day encountered; while you may, then, you must kill all you can. And if you cannot kill them all at once, you must wing them, so that they can be afterward killed at your leisure. Hence it is that at times like these, the drugg comes into requisition. Our boat was furnished with three of them. The first and second were successfully darted, and we saw the whales staggeringly running off, fettered by the enormous sidelong resistance of the towing drugg. They were cramped like malefactors with the chain and ball. But upon flinging the third, in the act of tossing overboard the clumsy wooden block, it caught under one of the seats of the boat, and in an instant tore it out and carried it away, dropping the oarsman in the boat's bottom as the seat slid from under him. On both sides the sea came in at the wounded planks, but we stuffed two or three drawers and shirts in, and so stopped the leaks for the time.

It had been next to impossible to dart these drugged harpoons, were it not that as we advanced into the herd, our whale's way greatly diminished; moreover, as we went still farther and farther from the circumference of commotion, the direful disorders seemed waning. So that when at last the jerking harpoon drew out, and the towing whale sideways vanished, then, with the tapering force of his parting momentum, we glided between two whales into the innermost heart of the shoal, as if from some mountain torrent we had slid into a serene valley lake.

Here the storms in the roaring glens between the outermost whales were heard but not felt. In this central expanse the sea presented that smooth satinlike surface called a sleek, produced by the subtle moisture thrown off by the whale in his quieter moods. Yes, we were now in that enchanted calm which they say lurks at the heart of every commotion. And still in the distracted distance we beheld the tumults of the outer concentric circles, and saw successive pods of whales, eight or ten in each, swiftly going round and round, like multiplied spans of horses in a ring. And so closely shoulder to shoulder were they, that a Titanic circus rider might easily have overarched the middle ones, and so have gone around on their backs. Owing to the density of the crowd of reposing whales more immediately surrounding the embayed axis of the herd, no possible chance of escape was at present afforded us. We must watch for a breach in the living wall that hemmed us in, the wall that had only admitted us in order to shut us up. Keeping at the center of the lake, we were occasionally visited by small tame cows and calves, the women and children of this routed host.

Now, inclusive of the occasional wide intervals between the revolving outer circles, and inclusive of the spaces between the various pods in any one of those circles, the entire area at this junction embraced by the whole multitude, must have contained at least two or

three square miles. At any rate—though indeed such a test
at such a time might be deceptive—spoutings might be
discovered from our low boat that seemed to be playing
up almost from the rim of the horizon. I mention this
circumstance because, as if the cows and calves had been
purposely locked up in this innermost fold, and as if the
wide extent of the herd had hitherto prevented them
from learning the precise cause of its stopping—or possibly, being so young, unsophisticated and every way innocent and inexperienced—however it may have been,
these smaller whales, now and then visiting our becalmed
boat from the margin of the lake, evinced a wondrous
fearlessness and confidence, or else a still becharmed
panic, which it was impossible not to marvel at. Like
household dogs they came snuffing around us, right up to
our gunwales and touching them, till it almost seemed
that some spell had suddenly domesticated them. Queequeg patted their foreheads; Starbuck scratched their
backs with his lance; but fearful of the consequences, for
the time refrained from darting it.

But far beneath this wondrous world upon the surface,
another and still stranger world met our eyes as we gazed
over the side. For, suspended in those watery vaults,
floated the forms of the nursing mothers of the whales,
and those that by their enormous girth seemed shortly to
become mothers. The lake, as I have hinted, was to a considerable depth exceedingly transparent; and as human
infants while suckling will calmly and fixedly gaze away
from the breast, as if leading two different lives at the

time; and while yet drawing mortal nourishment, be still spiritually feasting upon some unearthly reminiscence— even so did the young of these whales seem to be looking up toward us, but not at us, as if we were but a bit of gulfweed in their newborn sight. Floating on their sides, the mothers also seemed quietly eyeing us. One of the little infants, that from certain queer tokens seemed hardly a day old, might have measured some fourteen feet in length, and some six feet in girth. He was a little frisky, though his body seemed scarce yet recovered from that irksome position it had so lately occupied in the maternal reticule, where, tail to head and all ready for the final spring, the unborn whale lies bent like a Tartar's bow. The delicate side fins and the palms of his flukes still freshly retained the plaited crumpled appearance of a baby's ears newly arrived from foreign parts.

"Line! line!" cried Queequeg, looking over the gunwale. "Him fast! Him fast!—Who line him? Who struck? —Two whale; one big, one little!"

"What ails ye, man?" cried Starbuck.

"Look-e here," said Queequeg, pointing down.

As when the stricken whale, that from the tub has reeled out hundreds of fathoms of rope; as, after deep sounding, he floats up again, and shows the slackened curling line buoyantly rising and spiraling toward the air; so now Starbuck saw long coils of the umbilical cord of Madame Leviathan, by which the young cub seemed still tethered to its dam. Not seldom in the rapid vicissitudes of the chase this natural line, with the maternal end loose, becomes entangled with the hempen one, so that the cub is thereby trapped.

Some of the subtlest secrets of the seas seemed divulged to us in this enchanted pond. We saw young Leviathan amours in the deep.[1]

And thus, though surrounded by circle upon circle of consternations and affrights, did these inscrutable creatures at the center freely and fearlessly indulge in all peaceful concernments; yea, serenely reveled in dalliance and delight. But even so, amid the tornadoed Atlantic of my being do I myself still forever centrally disport in mute calm; and while ponderous planets of unwaning woe revolve around me, deep down and deep inland there I still bathe me in eternal mildness of joy.

Meanwhile, as we thus lay entranced, the occasional sudden frantic spectacles in the distance evinced the activity of the other boats still engaged in drugging the whales on the frontier of the host, or possibly carrying on the war within the first circle, where abundance of room and some convenient retreats were afforded them. But the sight of the enraged drugged whales now and

[1] The sperm whale, as with all other species of the Leviathan, but unlike most other fish, breeds indifferently at all seasons; after a gestation which may probably be set down at nine months, producing but one at a time; though in some few known instances giving birth to an Esau and Jacob, a contingency provided for in suckling by two teats, curiously situated, one on each side of the anus; but the breasts themselves extend upward from that. When by chance these pervious parts of a nursing whale are cut by the hunter's lance, the mother's pouring milk and blood rivalingly discolor the sea for rods. The milk is very sweet and rich; it has been tasted by man. It might do well with strawberries. When overflowing with mutual esteem, the whales salute *more hominum*.

then blindly darting to and fro across the circles, was nothing to what at last met our eyes. It is sometimes the custom, when fast to a whale more than commonly powerful and alert, to seek to hamstring him, as it were, by sundering or maiming his gigantic tail-tendon. It is done by darting a short-handled cutting-spade, to which is attached a rope for hauling it back again. A whale wounded (as we afterward learned) in this part, but not effectually, as it seemed, had broken away from the boat, carrying along with him half of the harpoon line; and in the extraordinary agony of the wound, he was now dashing among the revolving circles like the lone mounted desperado Arnold at the battle of Saratoga, carrying dismay wherever he went.

But agonizing as was the wound of this whale, and an appalling spectacle enough, anyway; yet the peculiar horror with which he seemed to inspire the rest of the herd was owing to a cause which at first the intervening distance obscured from us. But at length we perceived that by one of the unimaginable accidents of the fishery, this whale had become entangled in the harpoon line that he towed. He had also run away with the cutting-spade in him. And while the free end of the rope attached to that weapon had permanently caught the coils of the harpoon line around his tail, the cutting-spade itself had worked loose from his flesh. So that tormented to madness, he was now churning through the water, violently flailing with his flexible tail, and tossing the keen spade about him, wounding and murdering his own comrades.

This terrific object seemed to recall the whole herd

from their stationary fright. First, the whales forming the margin of our lake began to crowd a little and tumble against each other, as if lifted by half-spent billows from afar. Then the lake itself began faintly to heave and swell; the submarine bridal chambers and nurseries vanished; in more and more contracting orbits the whales in the more central circles began to swim in thickening clusters. Yes, the long calm was departing. A low advancing hum was soon heard; and then like to the tumultuous masses of block-ice when the great river Hudson breaks up in spring, the entire host of whales came tumbling upon their inner center, as if to pile themselves up in one common mountain. Instantly Starbuck and Queequeg changed places, Starbuck taking the stern.

"Oars! Oars!" he intensely whispered, seizing the helm —"gripe your oars, and clutch your souls, now! My God, men, stand by! Shove him off, you Queequeg—the whale there! Prick him!—hit him! Stand up—stand up, and stay so! Spring, men—pull, men; never mind their backs— scrape them!—scrape away!"

The boat was now all but jammed between two vast black bulks, leaving a narrow Dardanelles between their long lengths. But by desperate endeavor we at last shot into a temporary opening, then giving way rapidly, and at the same time earnestly watching for another outlet. After many similar hair-breadth escapes, we at last swiftly glided into what had just been one of the outer circles, but was now crossed by random whales, all violently making for one center. This lucky salvation was cheaply purchased by the loss of Queequeg's hat, who, while standing in the bows to prick the fugitive whales, had his hat taken clean from his head in the air-eddy made by the tossing of a pair of broad flukes close by.

Riotous and disordered as the universal commotion now was, it soon resolved into what seemed a systematic movement. For having clumped together at last in one dense body, they then renewed their onward flight with augmented fleetness. Further pursuit was useless; but the boats still lingered in their wake to pick up what drugged whales might be dropped astern, and likewise to secure one which Flask had killed and waifed. The waif is a pennoned pole. Two or three are carried by every boat; and when additional game is at hand, are inserted upright into the floating body of a dead whale, both to mark its place on the sea, and also as token of prior possession, should the boats of any other ship draw near.

The result of this lowering was somewhat illustrative of that sagacious saying in the fishery—the more whales the less fish. Of all the drugged whales only one was captured. The rest contrived to escape for the time, only to be taken by some other craft than the *Pequod*.

⚓

CHAPTER 35

The Castaway

IN THE WHALE SHIP, it is not everyone who goes in the boats. Some few hands are reserved, called shipkeepers, whose province it is to work the vessel while the boats are pursuing the whale. As a general thing these shipkeepers are as hardy fellows as the men comprising the boats' crews. But if there happens to be an unduly slender, clumsy or timorous wight in the ship, that wight is certain to be made a shipkeeper. It was so in the *Pequod* with the little Negro Pippin by nickname, Pip by abbreviation.

It came to pass, that Stubb's afteroarsman chanced so to sprain his hand, as for a time to become quite maimed, and temporarily Pip was put into his place.

The first time Stubb lowered with him Pip evinced much nervousness, but happily for that time escaped

close contact with the whale, and therefore came off not
altogether discreditably, though Stubb observing him,
took care afterward to exhort him to cherish his courage-
ousness to the utmost, for he might often find it needful.

Now upon the second lowering, the boat paddled upon
the whale; and as the fish received the darted iron, it
gave its customary rap, which happened in this instance
to be right under poor Pip's seat. The involuntary consternation of the moment caused him to leap, paddle in hand,
out of the boat, and in such a way that part of the slack
whale line coming against his chest, he breasted it overboard with him, so as to become entangled in it when at
last plumping into the water. That instant the stricken
whale started on a fierce run, the line swiftly straightened,
and presto! Poor Pip came all foaming up to the chocks
of the boat, remorselessly dragged there by the line
which had taken several turns around his chest and neck.

Tashtego stood in the bows. He was full of the fire of
the hunt. He hated Pip for a poltroon. Snatching the boat
knife from his sheath, he suspended its sharp edge over
the line, and turning toward Stubb, exclaimed interroga-
tively, "Cut?" Meantime Pip's blue choked face plainly
looked, Do, for God's sake! All passed in a flash. In less
than half a minute this entire thing happened.

"Damn him, cut!" roared Stubb; and so the whale was
lost and Pip was saved.

So soon as he recovered himself, the poor little Negro
was assailed by yells and execrations from the crew.
Tranquilly permitting these irregular cursings to evapo-
rate, Stubb then in a plain, businesslike, but still half-

humorous manner, cursed Pip officially; and that done, unofficially gave him much wholesome advice. The substance was, Never jump from a boat, Pip, except—but all the rest was indefinite, as the soundest advice ever is. Now in general, *Stick to the boat* is your true motto in whaling; but cases will sometimes happen when *Leap from the boat* is still better. Moreover, as if perceiving at last that if he should give undiluted conscientious advice to Pip, he would be leaving him too wide a margin to jump in for the future, Stubb suddenly dropped all advice, and concluded with a peremptory command, "Stick to the boat, Pip, or by the Lord, I won't pick you up if you jump. Bear that in mind, and don't jump any more."

But we are all in the hands of the gods; and Pip jumped again. It was under very similar circumstances to the first performance; but this time he did not breast out the line, and hence, when the whale started to run, Pip was left behind on the sea, like a hurried traveler's trunk. Alas! Stubb was but too true to his word. It was a beautiful, bounteous, blue day; the spangled sea calm and cool, and flatly stretching away, all around to the horizon, like gold-beater's skin hammered out to the extremest. Bobbing up and down in that sea, Pip's ebon head showed like a head of cloves. No boat knife was lifted when he fell so rapidly astern. Stubb's inexorable back was turned upon him; and the whale was winged. In three minutes a whole mile of shoreless ocean was between Pip and Stubb. Out from the center of the sea, poor Pip turned his crisp, curling black head to the sun, another lonely castaway, though the loftiest and the brightest.

Now in calm weather, to swim in the open ocean is as easy to the practiced swimmer as to ride in a spring-carriage ashore. But the awful lonesomeness is intolerable. The intense concentration of self in the middle of such a heartless immensity—my God! who can tell it? Mark how when sailors in a dead calm bathe in the open sea— mark how closely they hug their ship and only coast along her sides.

But had Stubb really abandoned the poor little Negro to his fate? No; he did not mean to, at least. Because there were two boats in his wake, he supposed, no doubt, that they would of course come up to Pip very quickly and pick him up; though, indeed, such considerateness toward oarsmen jeopardized through their own timidity is not always manifested by the hunters in all similar instances. And such instances not infrequently occur; almost invariably in the fishery a coward, so-called, is marked with the same ruthless detestation peculiar to military navies and armies.

But it so happened, that those boats, without seeing Pip, suddenly spying whales close to them on one side, turned and gave chase; and Stubb's boat was now so far away, and he and all his crew so intent upon his fish, that Pip's ringed horizon began to expand around him miserably. By the merest chance the ship itself at last rescued him; but from that hour the little Negro went about the deck an idiot; such, at least, they said he was. The sea had jeeringly kept his finite body up, but drowned the infinite of his soul. Not drowned entirely, though. Rather carried down alive to wondrous depths, where strange shapes of the unwarped primal world glided to and fro before his passive eyes; and the miser-merman, Wisdom, revealed his hoarded heaps; and among the joyous, heartless, ever-juvenile eternities, Pip saw the multitudinous, God-omnipresent coral insects, that out of the firmament of waters heaved the colossal orbs. He saw God's foot upon the treadle of the loom, and spoke it; and therefore his shipmates called him mad. So man's insanity is heaven's sense; and wandering from all mortal reason, man comes at last to that celestial thought, which, to reason, is absurd and frantic; and weal or woe, feels then uncompromised.

For the rest, blame not Stubb too hardly. The thing is common in that fishery; and in the sequel of the narrative it will then be seen what like abandonment befell myself.

CHAPTER 36

⚓

Leg and Arm

THE "PEQUOD" OF NANTUCKET MEETS
THE "SAMUEL ENDERBY" OF LONDON

SHIP AHOY! Hast seen the white whale?"

So cried Ahab, hailing a ship showing English colors, bearing down under the stern. Trumpet to mouth, the old man was standing in his hoisted quarter boat, his ivory leg plainly revealed to the stranger captain, who was carelessly reclining in his own boat's bow. He was a darkly tanned, burly, good-natured, fine-looking man of sixty or thereabouts, dressed in a spacious roundabout that hung around him in festoons of blue pilot-cloth; and one empty arm of his jacket streamed behind him like the broidered arm of a hussar's surcoat.

"Hast seen the white whale?"

240

"See you this?"—and withdrawing it from the folds that had hidden it, he held up a white arm of sperm whale bone terminating in a wooden head like a mallet.

"Man my boat!" cried Ahab impetuously, and tossing about the oars near him—"Stand by to lower!"

In less than a minute, without quitting his little craft, he and his crew were dropped to the water, and were soon alongside of the stranger. But here a curious difficulty presented itself. In the excitement of the moment Ahab had forgotten that since the loss of his leg he had never once stepped on board any vessel at sea but his own, and then it was always by an ingenious and very handy mechanical contrivance peculiar to the *Pequod*, and a thing not to be rigged and shipped in any other vessel at a moment's warning. Now, it is no very easy matter for anybody—except those who are almost hourly used to it, like whalemen—to clamber up a ship's side from a boat on the open sea; for the great swells now lift the boat high up towards the bulwarks, and then instantaneously drop it halfway down to the kelson. So, deprived of one leg, and the strange ship of course being altogether unsupplied with the kindly invention, Ahab now found himself abjectly reduced to a clumsy landsman again, hopelessly eyeing the uncertain changeful height he could hardly hope to attain.

It has before been hinted, perhaps, that every little untoward circumstance that befell him, and which indirectly sprang from his luckless mishap, almost invariably irritated or exasperated Ahab. And in the present instance, all this was heightened by the sight of the two officers of the strange ship leaning over the side, by the perpendicular ladder of nailed cleats there, and swinging toward him a pair of tastefully ornamented manropes; for at first they did not seem to bethink them that a one-legged man must be too much of a cripple to use their sea banisters. But this awkwardness lasted only a minute because the strange captain, observing at a glance how affairs stood, cried out: "I see, I see!—avast heaving there! Jump, boys, and swing over the cutting tackle."

As good luck would have it, they had had a whale alongside a day or two previous, and the great tackles were still aloft, and the massive curved blubber hook, now clean and dry, was still attached to the end. This was quickly lowered to Ahab, who at once comprehended it all, slid his solitary thigh into the curve of the hook (it was like sitting in the fluke of an anchor, or the crotch of an apple tree), and then giving the word, held himself fast, and at the same time also helped to hoist his own weight by pulling hand over hand upon one of the running parts of the tackle. Soon he was carefully swung inside the high bulwarks, and gently landed upon the capstan head. With his ivory arm frankly thrust forth in welcome the other captain advanced, and Ahab, putting out his ivory leg and crossing the ivory arm (like two swordfish blades) cried out in his walrus way, "Aye, aye, hearty! Let us shake bones together! An arm and a leg! An arm that never can shrink, d'ye see, and a leg that never can run. Where didst thou see the white whale?— how long ago?"

"The white whale," said the Englishman, pointing his ivory arm toward the east, and taking a rueful sight along it, as if had been a telescope. "There I saw him, on the Line, last season."

"And he took that arm off, did he?" asked Ahab, now sliding down from the capstan, and resting on the Englishman's shoulder as he did so.

"Aye, he was the cause of it, at least; and that leg, too?"

"Spin me the yarn," said Ahab; "how was it?"

"It was the first time in my life I ever cruised on the Line," began the Englishman. "I was ignorant of the white whale at that time. Well, one day we lowered for a pod of four or five whales, and my boat fastened to one of them; a regular circus horse he was, too, that went milling and milling round so, that my boat's crew could only trim dish, by sitting all their sterns on the outer gunwale. Presently up breaches from the bottom of the sea a bouncing great whale, with a milky-white head and hump, all crow's feet and wrinkles."

"It was he, it was he!" cried Ahab, suddenly letting out his suspended breath.

"And harpoons sticking in near his starboard fin."

"Aye, aye—they were mine—*my* irons," cried Ahab exultingly—"but on!"

"Give me a chance, then," said the Englishman, good-humoredly. "Well, this old great grandfather, with the white head and hump, runs all afoam into the pod, and goes to snapping furiously at my fast-line."

"Aye, I see!—wanted to part it; free the fast-fish—an old trick—I know him."

"How it was exactly," continued the one-armed commander, "I do not know; but in biting the line, it got foul of his teeth, caught there somehow; but we didn't know it then; so that when we afterwards pulled on the line, bounce we came plump onto *his* hump, instead of the other whale's, that went off to windward, all fluking. Seeing how matters stood, and what a noble great whale it was—the noblest and biggest I ever saw, sir, in my life—I resolved to capture him, spite of the boiling rage he seemed to be in. And thinking the haphazard line would get loose, or the tooth it was tangled to might draw (for I have a devil of a boat's crew for a pull on a whale line); seeing all this, I say, I jumped into my first mate's boat—Mr. Mounttop's here (by the way, captain—Mounttop; Mounttop—the captain)—as I was saying, I jumped into Mounttop's boat, which, d'ye see, was gunwale and gunwale with mine then; and snatching the first harpoon, let this old great grandfather have it.

"But, Lord look you, sir—hearts and souls alive, man—the next instant, in a jiff, I was blind as a bat—both eyes out—all befogged and bedeadened with black foam—the whale's tail looming straight up out of it, perpendicular in the air, like a marble steeple. No use sterning all, then; but as I was groping at midday, with a blinding sun, all crown jewels; as I was groping, I say, after the second iron to toss it overboard—down comes the tail like a Lima tower, cutting my boat in two, leaving each half in splinters; and, flukes first, the white hump backed through the wreck as though it was all chips. We all struck out.

"To escape his terrible flailings, I seized hold of my harpoon pole sticking in him, and for a moment clung to that like a sucking fish. But a combing sea dashed me off, and at the same instant the fish, taking one good dart forwards, went down like a flash; and the barb of that cursed second iron towing along near me caught me here" (clapping his hand just below his shoulder); "yes, caught me just here, I say, and bore me down to Hell's flames, I was thinking; when, when, all of a sudden, thank the good God, the barb ripped its way along the flesh—clear along the whole length of my arm—came out nigh my wrist, and up I floated. And that gentleman there will tell you the rest (by the way, captain—Dr. Bunger, ship's surgeon: Bunger, my lad—the captain). Now Bunger, boy, spin your part of the yarn."

The professional gentleman thus familiarly pointed out, had been all the time standing near them, with nothing specific visible to denote his gentlemanly rank on board. His face was an exceedingly round but sober one; he was dressed in a faded blue woolen frock or shirt, and patched trousers; and had thus far been dividing his attention between a marlinspike he held in one hand, and a pill box held in the other, occasionally casting a critical glance at the ivory limbs of the two crippled captains. But, at the superior's introduction of him to Ahab, he politely bowed and straightway went on to do his captain's bidding.

"It was a shocking bad wound," began the whale surgeon; "and, taking my advice, Captain Boomer here, stood our old Sammy—"

"*Samuel Enderby* is the name of my ship," interrupted the one-armed captain, addressing Ahab; "go on, boy."

"Stood our old Sammy off to the northward, to get out of the blazing hot weather there on the Line. But it was no use—I did all I could, sat up with him nights, was very severe with him in the matter of diet—"

"Oh, very severe!" chimed in the patient himself; then suddenly altering his voice, "drinking hot rum toddies with me every night, till he couldn't see to put on the bandages; and sending me to bed, half seas over, about three o'clock in the morning. Oh, ye stars! he sat up with me indeed, and was very severe in my diet. Oh! a great watcher, and very dietetically severe, is Dr. Bunger. (Bunger, you dog, laugh out! why don't ye? You know you're a precious jolly rascal.) But, heave ahead, boy, I'd rather be killed by you than kept alive by any other man."

"My captain, as you must have ere this perceived, respected sir," said the imperturbable godly-looking Bunger, slightly bowing to Ahab, "is apt to be facetious at times; he spins us many clever things of that sort. But I may as well say—*en passant*, as the French remark—that I myself—that is to say, Jack Bunger, late of the reverend clergy—am a strict total abstinence man; I never drink—"

"Water!" cried the captain. "He never drinks it; it's a sort of fits to him; fresh water throws him into the hydrophobia; but go on—go on with the arm story."

"Yes, I may as well," said the surgeon coolly. "I was

about observing, sir, before Captain Boomer's facetious interruption, that spite of my best and severest endeavors, the wound kept getting worse and worse. The truth was, sir, it was as ugly a gaping wound as surgeon ever saw, more than two feet and several inches long. I measured it with the lead-line. In short, it grew black; I knew what was threatened, and off it came. But I had no hand in shipping that ivory arm there; that thing is against all rule"—pointing at it with the marlinspike—"that is the captain's work, not mine; he ordered the carpenter to make it; he had that club-hammer there put to the end, to knock someone's brains out with, I suppose, as he tried mine once. He flies into diabolical passions sometimes. Do ye see this dent, sir"—removing his hat and brushing aside his hair, and exposing a bowl-like cavity in his skull, but which bore not the slightest scarry trace, or any token of ever having been a wound—"Well, the captain there will tell you how that came here; he knows."

"No, I don't," said the captain, "but his mother did; he was born with it. Oh, you solemn rogue, you—you Bunger! Was there ever such another Bunger in the watery world? Bunger, when you die, you ought to die in pickle, you dog; you should be preserved to future ages, you rascal."

"What became of the white whale?" now cried Ahab, who thus far had been impatiently listening to this by-play between the two Englishmen.

"Oh," cried the one-armed captain, "oh, yes! Well, after

he sounded, we didn't see him again for some time; in fact, as I before hinted, I didn't then know what whale it was that had served me such a trick, till sometime afterwards, when coming back to the Line, we heard about Moby Dick—as some call him—and then I knew it was he."

"Didst thou cross his wake again?"

"Twice."

"But could not fasten?"

"Didn't want to try to: ain't one limb enough? What should I do without this other arm? And I'm thinking Moby Dick doesn't bite so much as he swallows."

"Well, then," interrupted Bunger, "give him your left arm for bait to get the right. Do you know, gentlemen"— very gravely and mathematically bowing to each captain in succession—"do you know, gentlemen, that the digestive organs of the whale are so inscrutably constructed by Divine Providence, that it is quite impossible for him to completely digest even a man's arm? And he knows it too. So that what you take for the white whale's malice is only his awkwardness. For he never means to swallow a single limb; he only thinks to terrify by feints. But sometimes he is like the old juggling fellow, formerly a patient of mine in Ceylon, that making believe swallow jackknives, once upon a time let one drop into him in good earnest, and there it stayed for a twelvemonth or more; when I gave him an emetic, and he heaved it up in small tacks, d'ye see. No possible way for him to digest that jackknife, and fully incorporate it into his general bodily system. Yes, Captain Boomer, if you are quick enough about it, and have a mind to pawn one arm for the sake of the privilege of giving decent burial to the other, why in that case the arm is yours; only let the whale have another chance at you shortly, that's all."

"No, thank ye, Bunger," said the English captain; "he's welcome to the arm he has, since I can't help it, and didn't know him then, but not to another one. No more white whales for me; I've lowered for him once, and that has satisfied me. There would be great glory in killing him, I know that; and there is a shipload of precious sperm in him, but, hark ye, he's best let alone; don't you think so, captain?"—glancing at the ivory leg.

"He is, but he will still be hunted, for all that. What is best let alone, that accursed thing is not always what least allures. He's all a magnet. How long since thou saw'st him last? Which way heading?"

"Bless my soul, and curse the foul fiend's," cried Bunger stoopingly walking around Ahab, and like a dog strangely snuffing. "This man's blood—bring the thermometer!—it's at the boiling point! His pulse makes these planks beat! Sir!"—taking a lancet from his pocket, and drawing near to Ahab's arm.

"Avast!" roared Ahab, dashing him against the bulwarks—"Man the boat! Which way heading?"

"Good God!" cried the English captain, to whom the question was put. "What's the matter? He was leading east, I think. Is your captain crazy?" whispering to Fedallah.

But Fedallah, putting a finger on his lip, slid over the bulwarks to take the boat's steering-oar, and Ahab, swinging the cutting tackle toward him, commanded the ship's sailors to stand by to lower.

In a moment he was standing in the boat's stern, and the Manila men were springing to their oars. In vain the English captain hailed him. With back to the stranger ship, and face set like a flint to his own, Ahab stood upright till alongside of the *Pequod*.

⚓

CHAPTER 37

Ahab's Leg

THE PRECIPITATING MANNER in which Captain Ahab had quitted the *Samuel Enderby* of London, had not been unattended with some small violence to his own person. He had alighted with such energy upon a thwart of his boat that his ivory leg had received a half-splintering shock. And when after gaining his own deck, and his own pivot hole there, he so vehemently wheeled around with an urgent command to the steersman (it was, as ever, something about his not steering inflexibly enough); then, the already shaken ivory received such an additional twist and wrench that though it still remained entire and to all appearances lusty, yet Ahab did not deem it entirely trustworthy.

And, indeed, it seemed small matter for wonder, that for all his pervading mad recklessness, Ahab did at times give careful heed to the condition of that dead bone upon which he partly stood. For it had not been very long prior to the *Pequod's* sailing from Nantucket, that he had been found one night lying prone upon the ground, and insensible; by some unknown, and seemingly inexplicable, unimaginable casualty, his ivory limb having been so violently displaced, that it had stakewise smitten, and all but pierced his groin; nor was it without extreme difficulty that the agonizing wound was entirely cured.

Unwittingly here a secret has been divulged, which perhaps might more properly, in set way, have been disclosed before. With many other particulars concerning Ahab, always had it remained a mystery to some why it was, that for a certain period both before and after the sailing of the *Pequod,* he had hidden himself away with such Grand Lama-like exclusiveness; and for that one interval, sought speechless refuge, as it were, among the marble senate of the dead. Captain Peleg's bruited reason for this thing appeared by no means adequate; though, indeed, as touching all Ahab's deeper part, every revelation partook more of significant darkness than of explanatory light. But in the end it all came out; this one matter did, at least. That direful mishap was at the bottom of his temporary recluseness.

But be all this as it may; let the unseen, ambiguous synod in the air, or the vindictive princes and potentates of fire, have to do or not with earthly Ahab, yet, in this present matter of his leg, he took plain, practical procedures. He called the carpenter.

And when that functionary appeared before him, he bade him without delay set about making a new leg, and directed the mates to see him supplied with all the studs and joists of jaw ivory (sperm whale) which had thus far been accumulated on the voyage, in order that a careful selection of the stoutest, clearest-grained stuff might be secured. This done, the carpenter received orders to have the leg completed that night; and to provide all the fittings for it, independent of those pertaining to the distrusted one in use. Moreover the ship's forge was ordered to be hoisted out of its temporary idleness in the hold; and to accelerate the affair, the blacksmith was commanded to proceed at once to the forging of whatever iron contrivances might be needed.

⚓

CHAPTER 38

Ahab and Starbuck in the Cabin

ACCORDING TO USAGE they were pumping the ship next morning, and lo! No inconsiderable oil came up with the water; the casks below must have sprung a bad leak. Much concern was shown, and Starbuck went down into the cabin to report this unfavorable affair.[1]

Now, from the south and west the *Pequod* was drawing nigh to Formosa and the Bashee Isles, between which lies one of the tropical outlets from the China waters into the Pacific. And so Starbuck found Ahab with a general chart of the Oriental archipelagoes spread before him, and another separate one representing the long eastern

[1] In sperm-whalemen with any considerable quantity of oil on board, it is a regular semi-weekly duty to conduct a hose into the hold, and drench the casks with sea water; which afterward, at varying intervals is removed by the ship's pumps. Hereby the casks are sought to be kept damply tight, while by the changed character of the withdrawn water, the mariners readily detect any serious leakage in the precious cargo.

coasts of the Japanese islands. With his snow-white new ivory leg braced against the screwed leg of his table, and with a long pruning-hook of a jackknife in his hand, the wondrous old man, with his back to the gangway door, was wrinkling his brow, and tracing his old courses again.

"Who's there?"—hearing the footstep at the door, but not turning around to it. "On deck! Begone!"

"Captain Ahab mistakes; it is I. The oil in the hold is leaking, sir. We must up Burtons and break out."

"Up Burtons and break out? Now that we are nearing Japan—heave-to here for a week to tinker a parcel of old hoops?"

"Either do that, sir, or waste in one day more oil than we may make good in a year. What we come twenty thousand miles to get is worth saving, sir."

"So it is, so it is, if we get it."

"I was speaking of the oil in the hold, sir."

"And I was not speaking or thinking of that at all. Begone! Let it leak! I'm all aleak myself. Aye! Leaks in leaks! Not only full of leaky casks, but those leaky casks are in a leaky ship, and that's a far worse plight than the *Pequod's*, man. Yet I don't stop to plug my leak, for who can find it in the deep-loaded hull, or how hope to plug it, even if found, in this life's howling gale? Starbuck! I'll not have the Burtons hoisted."

"What will the owners say, sir?"

"Let the owners stand on Nantucket beach and outyell the typhoons. What cares Ahab? Owners, owners? Thou art always prating to me, Starbuck, about those miserly owners, as if the owners were my conscience. But look ye, the only real owner of anything is its commander; and hark ye, my conscience is in this ship's keel—On deck!"

"Captain Ahab," said the reddening mate, moving further into the cabin, with a daring so strangely respectful and cautious that it almost seemed not only every way seeking to avoid the slightest outward manifestation of itself, but inward also seemed more than half distrustful of itself, "a better man than I might well pass over in thee what he would quickly enough resent in a younger man; aye, and in a happier, Captain Ahab."

"Devils! Dost thou then so much as dare to critically think of me? On deck!"

"Nay, sir, not yet, I do entreat. And I do dare, sir—to be forbearing! Shall we not understand each other better than hitherto, Captain Ahab?"

Ahab seized a loaded musket from the rack (forming part of most south seamen's cabin furniture), and pointing it toward Starbuck, exclaimed, "There is one God that is Lord over the earth, and one captain that is lord over the *Pequod*—On deck!"

For an instant in the flashing eyes of the mate, and his fiery cheeks, you would have almost thought that he had really received the blaze of the leveled tube. But mastering his emotion, he half calmly rose, and as he quitted the cabin, paused for an instant and said: "Thou hast outraged, not insulted me, sir; but for that I ask thee not to beware of Starbuck; thou wouldst but laugh, but let Ahab beware of Ahab; beware of thyself, old man."

"He waxes brave, but nevertheless obeys; most careful bravery that!" murmured Ahab, as Starbuck disappeared. "What's that he said—Ahab beware of Ahab—there's something there!" Then unconsciously using the musket for a staff, with an iron brow he paced to and fro in the little cabin; but presently the thick plaits of his forehead relaxed, and returning the gun to the rack, he went to the deck.

"Thou art but too good a fellow, Starbuck," he said lowly to the mate; then raising his voice to the crew: "Furl the t'gallant-sails, and close-reef the topsails, fore and aft; back the mainyard; up Burtons, and break out in the mainhold."

It were perhaps vain to surmise exactly why it was that as respecting Starbuck, Ahab thus acted. It may have been a flash of honesty in him, or mere prudential policy which, under the circumstance, imperiously forbade the slightest symptom of open disaffection, however transient, in the important chief officer of his ship. However it was, his orders were executed, and the Burtons were hoisted.

CHAPTER 39

⚓

Queequeg in His Coffin

UPON SEARCHING, it was found that the casks last struck into the hold were perfectly sound, and that the leak must be further off. So, it being calm weather, they broke out deeper and deeper, disturbing the slumbers of the huge ground-tier butts; and from that black midnight sending those gigantic moles into the daylight above. So deep did they go, and so ancient and corroded and weedy the aspect of the lowermost puncheons, that you almost looked next for some moldy cornerstone cask containing coins of Captain Noah, with copies of the posted placards vainly warning the infatuated old world from the flood. Tierce after tierce, too, of water and bread and beef, and shooks of staves, and iron bundles of hoops were hoisted out, until at last the piled decks were hard to get about. The hollow hull echoed underfoot as if you were treading over empty catacombs, and reeled and rolled in the sea like an air-freighted demijohn. Top-heavy was the ship as a dinnerless student with all Aristotle in his head. Well was it that the typhoons did not visit us then.

Now, at this time it was that my poor pagan companion and fast bosom friend, Queequeg, was seized with a fever which brought him nigh to his endless end.

Be it said that in this vocation of whaling, sinecures are unknown. Dignity and danger go hand in hand. Until you get to be captain, the higher you rise the harder you toil. So with poor Queequeg, who, as harpooneer, must not only face all the rage of the living whale, but—as we have elsewhere seen—mount his dead back in a rolling sea, and finally descend into the gloom of the hold, and bitterly sweating all day in that subterraneous confinement, resolutely manhandle the clumsiest casks and see to their stowage. In short, among whalemen, the harpooners are the holders, so-called.

Poor Queequeg! when the ship was about half disemboweled, you should have stooped over the hatchway, and peered down upon him; there, stripped to his woolen drawers, the tattooed savage was crawling about amid that dampness and slime, like a green spotted lizard at the bottom of a well. And a well, or an ice house it somehow proved to him, poor pagan. Strange to say, for all the heat of his sweatings, he caught a terrible chill which lapsed into a fever; and at last, after some days' suffering, laid him in his hammock, close to the very sill of the door of death. How he wasted and wasted away in those few

long-lingering days, till there seemed but little left of
him but his frame and tattooing. But as all else in him
thinned, and his cheekbones grew sharper, his eyes,
nevertheless, seemed to grow fuller and fuller; they became of a strange softness of luster; and mildly but
deeply looked out at you there from his sickness, a wondrous testimony to that immortal health in him which
could not die, or be weakened. And like circles on the
water, which as they grow fainter, expand; so his eyes
seemed rounding and rounding, like the rings of Eternity.
An awe that cannot be named would steal over you as you
sat by the side of this waning savage, and saw as strange
things in his face as any beheld who were bystanders
when Zoroaster died. For whatever is truly wondrous and
fearful in man never yet was put into words or books. And
the drawing near of Death, which alike levels all, alike
impresses all with a last revelation, which only an author
from the dead could adequately tell. So that—let us say
it again—no dying Chaldee or Greek had higher and
holier thoughts than those whose mysterious shades you
saw creeping over the face of poor Queequeg, as he
quietly lay in his swaying hammock, and the rolling sea
seemed gently rocking him to his final rest, and the
ocean's invisible floodtide lifted him higher and higher
toward his destined heaven.

Not a man of the crew but gave him up; and, as for
Queequeg himself, what he thought of his case was
forcibly shown by a curious favor he asked. He called
one to him in the gray morning watch, when the day was
just breaking, and taking his hand, said that while in Nan-

tucket he had chanced to see certain little canoes of dark wood, like the rich warwood of his native isle. Upon inquiry, he had learned that all whalemen who died in Nantucket were laid in those same dark canoes, and that the fancy of being so laid had much pleased him; for it was not unlike the custom of of his own race, who, after embalming a dead warrior, stretched him out in his canoe, and so left him to be floated away to the starry archipelagoes—for not only do they believe that the stars are isles, but that far beyond all visible horizons, their own mild, uncontinented seas interflow with the blue heavens, and so form the white breakers of the milky way. After saying this, he added that he shuddered at the thought of being buried in his hammock, according to the usual sea custom, tossed like something vile to the death-devouring sharks. No: he desired a canoe like those of Nantucket, all the more congenial to him, being a whaleman, that like a whaleboat these coffin-canoes were without a keel, though that involved but uncertain steering, and much leeway adown the dim ages.

Now, when this strange circumstance was made known aft, the carpenter was at once commanded to do Quee-queg's bidding, whatever it might include. There was some heathenish coffin-colored old lumber aboard, which, upon a long previous voyage, had been cut from the aboriginal groves of the Lackaday Islands, and from these dark planks the coffin was recommended to be made. No sooner was the carpenter apprised of the order, than taking his rule, he forthwith with all the indifferent promptitude of his character, proceeded into the forecastle and took Queequeg's measure with great accuracy, regularly chalking Queequeg's person as he shifted the rule.

"Ah! poor fellow! He'll have to die now," ejaculated the Long Island sailor.

Going to his vice-bench, the carpenter for convenience sake and general reference, now transferringly measured on it the exact length the coffin was to be, and then made the transfer permanent by cutting two notches as its extremities. This done, he marshaled the planks and his tools, and went to work.

When the last nail was driven and the lid duly planed and fitted, he lightly shouldered the coffin and went forward with it, enquiring whether they were ready for it yet in that direction.

Overhearing the indignant but half-humorous cries with which the people on deck began to drive the coffin away, Queequeg, to every one's consternation, commanded that the thing should be instantly brought to him, nor was there any denying him, seeing that, of all mortals, some dying men are the most tyrannical; and certainly, since they will shortly trouble us so little forevermore, the poor fellows ought to be indulged.

Leaning over in his hammock, Queequeg long regarded the coffin with an attentive eye. He then called for his harpoon, had the wooden stock drawn from it, and then had the iron part placed in the coffin along with one of the paddles of his boat. All by his own request, also, biscuits were then ranged around the sides within. A flask of fresh water was placed at the head, a small bag of woody earth scraped up in the hold at the foot, and a piece of sailcloth being rolled up for a pillow, Queequeg now entreated to be lifted into his final bed, that he might make trial of its comforts, if any it had. He lay without moving a few minutes, then told someone to go to his bag and bring out his little god, Yojo. Then crossing his arms on his breast with Yojo between, he called for the coffin lid (hatch he called it) to be placed over him. The head part turned over with a leather hinge, and there lay Queequeg in his coffin with little but his composed countenance in view. "Rarmai" (it will do; it is easy), he murmured at last, and signed to be replaced in his hammock.

But ere this was done Pip, who had been slyly hovering near by all this while, drew nigh to him where he lay, and with soft sobbings, took him by the hand, in the other, holding his tambourine.

"Poor rover! will ye never have done with all this weary roving? where go ye now? But if the currents carry ye to those sweet Antilles where the beaches are only beat with water lilies, will ye do one little errand for me? Seek out one Pip, who's now been missing long: I think he's in those far Antilles. If ye find him, then comfort him; for he must be very sad; for look! He's left his tambourine behind; I found it. Rig-a-dig, dig, dig! Now, Queequeg, die; and I'll beat ye your dying march."

"I have heard," murmured Starbuck, gazing down the scuttle, "that in violent fevers, men, all ignorance, have talked in ancient tongues; and that when the mystery is probed, it turns out always that in their wholly forgotten

childhood those ancient tongues had been really spoken
in their hearing by some lofty scholars. So, to my fond
faith, poor Pip, in this strange sweetness of his lunacy,
brings heavenly vouchers of all our heavenly homes.
Where learned he that, but there?—Hark! He speaks
again but more wildly now."

"Form two and two! Let's make a General of him! Ho,
where's his harpoon? Lay it across here—rig-a-dig, dig,
dig! huzza! Oh, for a gamecock now to sit upon his head
and crow! Queequeg dies game!—mind ye that; Queequeg dies game!—take ye good heed of that; Queequeg
dies game! I say; game, game, game! but base little Pip,
he died a coward; died all a-shiver. Out upon Pip!
Hark ye: if ye find Pip, tell all the Antilles he's a runaway,
a coward, a coward, a coward! Tell them he jumped from
a whaleboat! I'd never beat my tambourine over base
Pip, and hail him General, if he were once more dying
here. No, no! Shame upon all cowards—shame upon
them! Let 'em go drown like Pip, that jumped from a
whaleboat. Shame! shame!"

During all this, Queequeg lay with closed eyes, as if in
a dream. Pip was led away, and the sick man was replaced in his hammock.

But now that he had apparently made every preparation for death; now that his coffin was proved a good fit,
Queequeg suddenly rallied. Soon there seemed no need
of the carpenter's box: and thereupon, when some expressed their delighted surprise, he in substance said
that the cause of his sudden convalescence was this: at
a critical moment, he had just recalled a little duty ashore

which he was leaving undone and therefore had changed his mind about dying. He could not die yet, he averred. They asked him, then, whether to live or die was a matter of his own sovereign will and pleasure. He answered, certainly. In a word, it was Queequeg's conceit that if a man made up his mind to live, mere sickness could not kill him—nothing but a whale, or a gale, or some violent, ungovernable, unintelligent destroyer of that sort.

Now, there is this noteworthy difference between savage and civilized; that while a sick, civilized man may be six months convalescing, generally speaking, a sick savage is almost half well again in a day. So, in good time my Queequeg gained strength; and at length after sitting on the windlass for a few indolent days (but eating with a vigorous appetite) he suddenly leaped to his feet, threw out his arms and legs, gave himself a good stretching, yawned a little bit, and then springing into the head of his hoisted boat, and poising a harpoon, pronounced himself fit for a fight.

With a wild whimsiness, he now used his coffin for a sea chest; and emptying into it his canvas bag of clothes, set them in order there. Many spare hours he spent in carving the lid with all manner of grotesque figures and drawings; and it seemed that hereby he was striving in his rude way to copy parts of the twisted tattooing on his body. This tattooing had been the work of a departed prophet and seer of his island, who, by those hieroglyphic marks, had written out on his body a complete theory of the heavens and the earth, and a mystical treatise on the art of attaining truth. So that Queequeg in his own proper person was a riddle to unfold, a wondrous work in one volume, but whose mysteries not even himself could read, though his own live heart beat against them. And these mysteries were therefore destined in the end to molder away with the living parchment whereon they were inscribed, and so be unsolved to the last. This thought it must have been which suggested to Ahab that wild exclamation of his, when one morning turning away from surveying poor Queequeg—"Oh, devilish tantalization of the gods!"

CHAPTER 40

⚓

The Forge

With matted beard and swathed in a bristling shark-skin apron, about midday Perth was standing between his forge and anvil, the latter placed upon an ironwood log. One hand was holding a pikehead in the coals with the other at his forge's lungs, when Captain Ahab came along carrying in his hand a small rusty-looking leathern bag. While yet a little distance from the forge, moody Ahab paused; till at last, Perth, withdrawing his iron from the fire, began hammering it upon the anvil—the red mass sending off the sparks in thick hovering flights, some of which flew close to Ahab.

"Are these thy Mother Carey's chickens, Perth? They are always flying in thy wake; birds of good omen, too, but not to all. Look here, they burn, but thou—thou liv'st among them without a scorch."

267

"Because I am scorched all over, Captain Ahab," answered Perth, resting for a moment on his hammer. "I am past scorching; not easily canst thou scorch a scar."

"Well, well, no more. Thy shrunk voice sounds too calmly, sanely woeful to me. In no paradise myself, I am impatient of all misery in others that is not mad. Thou shouldst go mad, blacksmith; say, why dost thou not go mad? How canst thou endure without being mad? Do the heavens yet hate thee, that thou canst not go mad?— What wert thou making there?"

"Welding an old pikehead, sir; there were seams and dents in it."

"And canst thou make it all smooth again, blacksmith, after such hard usage as it had?"

"I think so, sir."

"And I suppose thou canst smooth almost any seams and dents, never mind how hard the metal, blacksmith?"

"Aye, sir, I think I can, all seams and dents but one."

"Look ye here, then," cried Ahab, passionately advancing and leaning with both hands on Perth's shoulders. "Look ye here—*here*—can ye smooth out a seam like this, blacksmith," sweeping one hand across his ribbed brow. "If thou couldst, blacksmith, glad enough would I lay my head upon thy anvil, and feel thy heaviest hammer between my eyes. Answer! Canst thou smooth this seam?"

"Oh! That is the one, sir! Said I not all seams and dents but one?"

"Aye, blacksmith, it is the one. Aye, man, it is unsmoothable. For though thou only see'st it here in my flesh, it has worked down into the bone of my skull— *that* is all wrinkles! But away with child's play. No more gaffs and pikes today. Look ye here!"—jingling the leathern bag as if it were full of gold coins. "I too want a harpoon made, one that a thousand yoke of fiends could not part, Perth. Something that will stick in a whale like his own finbone. There's the stuff," flinging the pouch upon the anvil. "Look ye, blacksmith, these are the gathered nail stubs of the steel shoes of racing horses.

"Horseshoe stubs, sir? Why, Captain Ahab, thou hast here, then, the best and stubbornest stuff we blacksmiths ever worked."

"I know it, old man. These stubs will weld together like glue from the melted bones of murderers. Quick! forge me the harpoon. And forge me first twelve rods for its shank. Then wind and twist and hammer these twelve together like the yarns and strands of a towline. Quick! I'll blow the fire."

When at last the twelve rods were made, Ahab tried them, one by one, by spiraling them, with his own hand, around a long heavy iron bolt. "A flaw!"—rejecting the last one. "Work that over again, Perth."

This done, Perth was about to begin welding the twelve into one when Ahab stayed his hand, and said he would weld his own iron. As then, with regular gasping hems he hammered on the anvil, Perth passing to him the glowing rods one after the other, and the hard-pressed forge shooting up its intense straight flame, the Parsee passed silently, and bowing over his head toward the fire, seemed invoking some curse or some blessing on the toil. But as Ahab looked up he slid aside.

"What's that bunch of lucifers dodging about there for?" muttered Stubb, looking on from the forecastle. "That Parsee smells fire like a fusee and smells of it himself, like a hot musket's powder-pan."

At last the shank, in one complete rod, received its final heat. And as Perth to temper it plunged it all hissing into the cask of water near by, the scalding steam shot up into Ahab's bent face.

"Wouldst thou brand me, Perth?"—wincing for a moment with the pain. "Have I been but forging my own branding iron, then?"

"Pray God, not that. Yet I fear something, Captain Ahab. Is not this harpoon for the white whale?"

"For the white fiend! But now for the barbs; thou must make them thyself, man. Here are my razors—the best of steel. Here, and make the barbs sharp as the needle-sleet of the Icy Sea."

For a moment the old blacksmith eyed the razors as though he would fain not use them.

"Take them, man. I have no need for them for I now neither shave, sup nor pray till—but here—to work!"

Fashioned at last into an arrowy shape and welded by Perth to the shank, the steel soon pointed the end of the iron; and as the blacksmith was about to give the barbs their final heat prior to tempering them, he cried to Ahab to place the water cask near.

"No, no—no water for that. I want it of the true death-temper. Ahoy, there! Tashtego, Queequeg, Daggoo! What

say ye pagans? Will ye give me as much blood as will
cover this barb?"—holding it high up. A cluster of dark
nods replied "Yes." Three punctures were made in the
heathen flesh, and the barbs were then tempered.

"Ego non baptizo te in nomine patris, sed in nomine
diaboli!" deliriously howled Ahab, as the malignant iron
scorchingly devoured the baptismal blood.

Now, mustering the spare poles from below and selecting one of hickory with the bark still investing it, Ahab
fitted the end of the socket of the iron. A coil of new
towline was then unwound, and some fathoms of it taken
to the windlass and stretched to great tension. Pressing
his foot upon it until the rope hummed like a harp string,
then eagerly bending over it and seeing no strandings,
Ahab exclaimed, "Good! And now for the seizings."

At one extremity the rope was unstranded and the separate spread yarns were all braided and woven around
the socket of the harpoon. The pole was then driven
hard up into the socket. From the lower end the rope
was traced halfway along the pole's length and firmly
secured so, with intertwistings of twine. This done, pole,
iron and rope—like the Three Fates—remained inseparable, and Ahab moodily stalked away with the weapon,
the sound of his ivory leg and the sound of the hickory
pole both hollowly ringing along every plank. But ere
he entered his cabin, a light, unnatural, half-bantering,
yet most piteous sound was heard. Oh, Pip, thy wretched
laugh, thy idle unresting eye! All thy strange mum-
meries not unmeaningly blended with the black tragedy
of the melancholy ship, and mocked it!

CHAPTER 41

⚓

The *Pequod* Meets the *Bachelor*

AND JOLLY ENOUGH were the sights and the sounds that came bearing down before the wind some few weeks after Ahab's harpoon had been welded.

It was a Nantucket ship, the *Bachelor,* which had just wedged in her last cask of oil and bolted down her bursting hatches; and now, in glad holiday apparel was joyously, though somewhat vaingloriously, sailing around among the widely-separated ships on the ground, previous to pointing her prow for home.

The three men at her masthead wore long streamers of narrow red bunting at their hats. From the stern, a whaleboat was suspended bottom down. And hanging captive from the bowsprit was seen the long lower jaw of the last whale they had slain. Signals, ensigns and jacks of all colors were flying from her rigging on every side. Sideways lashed in each of her three basketed tops were two barrels of sperm. Above, in her topmast crosstrees, you saw slender breakers of the same precious fluid; and nailed to her main truck was a brazen lamp.

As was afterward learned, the *Bachelor* had met with the most surprising success, all the more wonderful, for that while cruising in the same seas numerous other vessels had gone entire months without securing a single fish. Not only had barrels of beef and bread been given away to make room for the far more valuable sperm, but additional supplemental casks had been bartered for, from the ships she had met; and these were stowed along the deck, and in the captain's and officers' staterooms. Even the cabin table itself had been knocked into kindling wood, and the cabin mess dined off the broad head of an oil-butt, lashed down to the floor for a centerpiece. In the forecastle, the sailors had actually caulked and pitched their chests, and filled them. It was humorously added that the cook had clapped a head on his larger boiler and filled it, that the steward had plugged his spare coffeepot and filled it, that the harpooneers had headed the sockets of their irons and filled them—that indeed everything was filled with sperm except the captain's pantaloons pockets, and those he reserved to thrust his hands into, in self-complacent testimony of his entire satisfaction.

As this glad ship of good luck bore down upon the moody *Pequod*, the barbarian sound of enormous drums came from her forecastle. And upon her drawing still nearer, a crowd of her men were seen standing around

her huge try-pots, which, covered with the parchmentlike
poke or stomach skin of the black fish, gave forth a loud
roar to every stroke of the clenched hands of the crew.
On the quarterdeck, the mates and harpooneers were
dancing with the olive-hued girls who had eloped with
them from the Polynesian Isles, while suspended in an
ornamented boat, firmly secured aloft between the foremast and mainmast, three Long Island Negroes, with
glittering fiddle bows of whale ivory, were presiding over
the hilarious jig. Meanwhile, others of the ship's company
were tumultuously busy at the masonry of the try-works,
from which the huge pots had been removed. You would
have almost thought they were pulling down the cursed
Bastille, such wild cries they raised as the now useless
brick and mortar were being hurled into the sea.

Lord and master over all this scene, the captain stood
erect on the ship's elevated quarterdeck, so that the
whole rejoicing drama was full before him, and seemed
merely contrived for his own individual diversion.

And Ahab, he too was standing on his quarterdeck,
shaggy and black, with a stubborn gloom. As the two
ships crossed each other's wakes—one all jubilations for
things passed, the other all forebodings as to things to
come—their two captains in themselves impersonated the
whole striking contrast of the scene.

"Come aboard, come aboard!" cried the gay *Bachelor's*
commander, lifting a glass and a bottle in the air.

"Hast seen the white whale?" gritted Ahab in reply.

"No, only heard of him, but don't believe in him at all,"
said the other good-humoredly. "Come aboard!"

"Thou art too damned jolly. Sail on. Hast lost any men?"

"Not enough to speak of—two islanders, that's all. But come aboard, old hearty, come along. I'll soon take that black from your brow. Come along, will ye (merry's the play). A full ship and homeward-bound!"

"How wondrous familiar is a fool!" muttered Ahab. Then aloud, "Thou art a full ship and homeward-bound, thou say'st. Well then, call me an empty ship, and out-ward-bound. So go thy ways, and I will mine. Forward there! Set all sail, and keep her to the wind!"

And thus while the one ship went cheerily before the breeze, the other stubbornly fought against it. And so the two vessels parted, the crew of the *Pequod* looking with grave lingering glances toward the receding *Bachelor,* but the *Bachelor's* men never heeding their gaze for the lively revelry they were in. And as Ahab leaning over the taffrail eyed the homeward-bound craft, he took from his pocket a small vial of sand, and then looking from the ship to the vial, seemed thereby bringing two remote as-sociations together, for that vial was filled with Nan-tucket soundings.

⚓

CHAPTER 42

The Whale Watch

THE FOUR WHALES slain that evening had died wide
apart—one far to windward, one less distant to leeward,
one ahead, one astern. These last three were brought
alongside ere nightfall, but the windward one could not
be reached until morning. The boat that had killed it lay
by its side all night; and that boat was Ahab's.

The waif pole was thrust upright into the dead whale's
spout-hole, and the lantern hanging from its top cast a
troubled flickering glare upon the black glossy back, and
far out upon the midnight waves, which gently chafed
the whale's broad flank, like soft surf upon a beach.

Ahab and all his boat's crew seemed asleep but the
Parsee. Crouching in the bow he sat watching the sharks

that spectrally played around the whale and tapped the light cedar planks with their tails. A sound like the moaning in squadrons over Asphaltites of unforgiven ghosts of Gomorrah, ran shuddering through the air.

Started from his slumbers Ahab saw the Parsee face to face; and hooped around by the gloom of the night they seemed the last men in a flooded world. "I have dreamed it again," said he.

"Of the hearses? Have I not said, old man, that neither hearse nor coffin can be thine?"

"And who are hearsed that die on the sea?"

"But I said, old man, that ere thou couldst die on this voyage, two hearses must verily be seen by thee on the sea, the first not made by mortal hands, and the visible wood of the last one must be grown in America."

"Aye, aye! A strange sight that, Parsee—a hearse and its plumes floating over the ocean with the waves for the pallbearers. Ha! Such a sight we shall not soon see."

"Believe it or not, thou canst not die till it be seen, old man."

"And what was that saying about thyself?"

"Though it come to the last, I shall still go before thee thy pilot."

"And when thou art so gone before—if that ever befall—then ere I can follow, thou must still appear to me, to pilot me still? Was it not so? Well then did I believe all ye say, oh my pilot! I have here two pledges that I shall yet slay Moby Dick and survive it."

"Take another pledge, old man," said the Parsee, as his

eyes lighted up like fireflies in the gloom—"Hemp only can kill thee."

"The gallows, ye mean. I am immortal then, on land and on sea," cried Ahab with a laugh of derision. "Immortal on land and on sea!"

Both were silent again, as one man. The gray dawn came on and the slumbering crew arose from the boat's bottom, and ere noon the dead whale was brought to the ship.

⚓

CHAPTER 43

The Quadrant

THE SEASON for the Line at length drew near; and every day when Ahab, coming from his cabin, cast his eyes aloft, the vigilant helmsman would ostentatiously handle his spokes. And the eager mariners would quickly run to the braces and stand there with all their eyes centrally fixed on the nailed doubloon, impatient for the order to point the ship's prow for the equator. In good time the order came. It was hard upon high noon, and Ahab, seated in the bows of his high-hoisted boat, was taking his wonted daily observation of the sun to determine his latitude.

Now in that Japanese sea the days in summer are as freshets of effulgences. That unblinkingly vivid Japanese sun seems the blazing focus of the glassy ocean's immeasurable burning-glass. The sky looks lacquered;

clouds there are none; the horizon floats; and this nakedness of unrelieved radiance is as the insufferable splen-
dors of God's throne. Well that Ahab's quadrant was
furnished with colored glasses through which to take
sight of that solar fire. So, swinging his seated form to
the roll of the ship and with his astrological-looking
instrument placed to his eye, he remained in that posture
for some moments to catch the precise instant when the
sun should gain the precise meridian. Meantime, while
his whole attention was absorbed, the Parsee was kneeling beneath him on the ship's deck, and with face thrown
up like Ahab's, was eyeing the same sun with him. Only
the lids of his eyes half hooded their orbs, and his wild
face was subdued to an earthly passionlessness. At length
the desired observation was taken, and with his pencil
upon his ivory leg Ahab soon calculated what his latitude
must be at that precise instant. Then falling into a
moment's reverie, he again looked up toward the sun and
murmured to himself: "Thou sea-mark! Thou high and
mighty Pilot! Thou tellest me truly where I *am*—but
canst thou cast the least hint where I *shall* be? Or canst
thou tell where some other thing besides me is this moment living? Where is Moby Dick? This instant thou must
be eyeing him. These eyes of mine look into the very eye
that is even now beholding him; aye, and into the eye
that is even now equally beholding the objects on the unknown, thither side of thee, thou sun!"

Then gazing at his quadrant, and handling one after
the other its numerous cabalistical contrivances, he pondered again, and muttered: "Foolish toy! Babies' play-

thing of haughty admirals, and commodores, and captains! The world brags of thee, of thy cunning and might. But what after all canst thou do but tell the poor pitiful point where thou thyself happenest to be on this wide planet, and the hand that holds thee. No! Not one jot more! Thou canst not tell where one drop of water or one grain of sand will be tomorrow noon. And yet with thy impotence thou insultest the sun! Science! Curse thee, thou vain toy. And cursed be all the things that cast man's eyes aloft to that heaven, whose live vividness but scorches him, as these old eyes are even now scorched with thy light, O sun! Level by nature to this earth's horizon are the glances of man's eyes, not shot from the crown of his head, as if God had meant him to gaze on his firmament. Curse thee, thou quadrant!"—dashing it to the deck. "No longer will I guide my earthly way by thee. The level ship's compass and the level dead reckoning, by log and by line: *these* shall conduct me, and show me my place on the sea. Aye," lighting from the boat to the deck, "thus I trample on thee, thou paltry thing that feebly pointest on high; thus I split and destroy thee!"

As the frantic old man thus spoke and thus trampled with his live and dead feet, a sneering triumph that seemed meant for Ahab, and a fatalistic despair that seemed meant for himself—these passed over the mute, motionless Parsee's face. Unobserved he rose and glided away; while, awestruck by the aspect of their commander, the seamen clustered together on the forecastle, till Ahab, troubledly pacing the deck, shouted out, "To the braces! Up helm!—square in!"

In an instant the yards swung round; and as the ship half wheeled upon her heel, her three firm-seated graceful masts erectly poised upon her long ribbed hull seemed as the three Horatii pirouetting on one sufficient steed.

Standing between the knightheads Starbuck watched the *Pequod's* tumultuous way, and Ahab's also, as he went lurching along the deck.

"I have sat before the dense coal fire and watched it all aglow, full of its tormented flaming life; and I have seen it wane at last, down, down to dumbest dust. Old man of oceans! Of all this fiery life of thine, what will at length remain but one little heap of ashes!"

"Aye," cried Stubb, "but sea-coal ashes—mind ye that, Mr. Starbuck. Sea coal, not your common charcoal. Well, well. I heard Ahab mutter, 'Here someone thrusts these cards into these old hands of mine, swears that I must play them and no others.' And damn me, Ahab, but thou actest right; live in the game, and die in it!"

CHAPTER 44

⚓

The Candles

WARMEST CLIMES but nurse the cruelest fangs; the tiger of Bengal crouches in spiced groves of ceaseless verdure. Skies the most effulgent but basket the deadliest thunders: gorgeous Cuba knows tornadoes that never swept the tame northern lands. So too, it is, that in these resplendent Japanese seas the mariner encounters the direst of all storms, the typhoon. It will sometimes burst from out that cloudless sky like an exploding bomb upon a dazed and sleepy town.

Toward evening of that day the *Pequod* was torn of her canvas, and bare-poled was left to fight a typhoon which had struck her directly ahead. When darkness came on, sky and sea roared and split with the thunder, and blazed with the lightning that showed the disabled masts fluttering here and there with the rags which the first fury of the tempest had left for its after sport.

Holding by a shroud, Starbuck was standing on the quarterdeck. At every flash of the lightning he glanced aloft to see what additional disaster might have befallen the intricate hamper there, while Stubb and Flask were directing the men in the higher hoisting and firmer lashing of the boats. But all their pains seemed naught. Though lifted to the very top of the cranes, the windward quarter boat (Ahab's) did not escape. A great rolling sea, dashing high up against the reeling ship's high tottering side, stove in the boat's bottom at the stern and left it again, all dripping through like a sieve.

"Bad work, bad work! Mr. Starbuck," said Stubb, regarding the wreck, "but the sea will have its way. Stubb, for one, can't fight it. You see, Mr. Starbuck, a wave has such a great long start before it leaps, all around the world it runs, and then comes the spring! But as for me, all the start I have to meet it is just across the deck here. But never mind. It's all in fun, so the old song says"— (*sings*):

> Oh! jolly is the gale,
> And a joker is the whale,
> A-flourishin' his tail,

Such a funny, sporty, gamy, jesty, joky, hoky-poky lad, is the ocean, oh!

> The scud all a-flyin',
> That's his flip only foamin';
> When he stirs in the spicin',

Such a funny, sporty, gamy, jesty, joky, hoky-poky lad, is the
    ocean, oh!

> Thunder splits the ships,
> But he only smacks his lips,
> A-tastin' of this flip,

Such a funny, sporty, gamy, jesty, joky, hoky-poky lad, is the
    ocean, oh!

"Avast, Stubb," cried Starbuck. "Let the typhoon sing
and strike his harp here in our rigging, but if thou art a
brave man thou wilt hold thy peace."

"But I am not a brave man, never said I was a brave
man. I am a coward, and I sing to keep up my spirits.
And I tell you what it is, Mr. Starbuck, there's no way
to stop my singing in this world but to cut my throat.
And when that's done, ten to one I sing ye the doxology
for a wind-up."

"Madman! Look through my eyes if thou hast none of
thine own."

"What! How can you see better of a dark night than
anybody else, never mind how foolish?"

"Here!" cried Starbuck, seizing Stubb by the shoulder,
and pointing his hand toward the weather bow. Markest
thou not that the gale comes from the eastward, the very
course Ahab is to run for Moby Dick? The very course he
swung to this day noon? Now mark his boat there!
Where is that stove! In the stern sheets, man, where he
is wont to stand—his standpoint is stove, man! Now jump
overboard, and sing away, if thou must!"

"I don't half understand ye; what's in the wind?"

"Yes, yes, round the Cape of Good Hope is the short-
est way to Nantucket," soliloquized Starbuck suddenly,
heedless of Stubb's question. "The gale that now hammers at us to stave us, we can turn it into a fair wind
that will drive us toward home. Yonder, to windward,
all is blackness of doom, but to leeward, homeward—I
see it lightens up there, but not with the lightning."

At that moment in one of the intervals of profound
darkness following the flashes, a voice was heard at his
side, and almost at the same instant a volley of thunder
peals rolled overhead.

"Who's there?"

"Old Thunder!" said Ahab, groping his way along the
bulwarks to his pivot-hole; but suddenly finding his
path made plain to him by elbowed lances of fire.

Now, as the lightning rod to a spire on shore is intended to carry off the perilous fluid into the soil, so
the kindred rod which at sea some ships carry to each
mast is intended to conduct it into the water. But this
conductor must descend to considerable depth that its
end may avoid all contact with the hull. Moreover, if
kept constantly towing there it would be liable to many
mishaps, besides interfering not a little with some of
the rigging and more or less impeding the vessel's way in
the water. Because of all this, the lower parts of a ship's
lightning rods are not always overboard, but are
generally made in long slender links so as to be the
more readily hauled up into the chains outside, or

thrown down into the sea, as occasion may require.

"The rods! the rods!" cried Starbuck to the crew, suddenly admonished to vigilance by the vivid lightning that had just been darting flambeaux, to light Ahab to his post. "Are they overboard? Drop them over, fore and aft. Quick!"

"Avast!" cried Ahab. Let's have fair play here though we be the weaker side. Yet I'll contribute to raise rods on the Himalayas and Andes that all the world may be secured, but out on privileges! Let them be, sir."

"Look aloft!" cried Starbuck. "The St. Elmo's Lights [corpus sancti]! Corposants! The corposants!"

All the yardarms were tipped with a pallid fire. And, touched at each tri-pointed lightning-rod end with three tapering white flames, each of the three tall masts was silently burning in that sulphurous air, like three gigantic wax tapers before an altar.

"Blast the boat! Let it go! cried Stubb at this instant as a swashing sea heaved up under his own little craft, so that its gunwale violently jammed his hand as he was passing a lashing. "Blast it!" But slipping backward on the deck his uplifted eyes caught the flames and immediately shifting his tone, he cried—"The corposants have mercy on us all!"

To sailors, oaths are household words. They will swear in the trance of the calm and in the teeth of the tempest. They will imprecate curses from the topsail-yardarms when most they teeter over to a seething sea. But in all my voyagings seldom have I heard a common oath when

God's burning finger has been laid on the ship, when His *mene, mene, tekel upharsin* has been woven into the shrouds and the cordage.

While this pallidness was burning aloft few words were heard from the enchanted crew, who in one thick cluster stood on the forecastle, all their eyes gleaming in that pale phosphorescence, like a faraway constellation of stars. Relieved against the ghostly light the gigantic jet Negro, Daggoo, loomed up to thrice his real stature, and seemed the black cloud from which the thunder had come. The parted mouth of Tashtego revealed his shark-white teeth, which strangely gleamed as if they too had been tipped by corposants, while lit up by the preternatural light, Queequeg's tattooing burned like Satanic blue flames on his body.

The tableau all waned at last with the pallidness aloft. And once more the *Pequod* and every soul on her decks were wrapped in a pall. A moment or two passed, when Starbuck, going forward, pushed against someone. It was Stubb. "What thinkest thou now, man? I heard thy cry; it was not the same in the song."

"No, no, it wasn't. I said the corposants have mercy on us all, and I hope they will, still. But do they only have mercy on long faces? Have they no bowels for a laugh? And look ye, Mr. Starbuck—but it's too dark to look. Hear me, then. Take that masthead flame we saw for a sign of good luck, for those masts are rooted in a hold that is going to be chock a' block with sperm oil, d'ye see; and so all that sperm will work up into the masts, like sap in a tree. Yes, our three masts will yet be as three spermaceti candles—that's the good promise we saw."

At that moment Starbuck caught sight of Stubb's face slowly beginning to glimmer into sight. Glancing upward, he cried, "See! see!" And once more the high tapering flames were beheld with what seemed redoubled supernaturalness in their pallor.

"The corposants have mercy on us all," cried Stubb again.

At the base of the mainmast, full beneath the doubloon and the flame, the Parsee was kneeling in Ahab's front, but with his head bowed away from him; while near by, from the arched and overhanging rigging where they had just been engaged securing a spar, a number of the seamen arrested by the glare, now cohered together, and hung pendulous, like a knot of numbed wasps from a drooping orchard twig. In various enchanted attitudes, like the standing or stepping or running skeletons in Herculaneum, others remained rooted to the decks; but all their eyes upcast.

"Aye, aye, men!" cried Ahab. "Look up at it; mark it well; the white flame but lights the way to the white whale! Hand me those mainmast links there; I would fain feel this pulse, and let mine beat against it, blood against fire! So." Then turning—the last link held fast in his left hand, he put his foot upon the Parsee, and with fixed upward eye and high-flung right arm, he stood erect before the lofty tri-pointed flames.

"Oh! thou clear spirit of clear fire, whom on these seas I as Persian once did worship till in the sacramental act so burned by thee that to this hour I bear the scar, I now know thee, thou clear spirit, and I know that thy right worship is defiance. To neither love nor reverence wilt thou be kind; and e'en for hate thou canst but kill, and all are killed. No fearless fool now fronts thee. I own thy speechless, placeless power; but to the last gasp of my earthquake life will dispute its unconditional, unintegral mastery in me. In the midst of the personified impersonal, a personality stands here. Though but a point at best, whencesoe'er I came, wheresoe'er I go, yet while I earthly live the queenly personality lives in me, and feels her royal rights. But war is pain and hate is woe. Come in thy lowest form of love and I will kneel and kiss thee; but at thy highest, come as mere supernal power. And though thou launchest navies of full-frighted worlds, there's that in here that still remains indifferent. Oh thou clear spirit, of thy fire thou madest me, and like a true child of fire I breathe it back to thee."

[*Sudden, repeated flashes of lightning; the nine flames leap to thrice their previous height; Ahab, with the rest, closes his eyes, his right hand pressed hard upon them.*]

"I own thy speechless, placeless power. Said I not so? Nor was it wrung from me; nor do I now drop these links. Thou canst blind, but I can then grope. Thou canst consume, but I can then be ashes. Take the homage of these poor eyes and shutter-hands. I would not take it. The lightning flashes through my skull; mine eyeballs ache and ache; my whole beaten brain seems as beheaded and rolling on some stunning ground. Oh, oh! Yet blindfolded, yet will I talk to thee. Light though thou be, thou leapest out of darkness; but I am darkness leaping out of light, leaping out of thee! The javelins cease; open eyes; see, or not? There burn in the flames! Oh, thou magnanimous! Now I do glory in my genealogy. But thou art but my fiery father; my sweet mother, I know not. Oh, cruel! What hast thou done with her? There lies my puzzle, but thine is greater. Thou knowest not how came ye, hence callest thyself unbegotten; I certainly knowest not thy beginning, hence callest thyself unbegun. I know that of me which thou knowest not of thyself, oh thou omniscient! There is some unsuffusing thing beyond thee, thou clear spirit, to whom all thy eternity is but time, all thy creativeness mechanical. Through thee, thy flaming self, my scorched eyes do dimly see it. Oh, thou foundling fire, thou hermit immemorial, thou too hast thy incommunicable riddle, thy unparticipated grief. Here again with haughty agony I read my sire. Leap! Leap up and lick the sky! I leap with thee; I burn with thee, would fain be welded with thee. Defyingly I worship thee!"

"The boat! The boat!" cried Starbuck. "Look at thy boat, old man!"

Ahab's harpoon, the one forged at Perth's fire, remained firmly lashed in its conspicuous crotch, so that it projected beyond his whaleboat's bow. But the sea that stove its bottom had caused the loose leather sheath to drop off, and from the keen steel barb there now came a leveled flame of pale forked fire. As the silent harpoon burned there like a serpent's tongue, Starbuck grasped Ahab by the arm. "God, God is against thee, old man;

forbear! 'Tis an ill voyage! Ill begun, ill continued; let me square the yards while we may, old man, and make a fair wind of it homeward, to go on a better voyage than this."

Overhearing Starbuck, the panic-stricken crew instantly ran to the braces—though not a sail was left aloft. For the moment all the aghast mate's thoughts seemed theirs; they raised a half mutinous cry. But dashing the rattling lightning links to the deck and snatching the burning harpoon, Ahab waved it like a torch among them, swearing to transfix with it the first sailor that but cast loose a rope's end. Petrified by his aspect, and still more shrinking from the fiery dart that he held, the men fell back in dismay, and Ahab again spoke:

"All your oaths to hunt the white whale are as binding as mine, and heart, soul and body, lungs and life, old Ahab is bound. And that ye may know to what tune this heart beats, look ye here: thus I blow out the last fear!" And with one blast of his breath he extinguished the flame.

As in the hurricane that sweeps the plain, men fly the neighborhood of some lone, gigantic elm, whose height and strength but render it so much the more unsafe because so much the more a mark for thunderbolts, so at those last words of Ahab's many of the mariners did run from him in a terror of dismay.

⚓

CHAPTER 45

The Deck

Toward the end of the first night watch
(Ahab standing by the helm. Starbuck approaching him.)

W E MUST SEND DOWN the maintopsail yard, sir. The band is working loose, and the lee lift is half stranded. Shall I strike it, sir?"

"Strike nothing; lash it. If I had skysail poles I'd sway them up now."

"Sir?—in God's name!—sir?"

"Well."

"The anchors are working, sir. Shall I get them inboard?"

"Strike nothing and stir nothing, but lash everything. The wind rises, but it has not got up to my tablelands yet. Quick and see to it. By masts and keels! He takes me for the hunchbacked skipper of some coasting smack. Send down my maintopsail yard! Ho, gluepots! Loftiest trucks were made for wildest winds, and this brain-truck of mine now sails amid the cloud scud. Shall I strike that? Oh, none but cowards send down their brain-trucks in tempest time. What a hooroosh aloft there! I would e'en take it for sublime, did I not know that the colic is a noisy malady. Oh, take medicine, take medicine!"

⚓

CHAPTER 46

Midnight—The Forecastle Bulwarks

(Stubb and Flask mounted on them, and passing additional lashings over the anchors hanging there.)

No, STUBB; you may pound that knot there as much as you please, but you will never pound into me what you were just now saying. And how long ago is it since you said the very contrary? Didn't you once say that whatever ship Ahab sails in, that ship should pay something extra on its insurance policy, just as though it were loaded with powder barrels aft and boxes of lucifers forward? Stop now, didn't you say so?"

"Well, suppose I did? What then? I've part changed my flesh since that time, why not my mind? Besides, supposing we *are* loaded with powder barrels aft and lucifers forward, how the devil could the lucifers get afire in this drenching spray here? Why, my little man, you have pretty red hair, but you couldn't get afire now. Shake yourself! You're Aquarius, or the water bearer, Flask. You might fill pitchers at your coat collar. Don't you see, then, that for these extra risks the marine insurance companies have extra guarantees? Here are hydrants, Flask. But hark again, and I'll answer ye the other thing. First take your leg off the crown of the anchor here, though, so I can pass the rope. Now listen. What's the mighty difference between holding a mast's lightning rod in the storm, and standing close by a mast that hasn't got any lightning rod at all in a storm? Don't you see, you timberhead, that no harm can come to the holder of the rod, unless the mast is first struck? What are you talking about, then? Not one ship in a hundred carries rods, and Ahab—aye, man, and all of us—were in no more danger then, in my poor opinion, than all the crews in ten thousand ships now sailing the seas. Why, you King Post, you, I suppose you would have every man in the world go about with a small lightning rod running up the corner of his hat, like a militia officer's skewered feather, and trailing behind like his sash. Why don't ye be sensible, Flask? It's easy to be sensible; why don't ye, then? Any man with half an eye can be sensible."

"I don't know that, Stubb. You sometimes find it rather hard."

"Yes, when a fellow's soaked through, it's hard to be sensible; that's a fact. And I am about drenched with this spray. Never mind; catch the turn there, and pass it.

Seems to me we are lashing down these anchors now as if they were never going to be used again. Tying these two anchors here, Flask, seems like tying a man's hands behind him. And what big generous hands they are, to be sure. These are your iron fists, hey? What a hold they have, too! I wonder, Flask, whether the world is anchored anywhere; if she is, she swings with an uncommon long cable, though. There, hammer that knot down, and we've done. So. Next to touching land, lighting on deck is the most satisfactory. I say, just wring out my jacket skirts, will ye? Thank ye. They laugh at long togs so, Flask. But it seems to me a long-tailed coat ought always to be worn in all storms afloat. The tails tapering down that way serve to carry off the water, d'ye see. Same with cocked hats; the cocks form gable-end eave troughs, Flask. No more monkey jackets and tarpaulins for me; I must mount a swallowtail and drive down a beaver, so! Halloa! Whew! there goes my tarpaulin overboard. Lord, Lord, that the winds that come from heaven should be so unmannerly! This is a nasty night, lad."

CHAPTER 47

⚓

The Musket

DURING the most violent shocks of the typhoons, the man at the *Pequod's* jawbone tiller had several times been reelingly hurled to the deck by its spasmodic motions, even though preventor tackles had been attached to it—for they were slack, because some play to the tiller was indispensable.

In a severe gale like this, while the ship is but a tossed shuttlecock to the blast, it is by no means uncommon to see the needles in the compasses, at intervals, go round and round. It was thus with the *Pequod's;* at almost every shock the helmsman had not failed to notice the whirling velocity with which they revolved upon the cards; it is a sight that hardly anyone can behold without some sort of unwonted emotion.

Some hours after midnight the typhoon abated so

much, that through the strenuous exertions of Starbuck
and Stubb—one engaged forward and the other aft—the
shivered remnants of the jib and fore and main topsails
were cut adrift from the spars and went eddying away
to leeward, like the feathers of an albatross, which sometimes are cast to the winds when that storm-tossed bird
is on the wing.

The three corresponding new sails were now bent and
reefed and a storm-trysail was set further aft, so that the
ship soon went through the water with some precision
again. The course—for the present, east-southeast—
which he was to steer, if practicable, was once more
given to the helmsman. For during the violence of the
gale he had only steered according to its vicissitudes. But
he was now bringing the ship as near her course as possible, watching the compass meanwhile, lo! A good sign!
The wind seemed to be coming around astern; aye, the
foul breeze became fair!

Instantly the yards were squared to the lively song of
"*Ho! the fair wind! oh-he-yo, cheerily, men!*" the crew
singing for joy that so promising an event should so soon
have falsified the evil portents preceding it.

In compliance with the standing order of his commander—to report immediately, and at every one of the
twenty-four hours, any decided change in the affairs of
the deck—Starbuck had no sooner trimmed the yards to
the breeze, however reluctantly and gloomily, than he
mechanically went below to appraise Captain Ahab of
the circumstance.

Ere knocking at his stateroom he involuntarily paused

before it a moment. The cabin lamp, taking long swings this way and that, was burning fitfully and casting fitful shadows upon the old man's bolted door—a thin one with fixed blinds inserted in place of upper panels. The isolated subterraneousness of the cabin made a certain humming silence to reign there, though it was hooped around by all the roar of the elements. The loaded muskets in the rack were shiningly revealed as they stood upright against the forward bulkhead. Starbuck was an honest, upright man. But out of Starbuck's heart at that instant when he saw the muskets there strangely evolved an evil thought, but so blended with its neutral or good accompaniments that for the instant he hardly knew it for itself.

"He would have shot me once," he murmured. "Yes, there's the very musket that he pointed at me—that one with the studded stock; let me touch it—lift it. Strange that I, who have handled so many deadly lances, strange that I should shake so now. Loaded? I must see. Aye, aye, and powder in the pan—that's not good. Best spill it? Wait, I'll cure myself of this. I'll hold the musket boldly while I think—I come to report a fair wind to him. But how fair? Fair for death and doom, *that's* fair for Moby Dick. It's a fair wind that's only fair for that accursed fish. The very tube he pointed at me! The very one, *this* one—I hold it here. He would have killed me with the very thing I handle now. Aye, and he would fain kill all his crew. Does he not say he will not strike his spars to any gale? Has he not dashed his heavenly quadrant? And in these same perilous seas gropes he not his way by mere dead reckoning of the error-abounding log? And in this very typhoon, did he not swear that he would have no lightning rods?

"But shall this crazed old man be tamely suffered to drag a whole ship's company down to doom with him? Yes, it would make him the wilful murderer of thirty men and more if this ship comes to any deadly harm; and come to deadly harm my soul swears this ship will, if Ahab have his way. If, then, he were this instant—put aside, that crime would not be his. Ha! Is he muttering in his sleep? Yes, just there—in there, he's sleeping. Sleeping? Aye, but still alive, and soon awake again. I can't withstand thee, then, old man. Not reasoning, not remonstrance, not entreaty wilt thou hearken to; all this thou scornest. Flat obedience to thy own flat commands, this is all thou breathest. Aye, and say'st the men have vowed thy vow; say'st all of us are Ahabs. Great God forbid!

"But is there no other way? No lawful way? Make him a prisoner to be taken home? What! Hope to wrest this old man's living power from his own living hands? Only a fool would try it. Say he were pinioned even, knotted all over with ropes and hawsers, chained down to ringbolts on this cabin floor; he would be more hideous than a caged tiger, then. I could not endure the sight, could not possibly fly his howlings. All comfort, sleep itself, inestimable reason would leave me on the long intolerable voyage. What then remains? The land is hundreds of leagues away, and locked Japan the nearest. I stand alone here upon an open sea with two oceans and a whole con-

tinent between me and law. Aye, aye, 'tis so. Is heaven
a murderer when its lightning strikes a would-be murderer in his bed, tindering sheets and skin together?
And would I be a murderer, then, if——" and slowly,
stealthily, and half sideways looking, he placed the
loaded musket's end against the door.

"On this level, Ahab's hammock swings within, his
head this way. A touch, and Starbuck may survive to hug
his wife and child again. Oh, Mary! Mary! Boy! boy! boy!
But if I wake thee not to death, old man, who can tell to
what unsounded deeps Starbuck's body this day week
may sink, with all the crew! Great God, where art thou?
Shall I? shall I——

"The wind has gone down and shifted, sir; the fore and
main topsails are reefed and set; she heads her course."

"Stern all! Oh, Moby Dick, I clutch thy heart at last!"

Such were the sounds that now came hurtling from
out the old man's tormented sleep, as if Starbuck's voice
had caused the long dumb dream to speak.

The yet leveled musket shook like a drunkard's arm
against the panel. Starbuck seemed wrestling with an
angel, but turning from the door, he placed the death-
tube in its rack and left the place.

"He's too sound asleep, Mr. Stubb. Go thou down and
wake him, and tell him. I must see to the deck here. Thou
know'st what to say."

⚓

CHAPTER 48

The Needle

NEXT MORNING the not yet subsided sea rolled in long slow billows of mighty bulk, and striving in the *Pequod's* gurgling track, pushed her on like giant palms outspread. The strong unstaggering breeze abounded so that sky and air seemed vast outbellying sails; the whole world boomed before the wind. Muffled in the full morning light, the invisible sun was only known by the spread intensity of his place, where his bayonet rays moved on in stacks. Emblazonings, as of crowned Babylonian kings and queens, reigned over everything. The sea was as a crucible of molten gold that bubblingly leaps with light and heat.

Long maintaining an enchanted silence, Ahab stood apart; and every time the teetering ship loweringly pitched down her bowsprit, he turned to eye the bright sun's rays produced ahead; and when she profoundly settled by the stern, he turned behind and saw the sun's rearward place, and how the same yellow rays were blending with his undeviating wake.

"Ha, ha, my ship! thou mightest well be taken now for the sea-chariot of the sun. Ho, ho! all ye nations before my prow, I bring the sun to ye! Yoke on the further billows; hallo! A-tandem, I drive the sea!"

But suddenly reigned back by some counter thought, he hurried toward the helm, huskily demanding how the ship was heading.

"East-sou' east, sir," said the frightened steersman.

"Thou liest!" smiting him with his clenched fist. "Heading east at this hour in the morning, and the sun astern?"

Upon this every soul was confounded; for the phenomenon just then observed by Ahab had unaccountably escaped every one else; but its very blinding palpableness must have been the cause.

Thrusting his head halfway into the binnacle Ahab caught one glimpse of the compass; his uplifted arm slowly fell; for a moment he almost seemed to stagger. Standing behind him Starbuck looked, and lo! The two compasses pointed east, yet the *Pequod* was as infallibly going west.

But ere the first wild alarm could get out abroad among the crew the old man with a rigid laugh exclaimed, "I have it! It has happened before. Mr. Starbuck, last night's thunder turned our compasses; that's all. Thou hast before now heard of such a thing, I take it."

"Aye; but never before has it happened to me, sir," said the pale mate, gloomily.

Here, it must needs be said that accidents like this have in more than one case occurred to ships in violent storms. The magnetic energy as developed in the mariner's needle is, as all know, essentially one with the electricity beheld in heaven; hence it is not to be much marveled at that such things should be. In instances where the lightning has actually struck the vessel, so as to smite down some of the spars and rigging, the effect upon the needle has at times been still more fatal; all its loadstone virtue being annihilated, so that the before magnetic steel was of no more use than an old wife's knitting needle. But in either case, the needle never again of itself recovers the original virtue thus marred or lost; and if the binnacle compasses be affected, the same fate reaches all the others that may be in the ship, even were the lowermost one inserted into the kelson.

Deliberately standing before the binnacle and eyeing the transpointed compasses, the old man, with the sharp of his extended hand, now took the precise bearing of the sun, and satisfied that the needles were exactly inverted, shouted out his orders for the ship's course to be changed accordingly. The yards were hard up; and once more the *Pequod* thrust her undaunted bows into the opposing wind, for the supposed fair one had only been juggling her.

Meanwhile, whatever were his own secret thoughts, Starbuck said nothing, but quietly he issued all requisite orders; while Stubb and Flask—who in some small degree seemed then to be sharing his feelings—likewise unmurmuringly acquiesced. As for the men, though some of them lowly rumbled, their fear of Ahab was greater than their fear of Fate. But as ever before, the pagan harpooneers remained almost wholly unimpressed; or if impressed, it was only with a certain magnetism shot into their congenial hearts from inflexible Ahab's.

For a space the old man walked the deck in rolling reveries. But chancing to slip with his ivory heel, he saw the crushed copper sight-tubes of the quadrant he had the day before dashed to the deck.

"Thou poor, proud heaven-gazer and sun's pilot! Yesterday I wrecked thee, and today the compasses would feign have wrecked me. So, so. But Ahab is lord over the level loadstone yet. Mr. Starbuck—a lance without a pole, top-maul, and the smallest of the sailmaker's needles. Quick!"

Accessory, perhaps, to the impulse dictating the thing he was now about to do were certain prudential motives, whose object might have been to revive the spirits of his crew by a stroke of his subtle skill in a matter so wondrous as that of the inverted compasses. Besides, the old man well knew that to steer by transpointed needles, though clumsily practicable, was not a thing to be passed over by superstitious sailors without some shudderings and evil portents.

"Men," said he, steadily turning upon the crew as the mate handed him the things he had demanded, "my men, the thunder turned old Ahab's needles; but out of this bit of steel Ahab can make one of his own that will point as true as any."

Abashed glances of servile wonder were exchanged

by the sailors, as this was said; and with fascinated eyes they waited whatever magic might follow. But Starbuck looked away.

With a blow from the top-maul Ahab knocked off the steel head of the lance, and then handing to the mate the long iron rod remaining, bade him hold it upright, without its touching the deck. Then, with the maul, after repeatedly smiting the upper end of this iron rod, he placed the blunted needle endwise on the top of it, and less strongly hammered that, several times, the mate still holding the rod as before. Then going through some small strange motions with it—whether indispensable to the magnetizing of the steel or merely intended to augment the awe of the crew is uncertain—he called for linen thread; and moving to the binnacle, slipped out the two reversed needles there and horizontally suspended the sail-needle by its middle, over one of the compass-cards. At first the steel went round and round, quivering and vibrating at either end; but at last it settled to its place. Then Ahab, who had been intently watching for this result, stepped frankly back from the binnacle, and pointing his stretched arm toward it, exclaimed, "Look ye for yourselves, if Ahab be not lord of the level loadstone! The sun is east and that compass swears it!"

One after another the crew peered in, for nothing but their own eyes could persuade such ignorance as theirs, and one after another they slunk away.

In his fiery eyes of scorn and triumph you then saw Ahab in all his fatal pride.

⚓

CHAPTER 49

The Log and Line

WHILE NOW the fated *Pequod* had been so long afloat this voyage, the log and line had but very seldom been in use. Owing to a confident reliance upon other means of determining the vessel's place some merchantmen and many whalemen, especially when cruising, wholly neglect to heave the log; at the same time, frequently more for form's sake than anything else, regularly putting down upon the customary slate the course steered by the ship, as well as the presumed average rate of progression every hour. It had been thus with the *Pequod*. The wooden reel and angular log attached hung, long untouched, just beneath the railing of the after bulwarks. Rains and spray had damped it; sun and wind had warped it; all the elements had combined to rot a thing that hung so idly. But heedless of all this, his mood seized Ahab as he happened to glance upon the reel, not many hours after the magnet scene. He remembered how his quadrant was no more and recalled his frantic oath about the level log and line. The ship was sailing plungingly; astern the billows rolled in riots.

"Forward, there! Heave the log!"

Two seamen came. The golden-hued Tahitian and the grizzly Manxman. "Take the reel, one of ye. I'll heave."

They went toward the extreme stern on the ship's lee-side, where the deck with the oblique energy of the wind was now almost dipping into the creamy, sidelong-rushing sea.

The Manxman took the reel, and holding it high up by the projecting handle-ends of the spindle around which the spool of line revolved, so stood with the angular log hanging downward, until Ahab advanced to him.

Ahab stood before him, and was lightly unwinding some thirty or forty turns to form a preliminary hand-coil to toss overboard when the old Manxman, who was intently eyeing both him and the line, made bold to speak.

"Sir, I mistrust it. This line looks far gone. Long heat and wet have spoiled it."

" 'Twill hold, old gentleman. Long heat and wet, have they spoiled thee? Thou seem'st to hold. Or, truer perhaps, life holds thee, not thou it."

"I hold the spool, sir. But just as my captain says. With these gray hairs of mine 'tis not worth while disputing, specially with a superior who'll ne'er confess."

"What's that? There's now a patched professor in

Queen Nature's granite-founded college; but methinks
he's too subservient. Where wert thou born?"

"In the little rocky Isle of Man, sir."

"Excellent! Thou'st hit the world by that."

"I know not, sir, but I was born there."

"In the Isle of Man, hey? Well, the other way, it's good.
Here's a man from Man; a man born in once independent
Man, and now unmanned of Man, which is sucked in—
by what? Up with the reel! The dead blind wall butts all
inquiring heads at last. Up with it! So."

The log was heaved. The loose coils rapidly straightened out in long dragging line astern, and then instantly
the reel began to whirl. In turn, jerkingly raised and lowered by the rolling billows, the towering resistance of the
log caused the old reelman to stagger strangely.

"Hold hard!"

Snap! The overstrained line sagged down in one long
festoon; the tugging log was gone.

"I crush the quadrant, the thunder turns the needles,
and now the mad sea parts the log line. But Ahab can
mend all. Haul in here, in, Tahitian. Reel up, Manxman.
And look ye, let the carpenter make another log, and
mend thou the line. See to it."

"There he goes now. To him nothing's happened, but
to me the skewer seems loosening out of the middle of
the world. Haul in, haul in, Tahitian. These lines run
whole and whirling out, come in broken and dragging
slow. Ha, Pip! Come to help, eh, Pip?"

"Pip? Whom call ye Pip? Pip jumped from the whaleboat. Pip's missing. Let's see now if we haven't fished him

up here, fishermen. It drags hard; I guess he's holding on. Jerk him, Tahiti! Jerk him off; we haul in no cowards here. Ho! There's his arm just breaking water. A hatchet! a hatchet! Cut it off—we haul in no cowards here. Captain Ahab! Sir, sir! Here's Pip trying to get on board again."

"Peace, thou crazy loon," cried the Manxman, seizing him by the arm. "Away from the quarterdeck!"

"The greater idiot ever scolds the lesser," muttered Ahab, advancing. "Hands off from that holiness! Where sayest thou Pip was, boy?"

"Astern there, sir, astern! Lo, lo!"

"And who art thou, boy? I see not my reflection in the vacant pupils of thy eyes. Oh God! That man should be a thing for immortal souls to sieve through! Who art thou, boy?"

"Bell-boy, sir; ship's-crier; ding, dong, ding! Pip! Pip! Pip! One hundred pounds of clay reward for Pip; five feet high—looks cowardly—quickest known by that! Ding, dong, ding! Who's seen Pip the coward?"

"There can be no hearts above the snowline. Oh, ye frozen heavens! look down here. Ye did beget this luckless child, and have abandoned him, ye creative libertines. Here, boy; Ahab's cabin shall be Pip's home henceforth, while Ahab lives. Thou touchest my inmost center, boy; thou art tied to me by cords woven of my heartstrings. Come, let's down."

"What's this? Here's velvet sharkskin,"—intently gazing at Ahab's hand and feeling it. "Ah now, had poor Pip but felt so kind a thing as this, perhaps he had ne'er been lost! This seems to me, sir, as a man-rope, something that weak souls may hold by. Oh, sir, let old Perth now come and rivet these two hands together, the black one with the white, for I will not let this go."

"Oh, boy, nor will I thee, unless I should thereby drag thee to worse horrors than are here. Come, then, to my cabin. Lo! Ye believers in gods all goodness, and in man all ill, lo, you! See the omniscient gods oblivious of suffering man; and man, though idiotic and knowing not what he does, yet full of the sweet things of love and gratitude. Come! I feel prouder leading thee by thy black hand, than though I grasped an emperor's!"

"There go two daft ones now," muttered the old Manxman. "One daft with strength, the other daft with weakness. But here's the end of the rotten line—all dripping too. Mend it, eh? I think we had best have a new line altogether. I'll see Mr. Stubb about it."

⚓

CHAPTER 50

The Life Buoy

STEERING now southeastward by Ahab's leveled steel, and her progress solely determined by Ahab's level log and line; the *Pequod* held on her path toward the equator. Making so long a passage through such unfrequented waters, descrying no ships, and ere long, sideways impelled by unvarying trade winds over waves monotonously mild; all these seemed the strange calm things preluding some riotous and desperate scene.

At last, when the ship drew near to the outskirts, as it were, of the equatorial fishing-ground, and in the deep darkness that goes before the dawn was sailing by a cluster of rocky islets, the watch—then headed by Flask —was startled by a cry so plaintively wild and unearthly, like half-articulated wailings of the ghosts of all Herod's murdered innocents, that one and all they started from

their reveries, and for the space of some moments stood
or sat or leaned all transfixedly listening, like the carved
Roman slave, while that wild cry remained within hearing. The Christian or civilized part of the crew said it was
mermaids, and shuddered, but the pagan harpooneers remained unappalled. Yet the gray Manxman—the oldest
mariner of all—declared that the wild thrilling sounds
that were heard were the voices of newly drowned men
in the sea.

Below in his hammock, Ahab did not hear of this until
gray dawn when he came to the deck; it was then recounted to him by Flask not unaccompanied with hinted
dark meanings. He hollowly laughed, and thus explained
the wonder.

Those rocky islands the ship had passed were the re-
sort of great numbers of seals, and some young seals that
had lost their dams, or some dams that had lost their
cubs, must have risen nigh the ship and kept company
with her, crying and sobbing with their human sort of
wail. But this only the more affected some of them, because most mariners cherish a very superstitious feeling
about seals, arising not only from their peculiar tones
when in distress, but also from the human look of their
round heads and semi-intelligent faces, seen peeringly
uprising from the water alongside. In the sea, under certain circumstances, seals have more than once been mistaken for men.

But the bodings of the crew were destined to receive
a most plausible confirmation in the fate of one of their

number that morning. At sunrise this man went from his hammock to his masthead at the fore; and whether it was that he was not yet half waked from his sleep (for sailors sometimes go aloft in a transition state), whether it was thus with the man there is now no telling; but, be that as it may, he had not been long at his perch when a cry was heard—a cry and a rushing—and looking up, they saw a falling phantom in the air, and looking down, a little tossed heap of white bubbles in the blue of the sea.

The life buoy—a long slender cask—was dropped from the stern where it always hung obedient to a cunning spring, but no hand rose to seize it, and the sun having long beat upon this cask it had shrunken, so that it slowly filled, and the parched wood also filled at its every pore, and the studded iron bound cask followed the sailor to the bottom, as if to yield him his pillow, though in sooth but a hard one.

And thus the first man of the *Pequod* that mounted the mast to look out for the white whale, on the white whale's own peculiar ground, that man was swallowed up in the deep. But few, perhaps, thought of that at the time. Indeed, in some sort, they were not grieved at this event, at least as a portent; for they regarded it, not as a foreshadowing of evil in the future, but as the fulfilment of an evil already presaged. They declared that now they knew the reason of those wild shrieks they had heard the night before. But again the old Manxman said nay.

The lost life buoy was now to be replaced. Starbuck was directed to see to it, but no cask of sufficient light-

ness could be found, and in the feverish eagerness of
what seemed the approaching crisis of the voyage, all
hands were impatient of any toil but what was directly
connected with its final end, whatever that might prove
to be. Therefore, they were going to leave the ship's stern
unprovided with a buoy, when by certain strange signs
and innuendoes Queequeg hinted a hint concerning his
coffin.

"A life buoy of a coffin!" cried Starbuck, staring.

"Rather queer, that, I should say," said Stubb.

"It will make a good enough one," said Flask, "the carpenter here can arrange it easily."

"Bring it up; there's nothing else for it," said Starbuck,
after a melancholy pause. "Rig it, carpenter; do not look
at me so—the coffin, I mean. Dost thou hear me? Rig it."

"And shall I nail down the lid, sir?" moving his hand
as with a hammer.

"Aye."

"And shall I caulk the seams, sir?" moving his hand as
with a caulking-iron.

"Aye."

"And shall I then pay over the same with pitch, sir?"
moving his hand as with a pitch-pot.

"Away! What possesses thee to this? Make a life buoy
of the coffin, and no more—Mr. Stubb, Mr. Flask, come
forward with me."

"He goes off in a huff. The whole he can endure; at the
parts he baulks. Now I don't like this. I make a leg for
Captain Ahab, and he wears it like a gentleman; but I

make a bandbox for Queequeg, and he won't put his head into it. Are all my pains to go for nothing with that coffin? And now I'm ordered to make a life buoy of it. It's like turning an old coat; going to bring the flesh on the other side now. I don't like this cobbling sort of business—I don't like it at all; it's undignified; it's not my place. Let tinkers' brats do tinkerings; we are their betters. I like to take in hand none but clean, virgin, fair-and-square mathematical jobs, something that regularly begins at the beginning, and is at the middle when midway, and comes to an end at the conclusion; not a cobbler's job, that's at an end in the middle, and at the beginning at the end. It's the old woman's tricks to be giving cobbling jobs. Lord! what an affection all old women have for tinkers. I know an old woman of sixty-five who ran away with a baldheaded young tinker once. And that's the reason I never would work for lonely widow old women ashore, when I kept my job-shop in the Vineyard; they might have taken it into their lonely old heads to run off with me. But heigh-ho! There are no caps at sea but snowcaps.

"Let me see. Nail down the lid; caulk the seams; pay over the same with pitch; batten them down tight, and hang it with the snap-spring over the ship's stern. Were ever such things done before with a coffin? Some superstitious old carpenters now, would be tied up in the rigging ere they would do the job. But I'm made of knotty Aroostook hemlock; I don't budge. Cruppered with a coffin! Sailing about with a graveyard tray! But never

mind. I'll do the job, now, tenderly. I'll have me—let's see
—how many in the ship's company, all told? But I've forgotten. Anyway, I'll have me thirty separate, Turk's-
headed lifelines, each three feet long hanging all around
to the coffin. Then, if the hull go down, there'll be thirty
lively fellows all fighting for one coffin, a sight not seen
very often beneath the sun! Come hammer, caulking-
iron, pitch-pot and marlinspike! Let's to it."

CHAPTER 51

⚓

The *Pequod* Meets the *Rachel*

EXT DAY a large ship, the *Rachel*, was descried, bearing directly down upon the *Pequod*, all her spars thickly clustering with men. At the time the *Pequod* was making good speed through the water; but as the broad-winged windward stranger shot nigh to her, the boastful sails all fell together as blank bladders that are burst, and all life fled from the smitten hull.

"Bad news, she brings bad news," muttered the old Manxman; but ere her commander, who, with trumpet to mouth, stood up in his boat, ere he could hopefully hail, Ahab's voice was heard.

"Hast seen the white whale?"

"Aye, yesterday. Have ye seen a whaleboat adrift?"

Throttling his joy, Ahab negatively answered this unexpected question, and would then have fain boarded the stranger when the stranger captain himself, having stopped his vessel's way, was seen descending her side. A few keen pulls, and his boathook soon clinched the *Pequod's* main-chains, and he sprang to the deck. Immediately he was recognized by Ahab for a Nantucketer he knew. But no formal salutation was exchanged.

"Where was he? Not killed!—not killed!" cried Ahab, closely advancing. "How was it?"

It seemed that somewhat late on the afternoon of the day previous, while three of the stranger's boats were engaged with a shoal of whales which had led them some four or five miles from the ship, and while they were yet in swift chase to windward, the white hump and head of Moby Dick had suddenly loomed up out of the blue water, not very far to leeward. Thereupon the fourth rigged boat—a reserved one—had been instantly lowered in chase. After a keen sail before the wind, this fourth boat—the swiftest keeled of all—seemed to have succeeded in fastening (at least as well as a man at the masthead could tell anything about it). In the distance he saw the diminished dotted boat, and then a swift gleam of bubbling white water, and after that nothing more. Whence it was concluded that the stricken whale must have indefinitely run away with his pursuers, as often happens. There was some apprehension, but no positive alarm as yet. The recall signals were placed in the rigging; darkness came on. And, forced to pick up her three far to windward boats ere going in quest of the fourth one in the precisely opposite direction, the ship had not only been necessitated to leave that boat to its fate till

near midnight, but for the time, to increase her distance
from it. But the rest of her crew being at last safe aboard,
she crowded all sail—stunsail on stunsail—after the missing boat, kindling a fire in her try-pots for a beacon; and
every man aloft on the lookout. But though when she
had thus sailed a sufficient distance to gain the presumed
place of the absent ones when last seen—though she then
paused to lower her spare boats to pull all around her,
and not finding anything, had again dashed on; again
paused and lowered her boats; and though she had thus
continued doing till daylight; yet not the least glimpse
of the missing keel had been seen.

The story told, the stranger captain immediately went
on to reveal his object in boarding the *Pequod*. He desired that ship to unite with his own in the search, by
sailing over the sea some four or five miles apart, on
parallel lines, and so sweeping a double horizon, as it
were.

"I will wager something now," whispered Stubb to
Flask, "that someone in that missing boat wore off that
captain's best coat, mayhap his watch—he's so cursed
anxious to get it back. Who ever heard of two pious
whaleships cruising after one missing whaleboat in the
height of the whaling season? See, Flask, only see how
pale he looks—pale in the very buttons of his eyes—look
—it wasn't the coat—it must have been the——"

"My boy, my own boy is among them. For God's sake
—I beg, I conjure"—here exclaimed the stranger captain
to Ahab, who thus far had but icily received his petition.
"For eight-and-forty hours let me charter your ship—I

will gladly pay for it, and roundly pay for it, if there be no other way. For eight-and-forty hours only—only that —you must, oh, you must, and you *shall* do this thing."

"His son!" cried Stubb, "oh, it's his son he's lost! I take back the coat and watch—what says Ahab? We must save that boy."

"He's drowned with the rest on 'em, last night," said the old Manx sailor standing behind them; "I heard; all of ye heard their spirits."

Now, as it shortly turned out, what made this incident of the *Rachel's* the more melancholy, was the circumstance that not only was one of the captain's sons among the number of the missing boat's crew, but among the number of the other boats' crews at the same time, and separated from the ship during the dark vicissitudes of the chase, there had been still another son. So that for a time the wretched father was plunged to the bottom of the cruelest perplexity, which was only solved for him by his chief mate's instinctively adopting the ordinary procedure of a whaleship in such emergencies—that is, when placed between jeopardized but divided boats, always to pick up the majority first. But the captain, for some unknown constitutional reason, had refrained from mentioning all this, and not until forced to it by Ahab's iciness did he allude to his one yet missing boy, a little lad but twelve years old, whose father with the earnest but unmisgiving hardihood of a Nantucketer's paternal love, had thus early sought to initiate him in the perils and wonders of a vocation almost immemorially the destiny of all his race. Nor does it unfrequently occur that Nantucket captains will send a son of such tender age away from them for a protracted three or four years' voyage in some other ship than their own. So that their first knowledge of a whaleman's career shall be unenervated by any chance display of a father's natural but untimely partiality, or undue apprehensiveness and concern.

Meantime now the stranger was still beseeching his poor boon of Ahab; and Ahab still stood like an anvil receiving every shock, but without the least quivering of his own.

"I will not go," said the stranger, "till you say *aye* to me. Do to me as you would have me do to you in the like case. For you too have a boy, Captain Ahab—though but a child, and nestling safely at home now—a child of your old age too. Yes, yes, you relent; I see it—run, run, men, now, and stand by to square in the yards."

"Avast," cried Ahab, "touch not a rope-yarn." Then in a voice that prolongingly molded every word, "Captain Gardiner, I will not do it. Even now I lose time. Good-bye, good-bye. God bless ye, man, and may I forgive myself, but I must go. Mr. Starbuck, look at the binnacle watch, and in three minutes from this present instant warn off all strangers. Then brace forward again, and let the ship sail as before."

Hurriedly turning with averted face, he descended into his cabin, leaving the strange captain transfixed at this unconditional and utter rejection of his so earnest suit. But starting from his enchantment, Gardiner silently hurried to the side, more fell than stepped into his boat, and returned to his ship.

Soon the two ships diverged their wakes; and as long as the strange vessel was in view, she was seen to yaw hither and thither at every dark spot, however small, on the sea. This way and that her yards were swung round; starboard and larboard, she continued to tack; now she beat against a head sea, and again it pushed her before it. Yet all the while her masts and yards were thickly clustered with men, as three tall cherry trees when the boys are cherrying among the boughs.

But by her still halting course and winding woful way, you plainly saw that this ship that so wept with spray, still remained without comfort. She was *Rachel*, weeping for her children because they were not.

⚓

CHAPTER 52

The *Pequod* Meets the *Delight*

THE INTENSE *Pequod* sailed on; the rolling waves and days went by; the life buoy-coffin still lightly swung; and another ship, most miserably misnamed the *Delight*, was descried. As she drew nigh, all eyes were fixed upon her broad beams, called shears, which, in some whaling ships, cross the quarterdeck at the height of eight or nine feet, serving to carry the spare, unrigged or disabled boats.

Upon the stranger's shears were beheld the shattered white ribs, and some few splintered planks, of what had once been a whaleboat. But you now saw through this wreck as plainly as you see through the peeled, half-unhinged and bleaching skeleton of a horse.

"Hast seen the white whale?"

"Look!" replied the hollow-cheeked captain from his

taffrail; and with his trumpet he pointed to the wreck.

"Hast killed him?"

"The harpoon is not yet forged that will ever do that," answered the other, sadly glancing upon a rounded hammock on the deck, whose gathered sides some noiseless sailors were busy in sewing together.

"Not forged!" and snatching Perth's leveled iron from the crotch, Ahab held it out, exclaiming, "Look ye, Nantucketer; here in this hand I hold his death! Tempered in blood, and tempered by lightning are these barbs; and I swear to temper them triply in that hot place behind the fin, where the white whale most feels his accursed life!"

"Then God keep thee, old man—see'st thou that"—pointing to the hammock. "I bury but one of five stout men who were alive only yesterday, but were dead ere night. Only *that* one I bury; the rest were buried before they died; you sail upon their tomb." Then turning to his crew—"Are ye ready there? Place the plank then on the rail, and lift the body; so, then—Oh God!"—advancing toward the hammock with uplifted hands, "may the resurrection and the life——"

"Brace forward! Up helm!" cried Ahab like lightning to his men.

But the suddenly started *Pequod* was not quick enough to escape the sound of the splash that the corpse soon made as it struck the sea; not so quick, indeed, but that some of the flying bubbles might have sprinkled her hull with their ghostly baptism.

As Ahab now glided from the dejected *Delight,* the strange life buoy hanging at the *Pequod's* stern came into conspicuous relief.

"Ha! yonder! Look yonder, men!" cried a foreboding voice in her wake. "In vain, oh, ye strangers, ye fly from our sad burial. Ye but turn us your taffrail to show us your coffin!"

⚓

CHAPTER 53

The Chase—First Day

T HAT NIGHT in the midwatch, when the old man—as his wont at intervals—stepped forth from the scuttle in which he leaned and went to his pivot hole, he suddenly thrust out his face fiercely, snuffing up the sea air as a sagacious ship's dog will in drawing nigh to some barbarous isle. He declared that a whale must be near. Soon that peculiar odor, sometimes to a great distance given forth by the living sperm whale, was palpable to all the watch; nor was any mariner surprised when, after inspecting the compass and then the dogvane, and then ascertaining the precise bearing of the odor as nearly as possible, Ahab rapidly ordered the ship's course to be slightly altered and the sail to be shortened.

The acute policy dictating these movements was sufficiently vindicated at daybreak by the sight of a long sleek on the sea directly and lengthwise ahead, smooth as oil, and resembling in the plaited watery wrinkles bordering it, the polished metalliclike marks of some swift tide rip at the mouth of a deep rapid stream.

"Man the mastheads! Call all hands!"

Thundering with the butts of three clubbed handspikes on the forecastle deck, Daggoo roused the sleepers with such judgment claps that they seemed to exhale from the scuttle, so instantaneously did they appear with their clothes in their hands.

"What d'ye see?" cried Ahab, flattening his face to the sky.

"Nothing, nothing, sir!" was the sound hailing down in reply.

"T'gallant sails! Stunsails alow and aloft, and on both sides!"

All sail being set, he now cast loose the lifeline, reserved for swaying him to the mainroyal masthead; and in a few moments they were hoisting him thither, when, while but two-thirds of the way aloft, and while peering ahead through the horizontal vacancy between the maintopsail and top gallant sail, he raised a gull-like cry in the air. "There she blows!—there she blows! A hump like a snowhill! It is Moby Dick!"

Fired by the cry which seemed simultaneously taken up by the three lookouts, the men on deck rushed to the rigging to behold the famous whale they had so long been pursuing. Ahab had now gained his final perch, some feet above the other lookouts, Tashtego standing just beneath him on the cap of the topgallant mast, so that the Indian's head was almost on a level with Ahab's heel. From this height the whale was now seen some mile or so ahead, at every roll of the sea revealing his high sparkling hump, and regularly jetting his silent spout into the air. To the credulous mariners it seemed the same silent spout they had so long ago beheld in the moonlit Atlantic and Indian Oceans.

"And did none of ye see it before?" cried Ahab, hailing the perched men all around him.

"I saw him almost the same instant, sir, that Captain Ahab did, and I cried out," said Tashtego.

"Not the same instant; not the same—no, the doubloon is mine. Fate reserved the doubloon for me. *I* only; none of ye could have raised the white whale first. There she blows! there she blows!—there she blows! There again! —there again!" he cried, in long-drawn, lingering, methodic tones, attuned to the gradual prolongings of the whale's visible jets. "He's going to sound! In stunsails! Down topgallant sails! Stand by three boats. Mr. Starbuck, remember, stay on board and keep the ship. Helm there! Luff, luff a point! So; steady, man, steady! There go flukes! No, no, only black water! All ready the boats there? Stand by, stand by! Lower me, Mr. Starbuck, lower, lower—quick, quicker!" and he slid through the air to the deck.

"He is heading straight to leeward, sir," cried Stubb, "right away from us, cannot have seen the ship yet."

"Be dumb, man! Stand by the braces! Hard down the

helm!—brace up! Shiver her! shiver her! So; well that!
Boats, boats!"

Soon all the boats but Starbuck's were dropped, all the
boat-sails set—all the paddles plying, with rippling swiftness, shooting to leeward, and Ahab heading the onset.
A pale death-glimmer lit up Fedallah's sunken eyes, a
hideous motion gnawed his mouth.

Like noiseless nautilus shells their light prows sped
through the sea, but only slowly they neared the foe. As
they neared him, the ocean grew still more smooth,
seemed to be drawing a carpet over its waves, seemed a
noon meadow so serenely it spread. At length the breathless hunter came so nigh his seemingly unsuspecting prey
that the whale's entire dazzling hump was distinctly visible, sliding along the sea as if an isolated thing, and continually set in a revolving ring of finest fleecy greenish
foam. He saw the vast involved wrinkles of the slightly
projecting head beyond. Before it, far out on the soft
Turkish-rugged waters, went the glistening white shadows from his broad milky forehead, a musical rippling
playfully accompanying the shade. Behind, the blue
waters interchangeably flowed over into the moving valley of his steady wake, and on either hand bright bubbles
arose and danced by his side. But these were broken
again by the light toes of hundreds of gay fowl softly
feathering the sea, alternate with their fitful flight. And
like to some flagstaff rising from the painted hull of an
argosy, the tall but shattered pole of a recent lance projected from the white whale's back; and at intervals one

of the cloud of soft-toed fowls hovering and to and from skimming like a canopy over the fish, silently perched and rocked on this pole, the long tail feathers streaming like pennons.

A gentle joyousness—a mighty mildness of repose in swiftness, invested the gliding whale. Not the white bull Jupiter swimming away with ravished Europa clinging to his graceful horns, his lovely, leering eyes sideways intent upon the maid, with smooth bewitching fleetness rippling straight for the nuptial bower in Crete; not Jove did surpass the glorified white whale as he so divinely swam.

On each soft side—coincident with the parted swell, that but once laving him, then flowed so wide away—on each bright side, the whale shed off enticings. No wonder there had been some among the hunters who, namelessly transported and allured by all this serenity, had ventured to assail it, and had fatally found that quietude but the vesture of tornadoes! Yet calm, enticing calm, oh whale! thou glidest on, to all who for the first time eye thee, no matter how many in that same way thou may'st have bejuggled and destroyed before.

And thus, through the serene tranquilities of the tropical sea, among waves whose handclappings were suspended by exceeding rapture, Moby Dick moved on, still withholding from sight the full terrors of his submerged trunk, entirely hiding the wretched hideousness of his jaw. But soon the fore part of him slowly rose from the water; for an instant his whole marbleized body formed

a high arch, like Virginia's Natural Bridge, and warn-
ingly waving his bannered flukes in the air, the grand god
revealed himself, sounded, and went out of sight. Hover-
ingly halting, and dipping on the wing, the white sea-
fowls longingly lingered over the agitated pool that he
left.

With oars apeak and paddles down, the sheets of their
sails adrift, the three boats now stilly floated, awaiting
Moby Dick's appearance.

"An hour," said Ahab, standing rooted in his boat's
stern, and he gazed beyond the whale's place toward the
dim blue spaces and wide wooing vacancies to leeward.
It was only an instant, for again his eyes seemed to be
whirling around in his head as he swept the watery circle.
The breeze now freshened; the sea began to swell.

"The birds!—the birds!" cried Tashtego.

In long Indian file, as when herons take wing, the
white birds were now all flying toward Ahab's boat, and
when within a few yards, began fluttering over the water
there, wheeling round and round with joyous expectant
cries. Their vision was keener than man's; Ahab could
discover no sign in the sea. But suddenly as he peered
down and into its depths, he profoundly saw a white
living spot no bigger than a white weasel, with a wonderful celerity uprising and magnifying as it rose, till it
turned, and then there were plainly revealed two long
crooked rows of white glistening teeth, floating up from
the undiscoverable bottom. It was Moby Dick's open
mouth and scrolled jaw, his vast, shadowed bulk still half

blending with the blue of the sea. The glittering mouth yawned beneath the boat like an open-doored marble tomb, and giving one sidelong sweep with his steering oar, Ahab whirled the craft aside from this tremendous apparition. Then calling upon Fedallah to change places with him, he went forward to the bows, and seizing Perth's harpoon, commanded his crew to grasp their oars and stand by to stern.

Now by reason of this timely spinning around of the boat upon its axis its bow, by anticipation, was made to face the whale's head while yet under water. But as if perceiving this stratagem Moby Dick, with that malicious intelligence ascribed to him, sidelingly transplanted himself, as it were, in an instant shooting his plaited head lengthwise beneath the boat.

Through and through, through every plank and each rib it thrilled for an instant, the whale obliquely lying on his back in the manner of a biting shark, slowly and feelingly taking its bows full within his mouth, so that the long narrow scrolled lower jaw curled high up into the open air, and one of the teeth caught in a rowlock. The bluish pearl-white of the inside of the jaw was within six inches of Ahab's head, and reached higher than that. In this attitude the white whale now shook the slight cedar as a mildly cruel cat her mouse. With unastonished eyes Fedallah gazed and crossed his arms; but the tiger-yellow crew were tumbling over each other's head to gain the uttermost stern.

And now, while both elastic gunwales were springing

in and out as the whale dallied with the doomed craft in this devilish way, from his body being submerged beneath the boat, he could not be darted at from the bows; the bows were almost inside of him, as it were. And while the other boats involuntarily paused, as before a quick crisis impossible to withstand, then it was that monomaniac Ahab, furious with this tantalizing vicinity of his foe which placed him all alive and helpless in the very jaws he hated, frenzied with all this, he seized the long bone with his naked hands and wildly strove to wrench it from its gripe. As now he thus vainly strove, the jaw slipped from him; the frail gunwales bent in, collapsed and snapped, as both jaws, like an enormous shears, sliding further aft, bit the craft completely in twain, and locked themselves fast again in the sea, midway between the two floating wrecks. These floated aside, the broken ends drooping, the crew at the stern-wreck clinging to the gunwales, and striving to hold fast to the oars to lash them across.

At that preluding moment, ere the boat was yet snapped, Ahab, the first to perceive the whale's intent by the crafty upraising of his head, a movement that loosed his hold for the time, had at that moment made one final effort to push the boat out of the bite. But only slipping further into the whale's mouth and tilting over sideways as it slipped, the boat had shaken off his hold on the jaw, and spilled him out of it as he leaned to the push; so he fell flat-faced upon the sea.

Ripplingly withdrawing from his prey, Moby Dick

now lay at a little distance, vertically thrusting his oblong white head up and down in the billows and at the same time slowly revolving his whole splendid body; so that when his vast wrinkled forehead rose—some twenty or more feet out of the water—the now rising swells, with all their confluent waves, dazzling broke against it, vindictively tossing their shivered spray still higher into the air.[1] So, in a gale, the but half baffled Channel billows only recoil from the base of the Eddystone, triumphantly to overlap its summit with their scud.

But soon resuming his horizontal attitude Moby Dick swam swiftly round and round the wrecked crew, sideways churning the water in his vengeful wake, as if lashing himself up to still another and more deadly assault. The sight of the splintered boat seemed to madden him, as the blood of grapes and mulberries cast before Antiochus's elephants in the book of Maccabees. Meanwhile Ahab was half smothered in the foam of the whale's insolent tail, and too much of a cripple to swim, though he could still keep afloat, even in the heart of such a whirlpool as that; helpless Ahab's head was seen, like a tossed bubble which the least chance shock might burst. From the boat's fragmentary stern Fedallah incuriously and mildly eyed him; the clinging crew at the other drifting end could not succor him; more than enough was it for them to look to themselves. For so revolvingly appall-

[1] This motion is peculiar to the Sperm whale. It receives its designation (pitchpoling) from its being likened to that preliminary up-and-down poise of the whale-lance, in the exercise called pitchpoling. By this motion the whale must best and most comprehensively view whatever objects may be encircling him.

ing was the white whale's aspect, and so planetarily swift the ever-contracting circles he made, that he seemed horizontally swooping upon them. And though the other boats, unharmed, still hovered hard by, still they dared not pull into the eddy to strike, lest that should be the signal for the instant destruction of the jeopardized castaways, Ahab and all. Nor in that case could they themselves hope to escape. With straining eyes, then, they remained on the outer edge of the direful zone, whose center had now become the old man's head.

Meantime, from the beginning all this had been descried from the ship's mastheads; and squaring her yards, she had borne down upon the scene, and was now so nigh that Ahab in the water hailed her, "Sail on the"—but that moment a breaking sea dashed on him from Moby Dick and whelmed him for the time. But struggling out of it again, and chancing to rise on a towering crest, he shouted, "Sail on the whale!—drive him off!"

The *Pequod's* prows were pointed; and breaking up the charmed circle, she effectually parted the white whale from his victim. As he sullenly swam off, the boats flew to the rescue.

Dragged into Stubb's boat with bloodshot blinded eyes, the white brine caking in his wrinkles, the long tension of Ahab's bodily strength did crack, and helplessly he yielded to his body's doom, for a time lying all crushed in the bottom of Stubb's boat, like one trodden underfoot of herds of elephants. Far inland, nameless wails came from him, as desolate sounds from out ravines.

But this intensity of his physical prostration did but so much the more abbreviate it. In an instant's compass, great hearts sometimes condense to one deep pang, the sum total of those shallow pains kindly diffused through feebler men's whole lives. And so such hearts, though summary in each one suffering, still, if the gods decree it, in their lifetime aggregate a whole age of woe, wholly made up of instantaneous intensities. For even in their pointless centers, those noble natures contain the entire circumferences of inferior souls.

"The harpoon," said Ahab, halfway rising and draggingly leaning on one bended arm—"is it safe?"

"Aye, sir, for it was not darted; this is it," said Stubb, showing it.

"Lay it before me; any missing men?"

"One, two, three, four, five; there were five oars, sir, and here are five men."

"That's good. Help me, man; I wish to stand. So, so, I see him! There!—there! Going to leeward still; what a leaping spout! Hands off from me! The eternal sap runs in Ahab's bones again! Set the sail; out oars; the helm!"

It is often the case that when a boat is stove, its crew, being picked up by another boat, help to work that second boat, and the chase is thus continued with what is called double-banked oars. It was thus now. But the added power of the boat did not equal the added power of the whale, for he seemed to have treble-banked his every fin, swimming with a velocity which plainly showed that if now, under these circumstances, pushed on, the chase would prove an indefinitely prolonged if not a hopeless one; nor could any crew endure for so long a period such an unintermitted, intense straining at the oar, a thing barely tolerable only in some one brief vicissitude. The ship itself, then, as it sometimes happens, offered the most promising intermediate means of overtaking the chase. Accordingly, the boats now made for her, and were soon swayed up to their cranes—the two parts of the wrecked boat having been previously secured by her— and then hoisting everything to her side, and stacking her canvas high up, and sideways outstretching it with stun-sails, like the double-jointed wings of an albatross; the *Pequod* bore down in the leeward wake of Moby Dick. At the well-known methodical intervals, the whale's glittering spout was regularly announced from the manned mastheads. And when he would be reported as just gone down, Ahab would take the time, and then pacing the deck, binnacle-watch in hand, as soon as the last second of the allotted hour expired his voice was heard—"Whose is the doubloon now? D'ye see him?" And if the reply was, "No, sir!" straightway he commanded them to lift him to his perch. In this way the day wore on, Ahab now aloft and motionless, anon, unrestingly pacing the planks.

As he was thus walking, uttering no sound except to hail the men aloft, or to bid them hoist a sail still higher, or to spread one to a still greater breadth—thus to and fro pacing, beneath his slouched hat, at every turn he passed his own wrecked boat which had been dropped upon the quarterdeck, and lay there reversed, broken bow to shattered stern. At last he paused before it; and as in an already overclouded sky fresh troops of clouds will sometimes sail across, so over the old man's face there now stole some such added gloom as this.

Stubb saw him pause. And perhaps intending, not vainly, though, to evince his own unabated fortitude and thus keep up a valiant place in his captain's mind, he advanced, and eyeing the wreck exclaimed—"The thistle the ass refused; it pricked his mouth too keenly, sir; ha! ha!"

"What soulless thing is this that laughs before a wreck? Man, man! Did I not know thee brave as fearless fire (and as mechanical) I could swear thou wert a poltroon. Groan nor laugh should be heard before a wreck."

"Aye, sir," said Starbuck, drawing near, " 'tis a solemn sight; an omen, and an ill one."

"Omen? Omen?—the dictionary! If the gods think to speak outright to man, they will honorably speak outright, not shake their heads and give an old wife's darkling hint. Begone! Ye two are the opposite poles of one thing! Starbuck is Stub reversed, and Stub is Starbuck; and ye two are all mankind; and Ahab stands alone among the millions of the peopled earth, nor gods nor men his neighbors! Cold, cold—I shiver! How now? Aloft there! D'ye see him? Sing out for every spout, though he spout ten times a second!"

The day was nearly done; only the hem of his golden robe was rustling. Soon it was almost dark, but the lookout men still remained unset.

"Can't see the spout now, sir—too dark," cried a voice from the air.

"How heading when last seen?"

"As before, sir—straight to leeward."

"Good! He will travel slower now 'tis night. Down royals and topgallant stunsails, Mr. Starbuck. We must not run over him before morning; he's making a passage now, and may heave-to a while. Helm there! Keep her full before the wind! Aloft! Come down! Mr. Stubb, send a fresh hand to the foremast head, and see it manned till morning."

Then advancing toward the doubloon in the mainmast: "Men, this gold is mine, for I earned it. But I shall let it abide here till the white whale is dead; and then, whosoever of ye first raises him upon the day he shall be killed, this gold is that man's. And if on that day I shall again raise him, then ten times its sum shall be divided among all of ye! Away now!—the deck is thine, sir."

And so saying, he placed himself halfway within the scuttle, and slouching his hat, stood there till dawn, except when at intervals rousing himself to see how the night wore on.

Chapter 54

⚓

The Chase—Second Day

A̲t daybreak, the three mastheads were punctually manned afresh.

"D'ye see him?" cried Ahab after allowing a little space for the light to spread.

"See nothing, sir."

"Turn up all hands and make sail! He travels faster than I thought for. The topgallant sails!—aye, they should have been kept on her all night. But no matter—'tis but resting for the rush."

Here be it said that this pertinacious pursuit of one particular whale, continued through day into night, and through night into day, is a thing by no means unprecedented in the south sea fishery. For such is the wonderful skill, prescience of experience, and invincible confidence acquired by some great natural geniuses among the Nan-

342

tucket commanders, that from the simple observation of a whale when last descried, they will, under certain given circumstances, pretty accurately foretell both the direction in which he will continue to swim for a time, while out of sight, as well as his probable rate of progression during that period.

And in these cases, somewhat as a pilot, when about losing sight of a coast, whose general trending he well knows, and which he desires shortly to return to again but at some further point; like as this pilot stands by his compass and takes the precise bearing of the cape at present visible, in order the more certainly to hit aright the remote, unseen headland eventually to be visited: so does the fisherman, at his compass, with the whale. For after being chased and diligently marked through several hours of daylight, then when night obscures the fish, the creature's future wake through the darkness is almost as established to the sagacious mind of the hunter, as the pilot's coast is to him. So that to this hunter's wondrous skill, the proverbial evanescence of a thing writ in water, a wake, is to all desired purposes well-nigh as reliable as the steadfast land.

And as the mighty iron Leviathan of the modern railway is so familiarly known in its every pace, that, with watches in their hands, men time his rate as doctors that of a baby's pulse, and lightly say of it, "the up train or the down train will reach such or such a spot, at such and such an hour;" even so, there are occasions when these Nantucketers time that other Leviathan of the deep according to the observed humor of his speed. And they say to themselves, "so many hours hence this whale will have gone two hundred miles, will have about reached this or that degree of latitude or longitude." But to render this acuteness at all successful in the end, the wind and the sea must be the whaleman's allies. For of what present avail to the becalmed or windbound mariner is the skill that assures him he is exactly ninety-three leagues and a quarter from this port? Inferable from these statements are many collateral subtle matters touching the chase of whales.

The ship tore on, leaving such a furrow in the sea as when a cannonball, missent, becomes a ploughshare and turns up the level field.

"By salt and hemp!" cried Stubb, "but this swift motion of the deck creeps up one's legs and tingles at the heart. This ship and I are two brave fellows!—Ha! ha! Someone take me up and launch me, spinewise, on the sea, for by live-oaks, my spine's a keel! Ha, ha! We go the gait that leaves no dust behind!"

"There she blows—she blows!—she blows!—right ahead!" was now the masthead cry.

"Aye, aye!" cried Stubb, "I knew it—ye can't escape—blow on and split your spout, O Whale! The mad fiend himself is after ye! Blow your trump—blister your lungs! Ahab will dam off your blood, as a miller shuts his watergate upon the stream!"

And Stubb did but speak out for well-nigh all that crew. The frenzies of the chase had by this time worked them bubblingly up, like old wine worked anew. Whatever pale fears and forebodings some of them might have felt before, these were not only now kept out of sight through the growing awe of Ahab, but they were broken up and on all sides routed, as timid prairie hares that scatter before the bounding bison. The hand of Fate had snatched all their souls; and by the stirring perils of the previous day, the rack of the past night's suspense, the fixed, unfearing, blind reckless way in which their wild craft went plunging toward its flying mark: by all these things, their hearts were bowled along. The wind that made great bellies of their sails and rushed the vessel on by arms invisible as irresistible, this seemed the symbol of that unseen agency which so enslaved them to the race.

They were one man, not thirty. For as the one ship that held them all, though it was put together of all contrasting things—oak and maple and pine wood, iron and pitch and hemp—yet all these ran into each other in the one concrete hull, which shot on its way both balanced and directed by the long central keel; even so, all the individualities of the crew—this man's valor, that man's fear, guilt and guiltiness—all varieties were welded into oneness, and were all directed to that fatal goal which Ahab their one lord and keel did point to.

The rigging lived. The mastheads, like the tops of tall palms, were outspreadingly tufted with arms and legs. Clinging to a spar with one hand, some reached forth the other with impatient wavings; others, shading their eyes from the vivid sunlight, sat far out on the rocking yards, all the spars in full bearing of mortals, ready and ripe for their fate. Ah! How they still strove through that infinite blueness to seek out the thing that might destroy them!

"Why sing ye not out for him, if ye see him?" cried Ahab, when, after the lapse of some minutes since the first cry, no more had been heard. "Sway me up, men; ye have been deceived; not Moby Dick casts one odd jet that way, and then disappears."

It was even so. In their headlong eagerness, the men had mistaken some other thing for the whale spout, as the event itself soon proved. For hardly had Ahab reached his perch, hardly was the rope belayed to its pin on deck, when he struck the keynote to an orchestra that made the air vibrate as with the combined discharges of rifles. The triumphant halloo of thirty buckskin lungs was heard, as —much nearer to the ship than the place of the imaginary jet, less than a mile ahead, Moby Dick bodily burst into view! For not by any calm and indolent spoutings; not by the peaceable gush of that mystic fountain in his head, did the white whale now reveal his vicinity, but by the far more wondrous phenomenon of breaching. Rising with his utmost velocity from the furthest depths, the sperm whale thus booms his entire bulk into the pure element of air, and piling up a mountain of dazzling foam, shows his place to the distance of seven miles and more. In those moments, the torn, enraged waves he shakes off seem his mane; in some cases this breaching is his act of defiance.

"There she breaches! There she breaches!" was the cry, as in his immeasurable bravadoes the white whale tossed himself salmonlike to heaven. So suddenly seen in the blue plain of the sea, and relieved against the still bluer margin of the sky, the spray that he raised, for the moment, intolerably glittered and glared like a glacier; and stood there gradually fading away from its first sparkling intensity, to the dim and fading mistiness of an advancing shower in a vale.

"Aye, breach your last to the sun, Moby Dick!" cried Ahab, "thy hour and thy harpoon are at hand! Down! down all of ye, but one man at the fore. The boats!— stand by!"

Unmindful of the tedious rope-ladders of the shrouds, the men, like shooting stars, slid to the deck by the isolated backstays and halyards, while Ahab, less dartingly but still rapidly, was dropped from his perch.

"Lower away," he cried as soon as he had reached his boat—a spare one, rigged the previous afternoon. "Mr. Starbuck, the ship is thine—keep away from the boats, but keep near them. Lower, all!"

As if to strike a quick terror into them by this time being the first assailant himself, Moby Dick had turned and was now coming for the three crews. Ahab's boat was central; and cheering his men, he told them he would take the whale head-and-head—that is, pull straight up to his forehead, a not uncommon thing; for when within a certain limit, such a course excludes the coming onset from the whale's sidelong vision. But ere that close limit was gained, and while yet all three boats were plain as the ship's three masts to his eye, the white whale churning himself into furious speed, almost in an instant as it were, rushing among the boats with open jaws and lashing tail, offered appalling battle on every side. And heedless of the irons darted at him from every boat, seemed only intent on annihilating each separate plank of which those boats were made. But skillfully maneuvered, incessantly wheeling like trained chargers in the field, the boats for a while eluded him, though at times but by a plank's breadth, while all the time Ahab's unearthly slogan tore every other cry but his to shreds.

But at last in his untraceable evolutions, the white whale so crossed and recrossed, and in a thousand ways entangled the slack of the three lines now fast to him, that they foreshortened, and of themselves, warped the devoted boats toward the planted irons in him, though now for a moment the whale drew aside a little, as if to rally for a more tremendous charge. Seizing that opportunity, Ahab first paid out more line, and then was rapidly hauling and jerking in upon it again—hoping that way to disencumber it of some snarls—when lo! A sight more savage than the embattled teeth of sharks!

Caught and twisted, corkscrewed in the mazes of the line, loose harpoons and lances, with all their bristling barbs and points, came flashing and dripping up to the chocks in the bows of Ahab's boat. Only one thing could be done. Seizing the boatknife, he critically reached within, through, and then, without—the rays of steel, dragged in the line beyond, passed it inboard to the bowsman, and then, twice sundering the rope near the chocks, dropped the intercepted fagot of steel into the sea, and was all fast again. That instant, the white whale made a sudden rush among the remaining tangles of the other lines. By so doing, he irresistibly dragged the more involved boats of Stubb and Flask toward his flukes, dashed them together like two rolling husks on a surf-beaten beach, and then diving down into the sea, disappeared in a coiling maelstrom, in which, for a space, the odorous cedar chips of the wrecks danced round and round, like the grated nutmeg in a swiftly stirred bowl of punch.

The two crews were yet circling in the waters, reaching out after the revolving line-tubs, oars and other floating furniture, while aslope little Flask bobbed up and down like an empty vial, twitching his legs upward to escape the dreaded jaws of sharks, and Stubb was lustily singing out for someone to ladle him up. And while the old man's line, now parting, admitted of his pulling into the creamy pool to rescue whom he could, in that wild simultaneousness of a thousand concreted perils—Ahab's yet unstricken boat seemed drawn up toward heaven by invisible wires.

Then, arrowlike shooting perpendicularly from the sea, the white whale dashed his broad forehead against its bottom and sent it, turning over and over, into the air, till it fell again—gunwale downward—and Ahab and his men struggled out from under it, like seals from a seaside cave.

The first uprising momentum of the whale—modifying its direction as he struck the surface—involuntarily launched him along it, to a little distance from the center of the destruction he had made. And with his back to it, he now lay for a moment slowly feeling with his flukes from side to side, and whenever a stray oar, bit of plank, the least chip or crumb of the boats touched his skin, his tail swiftly drew back and came sideways, smiting the sea. But soon, as if satisfied that his work for that time was done, he pushed his plaited forehead through the ocean, and trailing after him the intertangled lines, continued his leeward way at a traveler's methodic pace.

As before, the attentive ship having descried the whole fight, again came bearing down to the rescue, and dropping a boat, picked up the floating mariners, tubs, oars and whatever else could be caught at, and safely landed them upon her decks. Some sprained shoulders, wrists and ankles, livid contusions, wrenched harpoons and lances, inextricable intricacies of rope, shattered oars and planks: all these were there, but no fatal or even serious ill seemed to have befallen anyone. As with Fedallah the day before, so Ahab was now found grimly clinging to his boat's broken half, which offered a comparatively easy float, nor did it exhaust him as the previous day's mishap.

But when he was helped to the deck, all eyes were fastened upon him; instead of standing by himself he still half-hung upon the shoulder of Starbuck, who had thus far been the foremost to assist him. His ivory leg had been snapped off, leaving but one short sharp splinter.

"Aye, aye, Starbuck, 'tis sweet to lean sometimes, be the leaner who he will, and would old Ahab had leaned oftener than he has."

"The ferule has not stood, sir," said the carpenter, now coming up; "I put good work into that leg."

"But no bones broken, sir, I hope," said Stubb with true concern.

"Aye! And all splintered to pieces, Stubb!—d'ye see it? But even with a broken bone old Ahab is untouched; and

I account no living bone of mine one jot more me, than this dead one that's lost. Nor white whale, nor man, nor fiend, can so much as graze old Ahab in his own proper and inaccessible being. Can any lead touch yonder floor, any mast scrape yonder roof? Aloft there! Which way?"

"Dead to leeward, sir."

"Up helm, then; pile on the sail again, shipkeepers; down the rest of the spare boats and rig them—Mr. Starbuck, away, and muster the boat's crews."

"Let me first help thee toward the bulwarks, sir."

"Oh, oh, oh! how this splinter gores me now! Accursed fate! That the unconquerable captain in the soul should have such a craven mate!"

"Sir?"

"My body, man, not thee. Give me something for a cane—there, that shivered lance will do. Muster the men. Surely I have not seen him yet. By heaven, it cannot be! Missing?—quick! call them all."

The old man's hinted thought was true. Upon mustering the company, the Parsee was not there.

"The Parsee!" cried Stubb, "he must have been caught in——"

"The black vomit wrench thee!—run all of ye, above, alow, cabin, forecastle—find him—not gone—not gone!"

But quickly they returned to him with the tidings that the Parsee was nowhere to be found.

"Aye, sir," said Stubb, "caught among the tangles of your line—I thought I saw him dragged under."

"My line? *my* line? Gone?—gone? What means that little word? What death-knell rings in it, that old Ahab

shakes as if he were the belfry. The harpoon, too! Toss
over the litter there—d'ye see it? The forged iron, men,
the white whale's—no, no, no—blistered fool! This hand
did dart it!—'tis in the fish! Aloft there! Keep him nailed
—quick! All hands to the rigging of the boats—collect the
oars—harpooneers! The irons, the irons!—hoist the royals
higher—a pull on all the sheets! Helm there! steady,
steady for your life! I'll ten times girdle the unmeasured
globe, yea and dive straight through it, but I'll slay
him yet!"

"Great God! But for one single instant show thyself,"
cried Starbuck, "never, never wilt thou capture him, old
man. In Jesus' name no more of this, that's worse than
devil's madness. Two days chased; twice stove to splinters; thy very leg once more snatched from under thee;
thy evil shadow gone—all good angels mobbing thee with
warnings: what more wouldst thou have? Shall we keep
chasing this murderous fish till he swamps the last man?
Shall we be dragged by him to the bottom of the sea?
Shall we be towed by him to the infernal world? Oh, oh!
Impiety and blasphemy to hunt him more!"

"Starbuck, of late I've felt strangely moved to thee,
ever since that hour we both saw—thou know'st what, in
one another's eyes. But in this matter of the whale, be the
front of thy face to me as the palm of this hand—a lipless,
unfeatured blank. Ahab is forever Ahab, man. This whole
act's immutably decreed. 'Twas rehearsed by thee and me
a billion years before this ocean rolled. Fool! I am the
Fates' lieutenant; I act under orders. Look thou, underling, that thou obeyest mine! Stand round me, men. Ye

see an old man cut down to the stump, leaning on a shivered lance, propped up on a lonely foot. 'Tis Ahab—his body's part; but Ahab's soul's a centipede that moves upon a hundred legs. I feel strained, half stranded, as ropes that tow dismasted frigates in a gale; and I may look so. But ere I break, ye'll hear me crack; and till ye hear *that*, know that Ahab's hawser tows his purpose yet. Believe ye, men, in the things called omens? Then laugh aloud, and cry encore! For ere they drown, drowning things will twice rise to the surface; then rise again, to sink for evermore. So with Moby Dick—two days he's floated—tomorrow will be the third. Aye, men, he'll rise once more—but only to spout his last! D'ye feel brave men, brave?"

"As fearless fire," cried Stubb.

"And as mechanical," muttered Ahab. Then as the men went forward, he muttered on: "The things called omens! And yesterday I talked the same to Starbuck there, concerning my broken boat. Oh! How valiantly I seek to drive out of other's hearts what's clinched so fast in mine! The Parsee—the Parsee!—gone, gone? And he was to go before—but still was to be seen again ere I could perish. How's that? There's a riddle now might baffle all the lawyers backed by the ghosts of the whole line of judges—like a hawk's beak it pecks my brain. *I'll, I'll* solve it, though!"

When dusk descended, the whale was still in sight to leeward.

So once more the sail was shortened, and everything passed nearly as on the previous night; only, the sound of hammers and the hum of the grindstone were heard till nearly daylight, as the men toiled by lanterns in the complete and careful rigging of the spare boats and sharpening their fresh weapons for the morrow. Meantime, of the broken keel of Ahab's wrecked craft the carpenter made him another leg; while still as on the night before, slouched Ahab stood fixed within his scuttle, his hidden heliotrope glance anticipatingly gone backward on its dial, set due eastward for the earliest sun.

⚓

CHAPTER 55

The Chase—Third Day

T HE MORNING of the third day dawned fair and fresh, and once more the solitary night-man at the foremast head was relieved by crowds of the daylight lookouts, who dotted every mast and almost every spar.

"D'ye see him?" cried Ahab, but the whale was not yet in sight.

"In his infallible wake, though; but follow that wake, that's all. Helm there; steady, as thou goest, and hast been going. What a lovely day again! Were it a new-made world, and made for a summerhouse to the angels, and this morning the first of its throwing open to them, a fairer day could not dawn upon that world. Here's food for thought, had Ahab time to think; but Ahab never thinks; he only feels, feels, feels, *that's* tingling enough for mortal man! To think's audacity. God only has that right

and privilege. Tingling is, or ought to be, a coolness and
a calmness; and our poor hearts throb, and our poor
brains beat too much for that. And yet, I've sometimes
thought my brain was very calm—frozen calm, this old
skull cracks so, like a glass which the contents turn to
ice, and shiver it. And still this hair is growing now, this
moment growing, and heat must breed it; but no, it's like
that sort of common grass that will grow anywhere, between the earthy clefts of Greenland ice or in Vesuvius
lava. How the wild winds blow it; they whip it about me
as the torn shreds of split sails lash the tossed ship they
cling to. A vile wind that has no doubt blown ere this
through prison corridors and cells, and wards of hospitals,
and ventilated them, and now comes blowing hither as
innocent as fleeces. Out upon it!—it's tainted. Were I the
wind, I'd blow no more on such a wicked, miserable
world. I'd crawl somewhere to a cave, and slink there.
And yet, 'tis a noble and heroic thing, the wind! Who ever
conquered it? In every fight it has the last and bitterest
blow. Run tilting at it, and you but run through it. Ha! A
coward wind that strikes stark naked men, but will not
stand to receive a single blow. Even Ahab is a braver
thing—a nobler thing than *that*. Would now the wind but
had a body; but all the things that most exasperate and
outrage mortal man, all these things are bodiless, but
only bodiless as objects, not as agents. There's a most
special, a most cunning, oh, a most malicious difference!
And yet, I say again, and swear it now, that there's something all glorious and gracious in the wind. These warm
trade winds at least, that in the clear heavens blow

straight on, in strong and steadfast, vigorous mildness, and veer not from their mark, however the baser currents of the sea may turn and tack, and mightiest Mississippis of the land shift and swerve about, uncertain where to go at last. And by the eternal poles! These same trades that so directly blow my good ship on, these trades, or something like them—something so unchangeable, and full as strong, blow my keeled soul along! To it! Aloft there! What d'ye see?"

"Nothing, sir."

"Nothing! And noon at hand! The doubloon goes a-begging! See the sun! Aye, aye, it must be so. I've over-sailed him. How got the start? Aye, he's chasing *me* now, not I, *him*. That's bad; I might have known it, too. Fool! The lines—the harpoons he's towing. Aye, aye, I have run him by last night. About! about! Come down, all of ye, but the regular lookouts! Man the braces!"

Steering as she had done, the wind had been somewhat on the *Pequod's* quarter, so that now being pointed in the reverse direction, the braced ship sailed hard upon the breeze as she rechurned the cream in her own white wake.

"Against the wind he now steers for the open jaw," murmured Starbuck to himself, as he coiled the new-hauled mainbrace upon the rail. "God keep us, but already my bones feel damp within me, and from the inside wet my flesh. I misdoubt me that I disobeyed my God in obeying him!"

"Stand by to sway me up!" cried Ahab, advancing to the hempen basket. "We should meet him soon."

"Aye, aye, sir," and straightaway Starbuck did Ahab's bidding, and once more Ahab swung on high.

A whole hour now passed; gold-beaten out to ages. Time itself now held long breaths with keen suspense. But at last, some three points off the weather-bow, Ahab descried the spout again, and instantly from the three mastheads three shrieks went up as if the tongues of fire had voiced it.

"Forehead to forehead I meet thee, this third time, Moby Dick! On deck there!—brace sharper up; crowd her into the wind's eye. He's too far off to lower yet, Mr. Starbuck. The sails shake! Stand over that helmsman with a topmaul! So, so; he travels fast, and I must down. But let me have one more good round look aloft here at sea; there's time for that. An old, old sight, and yet somehow so young; aye, and not changed a wink since I first saw it, a boy, from the sandhills of Nantucket! The same!—the same! The same to Noah as to me. There's a soft shower to leeward. Such lovely leewardings! They must lead somewhere—to something else than common land, more palmy than the palms. Leeward! The white whale goes that way; look to windward, men; the better if the bitterer quarter. But good-bye, good-bye, old masthead! What's this?—green? Aye, tiny mosses in these warped cracks. No such green weather stains on Ahab's head! There's the difference now between man's old age and matter's. But aye, old mast, we both grow old together; sound in our hulls, though, are we not, my ship? Aye, minus a leg, that's all. By heaven! This dead wood has the better of my live flesh every way. I can't compare with it, and I've known some ships made of dead trees outlast the lives of men made of the most vital stuff of vital fathers. What's that he said? He should still go before me, my pilot; and yet to be seen again? But where? Shall I have eyes at the bottom of the sea, supposing I descend those endless stairs? And all night I've been sailing from him, wherever he did sink to. Aye, aye, like many more thou told'st direful truth as touching thyself, O Parsee, but Ahab, there thy shot fell short. Good-bye, masthead—keep a good eye upon the whale, the while I'm gone. We'll talk tomorrow, nay, tonight, when the white whale lies down there, tied by head and tail."

He gave the word; and still gazing around him, was steadily lowered through the cloven blue air to the deck.

In due time the boats were lowered, but as standing in his shallop's stern, Ahab just hovered upon the point of the descent, he waved to the mate—who held one of the tackle-ropes on deck—and bade him pause.

"Starbuck!"

"Sir?"

"For the third time my soul's ship starts upon this voyage, Starbuck."

"Aye, sir, thou wilt have it so."

"Some ships sailed from their ports, and ever afterward are missing, Starbuck!"

"Truth, sir, saddest truth."

"Some men die at ebb tide, some at low water, some at the full of the flood—and I feel now like a billow that's all one crested comb, Starbuck. I am old—shake hands with me, man."

Their hands met, their eyes fastened, Starbuck's tears the glue.

"Oh, my captain, my captain! Noble heart—go not—go not! See it's a brave man that weeps; how great the agony of the persuasion then!"

"Lower away!"—cried Ahab, tossing the mate's arm from him. "Stand by the crew!"

In an instant the boat was pulling round close under the stern.

"The sharks! the sharks!" cried a voice from the low cabin window there. "O master, my master, come back!"

But Ahab heard nothing, for his own voice was high-lifted then, and the boat leaped on.

Yet the voice spake true; for scarce had he pushed from the ship, when numbers of sharks, seemingly rising from out the dark waters beneath the hull, maliciously snapped at the blades of the oars every time they dipped in the water, and in this way accompanied the boat with their bites. It is a thing not uncommonly happening to the whaleboats in those swarming seas, the sharks at times apparently following them in the same prescient way that vultures hover over the banners of marching regiments in the east. But these were the first sharks that had been observed by the *Pequod* since the white whale had been first descried; and whether it was that Ahab's crew were all such tiger-yellow barbarians, and therefore their flesh more musky to the senses of the sharks—a matter sometimes well known to affect them—however it was, they seemed to follow that one boat without molesting the others.

"Heart of wrought steel!" murmured Starbuck, gazing over the side, and following with his eyes the receding boat, "canst thou yet ring boldly to that sight? Lowering thy keel among ravening sharks, and followed by them, open-mouthed, to the chase; and this the critical third day? For when three days flow together in one continuous intense pursuit, be sure the first is the morning, the second the noon, and the third the evening and the end of that thing—be that end what it may. Oh! my God! What is this that shoots through me, and leaves me so deadly calm, yet expectant—fixed at the top of a shudder! Future things swim before me, as in empty outlines and skeletons; all the past is somehow grown dim. Mary, girl! Thou fadest in pale glories behind me; boy! I seem to see but thine eyes grown wondrous blue. Strangest problems of life seem clearing, but clouds sweep between—is my journey's end coming? My legs feel faint, like his who has footed it all day. Feel thy heart—beats it yet? Stir thyself, Starbuck! Stave it off—move, move! Speak aloud! Masthead there! See ye my boy's hand on the hill? Crazed—aloft there! Keep thy keenest eye upon the boats —mark well the whale! Ho! Again!—drive off that hawk! See!—he pecks—he tears the vane"—pointing to the red flag flying at the main-truck—"ha! he soars away with it! Where's the old man now? See'st thou that sight, oh Ahab!—shudder, shudder!"

The boats had not gone very far, when by a signal from the mastheads—a downward pointed arm, Ahab knew that the whale had sounded; but intending to be near him at the next rising, he held on his way a little sideways from the vessel, the becharmed crew maintaining the profoundest silence as the head-beat waves hammered and hammered against the opposing bow.

"Drive, drive in your nails, oh ye waves! To their uttermost heads drive them in! Ye but strike a thing without a lid; and no coffin and no hearse can be mine—and hemp only can kill me! Ha! ha!"

Suddenly the waters around them slowly swelled in broad circles, then quickly upheaved, as if sideways sliding from a submerged berg of ice, swiftly rising to the surface. A low rumbling sound was heard, a subterraneous hum, and then all held their breaths, as bedraggled with trailing ropes and harpoons and lances, a vast form shot lengthwise, obliquely from the sea. Shrouded in a thin drooping veil of mist, it hovered for a moment in the rainbowed air, and then fell swamping back into the deep. Crushed thirty feet upwards, the waters flashed for an instant like heaps of fountains, then brokenly sank in a shower of flakes, leaving the circling surface creamed like new milk round the marble trunk of the whale.

"Give way!" cried Ahab to the oarsmen, and the boats darted forward to the attack. But maddened by yesterday's fresh irons that corroded in him, Moby Dick seemed combinedly possessed by all the angels that fell from heaven. The wide tiers of welded tendons overspreading his broad white forehead, beneath the transparent skin, looked knitted together as head on he came churning his tail among the boats, and once more flailed them apart, spilling out the irons and lances from the two mates' boats, and dashing in one side of the upper part of their bows, but leaving Ahab's almost without a scar.

While Daggoo and Queequeg were stopping the strained planks, and as the whale swimming out from them, turned, and showed one entire flank as he shot by them again, at that moment a quick cry went up. Lashed round and round to the fish's back, pinioned in the turns upon turns in which, during the past night, the whale had reeled the involutions of the lines around him, the half torn body of the Parsee was seen, his sable raiment frayed to shreds, his distended eyes turned full upon old Ahab.

The harpoon dropped from his hand.

"Befooled, befooled!"—drawing in a long lean breath— "Aye, Parsee! I see thee again—aye, and thou goest before; and this, *this* then is the hearse that thou didst promise. But I hold thee to the last letter of thy word. Where is the second hearse? Away, mates, to the ship! Those boats are useless now; repair them if ye can in time, and return to me; if not, Ahab is enough to die. Down, men! The first thing that but offers to jump from this boat I stand in, that thing I harpoon. Ye are not other men, but my arms and my legs; and so obey me. Where's the whale? Gone down again?"

But he looked too nigh the boat, for as if bent upon escaping with the corpse he bore, and as if the particular place of the last encounter had been but a stage in his leeward voyage, Moby Dick was now again steadily swimming forward and had almost passed the ship— which thus far had been sailing in the contrary direction to him, though for the present her headway had been stopped. He seemed swimming with his utmost velocity, and now only intent upon pursuing his own straight path in the sea.

"Oh! Ahab," cried Starbuck, "not too late is it, even now, the third day to desist. See! Moby Dick seeks thee not. It is thou, thou, that madly seekest him!"

Setting sail to the rising wind, the lonely boat was swiftly impelled to leeward by both oars and canvas. And at last when Ahab was sliding by the vessel, so near as plainly to distinguish Starbuck's face as he leaned over the rail, he hailed him to turn the vessel about, and follow him, not too swiftly, at a judicious interval. Glancing upward, he saw Tashtego, Queequeg and Daggoo, eagerly mounting to the three mastheads, while the oarsmen were rocking in the two staved boats which had just been hoisted to the side, and were busily at work in repairing them. One after the other, through the portholes, as he sped, he also caught flying glimpses of Stubb and Flask, busying themselves on deck among bundles of new irons and lances. As he saw all of this, as he heard the hammers in the broken boats, far other hammers seemed driving a nail into his heart. But he rallied. And now marking that the vane or flag was gone from the main masthead, he shouted to Tashtego, who had just gained that perch, to descend again for another flag, and a hammer and nails, and so nail it to the mast.

Whether fagged by the three days' running chase, and the resistance to his swimming in the knotted hamper he bore, or whether it was some latent deceitfulness and malice in him; whichever was true, the white whale's way now began to abate, as it seemed, from the boat so rapidly nearing him once more, though indeed the whale's last start had not been as long a one as before. And still as Ahab glided over the waves the unpitying sharks accompanied him; and so pertinaciously stuck to the boat; and so continually bit at the plying oars that the blades became jagged and crunched, and left small splinters in the sea at almost every dip.

"Heed them not! Those teeth but give new rowlocks to your oars. Pull on! 'Tis the better rest, the shark's jaw than the yielding water."

"But at every bite, sir, the thin blades grow smaller and smaller!"

"They will last long enough! Pull on!—but who can tell," he muttered, "whether these sharks swim to feast on a whale or on Ahab? But pull on! Aye, all alive, now—we near him. The helm! take the helm; let me pass"—and so saying, two of the oarsmen helped him forward to the bows of the still flying boat.

At length as the craft was cast to one side, and ran ranging along with the white whale's flank, he seemed strangely oblivious of its advance—as the whale sometimes will—and Ahab was fairly within the smoky mountain mist, which, thrown off from the whale's spout, curled round his great Monadnock hump. He was even thus close to him, when, with body arched back, and both arms lengthwise high-lifted to the poise, he darted his fierce iron, and his far fiercer curse into the hated whale. As both steel and curse sank to the socket, as if sucked into a morass, Moby Dick sideways writhed, spasmodically rolled his nigh flank against the bow, and without staving a hole in it, so suddenly canted the boat over, that had it not been for the elevated part of the gunwale to which he then clung, Ahab would have once more been tossed into the sea. As it was, three of the oarsmen—who foreknew not the precise instant of the dart, and were therefore unprepared for its effects—these were flung out; but so fell, that, in an instant two of them clutched the gunwale again, and rising to its level on a combing wave, hurled themselves bodily inboard again, the third man helplessly drooping astern, but still afloat and swimming.

Almost simultaneously, with a mighty volition of un-graduated, instantaneous swiftness, the white whale darted through the weltering sea. But when Ahab cried out to the steersman to take new turns with the line and hold it so, and commanded the crew to round on their seats and tow the boat up to the mark; that moment the treacherous line felt the double strain and tug, and snapped in the empty air!

"What breaks in me? Some sinew cracks!—'tis whole again; oars! oars! Burst in upon him!"

Hearing the tremendous rush of the sea-crashing boat, the whale wheeled round to present his blank forehead at bay; but in that evolution, catching sight of the nearing black hull of the ship, seemingly to see in it the source of all his persecutions, and bethinking it—it may be—a larger and nobler foe, of a sudden, he bore down upon its advancing prow, smiting his jaws amid fiery showers of foam.

Ahab staggered; his hand smote his forehead. "I grow blind. Hands! stretch out before me that I may yet grope my way. Is't nigh?"

"The whale! The ship!" cried the cringing oarsmen.

"Oars! oars! Slope downward to thy depths, O sea, that ere it be forever too late, Ahab may slide this last, last time upon his mark! I see; the ship!—the ship! Dash on, my men! Will ye not save my ship?"

But as the oarsmen violently forced their boat through the sledge-hammering seas, the before whale-smitten bow-ends of the two planks burst through, and in an instant almost, the temporarily disabled boat lay nearly level with the waves, its half-wading splashing crew trying hard to stop the gap and bail out the pouring water.

Meantime, for that one beholding instant, Tashtego's masthead hammer remained suspended in his hand; and the red flag, half-wrapping him as with a plaid, then streamed itself straight out from him, as his own forward-flowing heart; while Starbuck and Stubb, standing upon the bowsprit beneath, caught sight of the down-coming monster just as soon as he.

"The whale, the whale! Up helm, up helm! Oh, all ye sweet powers of air, now hug me close! Let not Starbuck die, if die he must, in a woman's fainting fit. Up helm, I say—ye fools, the jaw! The jaw! Is this the end of all my bursting prayers? All my lifelong fidelities? Oh, Ahab, Ahab, lo, thy work. Steady! Helmsman, steady. Nay, nay!

Up helm again! He turns to meet us! Oh, his unappeas-able brow drives on toward one, whose duty tells him he cannot depart. My God, stand by me now!

"Stand not by me, but stand under me, whoever you are that will now help Stubb, for Stubb, too, sticks here. I grin at thee, thou grinning whale! Whoever helped Stubb, or kept Stubb awake, but Stubb's own unwinking eye? And now poor Stubb goes to bed upon a mattress that is all too soft; would it were stuffed with brushwood! I grin at thee, thou grinning whale! Look ye, moon and stars! I call ye assassins of as good a fellow as ever spouted up his ghost. For all that, I would yet ring glasses with ye, would ye but hand the cup! Oh, oh, oh, oh! thou grinning whale, but there'll be plenty of gulping soon! Why fly ye not, O, Ahab? For me, off shoes and jacket to it; let Stubb die in his drawers! A most moldy and over-salted death, though—cherries!—cherries! Cherries! Oh, Flask, for one red cherry ere we die!"

"Cherries? I only wish that we were where they grow. Oh, Stubb, I hope my poor mother's drawn my part-pay ere this; if not, few coppers will come to her now, for the voyage is up."

From the ship's bows, nearly all the seamen now hung inactive; hammers, bits of plank, lances, and harpoons, mechanically retained in their hands, just as they had darted from their various employments. All their en-chanted eyes were intent upon the whale, which from side to side strangely vibrating his predestinating head, sent a broad band of overspreading semicircular foam be-fore him as he rushed. Retribution, swift vengeance, eternal malice were in his whole aspect, and spite of all that mortal man could do, the solid white buttress of his forehead smote the ship's starboard bow, till men and timbers reeled. Some fell flat upon their faces. Like dislodged trucks, the heads of the harpooneers aloft shook on their hull-like necks. Through the breach, they heard the waters pour, as mountain torrents down a flume.

"The ship! The hearse!—the second hearse!" cried Ahab from the boat; "its wood could only be American!"

Diving beneath the settling ship, the whale ran quivering along its keel, but turning under water, swiftly shot to the surface again, far off the other bow, but within a few yards of Ahab's boat, where, for a time, he lay quiescent.

"I turn my body from the sun. What ho, Tashtego! Let me hear thy hammer. Oh! Ye three unsurrendered spires of mine! Thou uncracked keel and only god-bullied hull, thou firm deck, and haughty helm, and pole-pointed prow —death-glorious ship! Must ye then perish, and without me? Am I cut off from the last fond pride of meanest shipwrecked captains? Oh, lonely death on lonely life! Oh, now I feel my topmost greatness lies in my topmost grief. Ho, ho! From all your furthest bounds, pour ye now in, ye bold billows of my whole foregone life, and top this one piled comber of my death! Toward thee I roll, thou all-destroying but unconquering whale; to the last I grapple with thee. From hell's heart I stab at thee; for hate's sake I spit my last breath at thee. Sink all coffins and all hearses to one common pool! And since neither can be mine let me then tow to pieces, while still chasing thee, though tied to thee, thou damned whale! *Thus*, I give up the spear!"

The harpoon was darted; the stricken whale flew forward; with igniting velocity the line ran through the groove, ran foul. Ahab stopped to clear it; he did clear it; but the flying turn caught him round the neck, and voicelessly as Turkish mutes bowstring their victims, he was shot out of the boat ere the crew knew he was gone. Next instant, the heavy eyesplice in the rope's final end flew out of the stark-empty tub, knocked down an oarsman, and smiting the sea, disappeared in its depths.

For an instant, the tranced boat's crew stood still, then turned. "The ship? Great God, where is the ship?" Soon they through dim, bewildering mediums saw her sidelong fading phantom, as in the gaseous Fata Morgana—only the uppermost masts out of water. While fixed by infatuation, or fidelity, or fate, to their once lofty perches, the pagan harpooneers still maintained their sinking lookouts on the sea. And now, concentric circles seized the lone boat itself, and all its crew, and each floating oar, and every lance-pole, and spinning, animate and inanimate, all round and round in one vortex, carried the smallest chip of the *Pequod* out of sight.

But as the last whelmings intermixingly poured themselves over the sunken head of the Indian at the mainmast, leaving a few inches of the erect spar yet visible, together with long streaming yards of the flag, which calmly undulated, with ironical coincidings, over the destroying billows they almost touched—at that instant, a red arm and a hammer hovered backwardly uplifted in the open air, in the act of nailing the flag faster and yet faster to the subsiding spar. A sky hawk that tauntingly had followed the main-truck downward from its natural home among the stars, pecking at the flag and incommoding Tashtego there, this bird now chanced to intercept its broad fluttering wing between the hammer and the wood. And simultaneously feeling that ethereal thrill, the submerged savage beneath, in his death-gasp, kept his hammer frozen there. And so the bird of heaven, with unearthly shrieks, and his imperial beak thrust upward, and his whole captive form folded in the flag of Ahab, went down with his ship, which, like Satan, would not sink to hell till she had dragged a living part of heaven along with her, and helmeted herself with it.

Now small fowls flew screaming over the yet yawning gulf; a sullen white surf beat against its steep sides; then all collapsed, and the great shroud of the sea rolled on as it rolled five thousand years ago.

⚓

Epilogue

"AND I ONLY AM ESCAPED ALONE TO TELL THEE."

Job.

THE DRAMA'S DONE. Why then here does anyone step forth?—Because one did survive the wreck.

It so chanced, that after the Parsee's disappearance, I was he whom the Fates ordained to take the place of Ahab's bowsman, when that bowsman assumed the vacant post—the same, who when on the last day the three men were tossed from out the rocking boat, was dropped astern. So, floating on the margin of the ensuing scene, and in full sight of it, when the half-spent suction of the sunk ship reached me, I was then, but slowly, drawn toward the closing vortex. When I reached it, it had subsided to a creamy pool. Round and round, then, and ever contracting toward the buttonlike black bubble at the axis of that slowly wheeling circle, like another Ixion I did revolve. Till, gaining that vital center, the black bubble upward burst. And now, liberated by reason of

372

its cunning spring, and owing to its great buoyancy, rising with great force, the coffin life buoy shot lengthwise from the sea, fell over, and floated by my side. Buoyed up by that coffin, for almost one whole day and night, I floated on a soft and dirgelike main. The unharming sharks, they glided by as if with padlocks on their mouths; the savage sea hawks with sheathed beaks. On the second day a sail drew near, nearer, and picked me up at last. It was the devious-cruising *Rachel,* that in her retracing search after her missing children, only found another orphan.

TYPEE

Selections

CHAPTER 1

⚓

Apprehensions of Evil

FRIGHTFUL DISCOVERY—SOME REMARKS ON CANNIBALISM—SECOND
BATTLE WITH THE HAPPARS—SAVAGE SPECTACLE—MYSTERIOUS
FEAST—SUBSEQUENT DISCLOSURES

FROM THE TIME of my casual encounter with Karky the artist, my life was one of absolute wretchedness. Not a day passed but I was prosecuted by the solicitations of some of the natives to subject myself to the odious operation of tattooing. Their importunities drove me half wild, for I felt how easily they might work their will upon me regarding this or anything else which they took into their heads. Still, however, the behavior of the islanders toward me was as kind as ever. Fayaway was quite as engaging, Kory-Kory was devoted, and Mehevi the King just as gracious and condescending as before.

But I had now been three months in their valley, as

nearly as I could estimate; I had grown familiar with the narrow limits to which my wanderings had been confined; and I began bitterly to feel the state of captivity in which I was held. There was no one with whom I could freely converse, no one to whom I could communicate my thoughts, no one who could sympathize with my sufferings. A thousand times I thought how much more endurable would have been my lot had Toby still been with me. But I was left alone, and the thought was terrible to me. Still, despite my griefs, I did all in my power to appear composed and cheerful, well knowing that by manifesting any uneasiness, or any desire to escape, I should only frustrate my object.

It was during the period I was in this unhappy frame of mind that the painful malady under which I had been laboring—after having almost completely subsided—began again to show itself, and with symptoms as violent as ever.[1] This added calamity nearly unmanned me. The recurrence of the complaint proved that without powerful remedial applications all hope of cure was futile. And when I reflected that just beyond the elevations which bound me in was the medical relief I needed, and that although so near, it was impossible for me to avail myself of it, the thought was misery.

In this wretched situation, every circumstance which evinced the savage nature of the beings at whose mercy I was, augmented the fearful apprehensions that con-

---

[1] The author had injured his leg badly while climbing the rugged terrain of the island, prior to meeting the Typees.—ED.

sumed me. An occurrence which happened about this time affected me most powerfully.

I have already mentioned that from the ridgepole of Marheyo's house were suspended a number of packages enveloped in tappa. Many of these I had often seen in the hands of the natives, and their contents had been examined in my presence. But there were three packages hanging very nearly over the place where I lay, which from their remarkable appearance had often excited my curiosity. Several times I had asked Kory-Kory to show me their contents. But my servitor, who in almost every other particular had acceded to my wishes, always refused to gratify me in this.

One day, returning unexpectedly from the Ti, my arrival seemed to throw the inmates of the house into the greatest confusion. They were seated together on the mats, and by the lines which extended from the roof to the floor I immediately perceived that the mysterious packages were for some purpose or other under inspection. The evident alarm the savages betrayed filled me with forebodings of evil, and with an uncontrollable desire to penetrate the secret so jealously guarded. Despite the efforts of Marheyo and Kory-Kory to restrain me, I forced my way into the midst of the circle, and just caught a glimpse of three human heads, which others of the party were hurriedly enveloping in the coverings from which they had been taken.

One of the three I distinctly saw. It was in a state of perfect preservation, and from the slight glimpse I had of it, seemed to have been subjected to some smoking operation which had reduced it to the dry, hard and mummylike appearance it presented. The two long scalp locks were twisted up into balls upon the crown of the head in the same way that the individual had worn them during life. The sunken cheeks were rendered yet more ghastly by the rows of glistening teeth which protruded from between the lips, while the sockets of the eyes—filled with oval bits of mother-of-pearl shell, with a black spot in the center—heightened the hideousness of its aspect.

Two of the three were heads of the islanders; but the third, to my horror, was that of a white man. Although it had been quickly removed from my sight, still the glimpse I had of it was enough to convince me that I could not be mistaken.

Gracious God! What dreadful thoughts entered my mind! In solving this mystery perhaps I had solved another, and the fate of my lost companion might be revealed in the shocking spectacle I had just witnessed. I longed to tear off the folds of cloth, and satisfy the awful doubts under which I labored. But before I had recovered from the consternation into which I had been thrown, the fatal packages were hoisted aloft and once more swung over my head. The natives now gathered round me tumultuously, and labored to convince me that what I had just seen were the heads of three Happar warriors, who had been slain in battle. This glaring falsehood added to my alarm, and it was not until I reflected that I had observed the packages swinging from their elevation before Toby's disappearance, that I could at all recover my composure.

But although this horrible apprehension had been dispelled, I had discovered enough to fill me, in my present state of mind, with the most bitter reflections. It was plain that I had seen the last relic of some unfortunate wretch, who must have been massacred on the beach by the savages, in one of their frequent perilous trading adventures.

It was not, however, alone the murder of the stranger that overcame me with gloom. I shuddered at the idea of the subsequent fate his inanimate body might have met with. Was the same doom reserved for me? Was I destined to perish like him—like him, perhaps, to be devoured, and my head to be preserved as a fearful memento of the event? My imagination ran riot in these horrid speculations, and I felt certain that the worst possible evils would befall me. But whatever were my misgivings, I studiously concealed them from the islanders, as well as the full extent of the discovery I had made.

Although the assurances which the Typees had often given me that they never eat human flesh had not convinced me that such was the case, yet having been so long a time in the valley without witnessing anything which indicated the existence of the practice, I began to hope that it was an event of very rare occurrence and that I should be spared the horror of witnessing it during my stay among them. But alas! These hopes were soon destroyed.

It is a singular fact that in all our accounts of cannibal tribes we have seldom received the testimony of an eyewitness to the revolting practice. The horrible conclusion has almost always been derived either from the second-hand evidence of Europeans, or else from the admissions of the savages themselves after they have in some degree become civilized. The Polynesians are aware of the detestation in which Europeans hold this custom, and therefore invariably deny its existence, and with the craft peculiar to savages endeavor to conceal every trace of it.

The excessive unwillingness betrayed by the Sandwich islanders, even at the present day, to allude to the unhappy fate of Cook, has been often remarked. And so well have they succeeded in covering that event with mystery that to this very hour, despite all that has been said and written on the subject, it still remains doubtful whether they wreaked upon his murdered body the vengeance they sometimes inflicted upon their enemies.

At Karakikova, the scene of that tragedy, a strip of ship's copper nailed against an upright post in the ground used to inform the traveler that beneath reposed the "remains" of the great circumnavigator. But I am strongly inclined to believe not only that the corpse was refused Christian burial, but that the heart which was brought to Vancouver some time after the event, and which the Hawaiians stoutly maintained was that of Captain Cook, was no such thing; and that the whole affair was a piece of imposture which they sought to palm off upon the credulous Englishman.

A few years since there was living on the island of Mowee (one of the Sandwich group) an old chief, who, actuated by a morbid desire for notoriety, gave himself out among the foreign residents of the place as the living tomb of Captain Cook's big toe! He affirmed that at the cannibal entertainment which ensued after the lamented Briton's death, that particular portion of his body had fallen to his share. His indignant countrymen actually caused him to be prosecuted in the native courts, on a charge nearly equivalent to what we term defamation of character; but the old fellow persisting in his assertion, and no invalidating proof being adduced, the plaintiffs were cast in the suit, and the cannibal reputation of the defendant fully established. This result was the making of his fortune; ever afterward he was in the habit of giving very profitable audiences to all curious travelers who were desirous of beholding the man who had eaten the great navigator's great toe.

About a week after my discovery of the contents of the mysterious packages, I happened to be at the Ti when another war alarm was sounded, and the natives rushing to their arms, sallied out to resist a second incursion of the Happar invaders. The same scene was again repeated, only that on this occasion I heard at least fifteen reports of muskets from the mountains during the time that the skirmish lasted. An hour or two after its termination, loud paeans chanted through the valley announced the approach of the victors. I stood with Kory-Kory leaning against the railing of the pi-pi awaiting their advance, when a tumultuous crowd of islanders emerged with wild clamors from the neighboring groves. In the midst of them marched four men, one preceding the other at regular intervals of eight or ten feet, with poles of corresponding length, extended from shoulder to shoulder, to which were lashed with thongs of bark three long narrow bundles, carefully wrapped in ample covering of freshly plucked palm leaves, tacked together with slivers of bamboo. Here and there upon these green winding sheets might be seen stains of blood, while the warriors who carried the frightful burdens displayed upon their naked limbs similar sanguinary marks.

The shaven head of the foremost had a deep gash upon it, and the clotted gore which had flowed from the wound remained in dry patches around it. This savage seemed to be sinking under the weight he bore. The bright tattooing upon his body was covered with blood and dust. His inflamed eyes rolled in their sockets, and his whole appearance denoted extraordinary suffering and exertion; yet, sustained by some powerful impulse, he continued to advance, while the throng around him with wild cheers sought to encourage him. The other three men were marked about the arms and breasts with several slight wounds, which they somewhat ostentatiously displayed.

These four individuals having been the most active in the last encounter, claimed the honor of bearing the bodies of their slain enemies to the Ti. Such was the conclusion I drew from my own observations, and as far as I could understand, from the explanation which Kory-Kory gave me.

The royal Mehevi walked by the side of these heroes. He carried in one hand a musket from the barrel of which was suspended a small canvas pouch of powder, and in the other he grasped a short javelin, which he held before him and regarded with fierce exultation. This javelin he had wrested from a celebrated champion of the Happars who had ignominiously fled, and was pursued by his foe beyond the summit of the mountain.

When within a short distance of the Ti, the warrior with the wounded head, who proved to be Narmonee, tottered forward two or three steps and fell helplessly to the ground; but not before another had caught the end of the pole from his shoulder and placed it upon his own.

The excited throng of islanders who surrounded the person of the king and the dead bodies of the enemy, approached the spot where I stood, brandishing their rude implements of warfare, many of which were bruised and broken, and uttering continual shouts of triumph. When the crowd drew up opposite the Ti, I set myself to watch their proceedings most attentively. But scarcely had they halted when my servitor, who had left my side for an instant, touched my arm and proposed our returning to Marheyo's house. To this I objected; but to my surprise Kory-Kory reiterated his request, and with an unusual vehemence of manner. Still, however, I refused to comply, and was retreating before him as in his importunity he pressed upon me, when I felt a heavy hand laid upon my shoulder. Turning around, I encountered the bulky form of Mow-Mow, a one-eyed chief who had just detached himself from the crowd below, and had mounted the rear of the pi-pi upon which we stood. His cheek had been pierced by the point of a spear, and the

wound imparted a still more frightful expression to his
hideously tattooed face, already deformed by the loss of
his eye. The warrior, without uttering a syllable, pointed
fiercely in the direction of Marheyo's house, while Kory-
Kory, at the same time presenting his back, desired me
to mount.

I declined this offer, but intimated my willingness to
withdraw, and moved slowly along the piazza, wondering what could be the cause of this unusual treatment. A
few minutes' consideration convinced me that the savages were about to celebrate some hideous rite in connection with their peculiar customs, and at which they were
determined I should not be present. I descended from
the pi-pi, and attended by Kory-Kory, who on this occasion did not show his usual commiseration for my
lameness, but seemed only anxious to hurry me on,
walked away from the place. As I passed through the
noisy throng, which by this time completely environed
the Ti, I looked with fearful curiosity at the three packages which now were deposited upon the ground. But
although I had no doubt as to their contents, still their
thick coverings prevented my actually detecting the form
of a human body.

The next morning, shortly after sunrise, the same
thundering sounds which had awakened me from sleep
on the second day of the Feast of Calabashes, assured me
that the savages were on the eve of celebrating another,
and, as I fully believed, a horrible solemnity.

All the inmates of the house, with the exception of

Marheyo, his son, and Tinor, after assuming their gala dresses, departed in the direction of the Taboo Groves.

Although I did not anticipate a compliance with my request, still, with a view to testing the truth of my suspicions, I proposed to Kory-Kory that according to our usual custom in the morning, we should take a stroll to the Ti. He positively refused, and when I renewed the request, he evinced his determination to prevent my going there. To divert my mind from the subject, he offered to accompany me to the stream. We accordingly went and bathed. On our coming back to the house I was surprised to find that all its inmates had returned and were lounging upon the mats as usual, although the drums still sounded from the groves.

The rest of the day I spent with Kory-Kory and Fayaway, wandering about a part of the valley situated in an opposite direction from the Ti. And whenever I so much as looked toward that building, although it was hidden from view by intervening trees and the distance was more than a mile, my attendant would exclaim, "Taboo! Taboo!"

At the various houses where we stopped I found many of the inhabitants reclining at their ease or pursuing some light occupation, as if nothing unusual were going forward. But among them all I did not perceive a single chief or warrior. When I asked several of the people why they were not at the Hoolah Hoolah (the feast), they uniformly answered the question in a manner which implied that it was not intended for them, but for Mehevi,

Narmonee, Mow-Mow, Kolor, Womonoo, Kalow—running over, in their desire to make me comprehend their meaning, the names of all the principal chiefs.

Everything, in short, strengthened my suspicions with regard to the nature of the festival they were now celebrating, and which amounted almost to a certainty. While in Nukuheva I had frequently been informed that the whole tribe were never present at these cannibal banquets, but the chiefs and priests only, and everything I now observed agreed with the account.

The sound of the drums continued without intermission the whole day, and falling continually upon my ear, caused me a sensation of horror which I am unable to describe. On the following day, hearing none of those noisy indications of revelry, I concluded that the inhuman feast was terminated. And feeling a kind of morbid curiosity to discover whether the Ti might furnish any evidence of what had taken place, I proposed to Kory-Kory to walk over there. To this proposition he replied by pointing with his finger to the newly risen sun and then up to the zenith, intimating that our visit must be deferred until noon. Shortly after that hour we accordingly proceeded to the Taboo Groves, and as soon as we entered their precincts, I looked fearfully around in quest of some memorial of the scenes which had so lately been acted there, but everything appeared as usual. On reaching the Ti, we found Mehevi and a few chiefs reclining on the mats. They gave me as friendly a reception as ever. No allusions of any kind were made by them to the recent events, and I refrained for obvious reasons from referring to them myself.

After staying a short time I took my leave. In passing along the piazza, previously to descending from the pi-pi, I observed a curiously carved vessel of wood of considerable size, with a cover placed over it of the same material, and which resembled in shape a small canoe. It was surrounded by a low railing of bamboos the top of which was scarcely a foot from the ground. As the vessel had been placed in its present position since my last visit, I at once concluded that it must have some connection with the recent festival. Prompted by a curiosity I could not repress, in passing it I raised one end of the cover. At the same moment the chiefs, perceiving my design, loudly ejaculated, "Taboo! Taboo!" But the slight glimpse sufficed. My eyes fell upon the disordered members of a human skeleton, the bones still fresh with moisture, and with particles of flesh clinging to them here and there!

Kory-Kory, who had been a little in advance of me, attracted by the exclamations of the chiefs, turned around in time to witness the expression of horror on my countenance. He now hurried toward me, pointing at the same time to the canoe, and exclaiming rapidly, "Puarkee! Puarkee!" (Pig, pig). I pretended to yield to the deception, and repeated the words after him several times as though acquiescing in what he said. The other savages, either deceived by my conduct or unwilling to manifest their displeasure at what could not now be remedied, took no further notice of the occurrence, and I immediately left the Ti.

All that night I lay awake, revolving in my mind the fearful situation in which I was placed. The last horrid revelation had now been made, and the full sense of my condition rushed upon my mind with a force I had never before experienced.

Where, thought I, desponding, is there the slightest prospect of escape? The only person who seemed to possess the ability to assist me was the stranger Marnoo; but would he ever return to the valley? And if he did, should I be permitted to hold any communication with him? It seemed as if I were cut off from every source of hope, and that nothing remained but passively to await whatever fate was in store for me.

A thousand times I endeavored to account for the mysterious conduct of the natives. For what conceivable purpose did they thus retain me a captive? What could be their object in treating me with such apparent kindness, and did it not cover some treacherous scheme? Or, if they had no other design than to hold me a prisoner, how should I be able to pass away my days in this narrow valley, deprived of all intercourse with civilized beings, and forever separated from friends and home?

One hope only remained to me. The French could not long defer a visit to the bay, and if they should permanently locate any of their troops in the valley the savages could not for any length of time conceal my existence from them. But what reason had I to suppose that I should be spared until such an event occurred—an event which might be postponed by a hundred different contingencies?

CHAPTER 2

⚓

The Stranger Again Arrives
in the Valley

SINGULAR INTERVIEW WITH HIM—ATTEMPT TO ESCAPE—FAILURE—
MELANCHOLY SITUATION—SYMPATHY OF MARHEYO

M ARNOO, MARNOO PEMI!" Such were the weclome
sounds which fell upon my ear some ten days after the
events related in the preceding chapter. Once more the
approach of the stranger was heralded, and the intelligence operated upon me like magic. Again I should be
able to converse with him in my own language. And I resolved at all hazards to concert with him some scheme,
however desperate, to rescue me from a condition that
had now become insupportable.

As he drew near I remembered with many misgivings
the inauspicious termination of our former interview.

391

When he entered the house I watched with intense anxiety the reception he met with from its inmates. To my joy his appearance was hailed with the liveliest pleasure; and accosting me kindly he seated himself by my side and entered into conversation with the natives around him. It soon appeared, however, that on this occasion he had not any intelligence of importance to communicate. I inquired of him from whence he had last come. He replied from Pueearka, his native valley, and that he intended to return to it the same day.

At once it struck me that, could I but reach the valley under his protection, I might easily from thence reach Nukuheva by water. And animated by the prospect which this plan held out, I disclosed it in a few brief words to the stranger and asked him how it could be best accomplished. My heart sunk within me when in his broken English he answered me that it could never be effected. "Kannaka no let you go nowhere," he said. "You taboo. Why you no like to stay? Plenty moee-moee (sleep)— plenty kiki (eat)—plenty whihenee (young girls)—Oh, very good place Typee! Suppose you no like this bay— why you come? You no hear about Typee. All white men afraid Typee, so no white men come."

These words distressed me beyond belief. And when I again related to him the circumstances under which I had descended into the valley, and sought to enlist his sympathies in my behalf by appealing to the bodily misery I endured, he listened to me with impatience and cut me short by exclaiming passionately, "Me no hear you talk any more. By by Kannaka get mad, kill you and me too. No you see he no want you to speak to me at all? You see? Ah! By by you no mind—you get well, he kill you, eat you, hang your head up there, like Happar Kannaka. Now you listen—but no talk anymore. By by I go; you see why I go. Ah! Then some night Kannaka all moee-moee—you run away, you come Pueearka. I speak Pueearka Kannaka—he no harm you—ah! Then I take you my canoe Nukuheva—and you no run away ship no more." With these words, enforced by a vehemence of gesture I cannot describe, Marnoo started from my side, and immediately engaged in conversation with some of the chiefs who had entered the house.

It would have been idle for me to have attempted to resume the interview so peremptorily terminated by Marnoo, who was evidently little disposed to compromise his own safety by any rash endeavors to ensure mine. But the plan he had suggested struck me as one which might possibly be accomplished, and I resolved to act upon it as speedily as possible.

Accordingly, when he rose to depart, I accompanied him with the natives outside of the house, with a view to carefully noting the path he would take in leaving the valley. Just before leaping from the pi-pi he clasped my hand, and looking significantly at me, exclaimed, "Now you see—you do what I tell you—ah! Then you do good. You no do so—ah! Then you die." The next moment he waved his spear in adieu to the islanders, and following the route that conducted to a defile in the mountains lying opposite the Happar side, was soon out of sight.

A mode of escape was now presented to me, but how

was I to avail myself of it? I was continually surrounded by the savages. I could not stir from one house to another without being attended by some of them. And even during the hours devoted to slumber the slightest movement which I made seemed to attract the notice of those who shared the mats with me. In spite of these obstacles, however, I determined forthwith to make the attempt. To do so with any prospect of success, it was necessary that I should have at least two hours' start before the islanders should discover my absence. For with such facility was any alarm spread through the valley, and so familiar, of course, were the inhabitants with the intricacies of the groves, that I could not hope, lame and feeble as I was and ignorant of the route, to secure my escape unless I had this advantage. It was also by night alone that I could hope to accomplish my object, and then only by adopting the utmost precaution.

The entrance to Marheyo's habitation was through a low narrow opening in its wickerwork front. This passage, for no conceivable reason that I could devise, was always closed after the household had retired to rest, by drawing a heavy slide across it composed of a dozen or more bits of wood, ingeniously fastened together by seizings of sinnate. When any of the inmates chose to go outside the noise occasioned by the removing of this rude door awakened everybody else. On more than one occasion I had remarked that the islanders were nearly as irritable as more civilized beings under similar circumstances.

The difficulty thus placed in my way I determined to obviate in the following manner. I would get up boldly in the course of the night, and drawing the slide, issue from the house, and pretend that my object was merely to procure a drink from the calabash, which always stood outside the dwelling on the corner of the pi-pi. On re-entering I would purposely omit closing the passage after me, and trusting that the indolence of the savages would prevent them from repairing my neglect, would return to my mat, and waiting patiently until all were again asleep, I would then steal forth and at once take the route to Pueearka.

The very night which followed Marnoo's departure, I proceeded to put this project into execution. About midnight, as I imagined, I rose and drew the slide. The natives, just as I had expected, started up, while some of them asked, "Arware poo awa, Tommo?" (Where are you going, Tommo?) "Wai," (water) I laconically answered, grasping the calabash. On hearing my reply they sank back again, and in a minute or two I returned to my mat, anxiously awaiting the result of the experiment.

One after another the savages turning restlessly, appeared to resume their slumbers. And rejoicing at the stillness which prevailed, I was about to rise again from my couch when I heard a slight rustling. A dark form was intercepted between me and the doorway. The slide was drawn across it, and the individual, whoever he was, returned to his mat. This was a sad blow to me; but as it might have roused the suspicions of the islanders to have made another attempt that night, I was reluctantly obliged to defer it until the next.

Several times afterward I repeated the same maneuver,

but with as little success as before. As my pretense for
withdrawing from the house was to allay my thirst, Kory-
Kory, either suspecting some design on my part or else
prompted by a desire to please me, regularly every evening placed a calabash of water by my side.

Even under these inauspicious circumstances I again
and again renewed the attempt. But when I did so my
valet always rose with me, as if determined I should not
remove myself from his observation. For the present,
therefore, I was obliged to abandon the attempt; but I
endeavored to console myself with the idea that by this
mode I might yet effect my escape.

Shortly after Marnoo's visit I was reduced to such a
state that it was with extreme difficulty I could walk,
even with the assistance of a spear, and Kory-Kory was
obliged to carry me daily to the stream.

For hours and hours during the warmest part of the
day I lay upon my mat, and while those around me were
nearly all dozing away in careless ease, I remained awake
gloomily pondering over the fate which it appeared now
idle for me to resist. When I thought of the loved friends
who were thousands and thousands of miles from the savage island in which I was held a captive, and when I
reflected that my dreadful fate would forever be concealed from them, and that with hope deferred they might
continue to await my return long after my inanimate
form had blended with the dust of the valley, I could not
repress a shudder of anguish.

How vividly is impressed upon my mind every minute

feature of the scene which met my view during those long days of suffering and sorrow! At my request my mats were always spread directly facing the door, opposite which, and at a little distance, was the hut of boughs Marheyo was building.

Whenever my gentle Fayaway and Kory-Kory, laying themselves down beside me, would leave me awhile to uninterrupted repose, I took a strange interest in the slightest movements of the eccentric old warrior. All alone during the stillness of the tropical midday he would pursue his quiet work, sitting in the shade and weaving together the leaflets of his coconut branches, or rolling upon his knee the twisted fibers of bark to form the cords with which he tied together the thatching of his tiny house. Frequently suspending his employment, and noticing my melancholy eye fixed upon him, he would raise his hand with a gesture expressive of deep commiseration. Then moving toward me slowly he would enter on tiptoe, fearful of disturbing the slumbering natives, and taking the fan from my hand would sit before me, swaying it gently to and fro and gazing earnestly into my face.

Just beyond the pi-pi, and disposed in a triangle before the entrance of the house, were three magnificent breadfruit trees. At this moment I can recall to my mind their slender shafts, and the graceful inequalities of their bark, on which my eye was accustomed to dwell day after day in the midst of my solitary musings. It is strange how inanimate objects will twine themselves into our affections, especially in the hour of affliction. Even now, amid all the bustle and stir of the proud and busy city in which I am dwelling, the image of those three trees seems to come as vividly before my eyes as if they were actually present, and I still feel the soothing quiet pleasure which I then had in watching hour after hour their topmost boughs waving gracefully in the breeze.

⚓

CHAPTER 3

The Escape

NEARLY THREE WEEKS had elapsed since the second visit of Marnoo, and it must have been more than four months since I entered the valley, when one day about noon, while everything lay in profound silence, Mow-Mow, the one-eyed chief, suddenly appeared at the door, and leaning toward me as I lay directly facing him, said in a low tone, "Toby pemi ena" (Toby has arrived). Gracious heaven! What a tumult of emotions rushed upon me at this startling intelligence! Insensible to the pain that had before distracted me, I leaped to my feet and called wildly to Kory-Kory, who was reposing by my side. The startled islanders sprang from their mats. The news was quickly communicated to them, and the next moment I was making my way to the Ti on the back of Kory-Kory, surrounded by the excited savages.

All that I could comprehend of the particulars which

Mow-Mow rehearsed to his auditors as we proceeded, was that my long-lost companion had arrived in a boat which had just entered the bay. These tidings made me most anxious to be carried at once to the sea, lest some untoward circumstance should prevent our meeting. But to this they would not consent, and continued their course toward the royal abode. As we approached it, Mehevi and several chiefs showed themselves from the piazza, and called upon us loudly to come to them.

As soon as we approached, I endeavored to make them understand that I was going down to the sea to meet Toby. To this the king objected and motioned Kory-Kory to bring me into the house. It was in vain to resist; and in a few moments I found myself within the Ti, surrounded by a noisy group engaged in discussing the recent intelligence. Toby's name was frequently repeated, coupled with violent exclamations of astonishment. It seemed as if they yet remained in doubt with regard to the fact of his arrival, and at every fresh report that was brought from the shore they betrayed the liveliest emotions.

Almost frenzied at being held in this state of suspense, I passionately besought Mehevi to permit me to proceed. Whether my companion had arrived or not, I felt a presentiment that my own fate was about to be decided. Again and again I renewed my petition to Mehevi. He regarded me with a fixed and serious eye, but at length yielding to my importunity, reluctantly granted my request.

Accompanied by some fifty of the natives, I now

rapidly continued my journey, every few moments being transferred from the back of one to another, and urging my bearer forward all the while with earnest entreaties. As I was thus hurried forward, no doubt as to the truth of the information I had received ever crossed my mind. I was alive only to the one overwhelming idea, that a chance of deliverance was now afforded me if the jealous opposition of the savages could be overcome.

Having been prohibited from approaching the sea during the whole of my stay in the valley, I had always associated with it the idea of escape. Toby too—if indeed he had ever voluntarily deserted me—must have effected his flight by the sea. Now that I was drawing near to it myself, I indulged in hopes which I had never felt before. It was evident that a boat had entered the bay, and I saw little reason to doubt the truth of the report that it had brought my companion. Every time therefore that we gained an elevation, I looked eagerly around, hoping to behold him.

In the midst of an excited throng, who by their violent gestures and wild cries appeared to be under the influence of some excitement as strong as my own, I was now borne along at a rapid trot, frequently stooping my head to avoid the branches which crossed their path, and never ceasing to implore those who carried me to accelerate their already swift pace.

In this manner we had proceeded about four or five miles, when we were met by a party of some twenty islanders, between whom and those who accompanied me ensued an animated conference. Impatient of the delay occasioned by this interruption, I was beseeching the man who carried me to proceed without his loitering companions, when Kory-Kory, running to my side, informed me, in three fatal words, that the news had all proved false—that Toby had not arrived—"Toby owlee permi." Heaven only knows how, in the state of mind and body I then was, I ever sustained the agony which this intelligence caused me. Not that the news was altogether unexpected, but I had trusted that the fact might not be made known until we had arrived at the beach. As it was, I at once foresaw the course the savages would pursue. They had only yielded thus far to my entreaties that I might give a joyful welcome to my long-absent comrade; but now that it was known he had not arrived they would at once oblige me to turn back.

My anticipations were but too correct. In spite of the resistance I made, they carried me into a house which was near the spot, and left me upon the mats. Shortly afterward several of those who had accompanied me from the Ti, detaching themselves from the others, proceeded in the direction of the sea. Those who remained—among whom were Marheyo, Mow-Mow, Kory-Kory, and Tinor —gathered about the dwelling and appeared to be awaiting their return.

This convinced me that strangers—perhaps some of my own countrymen—had for some cause or other entered the bay. Distracted at the idea of their vicinity and reckless of the pain which I suffered, I heeded not the assurances of the islanders that there were no boats at the beach, but starting to my feet endeavored to gain the door. Instantly the passage was blocked up by several men, who commanded me to resume my seat. The fierce looks of the irritated savages admonished me that I could gain nothing by force, and that it was by entreaty alone that I could hope to compass my object.

Guided by this consideration, I turned to Mow-Mow, the only chief present whom I had been much in the habit of seeing, and carefully concealing my real design, tried to make him comprehend that I still believed Toby to have arrived on the shore, and besought him to allow me to go forward to welcome him. To all his repeated assertions that my companion had not been seen I pretended to turn a deaf ear, while I urged my solicitations with an eloquence of gesture which the one-eyed chief appeared unable to resist. He seemed indeed to regard me as a forward child, to whose wishes he had not the heart to oppose force, and whom he must consequently humor. He spoke a few words to the natives, who retreated from the door and immediately passed out of the house.

Here I looked earnestly around for Kory-Kory; but that hitherto faithful servitor was nowhere to be seen. Unwilling to linger even for a single instant when every moment might be so important, I motioned to a muscular fellow near me to take me upon his back; to my surprise he angrily refused. I turned to another, but with a like result. A third attempt was as unsuccessful and I immediately perceived what had induced Mow-Mow to grant my request, and why the other natives conducted themselves in so strange a manner. It was evident that the chief had only given me liberty to continue my progress toward the sea because he supposed that I was deprived of the means of reaching it.

Convinced by this of their determination to retain me a captive, I became desperate; and almost insensible to the pain which I suffered I seized a spear which was leaning against the projecting eaves of the house, and supporting myself with it, resumed the path that swept by the dwelling. To my surprise I was suffered to proceed alone, all the natives remaining in front of the house and engaging in earnest conversation which every moment became more loud and vehement. And to my unspeakable delight I perceived that some difference of opinion had arisen between them. In short, two parties had been formed, and consequently in their divided counsels there was some chance of my deliverance.

Before I had proceeded a hundred yards I was again surrounded by the savages, who were still in all the heat of argument, and appeared every moment as if they would come to blows. In the midst of this tumult old Marheyo came to my side, and I shall never forget the benevolent expression of his countenance. He placed his arm upon my shoulder, and emphatically pronounced the only two English words I had taught him—"home" and "mother." I at once understood what he meant, and eagerly expressed my thanks to him. Fayaway and Kory-Kory were by his side, both weeping violently; and it was not until the old man had twice repeated the command that his son could bring himself to obey him, and take me again upon his back. The one-eyed chief opposed his doing so, but he was overruled, and, as it seemed to me, by some of his own party.

We proceeded onward, and never shall I forget the ecstasy I felt when I first heard the roar of the surf breaking upon the beach. Before long I saw the flashing billows themselves through the opening between the trees. Oh, glorious sight and sound of ocean! With what rapture did I hail you as familiar friend! By this time the shouts of the crowd upon the beach were distinctly audible, and in the blended confusion of sounds I almost fancied I could distinguish the voices of my own countrymen.

When we reached the open space which lay between the groves and the sea, the first object that met my view was an English whaleboat, lying with her bow pointed from the shore, only a few fathoms distant from it. It was manned by five islanders, dressed in short tunics of calico. My first impression was that they were in the very act of pulling out from the bay, and that after all my exertions I had come to late. My soul sunk within me: but a second glance convinced me that the boat was only hanging off to keep out of the surf; and the next moment I heard my own name shouted out by a voice from the midst of the crowd.

Looking in the direction of the sound, I perceived, to my indescribable joy, the tall figure of Karakoee, an Oahu Kannaka, who had often been aboard the *Dolly* while she lay in Nukuheva. He wore the green shooting jacket with gilt buttons which had been given to him by an officer of the *Reine Blanche*—the French flagship

—and in which I had always seen him dressed. I now remembered the Kannaka had frequently told me that his
person was tabooed in all the valleys of the island, and
the sight of him at such a moment as this filled my heart
with a tumult of delight.

Karakoee stood near the edge of the water with a large
roll of cotton cloth thrown over one arm, and holding
two or three canvas bags of powder, while with the other
hand he grasped a musket, which he appeared to be
proffering to several of the chiefs around him. But they
turned with disgust from his offers, and seemed to be impatient at his presence, with vehement gestures waving
him off to his boat, and commanding him to depart.

The Kannaka, however, still maintained his ground,
and I at once perceived that he was seeking to purchase
my freedom. Animated by the idea, I called upon him
loudly to come to me; but he replied, in broken English,
that the islanders had threatened to pierce him with their
spears if he stirred a foot toward me. At this time I was
still advancing, surrounded by a dense throng of the
natives, several of whom had their hands upon me, and
more than one javelin was threateningly pointed at me.
Still I perceived clearly that many of those least friendly
toward me looked irresolute and anxious.

I was still some thirty yards from Karakoee when my
further progress was prevented by the natives, who com-
pelled me to sit down upon the ground, while they still
retained their hold upon my arms. The din and tumult
now became tenfold, and I perceived that several of the
priests were on the spot, all of whom were evidently urg-

ing Mow-Mow and the other chiefs to prevent my departure; and the detestable word "Roo-ne! Roo-ne!" which
I had heard repeated a thousand times during the day,
was now shouted out on every side of me. Still I saw that
the Kannaka continued his exertions in my favor—that
he was boldly debating the matter with the savages and
was striving to entice them by displaying his cloth and
powder and snapping the lock of his musket. But all he
said or did appeared only to augment the clamors of
those around him, who seemed bent upon driving him
into the sea.

When I remembered the extravagant value placed by
these people upon the articles which were offered to
them in exchange for me, and which were so indignantly
rejected, I saw a new proof of the same fixed determination of purpose they had all along manifested with regard
to me, and in despair and reckless of consequences, I
exerted all my strength, and shaking myself free from
the grasp of those who held me, I sprang to my feet and
rushed toward Karakoee.

The rash attempt nearly decided my fate. For fearful
that I might slip from them, several of the islanders now
raised a simultaneous shout, and pressing upon Karakoee,
they menaced him with furious gestures and actually
forced him into the sea. Appalled at their violence, the
poor fellow, standing nearly to the waist in the surf, endeavored to pacify them; but at length, fearful that they
would do him some fatal violence, he beckoned to his
comrades to pull in at once, and take him into the boat.

It was at this agonizing moment, when I thought all

hope was ended, that a new contest arose between the two parties who had accompanied me to the shore. Blows were struck, wounds were given, and blood flowed. In the interest excited by the fray everyone had left me except Marheyo, Kory-Kory, and poor dear Fayaway, who clung to me, sobbing indignantly. I saw that now or never was the moment. Clasping my hands together, I looked imploringly at Marheyo, and moved toward the now almost deserted beach. The tears were in the old man's eyes, but neither he nor Kory-Kory attempted to hold me, and I soon reached the Kannaka who had been anxiously watching my movements. The rowers pulled in as near as they dared to the edge of the surf. I gave one parting embrace to Fayaway, who seemed speechless with sorrow, and the next instant I found myself safe in the boat. Karakoee by my side told the rowers at once to give way. Marheyo and Kory-Kory, and a great many of the women followed me into the water, and I was determined, as the only mark of gratitude I could show, to give them the articles which had been brought as my ransom. I handed the musket to Kory-Kory, with a rapid gesture which was equivalent to a "Deed of Gift," threw the roll of cotton to old Marheyo, pointing as I did so to poor Fayaway, who had retired from the edge of the water and was sitting down disconsolate on the beach, and tumbled the powder bags out to the nearest young ladies, all of whom were vastly willing to take them. This distribution did not occupy ten seconds, and before it was over the boat was under full way, the Kannaka all the while exclaiming loudly against what he considered a useless throwing away of valuable property.

Although it was clear that my movements had been noticed by several of the natives, still they had not suspended the conflict in which they were engaged, and it was not until the boat was above fifty yards from the shore that Mow-Mow and some six or seven other warriors rushed into the sea and hurled their javelins at us. Some of the weapons passed quite as close to us as was desirable, but no one was wounded, and the men pulled away gallantly. But although soon out of the reach of the spears, our progress was extremely slow. It blew strong upon the shore, and the tide was against us. I saw Kara-koee, who was steering the boat, give many a look toward a jutting point of the bay around which we had to pass.

For a minute or two after our departure the savages, who had formed into different groups, remained perfectly motionless and silent. All at once the enraged chief showed by his gestures that he had resolved what course he would take. Shouting loudly to his companions and pointing with his tomahawk toward the headland, he set off at full speed in that direction, and was followed by about thirty of the natives, among whom were several of the priests, all yelling out "Roo-ne! Roo-ne!" at the very top of their voices. Their intention was evidently to swim off from the headland and intercept us in our course. The wind was freshening every minute, and was right in our teeth, and it was one of those chopping angry seas in which it is so difficult to row. Still the chances seemed in our favor. But when we came within a hundred yards

of the point, the active savages were already dashing
into the water, and we all feared that within five minutes' time we should have a score of the infuriated
wretches around us. If so, our doom was sealed, for these
savages, unlike the feeble swimmers of civilized coun-
tries, are, if anything, more formidable antagonists in the
water than when on the land. It was all a trial of strength.
Our natives pulled till their oars bent again, and the
crowd of swimmers shot through the water despite its
roughness, with fearful rapidity.

By the time we had reached the headland, the savages
were spread right across our course. Our rowers got out
their knives and held them ready between their teeth,
and I seized the boathook. We were well aware that if
they succeeded in intercepting us they would practice
upon us the maneuver which has proved so fatal to many
a boat's crew in these seas. They would grapple the oars,
and seizing hold of the gunwale, capsize the boat, and
then we should be entirely at their mercy.

After a few breathless moments I discerned Mow-
Mow. The athletic islander, with his tomahawk between
his teeth, was dashing the water before him till it foamed
again. He was the nearest to us, and in another instant
he would have seized one of the oars. Even at the moment I felt horror at the act I was about to commit. But
it was no time for pity or compunction; with a true aim
and exerting all my strength, I dashed the boathook at
him. It struck him just below the throat, and forced
him downward. I had no time to repeat my blow, but

I saw him rise to the surface in the wake of the boat, and never shall I forget the ferocious expression of his countenance.

Only one other of the savages reached the boat. He seized the gunwale, but the knives of our rowers so mauled his wrist that he was forced to quit his hold, and the next minute we were past them all, and in safety. The strong excitement which had thus far kept me up, now left me, and I fell back fainting into the arms of Karakoee.

The circumstances connected with my most unexpected escape may be very briefly stated. The captain of an Australian vessel, being in distress for men in these remote seas, had put into Nukuheva in order to recruit his ship's company. Not a single man was to be obtained, and the barque was about to get under weigh when she was boarded by Karakoee, who informed the disappointed Englishman that an American sailor was detained by the savages in the neighboring bay of Typee; he then offered, that if supplied with suitable articles of traffic, he would undertake his release. The Kannaka had gained his intelligence from Marnoo, to whom, after all, I was indebted for my escape. The proposition was acceded to. Karakoee, taking with him five tabooed natives of Nukuheva, again repaired aboard the barque, which in a few hours sailed to that part of the island and threw her main topsail aback right off the entrance to the Typee bay. The whaleboat, manned by the tabooed crew, pulled toward the head of the inlet while the ship lay "off and on" awaiting its return.

The events which ensued have already been detailed, and little more remains to be related. On reaching the *Julia* I was lifted over the side, and my strange appearance and remarkable adventure occasioned the liveliest interest. Every attention was bestowed upon me that humanity could suggest. But to such a state was I reduced, that three months elapsed before I recovered my health.

The mystery which hung over the fate of my friend and companion Toby has never been cleared up. I still remain ignorant whether he succeeded in leaving the valley, or perished at the hands of the islanders.

BILLY BUDD

⚓

The Complete Novel

Dedicated to Jack Chase, Englishman, wherever that great heart may now be, here on earth or harbored in paradise. Captain of the maintop in the year 1843 in the U.S. Frigate *United States*.

BILLY BUDD

⚓

Author's Preface

THE year 1797, the year of this narrative, belongs to a period which, as every thinker now feels, involved a crisis for Christendom not exceeded in its undetermined momentousness at the time by any other era whereof there is record. The opening proposition made by the Spirit of that Age involved rectification of the Old World's hereditary wrongs. In France, to some extent, this was bloodily effected. But what then? Straightway the Revolution itself became a wrongdoer, one more oppressive than the kings. Under Napoleon it enthroned upstart kings, and initiated that prolonged agony of continual war whose final throe was Waterloo. During those years not the wisest could have foreseen that the outcome of all would be what to some thinkers apparently it has since turned out to be—a political advance along nearly the whole line for Europeans.

Now, as elsewhere hinted, it was something caught from the Revolutionary Spirit that at Spithead emboldened the man-of-war's men to rise against real abuses, long-standing ones, and afterwards at the Nore to make inordinate and aggressive demands—successful resistance to which was confirmed only when the ringleaders were hung for an admonitory spectacle to the anchored fleet. Yet, in a way analogous to the operation of the Revolution at large, the Great Mutiny, though by Englishmen naturally deemed monstrous at the time, doubtless gave the first latent prompting to most important reforms in the British navy.

⚓

Billy Budd

1

IN THE TIME before steamships, or then more frequently than now, a stroller along the docks of any considerable seaport would occasionally have his attention arrested by a group of bronzed mariners, man-of-war's men or merchant sailors in holiday attire ashore on liberty. In certain instances they would flank, or like a bodyguard, quite surround some superior figure of their own class, moving along with them like Aldebaran among the lesser lights of his constellation. That signal object was the "Handsome Sailor" of the less prosaic time alike of the military and merchant navies. With no perceptible trace of the vainglorious about him, rather with the offhand unaffectedness of natural regality, he seemed to accept the spontaneous homage of his shipmates.

A somewhat remarkable instance recurs to me. In Liverpool, now half a century ago, I saw under the shadow of the great dingy street-wall of Prince's Dock (an obstruction long since removed) a common sailor, so intensely black that he must needs have been a native African of the unadulterate blood of Ham. A symmetric figure much above the average height. The two ends of a gay silk handkerchief thrown loose about the neck danced upon the displayed ebony of his chest; in his ears were big hoops of gold, and a Scotch Highland bonnet with a tartan band set off his shapely head.

It was a hot noon in July, and his face, lustrous with perspiration, beamed with barbaric good humor. In jovial sallies right and left, his white teeth flashing into view, he rollicked along, the center of a company of his shipmates. These were made up of such an assortment of tribes and complexions as would have well fitted them to be marched up by Anacharsis Cloots before the bar of the first French Assembly as Representatives of the Human Race.[1] At each spontaneous tribute rendered by the wayfarers to this black pagoda of a fellow—the tribute of a pause and stare, and less frequently an exclamation—the motley retinue showed that they took that sort of pride in the evoker of it which the Assyrian priests doubtless showed for their grand sculptured Bull when the faithful prostrated themselves.

To return.

If in some cases a bit of a nautical Murat[2] in setting

---

[1] An incident described in Carlyle's *French Revolution.*
[2] A French military adventurer and conspirator with Napoleon.

forth his person ashore, the Handsome Sailor of the period in question evinced nothing of the dandified Billy-be-Damn, an amusing character all but extinct now, but occasionally to be encountered, and in a form yet more amusing than the original, at the tiller of the boats on the tempestuous Erie Canal, or, more likely, vaporing in the groggeries along the towpath. Invariably a proficient in his perilous calling, he was also more or less of a mighty boxer or wrestler. It was strength and beauty. Tales of his prowess were recited. Ashore he was the champion, afloat the spokesman; on every suitable occasion always foremost. Close-reefing topsails in a gale, there he was, astride the weather yardarm end, foot in the Flemish horse as "stirrup," both hands tugging at the "earing" as at a bridle, in very much the attitude of young Alexander curbing the fiery Bucephalus.[1] A superb figure, tossed up as by the horns of Taurus against the thunderous sky, cheerily hallooing to the strenuous file along the spar.

The moral nature was seldom out of keeping with the physical make. Indeed, except as toned by the former, the comeliness and power, always attractive in masculine conjunction, hardly could have drawn the sort of honest homage the Handsome Sailor in some examples received from his less gifted associates.

Such a cynosure, at least in aspect, and something such too in nature, though with important variations made apparent as the story proceeds, was welkin-eyed Billy Budd, or Baby Budd as more familiarly under cir-

---

[1] The famous war horse of Alexander the Great.

cumstances hereafter to be given he at last came to be called, aged twenty-one, a foretopman of the British fleet toward the close of the last decade of the eighteenth century. It was not very long prior to the time of the narration that follows that he had entered the King's Service, having been impressed on the Narrow Seas from a homeward-bound English merchantman into a seventy-four outward-bound, H.M.S. *Indomitable;* which ship, as was not unusual in those hurried days having been obliged to put to sea short of her proper complement of men. Plump upon Billy at first sight in the gangway the boarding officer Lieutenant Ratcliffe pounced, even before the merchantman's crew was formally mustered on the quarterdeck for his deliberate inspection. And him only he elected. For whether it was because the other men when ranged before him showed to ill advantage after Billy, or whether he had some scruples in view of the merchantman being rather short-handed, however it might be, the officer contented himself with his first spontaneous choice. To the surprise of the ship's company, though much to the lieutenant's satisfaction, Billy made no demur. But, indeed, any demur would have been as idle as the protest of a goldfinch popped into a cage.

Noting this uncomplaining acquiescence, all but cheerful one might say, the shipmates turned a surprise glance of silent reproach at the sailor. The shipmaster was one of those worthy mortals found in every vocation, even the humbler ones—the sort of person whom everybody agrees in calling "a respectable man." And—nor so strange to report as it may appear to be—though a plow-

man of the troubled waters, lifelong contending with the
intractable elements, there was nothing this honest soul
at heart loved better than simple peace and quiet. For
the rest, he was fifty or thereabouts, a little inclined
to corpulence, a prepossessing face, unwhiskered, and
of an agreeable color—a rather full face, humanely intelligent in expression. On a fair day with a fair wind and all
going well, a certain musical chime in his voice seemed
to be the veritable unobstructed outcome of the innermost man. He had much prudence, much conscientious-
ness, and there were occasions when these virtues were
the cause of overmuch disquietude in him. On a passage,
so long as his craft was in any proximity to land, no sleep
for Captain Graveling. He took to heart those serious
responsibilities not so heavily borne by some shipmasters.

Now while Billy Budd was down in the forecastle getting his kit together, the *Indomitable's* lieutenant, burly
and bluff, nowise disconcerted by Captain Graveling's
omitting to proffer the customary hospitalities on an occasion so unwelcome to him, an omission simply caused
by preoccupation of thought, unceremoniously invited
himself into the cabin, and also to a flask from the spirit-
locker, a receptacle which his experienced eye instantly
discovered. In fact he was one of those sea dogs in whom
all the hardship and peril of naval life in the great prolonged wars of his time never impaired the natural instinct for sensuous enjoyment. His duty he always faithfully did; but duty is sometimes a dry obligation, and he
was for irrigating its aridity, whensoever possible, with
a fertilizing decoction of strong waters. For the cabin's

proprietor there was nothing left but to play the part of the enforced host with whatever grace and alacrity were practicable. As necessary adjuncts to the flask, he silently placed tumbler and water-jug before the irrepressible guest. But excusing himself from partaking just then, he dismally watched the unembarrassed officer deliberately diluting his grog a little, then tossing it off in three swallows, pushing the empty tumbler away, yet not so far as to be beyond easy reach, at the same time settling himself in his seat and smacking his lips with high satisfaction, looking straight at the host.

These proceedings over, the master broke the silence, and there lurked a rueful reproach in the tone of his voice: "Lieutenant, you are going to take my best man from me, the jewel of 'em."

"Yes, I know," rejoined the other, immediately drawing back the tumbler preliminary to a replenishing. "Yes, I know. Sorry."

"Beg pardon, but you don't understand, Lieutenant. See here now. Before I shipped that young fellow, my forecastle was a rat-pit of quarrels. It was black times, I tell you aboard the *Rights* here. I was worried to that degree my pipe had no comfort for me. But Billy came, and it was like a Catholic priest striking peace in an Irish shindy. Not that he preached to them or said or did anything in particular, but a virtue went out of him, sugaring the sour ones. They took to him like hornets to treacle; all but the buffer of the gang, the big shaggy chap with the fire-red whiskers. He indeed, out of envy, perhaps, of the newcomer, and thinking such a 'sweet and pleasant fellow,' as he mockingly designated him to the others, could hardly have the spirit of a gamecock, must needs bestir himself in trying to get up an ugly row with him. Billy forebore with him and reasoned with him in a pleasant way—he is something like myself, Lieutenant, to whom aught like a quarrel is hateful—but nothing served. So, in the second dog watch one day the Red Whiskers, in presence of the others, under pretense of showing Billy just whence a sirloin steak was cut—for the fellow had once been a butcher—insultingly gave him a dig under the ribs. Quick as lightning Billy let fly his arm. I dare say he never meant to do quite as much as he did, but anyhow he gave the burly fool a terrible drubbing. It took about half a minute, I should think. And, Lord bless you, the lubber was astonished at the celerity. And will you believe it, Lieutenant, the Red Whiskers now really loves Billy—loves him, or is the biggest hypocrite that ever I heard of. But they all love him. Some of 'em do his washing, darn his old trousers for him; the carpenter is at odd times making a pretty little chest of drawers for him. Anybody will do anything for Billy Budd; and it's the happy family here. But now, Lieutenant, if that young fellow goes—I know how it will be aboard the *Rights*. Not again very soon shall I, coming up from dinner, lean over the capstan smoking a quiet pipe—no, not very soon again, I think. Aye, Lieutenant, you are going to take away the jewel of 'em; you are going to take away my peacemaker!" And with that the good soul had really some ado in checking a rising sob.

"Well," said the officer, who had listened with amused

interest to all this, and now waxing merry with his tipple,
"well, blessed are the peacemakers, especially the fighting
peacemakers! And such are the seventy-four beauties
some of which you see poking their noses out of the portholes of yonder warship lying to for me," pointing through
the cabin window at the *Indomitable*. "But courage!
don't you look so downhearted, man. Why, I pledge you
in advance the royal approbation. Rest assured that His
Majesty will be delighted to know that in a time when
his hardtack is not sought for by sailors with such avidity
as should be, a time also when some shipmasters privily
resent the borrowing from them a tar or two for the serv-
ices, His Majesty, I say, will be delighted to learn that
one shipmaster at least cheerfully surrenders to the King
the flower of his flock, a sailor who with equal loyalty
makes no dissent.—But where's my beauty? Ah," looking
through the cabin's open door, "here he comes; and, by
Jove—lugging along his chest—Apollo with his portman-
teau!—My man," stepping out to him, "you can't take that
big box aboard a warship. The boxes there are mostly
shot-boxes. Put your duds in a bag, lad. Boot and saddle
for the cavalrymen, bag and hammock for the man-of-
war's man."

The transfer from chest to bag was made. And, after
seeing his man into the cutter and then following him
down, the lieutenant pushed off from the *Rights-of-Man*.
That was the merchant ship's name, though by her master
and crew abbreviated in sailor fashion into the *Rights*.
The hard-headed Dundee owner was a staunch admirer
of Thomas Paine, whose book in rejoinder to Burke's

arraignment of the French Revolution had then been published for some time and had gone everywhere. In christening his vessel after the title of Paine's volume the man of Dundee was something like his contemporary shipowner, Stephen Girard of Philadelphia, whose sympathies, alike with his native land and its liberal philosophers, he evinced by naming his ships after Voltaire, Diderot, and so forth.

But now, when the boat swept under the merchantman's stern, and officer and oarsmen were noting—some bitterly and others with a grin—the name emblazoned there, just then it was that the new recruit jumped up from the bow where the coxswain had directed him to sit, and waving his hat to his silent shipmates sorrowfully looking over at him from the taffrail, bade the lads a genial good-bye. Then, making a salutation as to the ship herself, "And good-bye to you too, old *Rights of Man.*"

"Down, sir!" roared the lieutenant, instantly assuming all the rigor of his rank, though with difficulty repressing a smile.

To be sure, Billy's action was a terrible breach of naval decorum. But in that decorum he had never been instructed, in consideration of which the lieutenant would hardly have been so energetic in reproof but for the concluding farewell to the ship. This he rather took as meant to convey a covert sally on the new recruit's part, a sly slur at impressment in general, and that of himself in especial. And yet, more likely, if satire it was in effect, it was hardly so by intention, for Billy, though happily endowed with the gaiety of high health, youth, and a free

heart, was yet by no means of a satirical turn. The will to
it and the sinister dexterity were alike wanting. To deal
in double meanings and insinuations of any sort was quite
foreign to his nature.

As to his enforced enlistment, that he seemed to take
pretty much as he was wont to take any vicissitude of
weather. Like the animals, though no philosopher, he
was, without knowing it, practically a fatalist. And it may
be that he rather liked this adventurous turn in his affairs,
which promised an opening into novel scenes and martial
excitements.

Aboard the *Indomitable* our merchant sailor was forthwith rated as an able seaman and assigned to the starboard watch of the foretop. He was soon at home in the
service, not at all disliked for his unpretentious good
looks and a sort of genial happy-go-lucky air. No merrier
man in his mess, in marked contrast to certain other individuals included like himself among the impressed portion of the ship's company; for these when not actively
employed were sometimes, and more particularly in the
last dog watch when the drawing near of twilight induced reverie, apt to fall into a saddish mood which in
some partook of sullenness. But they were not so young
as our foretopman, and no few of them must have known
a hearth of some sort; others may have had wives and
children left, too probably, in uncertain circumstances,
and hardly any but must have had acknowledged kith
and kin, while for Billy, as will shortly be seen, his entire
family was practically invested in himself.

2

Though our new-made foretopman was well received in the top and on the gun decks, hardly here was he that cynosure he had previously been among those minor ship's companies of the merchant marine, with which companies only had he hitherto consorted.

He was young, and, despite his all but fully developed frame, in aspect looked even younger than he really was, owing to a lingering adolescent expression in the as yet smooth face all but feminine in purity of natural complexion but where, thanks to his seagoing, the lily was quite suppressed and the rose had some ado visibly to flush through the tan.

To one essentially such a novice in the complexities of factitious life, the abrupt transition from his former and simpler sphere to the ampler and more knowing world of a great warship—this might well have abashed him had there been any conceit or vanity in his composition. Among her miscellaneous multitude, the *Indomitable* mustered several individuals who, however inferior in grade, were of no common natural stamp, sailors more signally susceptive of that air which continuous martial discipline and repeated presence in battle can in some degree impart even to the average man. As the Handsome Sailor Billy Budd's position aboard the seventy-four was something analogous to that of a rustic beauty trans-

planted from the provinces and brought into competition
with the highborn dames of the court. But this change of
circumstances he scarce noted. As little did he observe
that something about him provoked an ambiguous smile
in one or two harder faces among the bluejackets. Nor less
unaware was he of the peculiar favorable effect his person and demeanor had upon the more intelligent gentlemen of the quarterdeck. Nor could this well have been
otherwise. Cast in a mold peculiar to the finest physical
examples of those Englishmen in whom the Saxon strain
would seem not at all to partake of any Norman or other
admixture, he showed in face that humane look of repose-
ful good nature which the Greek sculptor in some instances gave to his heroic strong man, Hercules. But this
again was subtly modified by another and pervasive quality. The ear, small and shapely, the arch of the foot, the
curve in mouth and nostril, even the indurated hand dyed
to the orange-tawny of the toucan's bill, a hand telling
alike of the halyards and tar bucket; but, above all, something in the mobile expression, and every chance attitude
and movement, something suggestive of a mother emi-
nently favored by Love and the Graces; all this strangely
indicated a lineage in direct contradiction to his lot. The
mysteriousness here became less mysterious through a
matter of fact elicited when Billy at the capstan was being formally mustered into the service. Asked by the
officer, a small brisk little gentleman, as it chanced among
other questions, his place of birth, he replied, "Please,
sir, I don't know."

"Don't know where you were born?—Who was your father?"

"God knows, sir."

Struck by the straightforward simplicity of these replies, the officer next asked, "Do you know anything about your beginning?"

"No, sir. But I have heard that I was found in a pretty silk-lined basket hanging one morning from the knocker of a good man's door in Bristol."

"*Found* say you? Well," throwing back his head and looking up and down the new recruit. "Well, it turns out to have been a pretty good find. Hope they'll find some more like you, my man; the fleet sadly needs them."

Yes, Billy Budd was a foundling, a presumable byblow, and, evidently, no ignoble one. Noble descent was as evident in him as in a blood horse.

For the rest, with little or no sharpness of faculty or any trace of the wisdom of the serpent, nor yet quite a dove, he possessed that kind and degree of intelligence going along with the unconventional rectitude of a sound human creature, one to whom not yet has been proffered the questionable apple of knowledge. He was illiterate; he could not read, but he could sing, and like the illiterate nightingale was sometimes the composer of his own song.

Of self-consciousness he seemed to have little or none, or about as much as we may reasonably impute to a dog of Saint Bernard's breed.

Habitually living with the elements and knowing little more of the land than as a beach, or, rather, that portion

of the terraqueous globe providentially set apart for
dance-houses, doxies, and tapsters, in short what sailors
call a "fiddlers' green," his simple nature remained unsophisticated by those moral obliquities which are not in
every case incompatible with that manufacturable thing
known as respectability. But are sailors, frequenters of
fiddlers' greens, without vices? No, but less often than
with landsmen do their vices, so-called, partake of
crookedness of heart, seeming less to proceed from vi-
ciousness than exuberance of vitality after long constraint,
frank manifestations in accordance with natural law. By
his original constitution aided by the cooperating influences of his lot, Billy in many respects was little more
than a sort of upright barbarian, much such perhaps as
Adam presumably might have been ere the urbane serpent wriggled himself into his company.

And here be it submitted that, apparently going to
corroborate the doctrine of man's fall, a doctrine now
popularly ignored, it is observable that where certain
virtues pristine and unadulterate peculiarly characterize
anybody in the external uniform of civilization, they will
upon scrutiny seem not to be derived from custom or convention, but rather to be out of keeping with these, as if
indeed exceptionally transmitted from a period prior to
Cain's city and citified man. The character marked by
such qualities has to an unvitiated taste an untampered-
with flavor like that of berries, while the man thoroughly
civilized even in a fair specimen of the breed has to the
same moral palate a questionable smack as of a com-

pounded wine. To any stray inheritor of these primitive qualities found, like Kaspar Hauser,[1] wandering dazed in any Christian capital of our time, the good-natured poet's famous invocation, near two thousand years ago, of the good rustic out of his latitude in the Rome of the Caesars, still appropriately holds:

> Honest and poor, faithful in word and thought,
> What has thee, Fabian, to the city brought.

Though our Handsome Sailor had as much of masculine beauty as one can expect anywhere to see, nevertheless, like the beautiful woman in one of Hawthorne's minor tales, there was just one thing amiss in him. No visible blemish indeed, as with the lady; no, but an occasional liability to a vocal defect. Though in the hour of elemental uproar or peril he was everything that a sailor should be, yet under sudden provocation of strong heart-feeling his voice, otherwise singularly musical, as if expressive of the harmony within, was apt to develop an organic hesitancy, in fact more or less of a stutter or even worse. In this particular Billy was a striking instance that the arch interferer, the envious marplot of Eden, still has more or less to do with every human consignment to this planet of earth. In every case, one way or another he is sure to slip in his little card, as much as to remind us—I too have a hand here.

The avowal of such an imperfection in the Handsome

[1] A stranger who appeared in Nuremburg, Germany, around 1830. Supposedly of noble birth, he aroused international attention.

Sailor should be evidence not alone that he is not presented as a conventional hero, but also that the story in which he is the main figure is no romance.

3

At the time of Billy Budd's arbitrary enlistment into the *Indomitable* that ship was on her way to join the Mediterranean fleet. No long time elapsed before the junction was effected. As one of that fleet the seventy-four participated in its movements, though at times on account of her superior sailing qualities, in the absence of frigates despatched on separate duty as a scout and at times on less temporary service. But with all this the story has little concernment, restricted as it is to the inner life of one particular ship and the career of an individual sailor.

It was the summer of 1797. In the April of that year had occurred the commotion at Spithead, followed in May by a second and yet more serious outbreak in the fleet at the Nore. The latter is known, and without exaggeration in the epithet, as the Great Mutiny. It was indeed a demonstration more menacing to England than the contemporary manifestoes and conquering and proselyting armies of the French Directory.

To the British Empire the Nore mutiny was what a strike in the fire brigade would be to London threatened by general arson. In a crisis when the kingdom might well have anticipated the famous signal that some years later published along the naval line of battle what it was that upon occasion England expected of Englishmen, *that* was the time when at the mastheads of the three-deckers and seventy-fours moored in her own roadstead—a fleet, the right arm of a Power then all but the sole free conservative one of the Old World—the bluejackets, to be numbered by thousands, ran up with huzzahs the British colors with the union and cross wiped out; by that cancellation transmuting the flag of founded law and freedom defined into the enemy's red meteor of unbridled and unbounded revolt. Reasonable discontent growing out of practical grievances in the fleet had been ignited into irrational combustion as by live cinders blown across the Channel from France in flames.

The event converted into irony for a time those spirited strains of Dibdin—as a songwriter no mean auxiliary to the English Government at the European conjuncture—strains celebrating, among other things, the patriotic devotion of the British tar:

And as for my life, 'tis the King's!

Such an episode in the Island's grand naval story her naval historians naturally abridge, one of them (G. P. R. James) candidly acknowledging that fain would he pass it over did not "impartiality forbid fastidiousness." And yet his mention is less a narration than a reference, having to do hardly at all with details. Nor are these readily to be found in the libraries. Like some other events in every age befalling states everywhere including America, the Great Mutiny was of such character that national pride along with views of policy would fain shade it off into the historical background. Such events cannot be ignored, but there is a considerate way of historically treating them. If a well-constituted individual refrains from blazoning aught amiss or calamitous in his family, a nation in the like circumstance may without reproach be equally discreet.

Though after parleyings between Government and the ringleaders, and concessions by the former as to some glaring abuses, the first uprising—that at Spithead—with difficulty was put down, or matters for the time pacified; yet at the Nore the unforeseen renewal of insurrection on a yet larger scale, and emphasized in the conferences that ensued by demands deemed by the authorities not only inadmissible but aggressively insolent, indicated—if the Red Flag did not sufficiently do so—what was the spirit animating the men. Final suppression, however, there was, but only made possible perhaps by the unswerving loyalty of the marine corps and voluntary resumption of loyalty among influential sections of the crews.

To some extent the Nore Mutiny may be regarded as analogous to the distempering irruption of contagious fever in a frame constitutionally sound, and which anon throws it off.

At all events, of these thousands of mutineers were some of the tars who not so very long afterward—whether

wholly prompted thereto by patriotism, or pugnacious
instinct, or by both—helped to win a coronet for Nelson
at the Nile, and the naval crown of crowns for him at
Trafalgar. To the mutineers those battles and especially
Trafalgar were a plenary absolution and a grand one: For
all that goes to make up scenic naval display, heroic magnificence in arms, those battles, especially Trafalgar,
stand unmatched in human annals.

4

CONCERNING
"The greatest sailor since our world began."
—Tennyson

In this matter of writing, resolve as one may to keep to
the main road, some bypaths have an enticement not
readily to be withstood. I am going to err into such a
bypath. If the reader will keep me company I shall be
glad. At the least we can promise ourselves that pleasure
which is wickedly said to be in sinning, for a literary sin
the divergence will be.

Very likely it is no new remark that the inventions of
our time have at last brought about a change in sea warfare in degree corresponding to the revolution in all

warfare effected by the original introduction from China
into Europe of gunpowder. The first European firearm, a
clumsy contrivance, was, as is well known, scouted by no
few of the knights as a base implement, good enough
peradventure for weavers too craven to stand up crossing
steel with steel in frank fight. But as ashore knightly valor,
though shorn of its blazonry, did not cease with the
knights, neither on the seas, though nowadays in encounters there a certain kind of displayed gallantry be fallen
out of date as hardly applicable under changed circumstances, did the nobler qualities of such naval magnates
as Don John of Austria, Doria, Van Tromp, Jean Bart, the
long line of British Admirals and the American Decaturs
of 1812, become obsolete with their wooden walls.

Nevertheless, to anybody who can hold the Present at
its worth without being inappreciative of the Past, it may
be forgiven, if to such a one the solitary old hulk at
Portsmouth, Nelson's *Victory*, seems to float there, not
alone as the decaying monument of a fame incorruptible,
but also as a poetic reproach, softened by its picturesque-
ness, to the *Monitors* and yet mightier hulls of the European ironclads. And this not altogether because such
craft are unsightly, unavoidably lacking the symmetry
and grand lines of the old battleships, but equally for
other reasons.

There are some, perhaps, who, while not altogether
inaccessible to that poetic reproach just alluded to, may
yet on behalf of the new order be disposed to parry it;
and this to the extent of iconoclasm, if need be. For
example, prompted by the sight of the star inserted in the

Victory's quarterdeck designating the spot where the
Great Sailor fell, these martial utilitarians may suggest
considerations implying that Nelson's ornate publication
of his person in battle was not only unnecessary, but not
military, nay, savored of foolhardiness and vanity. They
may add, too, that at Trafalgar it was in effect nothing
less than a challenge to death, and death came; and that
but for his bravado the victorious admiral might possibly
have survived the battle, and so, instead of having his
sagacious dying injunctions overruled by his immediate
successor in command, he himself when the contest was
decided might have brought his shattered fleet to anchor,
a proceeding which might have averted the deplorable
loss of life by shipwreck in the elemental tempest that
followed the martial one.

Well, should we set aside the more disputable point
whether for various reasons it was possible to anchor the
fleet, then plausibly enough the Benthamites of war may
urge the above.

But the *might-have-been* is but boggy ground to build
on. And, certainly, in foresight as to the larger issue of an
encounter, and anxious preparations for it—buoying the
deadly way and mapping it out, as at Copenhagen—few
commanders have been so painstakingly circumspect as
this same reckless declarer of his person in fight.

Personal prudence, even when dictated by quite other
than selfish considerations, surely is no special virtue in a
military man; while an excessive love of glory, impassion-
ing a less burning impulse, the honest sense of duty, is
the first. If the name *Wellington* is not so much of a

trumpet to the blood as the simpler name *Nelson,* the reason for this may perhaps be inferred from the above. Alfred in his funeral ode on the victor of Waterloo ventures not to call him the greatest soldier of all time, though in the same ode he invokes Nelson as "the greatest sailor since our world began."

At Trafalgar Nelson on the brink of opening the fight sat down and wrote his last brief will and testament. If under the presentiment of the most magnificent of all victories to be crowned by his own glorious death, a sort of priestly motive led him to dress his person in the jeweled vouchers of his own shining deeds; if thus to have adorned himself for the altar and the sacrifice were indeed vainglory, then affectation and fustian is each a more heroic line in the great epics and dramas, since in such lines the poet but embodies in verse those exaltations of sentiment that a nature like Nelson, the opportunity being given, vitalizes into acts.

5

Yes, the outbreak at the Nore was put down. But not every grievance was redressed. If the contractors, for example, were no longer permitted to ply some practices peculiar to their tribe everywhere, such as providing shoddy cloth, rations not sound or false in the measure, not the less impressment, for one thing, went on. By custom sanctioned for centuries, and judicially maintained by a Lord Chancellor as late as Mansfield, that mode of manning the fleet, a mode now fallen into a sort of abeyance but never formally renounced, it was not practicable to give up in those years. Its abrogation would have crippled the indispensable fleet, one wholly under canvas, no steam power, its innumerable sails and thousands of cannon, everything in short, worked by muscle alone; a fleet the more insatiate in demand for men, because then multiplying its ships of all grades against contingencies present and to come of the convulsed Continent.

Discontent foreran the two mutinies, and more or less it lurkingly survived them. Hence it was not unreasonable to apprehend some return of trouble sporadic or general. One instance of such apprehensions: In the same year with this story, Nelson, then Vice Admiral Sir Horatio, being with the fleet off the Spanish coast, was directed by the admiral in command to shift his pennant from the *Captain* to the *Theseus,* and for this reason: that the latter ship, having newly arrived on the station from home, where it had taken part in the Great Mutiny, danger was apprehended from the temper of the men, and it was thought that an officer like Nelson was the one, not indeed to terrorize the crew into base subjection, but to win them, by force of his mere presence, back to an allegiance, if not as enthusiastic as his own, yet as true. So it was that for a time on more than one quarterdeck anxiety did exist. At sea, precautionary vigilance was strained against relapse. At short notice an engagement

might come on. When it did, the lieutenants assigned to
batteries felt it incumbent on them, in some instances, to
stand with drawn swords behind the men working the
guns.

6

But on board the seventy-four in which Billy now swung
his hammock, very little in the manner of the men and
nothing obvious in the demeanor of the officers would
have suggested to an ordinary observer that the Great
Mutiny was a recent event. In their general bearing and
conduct the commissioned officers of a warship naturally
take their tone from the commander, that is if he have
that ascendancy of character that ought to be his.

Captain the Honorable Edward Fairfax Vere, to give
his full title, was a bachelor of forty or thereabouts, a
sailor of distinction even in a time prolific of renowned
seamen. Though allied to the higher nobility his advance-
ment had not been altogether owing to influences connected with that circumstance. He had seen much
service, been in various engagements, always acquitting
himself as an officer mindful of the welfare of his men, but
never tolerating an infraction of discipline; thoroughly
versed in the science of his profession, and intrepid to the
verge of temerity, though never injudiciously so. For his

gallantry in the West Indian waters as flag-lieutenant under Rodney in that admiral's crowning victory over De Grasse, he was made a post-captain.

Ashore in the garb of a civilian scarce anyone would have taken him for a sailor, more especially that he never garnished unprofessional talk with nautical terms, and, grave in his bearing, evinced little appreciation of mere humor. It was not out of keeping with these traits that on a passage when nothing demanded his paramount action, he was the most undemonstrative of men. Any landsman observing this gentleman not conspicuous by his stature and wearing no pronounced insignia, emerging from his cabin to the open deck, and noting the silent deference of the officers retiring to leeward, might have taken him for the King's guest, a civilian aboard the King's ship, some highly honorable discreet envoy on his way to an important post. But in fact this unobtrusiveness of demeanor may have proceeded from a certain unaffected modesty of manhood sometimes accompanying a resolute nature, a modesty evinced at all times not calling for pronounced action, and which, shown in any rank of life, suggests a virtue aristocratic in kind.

As with some other engaged in various departments of the world's more heroic activities, Captain Vere, though practical enough upon occasion, would at times betray a certain dreaminess of mood. Standing alone on the weather side of the quarterdeck, one hand holding by the rigging, he would absently gaze off at the blank sea. At the presentation to him then of some minor matter interrupting the current of his thoughts he would show

more or less irascibility, but instantly he would control it.
In the navy he was popularly known by the appellation
"Starry Vere." How such a designation happened to fall
upon one who, whatever his sterling qualities, was without any brilliant ones, was in this wise: A favorite kins-
man, Lord Denton, a free-hearted fellow, had been the
first to meet and congratulate him upon his return to
England from his West Indian cruise; and but the day
previous turning over a copy of Andrew Marvell's poems
had lighted, not for the first time however, upon the lines
entitled "Appleton House," the name of one of the seats
of their common ancestor, a hero in the German wars of
the seventeenth century, in which poem occur the lines,

> This 'tis to have been from the first
> In a domestic heaven nursed,
> Under the discipline severe
> Of Fairfax and the starry Vere.

And so, upon embracing his cousin fresh from Rodney's
great victory wherein he had played so gallant a part,
brimming over with just family pride in the sailor of their
house, he exuberantly exclaimed, "Give ye joy, Ed; give
ye joy, my starry Vere!" This got currency, and the novel
prefix serving in familiar parlance readily to distinguish
the *Indomitable's* captain from another Vere his senior,
a distant relative and officer of like rank in the navy, it
remained permanently attached to the surname.

7

In view of the part that the commander of the *Indomitable* plays in scenes shortly to follow, it may be well to fill out that sketch of him outlined in the previous chapter.

Aside from his qualities as a sea officer Captain Vere was an exceptional character. Unlike no few of England's renowned sailors, long and arduous service, with signal devotion to it, had not resulted in absorbing and *salting* the entire man. He had a marked leaning toward everything intellectual. He loved books, never going to sea without a newly replenished library, compact but of the best. The isolated leisure, in some cases so wearisome, falling at intervals to commanders even during a war cruise, never was tedious to Captain Vere. With nothing of that literary taste which less heeds the thing conveyed than the vehicle, his bias was toward those books to which every serious mind of superior order occupying any active post of authority in the world naturally inclines: books treating of actual men and events no matter of what era—history, biography, and unconventional writers, who, free from cant and convention, like Montaigne, honestly and in the spirit of common sense philosophize upon realities.

In this love of reading he found confirmation of his own more reasoned thoughts—confirmation which he had vainly sought in social converse—so that, as touching most

fundamental topics, there had got to be established in
him some positive convictions, which he forefelt would
abide in him essentially unmodified so long as his intelligent part remained unimpaired. In view of the troubled
period in which his lot was cast this was well for him. His
settled convictions were as a dike against those invading
waters of novel opinion, social, political, and otherwise,
which carried away as in a torrent no few minds in those
days, minds by nature not inferior to his own. While
other members of that aristocracy to which by birth he
belonged were incensed at the innovators mainly because
their theories were inimical to the privileged classes, not
alone Captain Vere disinterestedly opposed them because
they seemed to him incapable of embodiment in lasting
institutions, but at war with the peace of the world and
the true welfare of mankind.

With minds less stored than his and less earnest, some
officers of his rank, with whom at times he would necessarily consort, found him lacking in the companionable
quality, a dry and bookish gentleman as they deemed.
Upon any chance withdrawal from their company one
would be apt to say to another, something like this: "Vere
is a noble fellow, Starry Vere. Spite the gazettes, Sir
Horatio," meaning him with the Lord title, "is at bottom
scarce a better seaman or fighter. But between you and
me now don't you think there is a queer streak of the
pedantic running through him? Yes, like the King's yarn
in a coil of navy-rope?"

Some apparent ground there was for this sort of confidential criticism, since not only did the captain's dis-

course never fall into the jocosely familiar, but in illustrating of any point touching the stirring personages and events of the time he would be as apt to cite some historic character or incident of antiquity as that he would cite from the moderns. He seemed unmindful of the circumstance that to his bluff company such remote allusions, however pertinent they might really be, were altogether alien to men whose reading was mainly confined to the journals. But considerateness in such matters is not easy to natures constituted like Captain Vere's. Their honesty prescribes to them directness, sometimes far-reaching like that of a migratory fowl that in its flight never heeds when it crosses a frontier.

8

The lieutenants and other commissioned gentlemen forming Captain Vere's staff it is not necessary here to particularize, nor needs it to make any mention of any of the warrant officers. But among the petty officers was one who, having much to do with the story, may as well be forthwith introduced. His portrait I essay, but shall never hit it. This was John Claggart, the master-at-arms. But that sea title may to landsmen seem somewhat equivocal. Originally, doubtless, that petty officer's function was the instruction of the men in the use of arms, sword or cutlass.

But very long ago, owing to the advance in gunnery making hand-to-hand encounters less frequent and giving to niter and sulphur the preeminence over steel, that function ceased; the master-at-arms of a great warship becoming a sort of chief of police charged among other matters with the duty of preserving order on the populous lower gun decks.

Claggart was a man about five-and-thirty, somewhat spare and tall, yet of no ill figure upon the whole. His hand was too small and shapely to have been accustomed to hard toil. The face was a notable one, the features all except the chin cleanly cut as those on a Greek medallion; yet the chin, beardless as Tecumseh's, had something of strange protuberant heaviness in its make that recalled the prints of the Rev. Dr. Titus Oates, the historic deponent with the clerical drawl in the time of Charles II and the fraud of the alleged Popish Plot. It served Claggart in his office that his eye could cast a tutoring glance. His brow was of the sort phrenologically associated with more than average intellect; silken jet curls partly clustering over it, making a foil to the pallor below, a pallor tinged with a faint shade of amber akin to the hue of time-tinted marbles of old. This complexion, singularly contrasting with the red or deeply bronzed visages of the sailors, and in part the result of his official seclusion from the sunlight, though it was not exactly displeasing, nevertheless seemed to hint of something defective or abnormal in the constitution and blood. But his general aspect and manner were so suggestive of an education and career incongruous with his naval function that when not actively engaged in it he looked like a man of high quality, social and moral, who for reasons of his own was keeping incog. Nothing was known of his former life. It might be that he was an Englishman, and yet there lurked a bit of accent in his speech suggesting that possibly he was not such by birth, but through naturalization in early childhood. Among certain grizzled sea gossips of the gun decks and forecastle went a rumor perdue that the master-at-arms was a *chevalier* who had volunteered into the king's navy by way of compounding for some mysterious swindle whereof he had been arraigned at the King's Bench. The fact that nobody could substantiate this report was, of course, nothing against its secret currency. Such a rumor once started on the gun decks in reference to almost any-one below the rank of a commissioned officer would, during the period assigned to this narrative, have seemed not altogether wanting in credibility to the tarry old wise-acres of a man-of-war crew. And indeed a man of Clag-gart's accomplishments, without prior nautical experience entering the navy at mature life, as he did, and neces-sarily allotted at the start to the lowest grade in it; a man too who never made allusion to his previous life ashore, these were circumstances which in the dearth of exact knowledge as to his true antecedents opened to the invid-ious a vague field for unfavorable surmise.

But the sailors' dog-watch gossip concerning him de-rived a vague plausibility from the fact that now for some period the British navy could so little afford to be squeam-ish in the matter of keeping up the muster rolls, that not only were press gangs notoriously abroad both afloat and

ashore, but there was little or no secret about another
matter, namely that the London police were at liberty to
capture any questionable fellow at large, and summarily
ship him to the dockyard or fleet. Furthermore, even
among voluntary enlistments there were instances where
the motive thereto partook neither of patriotic impulse
nor yet of a random desire to experience a bit of sea life
and martial adventure. Insolvent debtors of minor grade,
together with the promiscuous lame ducks of morality,
found in the navy a convenient and secure refuge. Secure,
because once enlisted aboard a King's ship, they were as
much in sanctuary as the transgressor of the Middle Ages
harboring himself under the shadow of the altar. Such
sanctioned irregularities, which for obvious reasons the
government would hardly think to parade at the time and
which consequently, and as affecting the least influential
class of mankind, have all but dropped into oblivion, lend
color to something for the truth whereof I do not vouch,
and hence have some scruple in stating; something I
remember having seen in print, though the book I cannot
recall; but the same thing was personally communicated
to me now more than forty years ago by an old pensioner
in a cocked hat with whom I had a most interesting talk
on the terrace at Greenwich, a Baltimore Negro, a Trafalgar man. It was to this effect: In the case of a warship
short of hands whose speedy sailing was imperative, the
deficient quota, in lack of any other way of making it
good, would be eked out by drafts culled direct from the
jails. For reasons previously suggested it would not
perhaps be easy at the present day directly to prove or dis-

prove the allegation. But allowed as a verity, how significant would it be of England's straits at the time, confronted by those wars which like a flight of harpies rose shrieking from the din and dust of the fallen Bastille. That era appears measurably clear to us who look back at it, and but read of it. But to the grandfathers of us graybeards, the more thoughtful of them, the genius of it presented an aspect like that of Camöen's Spirit of the Cape, an eclipsing menace mysterious and prodigious. Not America was exempt from apprehension. At the height of Napoleon's unexampled conquests, there were Americans who had fought at Bunker Hill who looked forward to the possibility that the Atlantic might prove no barrier against the ultimate schemes of this French upstart from the revolutionary chaos who seemed in act of fulfilling judgment prefigured in the Apocalypse.

But the less credence was to be given to the gun-deck talk touching Claggart, seeing that no man holding his office in a man-of-war can ever hope to be popular with the crew. Besides, in derogatory comments upon anyone against whom they have a grudge, or for any reason or no reason mislike, sailors are much like landsmen—they are apt to exaggerate or romance it.

About as much was really known to the *Indomitable's* tars of the master-at-arms' career before entering the service as an astronomer knows about a comet's travels prior to its first observable appearance in the sky. The verdict of the sea quidnuncs has been cited only by way of showing what sort of moral impression the man made upon rude uncultivated natures whose conceptions of human wickedness were necessarily of the narrowest, limited to ideas of vulgar rascality—a thief among the swinging hammocks during a night watch, or the man-brokers and land sharks of the sea ports.

It was no gossip, however, but fact, that though, as before hinted, Claggart upon his entrance into the navy was, as a novice, assigned to the least honorable section of a man-of-war's crew, embracing the drudgery, he did not long remain there.

The superior capacity he immediately evinced, his constitutional sobriety, ingratiating deference to superiors, together with a peculiar ferreting genius manifested on a singular occasion, all this capped by a certain austere patriotism abruptly advanced him to the position of master-at-arms.

Of this maritime chief of police the ship's corporals, so called, were the immediate subordinates, and compliant ones, and this, as is to be noted in some business departments ashore, almost to a degree inconsistent with entire moral volition. His place put various converging wires of underground influence under the chief's control, capable when astutely worked through his understrappers of operating to the mysterious discomfort, if nothing worse, of any of the sea commonalty.

9

Life in the foretop well agreed with Billy Budd. There, when not actually engaged on the yards yet higher aloft, the topmen, who as such had been picked out for youth and activity, constituted an aerial club lounging at ease against the smaller stunsails rolled up into cushions, spinning yarns like the lazy gods, and frequently amused with what was going on in the busy world of the decks below. No wonder then that a young fellow of Billy's disposition was well content in such society. Giving no cause of offense to anybody, he was always alert at a call. So in the merchant service it had been with him. But now such a punctiliousness in duty was shown that his topmates would sometimes good-naturedly laugh at him for it. This heightened alacrity had its cause, namely, the impression made upon him by the first formal gangway punishment he had ever witnessed, which befell the day following his impressment. It had been incurred by a little fellow, young, a novice, an after-guardsman absent from his assigned post when the ship was being put about —a dereliction resulting in a rather serious hitch to that maneuver, one demanding instantaneous promptitude in letting go and making fast. When Billy saw the culprit's naked back under the scourge gridironed with red welts, and worse; when he marked the dire expression on the liberated man's face as with his woolen shirt flung over

him by the executioner he rushed forward from the spot
to bury himself in the crowd, Billy was horrified. He
resolved that never through remissness would he make
himself liable to such a visitation or do or omit aught that
might merit even verbal reproof. What then was his surprise and concern when ultimately he found himself getting into petty trouble occasionally about such matters as
the stowage of his bag or something amiss in his hammock, matters under the police oversight of the ship's
corporals of the lower decks, and which brought down on
him a vague threat from one of them.

So heedful in all things as he was, how could this be?
He could not understand it, and it more than vexed him.
When he spoke to his young topmates about it they were
either lightly incredulous or found something comical in
his unconcealed anxiety. "Is it your bag, Billy?" said one;
"well, sew yourself up in it, bully boy, and then you'll be
sure to know if anybody meddles with it."

Now there was a veteran aboard who because his years
began to disqualify him for more active work had been
recently assigned duty as mainmastman in his watch,
looking to the gear belayed at the rail roundabout that
great spar near the deck. At off times the foretopman had
picked up some acquaintance with him, and now in his
trouble it occurred to him that he might be the sort of
person to go to for wise counsel. He was an old Dansker
long anglicized in the service, of few words, many
wrinkles, and some honorable scars. His wizened face,
time-tinted and weather-stained to the complexion of an
antique parchment, was here and there peppered blue

by the chance explosion of a gun cartridge in action. He was an *Agamemnon* man; some two years prior to the time of this story having served under Nelson when but Sir Horatio in that ship immortal in naval memory, and which, dismantled and in part broken up to her bare ribs, is seen a grand skeleton in Haydon's etching. As one of a boarding party from the *Agamemnon* he had received a cut slantwise along one temple and cheek, leaving a long pale scar like a streak of dawn's light falling athwart the dark visage. It was on account of that scar and the affair in which it was known that he had received it, as well as from his blue-peppered complexion, that the Dansker went among the *Indomitable*'s crew by the name of "Board-her-in-the-smoke."

Now the first time that his small weazel eyes happened to light on Billy Budd, a certain grim internal merriment set all his ancient wrinkles into antic play. Was it that his eccentric unsentimental old sapience, primitive in its kind, saw or thought it saw something which in contrast with the warship's environment looked oddly incongruous in the Handsome Sailor? But after slyly studying him at intervals, the old Merlin's equivocal merriment was modified; for now when the twain would meet it would start in his face a quizzing sort of look, but it would be but momentary and sometimes replaced by an expression of speculative query as to what might eventually befall a nature like that, dropped into a world not without some man traps and against whose subtleties simple courage lacking experience and address and without any touch of defensive ugliness is of little avail; and where such innocence as man is capable of does yet in a moral emergency not always sharpen the faculties or enlighten the will.

However it was, the Dansker in his ascetic way rather took to Billy. Nor was this only because of a certain philosophic interest in such a character. There was another cause. While the old man's eccentricities, sometimes bordering on the ursine, repelled the junior, Billy, undeterred thereby, revering him as a salt hero would make advances, never passing the old *Agamemnon*-man without a salutation marked by that respect which is seldom lost on the aged, however crabbed at times or whatever their station in life.

There was a vein of dry humor, or what not, in the mastman; and, whether in freak of patriarchal irony touching Billy's youth and athletic frame or for some other and more recondite reason, from the first in addressing him he always substituted "Baby" for "Billy," the Dansker in fact being the originator of the name by which the foretopman eventually became known aboard ship.

Well then, in his mysterious little difficulty going in quest of the wrinkled one, Billy found him off duty in a dog watch ruminating by himself seated on a shot-box of the upper gun deck now and then surveying with a somewhat cynical regard certain of the more swaggering promenaders there. Billy recounted his trouble, again wondering how it all happened. The salt seer attentively listened, accompanying the foretopman's recital with queer twitchings of his wrinkles and problematical little sparkles of his small ferret eyes. Making an end of his story, the foretopman asked, "And now, Dansker, do tell me what you think of it."

The old man, shoving up the front of his tarpaulin and deliberately rubbing the long slant scar at the point where it entered the thin hair, laconically said, "Baby Budd, *Jimmy Legs*" (meaning the master-at-arms) "is down on you."

"*Jimmy Legs!*" ejaculated Billy, his welkin eyes expanding; "what for? Why he calls me *the sweet and pleasant young fellow*, they tell me."

"Does he so?" grinned the grizzled one; then said "Ay, Baby Lad, a sweet voice has *Jimmy Legs*."

"No, not always. But to me he has. I seldom pass him but there comes a pleasant word."

"And that's because he's down upon you, Baby Budd."

Such reiteration along with the manner of it, incomprehensible to a novice, disturbed Billy almost as much as the mystery for which he had sought explanation. Something less unpleasingly oracular he tried to extract; but the old sea-Chiron, thinking perhaps that for the nonce he had sufficiently instructed his young Achilles, pursed his lips, gathered all his wrinkles together, and would commit himself to nothing further.

Years, and those experiences which befell certain shrewder men subordinated lifelong to the will of superiors, all this had developed in the Dansker the pithy guarded cynicism that was his leading characteristic.

10

The next day an incident served to confirm Billy Budd in
his incredulity as to the Dansker's strange summing up
of the case submitted. The ship at noon going large before the wind was rolling on her course, and he below at
dinner and engaged in some sportful talk with the members of his mess chanced in a sudden lurch to spill the
entire contents of his soup pan upon the new scrubbed
deck. Claggart, the master-at-arms, official rattan in hand,
happened to be passing along the battery in a bay of
which the mess was lodged, and the greasy liquid
streamed just across his path. Stepping over it, he was
proceeding on his way without comment, since the matter was nothing to take notice of under the circumstances,
when he happened to observe who it was that had done
the spilling. His countenance changed. Pausing, he was
about to ejaculate something hasty at the sailor, but
checked himself, and, pointing down to the streaming
soup, playfully tapped him from behind with his rattan,
saying in a low musical voice peculiar to him at times:
"Handsomely done, my lad! And handsome is as handsome did it too!" And with that passed on. Not noted by
Billy, as not coming within his view, was the involuntary
smile, or rather grimace, that accompanied Claggart's
equivocal words. Aridly it drew down the thin corners of
his shapely mouth. But everybody taking his remark as

meant for humorous, and at which therefore as coming
from a superior they were bound to laugh, "with counter-
feited glee" acted accordingly; and Billy, tickled, it may
be, by the allusion to his being the Handsome Sailor,
merrily joined in; then addressing his messmates exclaimed: "There now, who says that Jimmy Legs is down
on me!" "And who said he was, Beauty?" demanded one
Donald with some surprise. Whereat the foretopman
looked a little foolish recalling that it was only one person, Board-her-in-the-smoke, who had suggested what to
him was the smoky idea that this master-at-arms was in
any peculiar way hostile to him. Meantime that functionary, resuming his path, must have momentarily worn
some expression less guarded than that of the bitter smile,
and usurping the face from the heart, some distorting expression perhaps, for a drummer-boy, heedlessly frolick-
ing along from the opposite direction and chancing to
come into light collision with his person, was strangely
disconcerted by his aspect. Nor was the impression
lessened when the official, impulsively giving him a sharp
cut with the rattan, vehemently exclaimed: "Look where
you go!"

11

What was the matter with the master-at-arms? And, be
the matter what it might, how could it have direct relation to Billy Budd, with whom, prior to the affair of the
spilled soup, he had never come into any special contact
official or otherwise? What indeed could the trouble have
to do with one so little inclined to give offense as the
merchant ship's *peacemaker*, even him who in Claggart's
own phrase was "the sweet and pleasant young fellow"?
Yes, why should *Jimmy Legs*, to borrow the Dansker's
expression, be *down* on the Handsome Sailor? But, at
heart and not for nothing, as the late chance encounter
may indicate to the discerning, down on him, secretly
down on him, he assuredly was.

Now to invent something touching the more private
career of Claggart, something involving Billy Budd, of
which something the latter should be wholly ignorant,
some romantic incident implying that Claggart's knowledge of the young bluejacket began at some period ante-
rior to catching sight of him on board the seventy-four
—all this, not so difficult to do, might avail in a way more
or less interesting to account for whatever of enigma may
appear to lurk in the case. But in fact there was nothing
of the sort. And yet the cause, necessarily to be assumed
as the sole one assignable, is in its very realism as much

charged with that prime element of Radcliffian romance, *the mysterious,* as any that the ingenuity of the author of the *Mysteries of Udolpho* could devise. For what can more partake of the mysterious than an antipathy spontaneous and profound, such as is evoked in certain exceptional mortals by the mere aspect of some other mortal however harmless he may be, if not called forth by this very harmlessness itself?

Now there can exist no irritating juxtaposition of dissimilar personalities comparable to that which is possible aboard a great warship fully manned and at sea. There, every day among all ranks, almost every man comes into more or less of contact with almost every other man. Wholly there to avoid even the sight of an aggravating object one must needs give it Jonah's toss or jump overboard himself. Imagine how all this might eventually operate on some peculiar human creature the direct reverse of a saint.

But for the adequate comprehending of Claggart by a normal nature these hints are insufficient. To pass from a normal nature to him one must cross "the deadly space between." And this is best done by indirection.

Long ago an honest scholar my senior said to me in reference to one who like himself is now no more, a man so unimpeachably respectable that against him nothing was ever openly said though among the few something was whispered, "Yes, X—— is a nut not to be cracked by the tap of a lady's fan. You are aware that I am the adherent of no organized religion, much less of any philosophy built into a system. Well, for all that, I think that to try and get into X——, enter his labyrinth and get out again, without a clue derived from some source other than what is known as *knowledge of the world*—that were hardly possible, at least for me."

"Why," said I, "X——, however singular a study to some, is yet human, and knowledge of the world assuredly implies the knowledge of human nature, and in most of its varieties."

"Yes, but a superficial knowledge of it, serving ordinary purposes. But for anything deeper, I am not certain whether to know the world and to know human nature be not two distinct branches of knowledge, which, while they may coexist in the same heart, yet either may exist with little or nothing of the other. Nay, in an average man of the world, his constant rubbing with it blunts that fine spiritual insight indispensable to the understanding of the essential in certain exceptional characters, whether evil ones or good. In a matter of some importance I have seen a girl wind an old lawyer about her little finger. Nor was it the dotage of senile love. Nothing of the sort. But he knew law better than he knew the girl's heart. Coke and Blackstone hardly shed so much light into obscure spiritual places as the Hebrew prophets. And who were they? Mostly recluses."

At the time my inexperience was such that I did not quite see the drift of all this. It may be that I see it now. And, indeed, if that lexicon which is based on Holy Writ were any longer popular, one might with less difficulty define and denominate certain phenomenal men. As it is, one must turn to some authority not liable to the charge of being tinctured with the Biblical element.

In a list of definitions included in the authentic translation of Plato, a list attributed to him, occurs this: "Natural Depravity: a depravity according to nature." A definition which, though savoring of Calvinism, by no means involves Calvin's dogmas as to total mankind. Evidently its intent makes it applicable but to individuals. Not many are the examples of this depravity, which the gallows and jail supply. At any rate, for notable instances, since these have no vulgar alloy of the brute in them but invariably are dominated by intellectuality, one must go elsewhere. Civilization, especially if of the austerer sort, is auspicious to it. It folds itself in the mantle of respectability. It has its certain negative virtues serving as silent auxiliaries. It never allows wine to get within its guard. It is not going too far to say that it is without vices or small sins. There is a phenomenal pride in it that excludes them from anything mercenary or avaricious. In short the depravity here meant partakes nothing of the sordid or sensual. It is serious, but free from acerbity. Though no flatterer of mankind it never speaks ill of it.

But the thing which in eminent instances signalizes so exceptional a nature is this: though the man's even temper and discreet bearing would seem to intimate a mind peculiarly subject to the law of reason, not the less in his heart he would seem to riot in complete exemption from that law, having apparently little to do with reason further than to employ it as an ambidexter implement for effecting the irrational. That is to say: Toward the accomplishment of an aim which in wantonness of malignity would seem to partake of the insane, he will direct a cool judgment sagacious and sound.

These men are true madmen, and of the most dangerous sort, for their lunacy is not continuous but occasional, evoked by some special object; it is probably secretive, which is as much to say it is self-contained, so that when, moreover, most active, it is to the average mind not distinguishable from sanity, and for the reason above suggested, that, whatever its aims may be—and the aim is never declared—the method and the outward proceeding are always perfectly rational.

Now something such a one was Claggart, in whom was the mania of an evil nature, not engendered by vicious training or corrupting books or licentious living but born with him and innate, in short "a depravity according to nature."

12

Lawyers, Experts, Clergy
AN EPISODE

By the way, can it be the phenomenon, disowned or at least concealed, that in some criminal cases puzzles the courts? For this cause have our juries at times not only to endure the prolonged contentions of lawyers with their fees, but also the yet more perplexing strife of the medical experts with theirs?—But why leave it to them? Why not subpoena as well the clerical proficients? their vocation bringing them into peculiar contact with so many human beings, and sometimes in their least guarded hour, in interviews very much more confidential than those of physician and patient; this would seem to qualify them to know something about those intricacies involved in the question of moral responsibility; whether in a given case, say, the crime proceeded from mania in the brain or rabies of the heart. As to any differences among themselves these clerical proficients might develop on the stand, these could hardly be greater than the direct contradictions exchanged between the remunerated medical experts.

Dark sayings are these, some will say. But why? Is it because they somewhat savor of Holy Writ in its phrase "mysteries of iniquity"? If they do, such savor was far from being intended, for little will it commend these pages to many a reader of today.

The point of the present story turning on the hidden nature of the master-at-arms has necessitated this chapter. With an added hint or two in connection with the incident at the mess, the resumed narrative must be left to vindicate, as it may, its own credibility.

13

Pale ire, envy and despair

That Claggart's figure was not amiss, and his face, save
the chin, well molded, has already been said. Of these
favorable points he seemed not insensible, for he was not
only neat but careful in his dress. But the form of Billy
Budd was heroic; and if his face was without the intellectual look of the pallid Claggart's, not the less was it lit
like his, from within, though from a different source. The
bonfire in his heart made luminous the rose-tan in his
cheek.

In view of the marked contrast between the persons of
the twain, it is more than probable that when the master-
at-arms in the scene last given applied to the sailor the
proverb *Handsome is as handsome does* he there let
escape an ironic inkling, not caught by the young sailors
who heard it, as to what it was that had first moved him
against Billy, namely, his significant personal beauty.

Now envy and antipathy, passions irreconcilable in
reason, nevertheless in fact may spring conjoined like
Chang and Eng in one birth. Is Envy then such a monster? Well, though many an arraigned mortal has in hopes
of mitigated penalty pleaded guilty to horrible actions,
did ever anybody seriously confess to envy? Something
there is in it universally felt to be more shameful than

even felonious crime. And not only does everybody disown it but the better sort are inclined to incredulity when it is in earnest imputed to an intelligent man. But since its lodgment is in the heart, not the brain, no degree of intellect supplies a guarantee against it. But Claggart's was no vulgar form of the passion. Nor, as directed toward Billy Budd, did it partake of that streak of apprehensive jealousy that marred Saul's visage perturbedly brooding on the comely young David. Claggart's envy struck deeper. If askance he eyed the good looks, cheery health, and frank enjoyment of young life in Billy Budd, it was because these went along with a nature that, as Claggart magnetically felt, had in its simplicity never willed malice or experienced the reactionary bite of that serpent. To him, the spirit lodged within Billy and looking out from his welkin eyes as from windows, that ineffability it was which made the dimple in his dyed cheek, suppled his joints, and, dancing in his yellow curls, made him preeminently the Handsome Sailor. One person excepted, the master-at-arms was perhaps the only man in the ship intellectually capable of adequately appreciating the moral phenomenon presented in Billy Budd. And the insight but intensified his passion, which, assuming various secret forms within him, at times assumed that of cynic disdain —disdain of innocence— To be nothing more than innocent! Yet in an esthetic way he saw the charm of it, the courageous free-and-easy temper of it, and fain would have shared it, but he despaired of it.

With no power to annul the elemental evil in him, though readily enough he could hide it; apprehending

the good, but powerless to be it; a nature like Claggart's
surcharged with energy as such natures almost invariably
are, what recourse is left to it but to recoil upon itself,
and, like the scorpion for which the Creator alone is
responsible, act out to the end the part allotted it.

14

Passion, and passion in its profoundest, is not a thing
demanding a palatial stage whereon to play its part.
Down among the groundlings, among the beggars and
rakers of the garbage, profound passion is enacted. And
the circumstances that provoke it, however trivial or
mean, are no measure of its power. In the present instance
the stage is a scrubbed gun deck, and one of the external
provocations a man-of-war's-man's spilled soup.

Now when the master-at-arms noticed whence came
that greasy fluid streaming before his feet, he must have
taken it—to some extent willfully, perhaps—not for the
mere accident it assuredly was, but for the sly escape of a
spontaneous feeling on Billy's part more or less answering
to the antipathy on his own. In effect a foolish demonstration he must have thought, and very harmless, like the
futile kick of a heifer, which yet, were the heifer a shod
stallion, would not be so harmless. Even so was it that
into the gall of Claggart's envy he infused the vitriol of

his contempt. But the incident confirmed to him certain telltale reports purveyed to his ear by "Squeak," one of his more cunning corporals, a grizzled little man, so nicknamed by the sailors on account of his squeaky voice and sharp visage ferreting about the dark corners of the lower decks after interlopers, satirically suggesting to them the idea of a rat in a cellar.

From his Chief's employing him as an implicit tool in laying little traps for the worriment of the foretopman— for it was from the master-at-arms that the petty persecutions heretofore adverted to had proceeded—the corporal, having naturally enough concluded that his master could have no love for the sailor, made it his business, faithful understrapper that he was, to foment the ill blood by perverting to his chief certain innocent frolics of the good-natured foretopman, besides inventing for his mouth sundry contumelious epithets he claimed to have overheard him let fall. The master-at-arms never suspected the veracity of these reports, more especially as to the epithets, for he well knew how secretly unpopular may become a master-at-arms, at least a master-at-arms of those days zealous in his function, and how the bluejackets shoot at him in private their raillery and wit; the nickname by which he goes among them (*Jimmy Legs*) implying under the form of merriment their cherished disrespect and dislike.

But in view of the greediness of hate for patrolmen, it hardly needed a purveyor to feed Claggart's passion. An uncommon prudence is habitual with the subtler depravity, for it has everything to hide. And in case of an injury

but suspected, its secretiveness voluntarily cuts it off
from enlightenment or disillusion; and, not unreluctantly,
action is taken upon surmise as upon certainty. And the
retaliation is apt to be in monstrous disproportion to the
supposed offense; for when in anybody was revenge in its
exactions aught else but an inordinate usurer? But how
with Claggart's conscience? For though consciences are
unlike as foreheads, every intelligence, not excluding the
Scriptural devils who "believe and tremble," has one.
But Claggart's conscience, being but the lawyer to his
will, made ogres of trifles, probably arguing that the
motive imputed to Billy in spilling the soup just when he
did, together with the epithets alleged, these, if nothing
more, made a strong case against him; nay, justified
animosity into a sort of retributive righteousness. The
Pharisee is the Guy Fawkes prowling in the hid chambers
underlying the Claggarts. And they can really form no
conception of an unreciprocated malice. Probably, the
master-at-arms' clandestine persecution of Billy was
started to try the temper of the man; but it had not
developed any quality in him that enmity could make
official use of or even pervert into plausible self-justifica-
tion; so that the occurrence at the mess, petty if it were,
was a welcome one to that peculiar conscience assigned
to be the private mentor of Claggart. And, for the rest,
not improbably it put him upon new experiments.

15

Not many days after the last incident narrated, something befell Billy Budd that more graveled him than aught that had previously occurred.

It was a warm night for the latitude, and the foretopman, whose watch at the time was properly below, was dozing on the uppermost deck, whither he had ascended from his hot hammock, one of hundreds suspended so closely wedged together over a lower gun deck that there was little or no swing to them. He lay as in the shadow of a hillside, stretched under the lee of the booms, a piled ridge of spare spars amidships between foremast and mainmast and among which the ship's largest boat, the launch, was stowed. Alongside of three other slumberers from below, he lay near that end of the booms which approaches the foremast, his station aloft on duty as a foretopman being just over the deck station of the forecastlemen, entitling him according to usage to make himself more or less at home in that neighborhood.

Presently he was stirred into semiconsciousness by somebody, who must have previously sounded the sleep of the others, touching his shoulder, and then, as the foretopman raised his head, breathing into his ear in a quick whisper, "Slip into the lee forechains, Billy; there is something in the wind. Don't speak. Quick, I will meet you there," and disappeared.

Now Billy, like sundry other essentially good-natured ones, had some of the weaknesses inseparable from essential good nature, and among these was a reluctance, almost an incapacity, of plumply saying *no* to an abrupt proposition not obviously absurd on the face of it, nor obviously unfriendly, nor iniquitous. And being of warm blood he had not the phlegm tacitly to negative any proposition by unresponsive inaction. Like his sense of fear, his apprehension as to aught outside of the honest and natural was seldom very quick. Besides, upon the present occasion, the drowse from his sleep still hung upon him.

However it was, he mechanically rose, and, sleepily wondering what could be in the wind, betook himself to the designated place, a narrow platform, one of six, outside of the high bulwarks and screened by the great dead-eyes and multiple columned lanyards of the shrouds and backstays, and, in a great warship of that time, of dimensions commensurate to the hull's magnitude, a tarry balcony in short overhanging the sea, and so secluded that one mariner of the *Indomitable,* a nonconformist old tar of a serious turn, made it even in daytime his private oratory.

In this retired nook the stranger soon joined Billy Budd. There was no moon as yet; a haze obscured the starlight. He could not distinctly see the stranger's face. Yet from something in the outline and carriage, Billy took him to be, and correctly, one of the after-guard.

"Hist! Billy," said the man in the same quick cautionary whisper as before; "you were impressed, weren't you? Well, so was I," and he paused, as to mark the effect.

But Billy, not knowing exactly what to make of this, said nothing. Then the other: "We are not the only impressed ones, Billy. There's a gang of us.—Couldn't you—help—at a pinch?"

"What do you mean?" demanded Billy, here thoroughly shaking off his drowse.

"Hist, hist!" the hurried whisper now growing husky, "See here"—and the man held up two small objects faintly twinkling in the nightlight—"see, they are yours, Billy, if you'll only——"

But Billy broke in, and in his resentful eagerness to deliver himself his vocal infirmity somewhat intruded: "D-D-Damme, I don't know what you are d-driving at, or what you mean, but you had better g-g-go where you belong!" For the moment the fellow, as confounded, did not stir; and Billy, springing to his feet, said, "If you d-don't start I'll t-t-toss you back over the r-rail!" There was no mistaking this, and the mysterious emissary decamped, disappearing in the direction of the mainmast in the shadow of the booms.

"Hallo, what's the matter?" here came growling from a forecastleman awakened from his deck doze by Billy's raised voice. And as the foretopman reappeared and was recognized by him: "Ah, Beauty, is it you? Well, something must have been the matter for you st-st-stuttered."

"Oh," rejoined Billy, now mastering the impediment, "I found an after-guardsman in our part of the ship here and I bid him be off where he belongs."

"And is that all you did about it, foretopman?" gruffly demanded another, an irascible old fellow of brick-colored visage and hair, and who was known to his associate forecastlemen as "Red Pepper." "Such sneaks I should like to marry to the gunner's daughter!" by that expression meaning that he would like to subject them to disciplinary castigation over a gun.

However, Billy's rendering of the matter satisfactorily accounted to these inquirers for the brief commotion, since of all the sections of a ship's company the forecastlemen, veterans for the most part and bigoted in their sea prejudices, are the most jealous in resenting territorial encroachments, especially on the part of any of the afterguard, of whom they have but a sorry opinion, chiefly landsmen, never going aloft except to reef or furl the mainsail, and in no wise competent to handle a marlinspike or turn in a deadeye, say.

16

This incident sorely puzzled Billy Budd. It was an entirely new experience, the first time in his life that he had ever been personally approached in underhand intriguing fashion. Prior to this encounter he had known nothing of the after-guardsman, the two men being stationed wide apart, one forward and aloft during his watch, the other on deck and aft.

What could it mean? And could they really be guineas,

those two glittering objects the interloper had held up to his eyes? Where could the fellow get guineas? Why even spare buttons are not so plentiful at sea. The more he turned the matter over, the more he was nonplused, and made uneasy and discomfited. In his disgustful recoil from an overture which though he but ill comprehended he instinctively knew must involve evil of some sort, Billy Budd was like a young horse fresh from the pasture suddenly inhaling a vile whiff from some chemical factory and by repeated snortings tries to get it out of his nostrils and lungs. This frame of mind barred all desire of holding further parley with the fellow, even were it but for the purpose of gaining some enlightenment as to his design in approaching him. And yet he was not without natural curiosity to see how such a visitor in the dark would look in broad day.

He espied him the following afternoon in his first dog watch below, one of the smokers on that forward part of the upper gun deck allotted to the pipe. He recognized him by his general cut and build, more than by his round freckled face and glassy eyes of pale blue, veiled with lashes all but white. And yet Billy was a bit uncertain whether indeed it were he—yonder chap about his own age chatting and laughing in free-hearted way, leaning against a gun, a genial young fellow enough to look at, and something of a rattlebrain, to all appearance. Rather chubby too for a sailor, even an after-guardsman. In short the last man in the world, one would think, to be overburthened with thoughts, especially those perilous thoughts that must needs belong to a conspirator in any serious project, or even to the underling of such a conspirator.

Although Billy was not aware of it, the fellow, with a sidelong watchful glance, had perceived Billy first, and then noting that Billy was looking at him thereupon nodded a familiar sort of friendly recognition as to an old acquaintance, without interrupting the talk he was engaged in with the group of smokers. A day or two afterwards, chancing in the evening promenade on a gun deck to pass Billy, he offered a flying word of good fellowship, as it were, which, by its unexpectedness and equivocalness under the circumstances, so embarrassed Billy that he knew not how to respond to it, and let it go unnoticed.

Billy was now left more at a loss than before. The ineffectual speculations into which he was led were so disturbingly alien to him that he did his best to smother them. It never entered his mind that here was a matter which, from its extreme questionableness, it was his duty as a loyal bluejacket to report in the proper quarter. And, probably, had such a step been suggested to him, he would have been deterred from taking it by the thought, one of novice magnanimity, that it would savor overmuch of the dirty work of a telltale. He kept the thing to himself. Yet upon one occasion he could not forbear a little disburthening himself to the old Dansker, tempted thereto perhaps by the influence of a balmy night when the ship lay becalmed; the twain, silent for the most part, sitting together on deck, their heads propped against the bulwarks. But it was only a partial and anonymous account that Billy gave, the unfounded scruples above referred to preventing full disclosure to anybody. Upon hearing Billy's version, the sage Dansker seemed to divine more than he was told, and, after a little meditation during which his wrinkles were pursed as into a point, quite effacing for the time that quizzing expression his face sometimes wore—"Didn't I say so, Baby Budd?"

"Say what?" demanded Billy.

"Why, *Jimmy Legs* is *down* on you."

"And what," rejoined Billy in amazement, "has *Jimmy Legs* to do with that cracked after-guardsman?"

"Ho, it was an after-guardsman then. A cat's-paw, a cat's-paw!" And with that exclamation, which, whether it had reference to a light puff of air just then coming over the calm sea, or subtler relation to the after-guardsman, there is no telling, the old Merlin gave a twisting wrench with his black teeth at his plug of tobacco, vouchsafing no reply to Billy's impetuous question, though now repeated, for it was his wont to relapse into grim silence when interrogated in skeptical sort as to any of his sententious oracles, not always very clear ones, rather partaking of that obscurity which invests most Delphic deliverances from any quarter.

Long experience had very likely brought this old man to that bitter prudence which never interferes in aught and never gives advice.

17

Yes, despite the Dansker's pithy insistence as to the master-at-arms being at the bottom of these strange experiences of Billy on board the *Indomitable,* the young sailor was ready to ascribe them to almost anybody but the man who, to use Billy's own expression, "always had a pleasant word for him." This is to be wondered at. Yet not so much to be wondered at. In certain matters, some sailors even in mature life remain unsophisticated enough. But a young seafarer of the disposition of our athletic foretopman is much of a child-man. And yet a child's utter innocence is but its blank ignorance, and the innocence more or less wanes as intelligence waxes. But in Billy Budd intelligence, such as it was, had advanced, while yet his simple-mindedness remained for the most part unaffected. Experience is a teacher indeed, yet did Billy's years make his experience small. Besides, he had none of that intuitive knowledge of the bad which in natures not good or incompletely so foreruns experience, and therefore may pertain, as in some instances it too clearly does pertain, even to youth.

And what could Billy know of man except of man as a mere sailor? And the old-fashioned sailor, the veritable man-before-the-mast, the sailor from boyhood up, he, though indeed of the same species as a landsman, is in some respects singularly distinct from him. The sailor is frankness, the landsman is finesse. Life is not a game with the sailor, demanding the long head; no intricate game of chess where few moves are made in straightforwardness, and ends are attained by indirection; an oblique, tedious, barren game hardly worth that poor candle burnt out in playing it.

Yes, as a class, sailors are in character a juvenile race. Even their deviations are marked by juvenility. And this more especially holding true with the sailors of Billy's time. Then, too, certain things which apply to all sailors do more pointedly operate here and there upon the junior one. Every sailor, too, is accustomed to obey orders without debating them; his life afloat is externally ruled for him; he is not brought into that promiscuous commerce with mankind where unobstructed free agency on equal terms—equal superficially, at least—soon teaches one that unless upon occasion he exercise a distrust keen in proportion to the fairness of the appearance, some foul turn may be served him. A ruled undemonstrative distrustfulness is so habitual, not with businessmen so much, as with men who know their kind in less shallow relations than business, namely, certain men-of-the-world, that they come at last to employ it all but unconsciously, and some of them would very likely feel real surprise at being charged with it as one of their general characteristics.

18

But after the little matter at the mess Billy Budd no more
found himself in strange trouble at times about his hammock or his clothes bag or what not. While, as to that
smile that occasionally sunned him, and the pleasant
passing word, these were, if not more frequent, yet if
anything more pronounced than before.

But, for all that, there were certain other demonstra-
tions now. When Claggart's unobserved glance happened
to light on belted Billy rolling along the upper gun deck
in the leisure of the second dog watch, exchanging
passing broadsides of fun with other young promenaders
in the crowd, that glance would follow the cheerful sea-
Hyperion with a settled meditative and melancholy expression, his eyes strangely suffused with incipient feverish tears. Then would Claggart look like the man of
sorrows. Yes, and sometimes the melancholy expression
would have in it a touch of soft yearning, as if Claggart
could even have loved Billy but for fate and ban. But this
was an evanescence, and quickly repented of, as it were,
by an immitigable look, pinching and shriveling the
visage into the momentary semblance of a wrinkled wal-
nut. But sometimes catching sight in advance of the foretopman coming in his direction, he would, upon their
nearing, step aside a little to let him pass, dwelling upon
Billy for the moment with the glittering dental satire of a

Guise. But upon any abrupt unforeseen encounter a red light would [flash] forth from his eye like a spark from an anvil in a dusk smithy. That quick fierce light was a strange one, darted from orbs which in repose were of a color nearest approaching a deeper violet, the softest of shades.

Though some of these caprices of the pit could not but be observed by their object, yet were they beyond the construing of such a nature. And the thews of Billy were hardly compatible with that sort of sensitive spiritual organization which in some cases instinctively conveys to ignorant innocence an admonition of the proximity of the malign. He thought the master-at-arms acted in a manner rather queer at times. That was all. But the occasional frank air and pleasant word went for what they purported to be, the young sailor never having heard as yet of the "too fair-spoken man."

Had the foretopman been conscious of having done or said anything to provoke the ill will of the official, it would have been different with him, and his sight might have been purged if not sharpened. As it was, innocence was his blinder.

So was it with him in yet another matter. Two minor officers—the armorer and captain of the hold, with whom he had never exchanged a word, his position in the ship not bringing him into contact with them—these men now for the first time began to cast upon Billy when they chanced to encounter him that peculiar glance which evidences that the man from whom it comes has been some way tampered with and to the prejudice of him upon whom the glance lights. Never did it occur to Billy as a thing to be noted or a thing suspicious, though he well knew the fact, that the armorer and captain of the hold, with the ship's yeoman, apothecary, and others of that grade, were, by naval usage, messmates of the master-at-arms, men with ears convenient to his confidential tongue.

But the general popularity that our Handsome Sailor's manly forwardness upon occasion, and his irresistible good nature, indicating no mental superiority tending to excite an invidious feeling—this good will on the part of most of his shipmates made him the less to concern himself about such mute aspects toward him as those whereto allusion has just been made.

As to the after-guardsman, though Billy for reasons already given necessarily saw little of him, yet when the two did happen to meet, invariably came the fellow's off-hand cheerful recognition, sometimes accompanied by a passing pleasant word or two. Whatever that equivocal young person's original design may really have been, or the design of which he might have been the deputy, certain it was from his manner upon these occasions that he had wholly dropped it.

It was as if his precocity of crookedness (and every vulgar villain is precocious) had for once deceived him, and the man he had sought to entrap as a simpleton had, through his very simplicity, ignominiously baffled him.

But shrewd ones may opine that it was hardly possible for Billy to refrain from going up to the after-guardsman

and bluntly demanding to know his purpose in the initial
interview, so abuptly closed in the forechains. Shrewd
ones may also think it but natural in Billy to set about
sounding some of the other impressed men of the ship in
order to discover what basis, if any, there was for the
emissary's obscure suggestions as to plotting disaffection
aboard. Yes, the shrewd may so think. But something
more, or rather something else than mere shrewdness
is perhaps needful for the due understanding of such a
character as Billy Budd's.

   As to Claggart, the monomania in the man—if that indeed it were, as involuntarily disclosed by starts in the
manifestations detailed, yet in general covered over by
his self-contained and rational demeanor—this, like a
subterranean fire was eating its way deeper and deeper
in him. Something decisive must come of it.

19

After the mysterious interview in the forechains, the
one so abruptly ended there by Billy, nothing especially
germane to the story occurred until the events now about
to be narrated.

   Elsewhere it has been said that in the lack of frigates
(of course better sailers than line-of-battle ships) in the
English squadron up the Straits at the period, the *Indom-*

itable was occasionally employed not only as an available substitute for a scout, but at times on detached service of more important kind. This was not alone because of her sailing qualities, not common in a ship of her rate, but quite as much, probably, that the character of her commander, it was thought, specially adapted him for any duty where under unforeseen difficulties a prompt initiative might have to be taken in some matter demanding knowledge and ability in addition to those qualities implied in good seamanship. It was on an expedition of the latter sort, a somewhat distant one, and when the *Indomitable* was almost at her furthest remove from the fleet, that in the latter part of an afternoon watch she unexpectedly came in sight of a ship of the enemy. It proved to be a frigate. The latter perceiving through the glass that the weight of men and metal would be heavily against her, invoking her light heels crowded sail to get away. After a chase urged almost against hope and lasting until about the middle of the first dog watch, she signally succeeded in effecting her escape.

Not long after the pursuit had been given up, and ere the excitement incident thereto had altogether waned away, the master-at-arms ascending from his cavernous sphere made his appearance cap in hand by the main-mast respectfully waiting the notice of Captain Vere, then solitary walking the weather side of the quarter-deck, doubtless somewhat chafed at the failure of the pursuit. The spot where Claggart stood was the place al-

lotted to men of lesser grades seeking some more particular interview either with the officer of the deck or
the captain himself. But from the latter it was not often
that a sailor or petty officer of those days would seek a
hearing; only some exceptional cause would, according
to established custom, have warranted that.

Presently, just as the commander absorbed in his reflections was on the point of turning aft in his promenade, he became sensible of Claggart's presence, and saw
the doffed cap held in deferential expectancy. Here be
it said that Captain Vere's personal knowledge of this
petty officer had only begun at the time of the ship's
last sailing from home, Claggart then for the first, in
transfer from a ship detained for repairs, supplying on
board the *Indomitable* the place of a previous master-
at-arms disabled and ashore.

No sooner did the commander observe who it was
that now deferentially stood awaiting his notice, than a
peculiar expression came over him. It was not unlike
that which uncontrollably will flit across the countenance
of one at unawares encountering a person who though
known to him indeed has hardly been long enough
known for thorough knowledge, but something in whose
aspect nevertheless now for the first provokes a vaguely
repellent distaste. But coming to a stand, and resuming
much of his wonted official manner, save that a sort of
impatience lurked in the intonation of the opening word,
he said: "Well? What is it, Master-at-Arms?"

With the air of a subordinate grieved at the necessity

of being a messenger of ill tidings, and while conscien-
tiously determined to be frank, yet equally resolved upon
shunning overstatement, Claggart, at this invitation or
rather summons to disburthen, spoke up. What he said,
conveyed in the language of no uneducated man, was
to the effect following if not altogether in these words,
namely, that during the chase and preparations for the
possible encounter he had seen enough to convince him
that at least one sailor aboard was a dangerous character
in a ship mustering some who not only had taken a
guilty part in the late serious troubles, but others also
who, like the man in question, had entered His Majesty's
service under another form than enlistment.

At this point Captain Vere with some impatience interrupted him: "Be direct, man; say impressed men."

Claggart made a gesture of subservience and proceeded.

Quite lately he (Claggart) had begun to suspect that
on the gun decks some sort of movement prompted by
the sailor in question was covertly going on, but he had
not thought himself warranted in reporting the suspicion
so long as it remained indistinct. But, from what he had
that afternoon observed in the man referred to, the suspicion of something clandestine going on had advanced
to a point less removed from certainty. He deeply felt,
he added, the serious responsibility assumed in making a
report involving such possible consequences to the individual mainly concerned, besides tending to augment
those natural anxieties which every naval commander
must feel in view of extraordinary outbreaks so recent

as those which, he sorrowfully said it, it needed not to name.

Now at the first broaching of the matter Captain Vere, taken by surprise, could not wholly dissemble his disquietude. But as Claggart went on, the former's aspect changed into restiveness under something in the witness's manner in giving his testimony. However, he refrained from interrupting him. And Claggart, continuing, concluded with this:

"God forbid, your honor, that the *Indomitable's* should be the experience of the——"

"Never mind that!" here peremptorily broke in the superior, his face altering with anger, instinctively divining the ship that the other was about to name, one in which the Nore Mutiny had assumed a singularly tragical character that for a time jeopardized the life of its commander. Under the circumstances he was indignant at the purposed allusion. When the commissioned officers themselves were on all occasions very heedful how they referred to the recent events, for a petty officer unnecessarily to allude to them in the presence of his captain, this struck him as a most immodest presumption. Besides, to his quick sense of self-respect, it even looked under the circumstances something like an attempt to alarm him. Nor at first was he without some surprise that one who so far as he had hitherto come under his notice had shown considerable tact in his function should in this particular evince such lack of it.

But these thoughts and kindred dubious ones flitting across his mind were suddenly replaced by an intuitional

surmise which though as yet obscure in form served practically to affect his reception of the ill tidings. Certain it
is that, long versed in everything pertaining to the complicated gun-deck life, which like every other form of life
has its secret mines and dubious side, the side popularly
disclaimed, Captain Vere did not permit himself to be
unduly disturbed by the general tenor of his subordinate's report. Furthermore, if in view of recent events
prompt action should be taken at the first palpable sign
of recurring insubordination, for all that, not judicious
would it be, he thought, to keep the idea of lingering
disaffection alive by undue forwardness in crediting an
informer even if his own subordinate and charged among
other things with police surveillance of the crew. This
feeling would not perhaps have so prevailed with him
were it not that upon a prior occasion the patriotic zeal
officially evinced by Claggart had somewhat irritated
him as appearing rather supersensible and strained.
Furthermore, something even in the official's self-
possessed and somewhat ostentatious manner in making
his specifications strangely reminded him of a bandsman,
a prejurious witness in a capital case before a court
martial ashore of which, when a lieutenant he, Captain
Vere, had been a member.

Now the peremptory check given to Claggart in the
matter of the arrested allusion was quickly followed up
by this: "You say that there is at least one dangerous
man aboard. Name him."

"William Budd, a foretopman, your honor———"

"William Budd," repeated Captain Vere with unfeigned astronishment; "and mean you the man that lieutenant Ratcliffe took from the merchantman not very long ago—the young fellow who seems to be so popular with the men—Billy, the Handsome Sailor, as they call him?"

"The same, your honor; but, for all his youth and good looks, a deep one. Not for nothing does he insinuate himself into the good will of his shipmates, since at the least all hands will at a pinch say a good word for him at all hazards. Did Lieutenant Ratcliffe happen to tell your honor of that adroit fling of Budd's, jumping up in the cutter's bow under the merchantman's stern when he was being taken off? It is even masked by that sort of good-humored air that at heart he resents his impressment. You have but noted his fair cheek. A man trap may be under his ruddy-tipped daisies."

Now the Handsome Sailor, as a signal figure among the crew, had naturally enough attracted the captain's attention from the first. Though in general not very demonstrative to his officers, he had congratulated Lieutenant Ratcliffe upon his good fortune in lighting on such a fine specimen of the *genus homo,* who in the nude might have posed for a statue of young Adam before the Fall. As to Billy's adieu to the ship *Rights-of-Man,* which the boarding lieutenant had indeed reported to him but in a deferential way more as a good story than aught else, Captain Vere, though mistakenly understanding it as a satiric sally, had but thought so much the better of the impressed man for it, as a military sailor, admiring the spirit that could take an arbitrary enlistment so merrily and sensibly. The foretopman's conduct, too, so far as it had fallen under the captain's notice, had confirmed the first happy augury, while the new recruit's qualities as a *sailorman* seemed to be such that he had thought of recommending him to the executive officer for promotion to a place that would more frequently bring him under his own observation, namely, the captaincy of the mizzentop, replacing there in the starboard watch a man not so young whom partly for that reason he deemed less fitted for the post. Be it parenthesized here that since the mizzentopmen, having not to handle such breadths of heavy canvas as the lower sails on the mainmast and foremast, a young man if of the right stuff not only seems best adapted to duty there, but in fact is generally selected for the captaincy of that top, and the company under him are light hands and often but striplings. In sum, Captain Vere had from the beginning deemed Billy Budd to be what in the naval parlance of the time was called a *"King's bargain,"* that is to say, for His Britannic Majesty's navy a capital investment at small outlay or none at all.

After a brief pause during which the reminiscences above mentioned passed vividly through his mind and he weighed the import of Claggart's last suggestion conveyed in the phrase "pitfall under the daisies," and the more he weighed it the less reliance he felt in the informer's good faith, suddenly he turned upon him and in a low voice: "Do you come to me, Master-at-Arms, with so foggy a tale? As to Budd, cite me an act or spoken word of his confirmatory of what you in general charge against him. Stay," drawing nearer to him, "heed what you speak. Just now, and in a case like this, there is a yardarm-end for the false witness."

"Ah, your honor!" sighed Claggart, mildly shaking his shapely head as in sad deprecation of such unmerited severity of tone. Then, bridling—erecting himself as in virtuous self-assertion, he circumstantially alleged certain words and acts, which collectively, if credited, led to presumptions mortally inculpating Budd. And for some of these averments, he added, substantiating proof was not far.

With gray eyes impatient and distrustful essaying to fathom to the bottom Claggart's calm violet ones, Captain Vere again heard him out, then for the moment stood ruminating. The mood he evinced, Claggart, himself for the time liberated from the other's scrutiny, steadily regarded with a look difficult to render—a look curious of the operation of his tactics, a look such as might have been that of the spokesman of the envious children of Jacob deceptively imposing upon the troubled patriarch the blood-dyed coat of young Joseph.

Though something exceptional in the moral quality of Captain Vere made him, in earnest encounter with a fellow man, a veritable touchstone of that man's essential nature, yet now as to Claggart and what was really going on in him his feeling partook less of intuitional conviction than of strong suspicion clogged by strange dubieties. The perplexity he evinced proceeded less from aught

touching the man informed against—as Claggart doubtless opined—than from considerations how best to act in
regard to the informer. At first indeed he was naturally
for summoning that substantiation of his allegations
which Claggart said was at hand. But such a proceeding
would result in the matter at once getting abroad, which
in the present stage of it, he thought, might undesirably
affect the ship's company. If Claggart was a false witness—that closed the affair. And therefore before trying
the accusation he would first practically test the accuser,
and he thought this could be done in a quiet undemonstrative way.

The measure he determined upon involved a shifting
of the scene, a transfer to a place less exposed to observation than the broad quarterdeck. For although the few
gun-room officers there at the time had, in due observance of naval etiquette, withdrawn to leeward the
moment Captain Vere had begun his promenade on the
deck's weather side; and though during the colloquy
with Claggart they of course ventured not to diminish
the distance, and though throughout the interview Captain Vere's voice was far from high and Claggart's silvery
and low, and the wind in the cordage and the wash of
the sea helped the more to put them beyond earshot;
nevertheless, the interview's continuance already had
attracted observation from some topmen aloft and other
sailors in the waist or further forward.

Having determined upon his measures, Captain Vere
forthwith took action. Abruptly turning to Claggart he
asked, "Master-at-Arms, is it now Budd's watch aloft?"

"No, your honor." Whereupon, "Mr. Wilkes!" summoning the nearest midshipman, "tell Albert to come to me." Albert was the captain's hammock-boy, a sort of sea-valet in whose discretion and fidelity his master had much confidence. The lad appeared. "You know Budd the foretopman?"

"I do, sir."

"Go find him. It is his watch off. Manage to tell him out of earshot that he is wanted aft. Contrive it that he speaks to nobody. Keep him in talk yourself. And not till you get well aft here, not till then let him know that the place where he is wanted is my cabin. You understand. Go.—Master-at-Arms, show yourself on the decks below, and when you think it time for Albert to be coming with his man, stand by quietly to follow the sailor in."

20

Now when the foretopman found himself closeted there, as it were, in the cabin with the captain and Claggart, he was surprised enough. But it was a surprise unaccompanied by apprehension or distrust. To an immature nature essentially honest and humane, forewarning intimations of subtler danger from one's kind come tardily if at all. The only thing that took shape in the young sailor's mind was this: Yes, the captain, I have always thought, looks kindly upon me. Wonder if he's going to make me his coxswain. I should like that. And maybe now he is going to ask the master-at-arms about me.

"Shut the door there, sentry," said the commander; "stand without, and let nobody came in.—Now, Master-at-Arms, tell this man to his face what you told of him to me," and stood prepared to scrutinize the mutually confronting visages.

With the measured step and calm collected air of an asylum physician approaching in the public hall some patient beginning to show indications of a coming paroxysm, Claggart deliberately advanced within short range of Billy, and, mesmerically looking him in the eye, briefly recapitulated the accusation.

Not at first did Billy take it in. When he did, the rose-tan of his cheek looked struck as by white leprosy. He stood like one impaled and gagged. Meanwhile the accuser's eyes removing not as yet from the blue dilated ones, underwent a phenomenal change, their wonted rich violet color blurring into a muddy purple, those lights of human intelligence losing human expression, gelidly protruding like the alien eyes of certain uncatalogued creatures of the deep. The first mesmeric glance was one of serpent fascination; the last was as the hungry lurch of the torpedo-fish.

"Speak, man!" said Captain Vere to the transfixed one, struck by his aspect even more than by Claggart's. "Speak! Defend yourself." Which appeal caused but a strange dumb gesturing and gurgling in Billy, amazement at such an accusation so suddenly sprung on inexperienced nonage; this, and it may be, horror of the accuser serving to bring out his lurking defect and in this instance for the time intensifying it into a convulsed tongue-tie; while the intent head and entire form straining forward in an agony of ineffectual eagerness to obey the injunction to speak and defend himself, gave an expression to the face like that of a condemned Vestal priestess in the moment of being buried alive, and in the first struggle against suffocation.

Though at the time Captain Vere was quite ignorant of Billy's liability to vocal impediment, he now immediately divined it, since vividly Billy's aspect recalled to him that of a bright young schoolmate of his whom he had once seen struck by much the same startling impotence in the act of eagerly rising in the class to be foremost in response to a testing question put to it by the master. Going close up to the young sailor, and laying a soothing hand on his shoulder, he said: "There is no hurry, my boy. Take your time, take your time." Contrary to the effect intended, these words so fatherly in tone doubtless touching Billy's heart to the quick, prompted yet more violent efforts at utterance—efforts soon ending for the time in confirming the paralysis, and bringing to his face an expression which was as a crucifixion to behold. The next instant, quick as the flame from a discharged cannon at night, his right arm shot out, and Claggart dropped to the deck. Whether intentionally or but owing to the young athlete's superior height, the blow had taken effect full upon the forehead,

so shapely and intellectual-looking a feature in the
master-at-arms, so that the body fell over lengthwise,
like a heavy plank tilted from erectness. A gasp or two,
and he lay motionless.

"Fated boy," breathed Captain Vere in tone so low as
to be almost a whisper, "what have you done! But here,
help me."

The twain raised the felled one from the loins up into
a sitting position. The spare form flexibly acquiesced,
but inertly. It was like handling a dead snake. They lowered it back. Regaining erectness Captain Vere with one
hand covering his face stood to all appearance as im-
passive as the object at his feet. Was he absorbed in
taking in all the bearings of the event and what was best,
not only now at once to be done, but also in the sequel?
Slowly he uncovered his face, and the effect was as if
the moon emerging from eclipse should reappear with
quite another aspect than that which had gone into hiding. The father in him, manifested toward Billy thus far
in the scene, was replaced by the military disciplinarian.
In his official tone he bade the foretopman retire to a
stateroom aft (pointing it out) and there remain till thence
summoned. This order Billy in silence mechanically
obeyed. Then, going to the cabin door where it opened
on the quarterdeck, Captain Vere said to the sentry without, "Tell somebody to send Albert here." When the lad
appeared his master so contrived it that he should not
catch sight of the prone one. "Albert," he said to him,
"tell the surgeon I wish to see him. You need not come
back until called." When the surgeon entered—a self-

poised character of that grave sense and experience that hardly anything could take him aback—Captain Vere advanced to meet him, thus unconsciously intercepting his view of Claggart, and interrupting the other's wonted ceremonious salutation, said, "Nay, tell me how it is with yonder man," directing his attention to the prostrate one.

The surgeon looked, and for all his self-command, somewhat started at the abrupt revelation. On Claggart's always pallid complexion, thick black blood was now oozing from nostril and ear. To the gazer's professional eye it was unmistakably no living man that he saw.

"Is it so then?" said Captain Vere, intently watching him. "I thought it. But verify it." Whereupon the customary tests confirmed the surgeon's first glance, who now, looking up in unfeigned concern, cast a look of intense inquisitiveness upon his superior. But Captain Vere, with one hand to his brow, was standing motionless. Suddenly, catching the surgeon's arm convulsively, he exclaimed, pointing down to the body—"It is the divine judgment on Ananias! Look!"

Disturbed by the excited manner he had never before observed in the *Indomitable's* captain, and as yet wholly ignorant of the affair, the prudent surgeon nevertheless held his peace, only again looking an earnest interrogation as to what it was that had resulted in such a tragedy.

But Captain Vere was now again motionless, standing absorbed in thought. But again starting, he vehemently exclaimed—"Struck dead by an angel of God! Yet the angel must hang!"

At these passionate interjections, mere incoherences

to the listener as yet unapprised of the antecedents, the surgeon was profoundly discomposed. But now, as recollecting himself, Captain Vere in less passionate tone briefly related the circumstances leading up to the event.

"But come, we must despatch," he added. "Help me to remove him (meaning the body) to yonder compartment," designating one opposite that where the foretopman remained immured. Anew disturbed by a request that, as implying a desire for secrecy, seemed unaccountably strange to him, there was nothing for the subordinate to do but comply.

"Go now," said Captain Vere with something of his wonted manner—"go now. I shall presently call a drumhead court. Tell the lieutenants what happened, and tell Mr. Mordant," meaning the captain of marines, "and charge them to keep the matter to themselves."

21

Full of disquietude and misgiving, the surgeon left the cabin. Was Captain Vere suddenly affected in his mind, or was it but a transient excitement, brought about by so strange and extraordinary a happening? As to the drumhead court, it struck the surgeon as impolitic, if nothing more. The thing to do, he thought, was to place Billy Budd in confinement and in a way dictated by us-

age, and postpone further action in so extraordinary a case
to such time as they should rejoin the squadron, and then
refer it to the admiral. He recalled the unwonted agita-
tion of Captain Vere and his excited exclamations so at
variance with his normal manner. Was he unhinged? But
assuming that he is, it is not so susceptible of proof.
What then can he do? No more trying situation is conceivable than that of an officer subordinate under a captain whom he suspects to be, not mad indeed, but yet
not quite unaffected in his intellect. To argue his order
to him would be insolence. To resist him would be
mutiny.

In obedience to Captain Vere he communicated what
had happened to the lieutenants and captain of marines,
saying nothing as to the captain's state. They fully shared
his own surprise and concern. Like him too they seemed
to think that such a matter should be referred to the
admiral.

22

Who in the rainbow can show the line where the violet
tint ends and the orange tint begins? Distinctly we see
the difference of the colors, but when exactly does the
one first blendingly enter into the other? So with sanity
and insanity. In pronounced cases, there is no question

about them. But in some supposed cases, in various degrees supposedly less pronounced, to draw the exact line
of demarcation few will undertake—though for a fee
some professional experts will. There is nothing namable
but that some men will undertake to do it for pay.

Whether Captain Vere, as the surgeon professionally
and privately surmised, was really the sudden victim of
any degree of aberration, one must determine for himself by such light as this narrative may afford.

That the unhappy event which has been narrated
could not have happened at a worse juncture was but
too true. For it was close on the heel of the suppressed
insurrections, an aftertime very critical to naval authority, demanding from every English sea commander
two qualities not readily interfusible—prudence and
rigor. Moreover, there was something crucial in the case.

In the jugglery of circumstances preceding and attending the event on board the *Indomitable,* and in the light
of that martial code whereby it was formally to be
judged, innocence and guilt personified in Claggart and
Budd in effect changed places. In a legal view the apparent victim of the tragedy was he who had sought to
victimize a man blameless; and the indisputable deed of
the latter, navally regarded, constituted the most hei-
nous of military crimes. Yet more. The essential right and
wrong involved in the matter, the clearer that might be,
so much the worse for the responsibility of a loyal sea
commander inasmuch as he was not authorized to determine the matter on that primitive basis.

Small wonder then that the *Indomitable's* captain,

though in general a man of rapid decision, felt that circumspectness not less than promptitude was necessary. Until he could decide upon his course, and in each detail, and not only so, but until the concluding measure was upon the point of being enacted, he deemed it advisable in view of all the circumstances to guard as much as possible against publicity. Here he may or may not have erred. Certain it is, however, that subsequently in the confidential talk of more than one or two gun rooms and cabins he was not a little criticized by some officers, a fact imputed by his friends and vehemently by his cousin Jack Denton to professional jealousy of "Starry Vere." Some imaginative ground for invidious comment there was. The maintenance of secrecy in the matter, the confining all knowledge of it for a time to the place where the homicide occurred, the quarterdeck cabin—in these particulars lurked some resemblance to the policy adopted in those tragedies of the palace which have occurred more than once in the capital founded by Peter the Barbarian.

The case indeed was such that fain would the *Indomitable's* captain have deferred taking any action whatever respecting it further than to keep the foretopman a close prisoner till the ship rejoined the squadron and then submitting the matter to the judgment of his admiral.

But a true military officer is in one particular like a true monk. Not with more of self-abnegation will the latter keep his vows of monastic obedience than the former his vows of allegiance to martial duty.

Feeling that unless quick action was taken on it, the

deed of the foretopman, as soon as it should be known on the gun decks, would tend to awaken any slumbering embers of the Nore among the crew, a sense of the urgency of the case overruled in Captain Vere every other consideration. But though a conscientious disciplinarian he was no lover of authority for mere authority's sake. Very far was he from embracing opportunities for monopolizing to himself the perils of moral responsibility, none at least that could properly be referred to an official superior or shared with him by his official equals or even subordinates. So thinking, he was glad it would not be at variance with usage to turn the matter over to a summary court of his own officers, reserving to himself as the one on whom the ultimate accountability would rest, the right of maintaining a supervision of it, or formally or informally interposing at need. Accordingly a drumhead court was summarily convened, he electing the individuals composing it, the first lieutenant, the captain of marines, and the sailing master.

In associating an officer of marines with the sea lieutenants in a case having to do with a sailor, the commander perhaps deviated from general custom. He was prompted thereto by the circumstance that he took that soldier to be a judicious person, thoughtful, and not altogether incapable of grappling with a difficult case unprecedented in his prior experience. Yet even as to him he was not without some latent misgiving, for withal he was an extremely good-natured man, an enjoyer of his dinner, a sound sleeper, and inclined to obesity. A man who though he would always maintain his manhood in battle might not prove altogether reliable in a moral dilemma involving aught of the tragic. As to the first lieutenant and the sailing master, Captain Vere could not but be aware that though honest natures, of approved gallantry upon occasion, their intelligence was mostly confined to the matter of active seamanship and the fighting demands of their profession. The court was held in the same cabin where the unfortunate affair had taken place. This cabin, the commander's, embraced the entire area under the poop deck. Aft, and on either side, was a small stateroom, the one room temporarily a jail and the other a dead-house, and a yet smaller compartment leaving a space between, expanding forward into a goodly oblong of length coinciding with the ship's beam. A skylight of moderate dimension was overhead, and at each end of the oblong space were two sashed porthole windows easily convertible back into embrasures for short carronades.

All being quickly in readiness, Billy Budd was arraigned, Captain Vere necessarily appearing as the sole witness in the case, and as such temporarily sinking his rank, though singularly maintaining it in a matter apparently trivial, namely, that he testified from the ship's weather side, with that object having caused the court to sit on the lee side. Concisely he narrated all that had led up to the catastrophe, omitting nothing in Claggart's accusation and deposing as to the manner in which the prisoner had received it. At this testimony the three officers glanced with no little surprise at Billy Budd, the last man they would have suspected either of the muti-

nous design alleged by Claggart or the undeniable deed
he himself had done.

The first lieutenant, taking judicial primacy and turning toward the prisoner, said, "Captain Vere has spoken.
Is it or is it not as Captain Vere says?" In response came
syllables not so much impeded in the utterance as might
have been anticipated. They were these: "Captain Vere
tells the truth. It is just as Captain Vere says, but it is
not as the master-at-arms said. I have eaten the King's
bread and I am true to the King."

"I believe you, my man," said the witness, his voice
indicating a suppressed emotion not otherwise betrayed.

"God will bless you for that, your honor!" not without
stammering said Billy, and all but broke down. But immediately was recalled to self-control by another question, to which with the same emotional difficulty of utterance he said, "No, there was no malice between us. I
never bore malice against the master-at-arms. I am sorry
that he is dead. I did not mean to kill him. Could I
have used my tongue I would not have struck him. But
he foully lied to my face and in presence of my captain, and I had to say something, and I could only say it
with a blow, God help me!"

In the impulsive aboveboard manner of the frank one
the court saw confirmed all that was implied in words
that just previously had perplexed them, coming as they
did from the testifier to the tragedy and promptly following Billy's impassioned disclaimer of mutinous intent—Captain Vere's words, "I believe you, my man."

Next it was asked of him whether he knew of or

suspected aught savoring of incipient trouble (meaning mutiny, though the explicit term was avoided) going on in any section of the ship's company.

The reply lingered. This was naturally imputed by the court to the same vocal embarrassment which had retarded or obstructed previous answers. But in main it was otherwise here, the question immediately recalling to Billy's mind the interview with the after-guardsman in the forechains. But an innate repugnance to playing a part at all approaching that of an informer against one's own shipmates—the same erring sense of uninstructed honor which had stood in the way of his reporting the matter at the time though as a loyal man-of-war-man it was incumbent on him, and failure so to do if charged against him and proven, would have subjected him to the heaviest of penalties—this, with the blind feeling now his, that nothing really was being hatched, prevailed with him. When the answer came it was a negative.

"One question more," said the officer of marines, now first speaking and with a troubled earnestness. "You tell us that what the master-at-arms said against you was a lie. Now why should he have so lied, so maliciously lied, since you declare there was no malice between you?"

At that question unintentionally touching on a spiritual sphere wholly obscure to Billy's thoughts, he was nonplused, evincing a confusion indeed that some observers, such as can readily be imagined, would have construed into involuntary evidence of hidden guilt. Nevertheless he strove some way to answer, but all at once relinquished the vain endeavor, at the same time

turning an appealing glance toward Captain Vere, as
deeming him his best helper and friend. Captain Vere,
who had been seated for a time, rose to his feet, addressing the interrogator. "The question you put to him comes
naturally enough. But how can he rightly answer it? Or
anybody else? Unless indeed it be he who lies within
there," designating the compartment where lay the
corpse. "But the prone one there will not rise to our summons. In effect, though, as it seems to me, the point you
make is hardly material. Quite aside from any conceivable motive actuating the master-at-arms, and irrespective of the provocation to the blow, a martial court
must needs in the present case confine its attention to the
blow's consequence, which consequence justly is to be
deemed not otherwise than as the striker's deed."

This utterance, the full significance of which it was not
at all likely that Billy took in, nevertheless caused him to
turn a wistful interrogative look toward the speaker, a
look in its dumb expressiveness not unlike that which a
dog of generous breed might turn upon his master,
seeking in his face some elucidation of a previous gesture
ambiguous to the canine intelligence. Nor was the same
utterance without marked effect upon the three officers,
more especially the soldier. Couched in it seemed to
them a meaning unanticipated, involving a prejudgment
on the speaker's part. It served to augment a mental dis-
turbance previously evident enough.

The soldier once more spoke, in a tone of suggestive
dubiety addressing at once his associates and Captain
Vere: "Nobody is present—none of the ship's company, I

mean—who might shed lateral light, if any is to be had, upon what remains mysterious in this matter."

"That is thoughtfully put," said Captain Vere; "I see your drift. Aye, there is a mystery; but, to use a Scriptural phrase, it is 'a mystery of iniquity,' a matter for psychologic theologians to discuss. But what has a military court to do with it? Not to add that for us any possible investigation of it is cut off by the lasting tongue-tie of—him—in yonder," again designating the mortuary stateroom. "The prisoner's deed—with that alone we have to do."

To this, and particularly the closing reiteration, the marine soldier, knowing not how aptly to reply, sadly abstained from saying aught. The first lieutenant, who at the outset had not unnaturally assumed primacy in the court, now overrulingly instructed by a glance from Captain Vere, a glance more effective than words, resumed that primacy. Turning to the prisoner, "Budd," he said, and scarce in equable tones, "Budd, if you have aught further to say for yourself, say it now."

Upon this the young sailor turned another quick glance toward Captain Vere; then, as taking a hint from that aspect, a hint confirming his own instinct that silence was now best, replied to the lieutenant, "I have said all, sir."

The marine—the same who had been the sentinel without the cabin door at the time that the foretopman, followed by the master-at-arms, entered it—he, standing by the sailor throughout these judicial proceedings, was now directed to take him back to the after-compartment

originally assigned to the prisoner and his custodian. As
the twain disappeared from view the three officers, as
partially liberated from some inward constraint associated with Billy's mere presence, simultaneously stirred in
their seats. They exchanged looks of troubled indecision,
yet feeling that decide they must and without long delay.
As for Captain Vere, he for the time stood unconsciously
with his back toward them, apparently in one of his absent
fits, gazing out from a sashed porthole to windward upon
the monotonous blank of the twilight sea. But the court's
silence continuing, broken only at moments by brief con-
sultations in low earnest tones, this seemed to arm him
and energize him. Turning, he to-and-fro paced the
cabin athwart, in the returning ascent to windward climbing the slant deck in the ship's lee roll, without knowing
it symbolizing thus in his action a mind resolute to sur-
mount difficulties even if against primitive instincts
strong as the wind and the sea. Presently he came to a
stand before the three. After scanning their faces he stood
less as mustering his thoughts for expression than as one
only deliberating how best to put them to well-meaning
men not intellectually mature, men with whom it was
necessary to demonstrate certain principles that were
axioms to himself. Similar impatience as to talking is perhaps one reason that deters some minds from addressing
any popular assemblies.

When speak he did, something both in the substance of
what he said and his manner of saying it showed the influence of unshared studies modifying and tempering the
practical training of an active career. This, along with his

phraseology now and then was suggestive of the grounds whereon rested that imputation of a certain pedantry socially alleged against him by certain naval men of wholly practical cast, captains who nevertheless would frankly concede that His Majesty's navy mustered no more efficient officer of their grade than "Starry Vere."

What he said was to this effect: "Hitherto I have been but the witness, little more; and I should hardly think now to take another tone, that of your coadjutor, for the time, did I not perceive in you—at the crisis too—a troubled hesitancy, proceeding, I doubt not, from the clash of military duty with moral scruple—scruple vitalized by compassion. For the compassion, how can I otherwise than share it? But, mindful of paramount obligations, I strive against scruples that may tend to enervate decision. Not, gentlemen, that I hide from myself that the case is an exceptional one. Speculatively regarded, it well might be referred to a jury of casuists. But for us here acting not as casuists or moralists, it is a case practical, and under martial law practically to be dealt with.

"But your scruples: do they move as in a dusk? Challenge them. Make them advance and declare themselves. Come now: do they import something like this: if, mindless of palliating circumstances, we are bound to regard the death of the master-at-arms as the prisoner's deed, then does that deed constitute a capital crime whereof the penalty is a mortal one? But in natural justice is nothing but the prisoner's overt act to be considered? How can we adjudge to summary and shameful death a fellow creature innocent before God, and whom we feel to be so?—Does that state it aright? You sign sad assent. Well, I too feel that, the full force of that. It is Nature. But do these buttons that we wear attest that our allegiance is to Nature? No, to the King. Though the ocean, which is inviolate Nature primeval, though this be the element where we move and have our being as sailors, yet as the King's officers lies our duty in a sphere correspondingly natural? So little is that true that, in receiving our commissions, we in the most important regards ceased to be natural free agents. When war is declared are we, the commissioned fighters, previously consulted? We fight at command. If our judgments approve the war, that is but coincidence. So in other particulars. So now. For suppose condemnation to follow these present proceedings. Would it be so much we ourselves that would condemn as it would be martial law operating through us? For that law and the rigor of it, we are not responsible. Our vowed responsibility is in this: that however pitilessly that law may operate, we nevertheless adhere to it and administer it.

"But the exceptional in the matter moves the hearts within you. Even so too is mine moved. But let not warm hearts betray heads that should be cool. Ashore in a criminal case will an upright judge allow himself off the bench to be waylaid by some tender kinswoman of the accused seeking to touch him with her tearful plea? Well the heart here denotes the feminine in man, is as that piteous woman and, hard though it be, she must here be ruled out."

He paused, earnestly studying them for a moment, then resumed.

"But something in your aspect seems to urge that it is not solely the heart that moves in you, but also the conscience, the private conscience. But tell me whether or not, occupying the position we do, private conscience should not yield to that imperial one formulated in the code under which alone we officially proceed?"

Here the three men moved in their seats, less convinced than agitated by the course of an argument troubling but the more, the spontaneous conflict within.

Perceiving which, the speaker paused for a moment, then abruptly changing his tone went on.

"To steady us a bit, let us recur to the facts. In wartime at sea a man-of-war's-man strikes his superior in grade, and the blow kills. Apart from its effect, the blow itself is, according to the Articles of War, a capital crime. Furthermore——"

"Aye, sir," emotionally broke in the officer of marines, "in one sense it was. But surely Budd purposed neither mutiny nor homicide."

"Surely not, my good man. And before a court less arbitrary and more merciful than a martial one that plea would largely extenuate. At the Last Assizes it shall acquit. But how here? We proceed under the law of the Mutiny Act. In feature no child can resemble his father more than that Act resembles in spirit the thing from

which it derives—War. In His Majesty's service—in this
ship indeed—there are Englishmen forced to fight for the
King against their will. Against their conscience, for
aught we know. Though as their fellow creatures some
of us may appreciate their position, yet as navy officers,
what reck we of it? Still less recks the enemy. Our impressed men he would fain cut down in the same swath
with our volunteers. As regards the enemy's naval con-
scripts, some of whom may even share our own abhor-
rence of the regicidal French Directory, it is the same
on our side. War looks but to the frontage, the appearance. And the Mutiny Act, War's child, takes after the
father. Budd's intent or non-intent is nothing to the purpose.

"But while, put to it by those anxieties in you which
I cannot but respect, I only repeat myself—while thus
strangely we prolong proceedings that should be summary—the enemy may be sighted and an engagement
result. We must do; and one of two things must we do—
condemn or let go."

"Can we not convict and yet mitigate the penalty?"
asked the junior lieutenant here speaking, and falter-
ingly, for the first.

"Lieutenant, were that clearly lawful for us under the
circumstances, consider the consequences of such clem-
ency. The people" (meaning the ship's company) "have
native sense; most of them are familiar with our naval
usage and tradition, and how would they take it? Even
could you explain to them—which our official position
forbids—they, long molded by arbitrary discipline, have

not that kind of intelligent responsiveness that might qualify them to comprehend and discriminate. No, to the people the foretopman's deed, however it be worded in the announcement, will be plain homicide committed in a flagrant act of mutiny. What penalty for that should follow, they know. But it does not follow. *Why?* they will ruminate. You know what sailors are. Will they not revert to the recent outbreak at the Nore? Aye. They know the well-founded alarm—the panic it struck throughout England. Your clement sentence they would account pusillanimous. They would think that we flinch, that we are afraid of them—afraid of practicing a lawful rigor singularly demanded at this juncture lest it should provoke new troubles. What shame to us such a conjecture on their part, and how deadly to discipline. You see then whither, prompted by duty and the law, I steadfastly drive. But I beseech you, my friends, do not take me amiss. I feel as you do for this unfortunate boy. But did he know our hearts, I take him to be of that generous nature that he would feel even for us on whom in this military necessity so heavy a compulsion is laid."

With that, crossing the deck he resumed his place by the sashed porthole, tacitly leaving the three to come to a decision. On the cabin's opposite side the troubled court sat silent. Loyal lieges, plain and practical, though at bottom they dissented from some points Captain Vere had put to them, they were without the faculty, hardly had the inclination, to gainsay one whom they felt to be an earnest man, one, too, not less their superior in mind than in naval rank. But it is not improbable that even

such of his words as were not without influence over
them, less came home to them than his closing appeal to
their instinct as sea officers in the forethought he threw
out as to the practical consequences to discipline, considering the unconfirmed tone of the fleet at the time,
should a man-of-war's-man's violent killing at sea of a
superior in grade be allowed to pass for aught else than
a capital crime demanding prompt infliction of the
penalty.

Not unlikely they were brought to something more or
less akin to that harassed frame of mind which in the year
1842 actuated the commander of the U.S. brig-of-war
Somers to resolve, under the so-called Articles of War,
Articles modeled upon the English Mutiny Act, to resolve
upon the execution at sea of a midshipman and two
petty officers as mutineers designing the seizure of the
brig. Which resolution was carried out though in a time
of peace and within not many days sail of home—an act
vindicated by a naval court of inquiry subsequently convened ashore. History, and here cited without comment.
True, the circumstances on board the *Somers* were different from those on board the *Indomitable*. But the urgency felt, well-warranted or otherwise, was much the
same.

Says a writer whom few know, "Forty years after a
battle it is easy for a noncombatant to reason about how
it ought to have been fought. It is another thing personally and under fire to direct the fighting while involved in the obscuring smoke of it. Much so with respect
to other emergencies involving considerations both prac-

tical and moral, and when it is imperative promptly to act. The greater the fog the more it imperils the steamer, and speed is put on though at the hazard of running somebody down. Little ween the snug card players in the cabin of the responsibilities of the sleepless man on the bridge."

In brief, Billy Budd was formally convicted and sentenced to be hung at the yardarm in the early morning watch, it being now night. Otherwise, as is customary in such cases, the sentence would forthwith have been carried out. In wartime, on the field or in the fleet, a mortal punishment decreed by a drumhead court—on the field sometimes decreed by but a nod from the general—follows without delay on the heel of conviction, without appeal.

23

It was Captain Vere himself who of his own motion communicated the finding of the court to the prisoner, for that purpose going to the compartment where he was in custody and bidding the marine there to withdraw for the time.

Beyond the communication of the sentence, what took place at this interview was never known. But in view of the character of the twain briefly closeted in that stateroom, each radically sharing in the rarer qualities of our nature—so rare indeed as to be all but incredible to average minds however much cultivated—some conjectures may be ventured.

It would have been in consonance with the spirit of Captain Vere should he on this occasion have concealed nothing from the condemned one—should he indeed have frankly disclosed to him the part he himself had played in bringing about the decision, at the same time revealing his actuating motives. On Billy's side it is not improbable that such a confession would have been received in much the same spirit that prompted it. Not without a sort of joy indeed he might have appreciated the brave opinion of him implied in his captain making such a confidant of him. Nor as to the sentence itself could he have been insensible that it was imparted to him as to one not afraid to die. Even more may have been. Captain Vere in the end may have developed the passion sometimes latent under an exterior stoical or indifferent. He was old enough to have been Billy's father. The austere devotee of military duty letting himself melt back into what remains primeval in our formalized humanity may in the end have caught Billy to his heart even as Abraham may have caught young Isaac on the brink of resolutely offering him up in obedience to the exacting behest. But there is no telling the sacrament, seldom if in any case revealed to the gadding world, wherever under circumstances at all akin to those here attempted to be set forth, two of great Nature's nobler order embrace. There is privacy at the time, inviolable to the survivor, and holy oblivion, the sequel to each diviner magnanimity, providentially covers all at last.

The first to encounter Captain Vere in act of leaving the compartment was the senior lieutenant. The face he beheld for the moment, one expressive of the agony of the strong, was to that officer, though a man of fifty, a startling revelation. That the condemned one suffered less than he who mainly had effected the condemnation was apparently indicated by the former's exclamation in the scene soon perforce to be touched upon.

24

Of a series of incidents within a brief term rapidly following each other, the adequate narration may take up a term less brief, especially if explanation or comment here and there seem requisite to the better understanding of such incidents. Between the entrance into the cabin of him who never left it alive, and him who when he did leave it left it as one condemned to die, between this and the closeted interview just given, less than an hour and a half had elapsed. It was an interval long enough, however, to awaken speculations among no few of the ship's company as to what it was that could be detaining in the cabin the master-at-arms and the sailor; for a rumor that both of them had been seen to enter it and neither

of them had been seen to emerge, this rumor had got
abroad upon the gun decks and in the tops; the people of
a great warship being in one respect like villagers taking
microscopic note of every outward movement or non-
movement going on. When therefore, in weather not at
all tempestuous, all hands were called in the second dog
watch, a summons under such circumstances not usual
in those hours, the crew were not wholly unprepared
for some announcement extraordinary, one having connection too with the continued absence of the two men
from their wonted haunts.

There was a moderate sea at the time, and the moon,
newly risen and near to being at its full, silvered the
white spar deck wherever not blotted by the clear-cut
shadows horizontally thrown of fixtures and moving men.
On either side the quarterdeck the marine guard under
arms was drawn up; and Captain Vere, standing in his
place surrounded by all the wardroom officers, addressed
his men. In so doing his manner showed neither more nor
less than that property pertaining to his supreme position aboard his own ship. In clear terms and concise he
told them what had taken place in the cabin: that the
master-at-arms was dead; that he who had killed him had
been already tried by a summary court and condemned to
death; and that the execution would take place in the
early morning watch. The word *mutiny* was not named in
what he said. He refrained too from making the occasion
an opportunity for any preachment as to the maintenance
of discipline, thinking perhaps that under existing circumstances in the navy the consequence of violating dis-

cipline should be made to speak for itself.

Their captain's announcement was listened to by the throng of standing sailors in a dumbness like that of a seated congregation of believers in hell listening to the clergyman's announcement of his Calvinistic text.

At the close, however, a confused murmur went up. It began to wax. All but instantly, then, at a sign, it was pierced and suppressed by shrill whistles of the boatswain and his mates piping down one watch.

To be prepared for burial Claggart's body was delivered to certain petty officers of his mess. And here, not to clog the sequel with lateral matters, it may be added that, at a suitable hour, the master-at-arms was committed to the sea with every funeral honor properly belonging to his naval grade.

In this proceeding, as in every public one growing out of the tragedy, strict adherence to usage was observed. Nor in any point could it have been at all deviated from, either with respect to Claggart or Billy Budd, without begetting undesirable speculations in the ship's company, sailors, and more particularly men-of-war's men, being of all men the greatest sticklers for usage.

For similar cause, all communication between Captain Vere and the condemned one ended with the closeted interview already given, the latter being now surrendered to the ordinary routine preliminary to the end. This transfer under guard from the captain's quarters was effected without unusual precautions—at least no visible ones.

If possible not to let the men so much as surmise that

their officers anticipate aught amiss from them is the
tacit rule in a military ship. And the more that some sort
of trouble should really be apprehended, the more do
the officers keep that apprehension to themselves, though
not the less unostentatious vigilance may be augmented.

In the present instance the sentry placed over the
prisoner had strict orders to let no one have communication with him but the chaplain. And certain unobtrusive
measures were taken absolutely to insure this point.

25

In a seventy-four of the old order the deck known as
the upper gun deck was the one covered over by the spar
deck, which last, though not without its armament, was
for the most part exposed to the weather. In general
it was at all hours free from hammocks; those of the crew
swinging on the lower gun deck and berth deck, the latter
being not only a dormitory but also the place for the
stowing of the sailors' bags, and on both sides lined with
the large chests or movable pantries of the many messes
of the men.

On the starboard side of the *Indomitable's* upper gun
deck, behold Billy Budd under sentry lying prone in
irons in one of the bays formed by the regular spacing of

the guns comprising the batteries on either side. All these pieces were of the heavier caliber of that period. Mounted on lumbering wooden carriages, they were hampered with cumbersome harness of breeching and strong side tackles for running them out. Guns and carriages, together with the long rammers and shorter lintstocks lodged in loops overhead—all these, as customary, were painted black; and the heavy hempen breechings, tarred to the same tint, wore the like livery of the undertakers. In contrast with the funereal hue of these surroundings the prone sailor's exterior apparel, white jumper and white duck trousers, each more or less soiled, dimly glimmered in the obscure light of the bay like a patch of discolored snow in early April lingering at some upland cave's black mouth. In effect he is already in his shroud, or the garments that shall serve him in lieu of one. Over him but scarce illuminating him, two battle lanterns swing from two massive beams of the deck above. Fed with the oil supplied by the war contractors (whose gains, honest or otherwise, are in every land an anticipated portion of the harvest of death) with flickering splashes of dirty yellow light, they pollute the pale moonshine, all but ineffectually struggling in obstructed flecks through the open ports from which the tompioned cannon protrude. Other lanterns at intervals serve but to bring out somewhat the obscurer bays, which, like small confessionals or side chapels in a cathedral, branch from the long dim-vistaed broad aisle between the two batteries of that covered tier

Such was the deck where now lay the Handsome

Sailor. Through the rose-tan of his complexion no pallor
could have shown. It would have taken days of seques-
tration from the winds and the sun to have brought about
the effacement of that. But the skeleton in the cheekbone
at the point of its angle was just beginning delicately to
be defined under the warm-tinted skin. In fervid hearts,
self-contained, some brief experiences devour our human tissue as secret fire in a ship's hold consumes cotton
in the bale.

But now lying between the two guns, as nipped in the
vice of fate, Billy's agony, mainly proceeding from a
generous young heart's virgin experience of the diabolical incarnate and effective in some men—the tension
of that agony was over now. It survived not the something healing in the closeted interview with Captain
Vere. Without movement he lay as in a trance. That
adolescent expression previously noted as his, taking on
something akin to the look of a slumbering child in the
cradle when the warm hearth-glow of the still chamber
at night plays on the dimples that at whiles mysteriously
form in the cheek, silently coming and going there. For
now and then in the gyved one's trance a serene happy
light born of some wandering reminiscence or dream
would diffuse itself over his face, and then wane away
only anew to return.

The Chaplain coming to see him and finding him thus,
and perceiving no sign that he was conscious of his
presence, attentively regarded him for a space, then
slipping aside, withdrew for the time, peradventure feeling that even he, the minister of Christ, though receiving

his stipend from Mars had no consolation to proffer which could result in a peace transcending that which he beheld. But in the small hours he came again. And the prisoner now awake to his surroundings noticed his approach and civilly, all but cheerfully, welcomed him. But it was to little purpose that in the interview following the good man sought to bring Billy Budd to some godly understanding that he must die, and at dawn. True, Billy himself freely referred to his death as a thing close at hand; but it was something in the way that children will refer to death in general, who yet among their other sports will play a funeral with hearse and mourners.

Not that like children Billy was incapable of conceiving what death really is. No; but he was wholly without irrational fear of it, a fear more prevalent in highly civilized communities than those so-called barbarous ones which in all respects stand nearer to unadulterate Nature. And, as elsewhere said, a barbarian Billy radically was; as much so, for all the costume, as his countrymen the British captives, living trophies, made to march in the Roman triumph of Germanicus. Quite as much so as those later barbarians, young men probably, and picked specimens among the earlier British converts to Christianity, at least nominally such and taken to Rome (as today converts from lesser isles of the sea may be taken to London) of whom the pope of that time, admiring the strangeness of their personal beauty so unlike the Italian stamp, their clear ruddy complexion and curled flaxen locks, exclaimed, "Angles" (meaning *English,* the modern derivative) "Angles do you call them?

And is it because they look so like angels?" Had it been later in time one would think that the Pope had in mind Fra Angelico's seraphs, some of whom, plucking apples in gardens of the Hesperides, have the faint rosebud complexion of the more beautiful English girls.

If in vain the good chaplain sought to impress the young barbarian with ideas of death akin to those conveyed in the skull, dial and crossbones on old tombstones, equally futile to all appearance were his efforts to bring home to him the thought of salvation and a Saviour. Billy listened, but less out of awe or reverence perhaps than from a certain natural politeness, doubtless at bottom regarding all that in much the same way that most mariners of his class take any discourse abstract or out of the common tone of the workaday world. And this sailor way of taking clerical discourse is not wholly unlike the way in which the pioneer of Christianity, full of transcendent miracles, was received long ago on tropic isles by any superior *savage* so-called—a Tahitian, say, of Captain Cook's time or shortly after that time. Out of natural courtesy he received, but did not appropriate. It was like a gift placed in the palm of an outreached hand upon which the fingers do not close.

But the *Indomitable's* chaplain was a discreet man, possessing the good sense of a good heart. So he insisted not in his vocation here. At the instance of Captain Vere, a lieutenant had apprised him of pretty much everything as to Billy; and since he felt that innocence was even a better thing than religion wherewith to go to Judgment, he reluctantly withdrew, but in his emotion not without first performing an act strange enough in an Englishman, and under the circumstances yet more so in any regular priest. Stooping over, he kissed on the fair cheek his fellow man, a felon in martial law, one who, though on the confines of death, he felt he could never convert to a dogma; nor for all that did he fear for his future.

Marvel not that having been made acquainted with the young sailor's essential innocence (an irruption of heretic thought hard to suppress) the worthy man lifted not a finger to avert the doom of such a martyr to martial discipline. So to do would not only have been as idle as invoking the desert, but would also have been an audacious transgression of the bounds of his function, one as exactly prescribed to him by military law as that of the boatswain or any other naval officer. Bluntly put, a chaplain is the minister of the Prince of Peace serving in the host of the God of War—Mars. As such, he is as incongruous as that musket of Blücher, etc., at Christmas. Why then is he there? Because he indirectly subserves the purpose attested by the cannon; because too he lends the sanction of the religion of the meek to that which practically is the abrogation of everything but brute Force.

26

The night so luminous on the spar deck but otherwise
on the cavernous ones below, levels so like the tiered gal-
leries in a coal mine—the luminous night passed away.
But, like the prophet in the chariot disappearing in
heaven and dropping his mantle to Elisha, the withdrawing night transferred its pale robe to the breaking day.
A meek shy light appeared in the East, where stretched a
diaphanous fleece of white furrowed vapor. That light
slowly waxed. Suddenly *eight bells* was struck aft, re-
sponded to by one louder metallic stroke from forward.
It was four o'clock in the morning. Instantly the silver
whistles were heard summoning all hands to witness
punishment. Up through the great hatchways rimmed
with racks of heavy shot, the watch below came pouring,
overspreading with the watch already on deck the space
between the mainmast and foremast, including that occupied by the capacious launch and the black booms
tiered on either side of it, boat and booms making a summit of observation for the powder-boys and younger tars.
A different group comprising one watch of topmen leaned
over the rail of that sea balcony, no small one in a
seventy-four, looking down on the crowd below. Man or
boy none spake but in whisper, and few spake at all.
Captain Vere—as before, the central figure among the
assembled commissioned officers—stood nigh the break

of the poop deck facing forward. Just below him on the quarterdeck the marines in full equipment were drawn up much as at the scene of the promulgated sentence.

At sea in the old time, the execution by halter of a military sailor was generally from the foreyard. In the present instance, for special reasons the mainyard was assigned. Under an arm of that lee yard the prisoner was presently brought up, the chaplain attending him. It was noted at the time, and remarked upon afterward, that in this final scene the good man evinced little or nothing of the perfunctory. Brief speech indeed he had with the condemned one, but the genuine Gospel was less on his tongue than in his aspect and manner toward him. The final preparations personal to the latter being speedily brought to an end by two boatswain's mates, the consummation impended. Billy stood facing aft. At the penultimate moment, his words, his only ones, words wholly unobstructed in the utterance, were these—"God bless Captain Vere!" Syllables so unanticipated coming from one with the ignominious hemp about his neck— a conventional felon's benediction directed aft toward the quarters of honor; syllables, too, delivered in the clear melody of a singing bird on the point of launching from the twig, had a phenomenal effect, not unenhanced by the rare personal beauty of the young sailor spiritualized now through late experiences so poignantly profound.

Without volition as it were, as if indeed the ship's populace were but the vehicles of some vocal current electric, with one voice from alow and aloft came a resonant sympathetic echo—"God bless Captain Vere!"

And yet at that instant Billy alone must have been in
their hearts, even as he was in their eyes.

At the pronounced words and the spontaneous echo
that voluminously rebounded them, Captain Vere, either
through stoic self-control or a sort of momentary paralysis
induced by emotional shock, stood erectly rigid as a
musket in the ship-armorer's rack.

The hull deliberately recovering from the periodic roll
to leeward was just regaining an even keel, when the last
signal, a preconcerted dumb one, was given. At the same
moment it chanced that the vapory fleece hanging low in
the East was shot through with a soft glory as of the
fleece of the Lamb of God seen in mystical vision, and
simultaneously therewith, watched by the wedged mass
of upturned faces, Billy ascended, and, ascending, took
the full rose of the dawn.

In the pinioned figure arrived at the yard-end, to the
wonder of all no motion was apparent, none save that
created by the ship's motion, in moderate weather so
majestic in a great ship ponderously cannoned.

27

A *digression*

When some days afterward, in reference to the singularity just mentioned the purser, a rather ruddy rotund person more accurate as an accountant than profound as a philosopher, said at mess to the surgeon, "What testimony to the force lodged in willpower," the latter—saturnine, spare and tall, one in whom a discreet causticity went along with a manner less genial than polite, replied, "Your pardon, Mr. Purser. In a hanging scientifically conducted—and under special orders I myself directed how Budd's was to be effected—any movement following the completed suspension and originating in the body suspended, such movement indicates mechanical spasm in the muscular system. Hence the absence of that is no more attributable to willpower as you call it than to horsepower—begging your pardon."

"But this muscular spasm you speak of, is not that in a degree more or less invariable in these cases?"

"Assuredly so, Mr. Purser."

"How then, my good sir, do you account for its absence in this instance?"

"Mr. Purser, it is clear that your sense of the singularity in this matter equals not mine. You account for it by what you call willpower, a term not yet included in the lexicon of science. For me, I do not, with my present knowledge, pretend to account for it at all. Even should we assume the hypothesis that at the first touch of the halyards the action of Budd's heart, intensified by extraordinary emotion at its climax, abruptly stopped—much like a watch when in carelessly winding it up you strain at the finish, thus snapping the chain—even under that hypothesis how account for the phenomenon that followed?"

"You admit, then, that the absence of spasmodic movement was phenomenal."

"It was phenomenal, Mr. Purser, in the sense that it was an appearance the cause of which is not immediately to be assigned."

"But tell me, my dear sir," pertinaciously continued the other, "was the man's death effected by the halter, or was it a species of euthanasia?"

" 'Euthanasia,' Mr. Purser, is something like your 'will-power': I doubt its authenticity as a scientific term—begging your pardon again. It is at once imaginative and metaphysical—in short, Greek. But," abruptly changing his tone, "there is a case in the sick bay that I do not care to leave to my assistants. Beg your pardon, but excuse me." And rising from the mess he formally withdrew.

28

The silence at the moment of execution and for a moment or two continuing thereafter, a silence but emphasized by the regular wash of the sea against the hull or the flutter of a sail caused by the helmsman's eyes being tempted astray, this emphasized silence was gradually disturbed by a sound not easily to be verbally rendered. Whoever has heard the freshet-wave of a torrent suddenly swelled by pouring showers in tropical mountains, showers not shared by the plain; whoever has heard the first muffled murmur of its sloping advance through precipitous woods, may form some conception of the sound now heard. The seeming remoteness of its source was because of its murmurous indistinctness since it came from close by, even from the men massed on the ship's open deck. Being inarticulate, it was dubious in significance further than it seemed to indicate some capricious revulsion of thought or feeling such as mobs ashore are liable to, in the present instance possibly implying a sullen revocation on the men's part of their involuntary echoing of Billy's benediction. But ere the murmur had time to wax into clamor it was met by a strategic command, the more telling that it came with abrupt unexpectedness.

"Pipe down the starboard watch, Boatswain, and see that they go."

Shrill as the shriek of the sea hawk the whistles of the
boatswain and his mates pierced that ominous low sound,
dissipating it, and yielding to the mechanism of discipline
the throng was thinned by one half. For the remainder,
most of them were set to temporary employments connected with trimming the yards and so forth, business
readily to be got up to serve occasion by any officer-of-
the-deck.

Now each proceeding that follows a mortal sentence
pronounced at sea by a drumhead court is characterized
by promptitude not perceptibly merging into hurry,
though bordering that. The hammock, the one which
had been Billy's bed when alive, having already been
ballasted with shot and otherwise prepared to serve for
his canvas coffin, the last offices of the sea-undertakers,
the sailmaker's mates, were now speedily completed.
When everything was in readiness a second call for all
hands, made necessary by the strategic movement before
mentioned, was sounded, and now to witness burial.

The details of this closing formality it needs not to
give. But when the tilted plank let slide its freight into
the sea, a second strange human murmur was heard,
blended now with another inarticulate sound proceeding
from certain larger seafowl, whose attention having been
attracted by the peculiar commotion in the water resulting from the heavy sloped dive of the shotted hammock
into the sea, flew screaming to the spot. So near the hull
did they come that the stridor or bony creak of their
gaunt double-jointed pinions was audible. As the ship
under light airs passed on, leaving the burial spot astern,

they still kept circling it low down with the moving
shadow of their outstretched wings and the croaked
requiem of their cries.

Upon sailors as superstitious as those of the age preceding ours, men-of-war's men, too, who had just beheld
the prodigy of repose in the form suspended in air and
now foundering in the deeps; to such mariners the action
of the seafowl, though dictated by mere animal greed
for prey, was big with no prosaic significance. An uncertain movement began among them, in which some en-
croachment was made. It was tolerated but for a moment.
For suddenly the drum beat to quarters, which familiar
sound, happening at least twice every day, had upon the
present occasion a signal peremptoriness in it. True
martial discipline long continued superinduces in average man a sort of impulse of docility whose operation at
the official sound of command much resembles in its
promptitude the effect of an instinct.

The drumbeat dissolved the multitude, distributing
most of them along the batteries of the two covered gun
decks. There, as wont, the guns' crews stood by their
respective cannon erect and silent. In due course the first
officer, sword under arm and standing in his place on the
quarterdeck, formally received the successive reports of
the sworded lieutenants commanding the sections of batteries below, the last of which reports being made, the
summed report he delivered with the customary salute to
the commander. All this occupied time, which in the
present case was the object of beating to quarters at an
hour prior to the customary one. That such variance from

usage was authorized by an officer like Captain Vere, a martinet as some deemed him, was evidence of the necessity for unusual action implied in what he deemed to be temporarily the mood of his men. "With mankind," he would say, "forms, measured forms, are everything; and that is the import couched in the story of Orpheus with his lyre spellbinding the wild denizens of the wood." And this he once applied to the disruption of forms going on across the Channel and the consequences thereof.

At this unwonted muster at quarters, all proceeded as at the regular hour. The band on the quarterdeck played a sacred air, after which the chaplain went through the customary morning service. That done, the drum beat the retreat, and, toned by music and religious rites subserving the discipline and purpose of war, the men in their wonted orderly manner dispersed to the places allotted them when not at the guns.

And now it was full day. The fleece of low-hanging vapor had vanished, licked up by the sun that late had so glorified it. And the circumambient air in the clearness of its serenity was like smooth white marble in the polished block not yet removed from the marble dealer's yard.

29

The symmetry of form attainable in pure fiction cannot so readily be achieved in a narration essentially having less to do with fable than with fact. Truth uncompromisingly told will always have its ragged edges; hence the conclusion of such a narration is apt to be less finished than an architectural finial.

How it fared with the Handsome Sailor during the year of the Great Mutiny has been faithfully given. But though properly the story ends with his life, something in way of sequel will not be amiss. Three brief chapters will suffice.

In the general rechristening under the Directory of the craft originally forming the navy of the French monarchy, the *St. Louis* line-of-battle ship was named the *Athéiste*. Such a name, like some other substituted ones in the Revolutionary fleet, while proclaiming the infidel audacity of the ruling power was yet, though not so intended to be, the aptest name, if one consider it, ever given to a warship, far more so indeed than the *Devastation*, the *Erebus* (the *Hell*) and similar names bestowed upon fighting ships.

On the return passage to the English fleet from the detached cruise during which occurred the events already recorded, the *Indomitable* fell in with the *Athéiste*. An engagement ensued, during which Captain Vere, in the act of putting his ship alongside the enemy with a view of throwing his boarders across her bulwarks, was hit by a musket ball from a porthole of the enemy's main cabin. More than disabled he dropped to the deck and was carried below to the same cockpit where some of his men already lay. The senior lieutenant took command. Under him the enemy was finally captured and though much crippled was by rare good fortune successfully taken into Gibraltar, an English port not very distant from the scene of the fight. There Captain Vere with the rest of the wounded was put ashore. He lingered for some days, but the end came. Unhappily he was cut off too early for the Nile and Trafalgar. The spirit that spite its philosophic austerity may yet have indulged in the most secret of all passions, ambition, never attained to the fullness of fame.

Not long before death, while lying under the influence of that magical drug which, soothing the physical frame, mysteriously operates on the subtler element in man, he was heard to murmur words inexplicable to his attendant —"Billy Budd, Billy Budd." That these were not the accents of remorse would seem clear from what the attendant said to the *Indomitable's* senior officer of marines. As the most reluctant to condemn of the members of the drumhead court, he knew too well, though here he kept the knowledge to himself, who Billy Budd was.

30

Some few weeks after the execution, among other matters under the head of *News from the Mediterranean,* there appeared in a naval chronicle of the time, an authorized weekly publication, an account of the affair. It was doubtless for the most part written in good faith, though the medium, partly rumor, through which the facts must have reached the writer, served to deflect and in part falsify them. The account was as follows:

"On the tenth of the last month a deplorable occurrence took place on board H.M.S. *Indomitable.* John Claggart, the ship's master-at-arms, discovering that some sort of plot was incipient among an inferior section of the ship's company, and that the ringleader was one William Budd, he, Claggart, in the act of arraigning the man before the captain was vindictively stabbed to the heart by the suddenly drawn sheath knife of Budd.

"The deed and the implement employed sufficiently suggest that, though mustered into the service under an English name, the assassin was no Englishman, but one of those aliens adopting English cognomens whom the present extraordinary necessities of the service have caused to be admitted into it in considerable numbers.

"The enormity of the crime and the extreme depravity of the criminal appear the greater in view of the character of the victim, a middle-aged man respectable and discreet, belonging to that minor official grade, the petty officers upon whom, as none know better than the commissioned gentlemen, the efficiency of His Majesty's navy so largely depends. His function was a responsible one, at once onerous and thankless, and his fidelity in it the greater because of his strong patriotic impulse. In this instance as in so many other instances in these days, the character of this unfortunate man signally refutes, if refutation were needed, that peevish saying attributed to the late Dr. Johnson, that patriotism is the last refuge of a scoundrel.

"The criminal paid the penalty of his crime. The promptitude of the punishment has proved salutary. Nothing amiss is now apprehended aboard H.M.S. *Indomitable.*"

The above, appearing in a publication now long ago superannuated and forgotten, is all that hitherto has stood in human record to attest what manner of men respectively were John Claggart and Billy Budd.

31

Everything is for a term remarkable in navies. Any tangible object associated with some striking incident of the service is converted into a monument. The spar from which the foretopman was suspended was for some few

years kept trace of by the bluejackets. Their knowledge
followed it from ship to dockyard and again from dockyard to ship, still pursuing it even when at last reduced
to a mere dockyard boom. To them a chip of it was as a
piece of the Cross. Ignorant though they were of the
secret facts of the tragedy, and not thinking but that the
penalty was somehow unavoidably inflicted from the
naval point of view, for all that they instinctively felt
that Billy was a sort of man as incapable of mutiny as of
willful murder. They recalled the fresh young image of
the Handsome Sailor, that face never deformed by a
sneer or subtler vile freak of the heart within. Their impression of him was doubtless deepened by the fact that
he was gone, and in a measure mysteriously gone. At
the time, on the gun decks of the *Indomitable* the general
estimate of his nature and its unconscious simplicity
eventually found rude utterance from another foretopman, one of his own watch, gifted as some sailors are,
with an artless poetic temperament; the tarry hands
made some lines which after circulating among the shipboard crew for a while, finally got rudely printed at
Portsmouth as a ballad. The title given to it was the
sailor's.

Billy in the Darbies

Good of the Chaplain to enter Lone Bay
And down on his marrow-bones here and pray
For the likes just o' me, Billy Budd.—But look:
Through the port comes the moonshine astray!

It tips the guard's cutlass and silvers this nook;
But 'twill die in the dawning of Billy's last day.
A jewel-block they'll make of me tomorrow,
Pendant pearl from the yardarm-end
Like the eardrop I gave to Bristol Molly—
Oh, 'tis me, not the sentence they'll suspend.
Aye, Aye, all is up; and I must up too
Early in the morning, aloft from alow.
On an empty stomach, now, never it would do.
They'll give me a nibble—bit o' biscuit ere I go.
Sure, a messmate will reach me the last parting cup;
But, turning heads away from the hoist and the belay,
Heaven knows who will have the running of me up!
No pipe to those halyards.—But aren't it all sham?
A blur's in my eyes; it is dreaming that I am.
A hatchet to my hawser? all adrift to go?
The drum roll to grog, and Billy never know?
But Donald he has promised to stand by the plank;
So I'll shake a friendly hand ere I sink.
But—no! It is dead then I'll be, come to think.—
I remember Taff the Welshman when he sank.
And his cheek it was like the budding pink
But me they'll lash me in hammock, drop me deep.
Fathoms down, fathoms down, how I'll dream fast asleep.
I feel it stealing now. Sentry, are you there?
Just ease this darbies at the wrist, and roll me over fair,
I am sleepy, and the oozy weeds about me twist.

END OF BOOK

April 19th, 1891

About

HERMAN MELVILLE

⚓

About Herman Melville

HERMAN MELVILLE, one of the greatest and most interesting of American writers, was of the era when his native
New York City's bustling harbor bristled with the spars
and masts of sailing ships.

His heritage, on both the paternal and maternal sides of
the family, was steeped in American tradition. His grandfather Melville had taken part in the Boston Tea Party,
and Peter Gansevoort on his mother's side had commanded Fort Stanwix during the American Revolution.
One of eight children, Herman was born in 1819 and
reared in an atmosphere of close family ties, Presbyte-
rianism, books and a gentleman's way of life—tinged,
however, with worry and financial strain. These fiscal
difficulties mounted until at last, unable to finish his
schooling, he went to sea at age 19 on an English packet
ship bound for Liverpool. His sporadic schooling and
previous odd jobs as bank clerk and country schoolmaster
scarcely qualified him for either business or a profession

equal to the family's needs. And after several fruitless
attempts on land, he again turned seaward aboard the
New Bedford whaler *Acushnet* bound for the Pacific.

This adventure that was to give him material for his
greatest books began auspiciously. Whales were sighted
and slain early in the cruise. Then luck ran out. When the
ship touched at the Marquesas Islands in the South Seas
Melville deserted, at Nukuheva, and lived for several
months with the cannibal Typees or Taipis, before being
rescued by an Australian whaler. Melville roved the Pacific for awhile as whaleman, beachcomber and general
sailor, even participating in a mutiny, before he joined
the United States navy and returned home on the frigate,
United States.

The adventure lasted only four years, but his experiences had carried him forever beyond the conventional
thinking and writing of his time. For write he soon did,
partly to ease the family's perennial financial difficulties.

With *Typee* and *Omoo,* among the first books to
present South Sea island life in the days before the white
man came to exploit it, Melville achieved immediate fame
as a best-selling author. His future seemingly assured, he
married and settled on a farm in the Berkshires to write
his great epic, *Moby Dick,* published in 1851.

Although based on his whaling experiences, the book
also reflected his immense reading and developing ma-
turity. Thus at first it disappointed his travel-hungry
readers, and its realism dismayed the critics. Increasingly
given to introspection and concerned with the ambiguity
of good and evil, and with a poet's love of symbolism,

Melville in his later books moved ever further from the realism and genial traveler's observations that had lightened his earlier work.

Twenty years after his triumphant debut with *Typee*, he went to work to support his family as customs inspector in New York City, a job which he held for the next two decades. In contrast to the previous period of literary, family and financial turmoil relieved only by occasional travel, Melville spent these remaining years of his life quietly, writing in the relative obscurity of a small circle of admirers.

Shortly before his death in 1891 he turned again to the sea, with *Billy Budd.* In this short tense novel he dramatically posed his mature thoughts on the problem of good and evil as it operates in human affairs. Melville died convinced that he would be remembered only as "the man who had lived with cannibals." But in the 1920's thought and literary taste finally caught up with him. Today Melville is fully recognized as one of the greatest of American writers.